WHEN THE SLEEPER WAKES

A STORY OF THE DAYS TO COME

THE TIME MACHINE

THREE PROPHETIC
SCIENCE FICTION
NOVELS OF
H.G. WELLS

SELECTED AND
WITH AN INTRODUCTION BY
E. F. BLEILER

DOVER PUBLICATIONS, INC.
NEW YORK

This new Dover edition, first published in 1960, is an
unabridged reproduction of the novels, *When the
Sleeper Wakes, A Story of the Days to Come*, and
The Time Machine.   E. F. Bleiler selected the novels
and wrote the Introduction to this Dover edition.

International Standard Book Number: 0-486-20605-X
Library of Congress Catalog Card Number: 59-14229

Manufactured in the United States of America

Dover Publications, Inc.
180 Varick Street
New York 14, New York

CONTENTS

To
WILLIAM ERNEST HENLEY

INTRODUCTION TO THE DOVER EDITION

MORE THAN any other major English novelist H. G. Wells was obsessed with the future. His better-known early novels and short stories are mostly set in the future, while about one-third of his non-fiction is devoted to speculation about things to come. He may have strayed at times into satire, the social novel, or other fields of writing, but as a glance at his bibliography will show he always returned to prediction.

His score as a prophet was mixed, and sometimes both his failures and his successes at prophecy were spectacular. During World War I, when he worked for the Northcliffe newspapers, he made as bad a series of predictions about the course of the War as could be imagined. In the early 1920's, on the other hand, he wrote an astonishingly accurate account of the invention of the atomic bomb; his speculation, which appeared in the novel *The Undying Fire*, corresponded almost point by point, year by year, with factual history.

It is no surprise, therefore, to read in his *Experiment in Autobiography* that Wells wrote much of his earlier fiction to express serious ideas about the future of mankind, and that a single conceptual scheme of history lay behind the stories written from about 1895 to about 1900. Wells had saturated himself in both the physical sciences and social philosophy, and believed that he had isolated the conflicts, trends, and threats that were basic to the late 19th century. Their projection, he thought, would give a consistent history of the human race.

Wells was not optimistic about the future. He believed that power had escaped moral control, and that injustice was in a position to perpetuate itself indefinitely with the new tools created for it by the physical and psychological sciences. He believed that advances in the control of matter would be paralleled by new techniques in controlling man, both as an individual and as a member of a group.

Wells predicted that the 20th century would be a welter of merciless wars, and that the wars would be followed by an increasingly oppressive capitalism, in which giant trusts would unify the world by literally buying most of mankind. He saw that the great politicians of the future would not be the Napoleonic figures of the past (a mistake into which many of his contemporaries had fallen), but "bosses" (in the political sense) who had managed to escape their duties to their followers. The political bosses would deliberately keep the people of servitor continents in jungle savagery, and would herd the peoples of America and Europe into giant cities that were glass-covered mazes of girders and cables. Most of the world would consist of blue-canvas-clad proletariat, who would be governed by the police rules of the Labor Company and the instincts of the primal herd, while a numerically small owner and controller class would live like Nero and Petronius, and would flit in airplanes to pleasure cities in the Mediterranean.

Such a society would arrive, Wells believed, some time during the late 20th century. By the end of the 21st century it would become unshakeable, despite occasional uprisings by the people, for great advances in the sciences would be privately owned, and would be used to maintain the ruler class in power.

Both *When the Sleeper Wakes* and *A Story of the Days to Come* share a common moment in this society. They are sister stories, moving within the same background of television, moving sidewalks, gigantic airplanes capable of jet speeds, omnipresent blaring propaganda machines, and the Labor Company. In both stories sham political institutions persist in the last degeneracy permitted by Grimm's law of cultural change. The King of England earns a living by skipping in crown and robes upon a vaudeville stage, and a calculated religious cult both focuses and nullifies the hope of the downtrodden.

When the Sleeper Wakes is slightly the earlier of the two stories, taking place in the spring of A.D. 2100. It analyzes the future world in terms of an adventure plot, and shows how syndicalism and thought-control would seem to a rationalistic liberal from the late 19th century. It is not necessary to belabor the point that the opinions about race which the Sleeper expresses are not Wells's own, and are used only for fictional purposes. *A Story of the Days to Come*, which begins late in A.D. 2100, and extends to 2103 or 2104, is more elaborate in its structure. It endeavors to explore the dynamics of conformity and class in the future anthill by means of logical situations built relatively rigorously from social patterns.

In many small ways these two novels are important in the history of English literature. In them Wells first exhibited one of his great gifts: the ability he shared with Dickens of taking subliterary forms and transforming them into intelligent literature. He managed, for the first time in English literature, to intermesh credible characterizations and a good story vehicle with the exposition necessary to a utopia. One need read only a few earlier utopias, negative utopias, or imaginary societies to see how great Wells's achievement was in this area. He seems to have been the first to recognize that a society different from our own will have different social dynamics, and that the plot must grow out of the stresses peculiar to each imaginary society. In many ways this is one of the greatest steps in the history of the novel of social theory since William Godwin showed the interrelation of miseducation, injustice, and the police state in his *Caleb Williams*.

When the Sleeper Wakes and *A Story of the Days to Come* are also the first important novels of any literary merit to question the contemporary concept of "progress." They showed clearly, by example and theory, that scientific advances do not necessarily imply social progress; they demonstrate that the sciences can be appropriated by a ruling class and used for human engineering. Not that Wells was the first to have such ideas: they had appeared in germ in the early 19th century, and had grown strong in the reaction to Bellamy's utopia *Looking Backward*. In the three novels reprinted in this volume, however, these ideas were first worked out clearly and consciously, and presented with literary ability.

It is hardly necessary to point out either the charm or the historical importance of *The Time Machine*, the third novel in this book. This has been done many times elsewhere. Let us only say that although *The Time Machine* is more wilfully fantastic than the two other novels, it is based upon the same ideas. Wells was a follower of both Herbert Spencer and Charles Darwin, and in this story he equated Spencer's social evolutionism with Darwin's biological evolution. Wells believed (for fictional purposes, at least) that the cultural and linguistic gaps between the worker and the enjoyer would eventually develop into biological differences. Within this interpretation of history, therefore, the social weaknesses of the late 19th century will damn humanity, by the 830rd century, to both an infantile fairyland and lightless tunnels beneath a fair surface.

All three of these novels are still alive to-day. The problems they discuss are still pertinent, and they are very enjoyable reading. As prophecy —it is best to leave a decision to the individual reader. There are obvious successes and equally obvious failures in Wells's sense for the future, but it must remain a matter of opinion whether he was right in important matters and wrong in minor, or vice versa. Wells did not consider this trilogy his final considered opinion about the future. He changed his mind several times—as did Isaiah and other prophets who are accounted great. As Wells goes on to say in his autobiography, he soon saw that other, very different futures were equally possible. In any case, let us remember that the Wells of these three novels stood as a prophet for many men whom we now consider prophets: Huxley, Orwell, Zamiatin, and Forster, all of whom have their followings. Wells heard the voice in the wilderness before they, and wrote its message before they, sometimes in the same symbols.

A note should be added about the text of these three stories. *When the Sleeper Wakes* follows the text of the first edition published by Harpers in 1899, rather than the slightly altered text published in 1910 under the title *The Sleeper Wakes*. *A Story of the Days to Come* has been reprinted without alteration from *Tales of Space and Time*, first published in 1899.

For *The Time Machine* the text of the 1895 Heinemann edition has been followed rather than the abridged contemporary American texts. One change, however, has been made. When *The Time Machine* appeared serially (under a different title) in the *National Review*, before book publication, besides minor textual differences, it contained an episode which was omitted from all book editions. This is the adventure with the kangaroo-rat men and giant insects, which starts on page 325 of the present book.

It is not known why Wells omitted this episode from later printings. Perhaps he felt that it was too fantastic, or perhaps he thought it weakened the structural development of his story. In this edition this interesting episode has been restored to the text, making the present printing of *The Time Machine* the first book edition, to my knowledge, to include the full range of the Time Traveller's wanderings and the full inevitability of human history.

New York

E. F. BLEILER

WHEN THE SLEEPER WAKES

By

H. G. WELLS

CONTENTS

CHAPTER I

INSOMNIA

ONE AFTERNOON, at low water, Mr. Isbister, a young artist lodging at Boscastle, walked from that place to the picturesque cove of Pentargen, desiring to examine the caves there. Halfway down the precipitous path to the Pentargen beach he came suddenly upon a man sitting in an attitude of profound distress beneath a projecting mass of rock. The hands of this man hung limply over his knees, his eyes were red and staring before him, and his face was wet with tears.

He glanced round at Isbister's footfall. Both men were disconcerted, Isbister the more so, and, to override the awkwardness of his involuntary pause, he remarked, with an air of mature conviction, that the weather was hot for the time of year.

"Very," answered the stranger shortly, hesitated a second, and added in a colourless tone, "I can't sleep."

Isbister stopped abruptly. "No?" was all he said, but his bearing conveyed his helpful impulse.

"It may sound incredible," said the stranger, turning weary eyes to Isbister's face and emphasizing his words with a languid hand, "but I have had no sleep—no sleep at all for six nights."

"Had advice?"

"Yes. Bad advice for the most part. Drugs. My nervous system. . . . They are all very well for the run of people. It's hard to explain. I dare not take . . . sufficiently powerful drugs."

"That makes it difficult," said Isbister.

He stood helplessly in the narrow path, perplexed what to do. Clearly the man wanted to talk. An idea natural enough under the circumstances, prompted him to keep the conversation going. "I've never suffered from sleeplessness myself," he said in a tone of commonplace gossip, "but in those cases I have known, people have usually found something——"

"I dare make no experiments."

He spoke wearily. He gave a gesture of rejection, and for a space both men were silent.

"Exercise?" suggested Isbister diffidently, with a glance from his interlocutor's face of wretchedness to the touring costume he wore.

"That is what I have tried. Unwisely perhaps. I have followed the coast, day after day—from New Quay. It has only added muscular fatigue to the mental. The cause of this unrest was overwork—trouble. There was something——"

He stopped as if from sheer fatigue. He rubbed his forehead with a lean hand. He resumed speech like one who talks to himself.

"I am a lone wolf, a solitary man, wandering through a world in which I have no part. I am wifeless—childless—who is it speaks of the childless as the dead twigs on the tree of life? I am wifeless, childless—I could find no duty to do. No desire even in my heart. One thing at last I set myself to do.

"I said, I *will* do this, and to do it, to overcome the inertia of this dull body, I resorted to drugs. Great God, I've had enough of drugs! I don't know if *you* feel the heavy inconvenience of the body, its exasperating demand of time from the mind—time—life! Live! We only live in patches. We have to eat, and then comes the dull digestive complacencies—or irritations. We have to take the air or else our thoughts grow sluggish, stupid, run into gulfs and blind alleys. A thousand distractions arise from within and without, and then comes drowsiness and sleep. Men seem to live for sleep. How little of a man's day is his own—even at the best! And then come those false friends, those Thug helpers, the alkaloids that stifle natural fatigue and kill rest—black coffee, cocaine——"

"I see," said Isbister.

"I did my work," said the sleepless man with a querulous intonation.

"And this is the price?"

"Yes."

For a little while the two remained without speaking.

"You cannot imagine the craving for rest that I feel—a hunger and thirst. For six long days, since my work was done, my mind has been a whirlpool, swift, unprogressive and incessant, a torrent of thoughts leading nowhere, spinning round swift and steady——"

He paused. "Towards the gulf."

"You must sleep," said Isbister decisively, and with an air of a remedy discovered. "Certainly you must sleep."

"My mind is perfectly lucid. It was never clearer. But I know I am drawing towards the vortex. Presently——"

"Yes?"

"You have seen things go down an eddy? Out of the light of the day, out of this sweet world of sanity—down——"

"But," expostulated Isbister.

The man threw out a hand towards him, and his eyes were wild, and his voice suddenly high. "I shall kill myself. If in no other way—at the foot of yonder dark precipice there, where the waves are green, and the white surge lifts and falls, and that little thread of water trembles down. There at any rate is . . . sleep."

"That's unreasonable," said Isbister, startled at the man's hysterical gust of emotion. "Drugs are better than that."

"There at any rate is sleep," repeated the stranger, not heeding him.

Isbister looked at him and wondered transitorily if some complex Providence had indeed brought them together that afternoon. "It's not a cert, you know," he remarked. "There's a cliff like that at Lulworth Cove—as high, anyhow—and a little girl fell from top to bottom. And lives to-day—sound and well."

"But those rocks there?"

"One might lie on them rather dismally through a cold night, broken bones grating as one shivered, chill water splashing over you. Eh?"

Their eyes met. "Sorry to upset your ideals," said Isbister with a sense of devil-may-careish brilliance. "But a suicide over that cliff (or any cliff for the matter of that), really, as an artist——" He laughed. "It's so damned amateurish."

"But the other thing," said the sleepless man irritably, "the other thing. No man can keep sane if night after night——"

"Have you been walking along this coast alone?"

"Yes."

"Silly sort of thing to do. If you'll excuse my saying so. Alone! As you say; body fag is no cure for brain fag. Who told you to? No wonder; walking! And the sun on your head, heat, fag, solitude, all the day long, and then, I suppose, you go to bed and try very hard—eh?"

Isbister stopped short and looked at the sufferer doubtfully.

"Look at those rocks!" cried the seated man with a sudden force of gesture. "Look at that sea that has shone and quivered there for ever! See the white spume rush into darkness under that great cliff. And this blue vault, with the blinding sun pouring from the dome of it. It is your world. You accept it, you rejoice in it. It warms and supports and delights you. And for me——"

He turned his head and showed a ghastly face, bloodshot pallid eyes and bloodless lips. He spoke almost in a whisper. "It is the garment of my misery. The whole world . . . is the garment of my misery."

Isbister looked at all the wild beauty of the sunlit cliffs about them and back to that face of despair. For a moment he was silent.

He started, and made a gesture of impatient rejection. "You get a night's sleep," he said, "and you won't see much misery out here. Take my word for it."

He was quite sure now that this was a providential encounter. Only half an hour ago he had been feeling horribly bored. Here was employment the bare thought of which was righteous self-applause. He took possession forthwith. It seemed to him that the first need of this exhausted being was companionship. He flung himself down on the steeply sloping turf beside the motionless seated figure, and deployed forthwith into a skirmishing line of gossip.

His hearer seemed to have lapsed into apathy; he stared dismally seaward, and spoke only in answer to Isbister's direct questions—and not to all of those. But he made no sign of objection to this benevolent intrusion upon his despair.

In a helpless way he seemed even grateful, and when presently Isbister, feeling that his unsupported talk was losing vigour, suggested that they should reascend the steep and return towards Boscastle, alleging the view into Blackapit, he submitted quietly. Halfway up he began talking to himself, and abruptly turned a ghastly face on his helper. "What can be happening?" he asked with a gaunt illustrative hand. "What can be happening? Spin, spin, spin, spin. It goes round and round, round and round for evermore."

He stood with his hand circling.

"It's all right, old chap," said Isbister with the air of an old friend. "Don't worry yourself. Trust to me."

The man dropped his hand and turned again. They went over the brow in single file and to the headland beyond Penally, with the sleepless man gesticulating ever and again, and speaking fragmentary things concerning his whirling brain. At the headland they stood for a space by the seat that looks into the dark mysteries of Blackapit, and then he sat down. Isbister had resumed his talk whenever the path had widened sufficiently for them to walk abreast. He was enlarging upon the complex difficulty of making Boscastle Harbour in bad weather, when suddenly and quite irrelevantly his companion interrupted him again.

"My head is not like what it was," he said, gesticulating for want of expressive phrases. "It's not like what it was. There is a sort of oppression, a weight. No—not drowsiness, would God it were! It is like a shadow, a deep shadow falling suddenly and swiftly across something busy. Spin, spin into the darkness. The tumult of thought, the confusion, the eddy and eddy. I can't express it. I can hardly keep my mind on it—steadily enough to tell you."

He stopped feebly.

"Don't trouble, old chap," said Isbister. "I think I can understand.

At any rate, it don't matter very much just at present about telling me, you know."

The sleepless man thrust his knuckles into his eyes and rubbed them. Isbister talked for awhile while this rubbing continued, and then he had a fresh idea. "Come down to my room," he said, "and try a pipe. I can show you some sketches of this Blackapit. If you'd care?"

The other rose obediently and followed him down the steep.

Several times Isbister heard him stumble as they came down, and his movements were slow and hesitating. "Come in with me," said Isbister, "and try some cigarettes and the blessed gift of alcohol. If you take alcohol?"

The stranger hesitated at the garden gate. He seemed no longer clearly aware of his actions. "I don't drink," he said slowly, coming up the garden path, and after a moment's interval repeated absently, "No—I don't drink. It goes round. Spin, it goes—spin——"

He stumbled at the doorstep and entered the room with the bearing of one who sees nothing.

Then he sat down abruptly and heavily in the easy chair, seemed almost to fall into it. He leant forward with his brows on his hands and became motionless.

Presently he made a faint sound in his throat. Isbister moved about the room with the nervousness of an inexperienced host, making little remarks that scarcely required answering. He crossed the room to his portfolio, placed it on the table and noticed the mantel clock.

"I don't know if you'd care to have supper with me," he said with an unlighted cigarette in his hand—his mind troubled with a design of the furtive administration of chloral. "Only cold mutton, you know, but passing sweet. Welsh. And a tart, I believe." He repeated this after momentary silence.

The seated man made no answer. Isbister stopped, match in hand, regarding him.

The stillness lengthened. The match went out, the cigarette was put down unlit. The man was certainly very still. Isbister took up the portfolio, opened it, put it down, hesitated, seemed about to speak. "Perhaps," he whispered doubtfully. Presently he glanced at the door and back to the figure. Then he stole on tiptoe out of the room, glancing at his companion after each elaborate pace.

He closed the door noiselessly. The house door was standing open, and he went out beyond the porch, and stood where the monkshood rose at the corner of the garden bed. From this point he could see the stranger through the open window, still and dim, sitting head on hand. He had not moved.

A number of children going along the road stopped and regarded the artist curiously. A boatman exchanged civilities with him. He felt that possibly his circumspect attitude and position seemed peculiar and un-accountable. Smoking, perhaps, might seem more natural. He drew pipe and pouch from his pocket, filled the pipe slowly.

"I wonder,"... he said, with a scarcely perceptible loss of complacency. "At any rate one must give him a chance." He struck a match in the virile way, and proceeded to light his pipe.

Presently he heard his landlady behind him, coming with his lamp lit from the kitchen. He turned, gesticulating with his pipe, and stopped her at the door of his sitting-room. He had some difficulty in explaining the situation in whispers, for she did not know he had a visitor. She retreated again with the lamp, still a little mystified to judge from her manner, and he resumed his hovering at the corner of the porch, flushed and less at his ease.

Long after he had smoked out his pipe, and when the bats were abroad, his curiosity dominated his complex hesitations, and he stole back into his darkling sitting-room. He paused in the doorway. The stranger was still in the same attitude, dark against the window. Save for the singing of some sailors aboard one of the little slate-carrying ships in the harbour, the evening was very still. Outside, the spikes of monkshood and del-phinium stood erect and motionless against the shadow of the hillside. Something flashed into Isbister's mind; he started, and leaning over the table, listened. An unpleasant suspicion grew stronger; became convic-tion. Astonishment seized him and became—dread!

No sound of breathing came from the seated figure!

He crept slowly and noiselessly round the table, pausing twice to listen. At last he could lay his hand on the back of the armchair. He bent down until the two heads were ear to ear.

Then he bent still lower to look up at his visitor's face. He started violently and uttered an exclamation. The eyes were void spaces of white.

He looked again and saw that they were open and with the pupils rolled under the lids. He was suddenly afraid. Overcome by the strangeness of the man's condition, he took him by the shoulder and shook him. "Are you asleep?" he said, with his voice jumping into alto, and again, "Are you asleep?"

A conviction took possession of his mind that this man was dead. He suddenly became active and noisy, strode across the room, blundering against the table as he did so, and rang the bell.

"Please bring a light at once," he said in the passage. "There is something wrong with my friend."

Then he returned to the motionless seated figure, grasped the shoulder, shook it, and shouted. The room was flooded with yellow glare as his astonished landlady entered with the light. His face was white as he turned blinking towards her. "I must fetch a doctor at once," he said. "It is either death or a fit. Is there a doctor in the village? Where is a doctor to be found?"

CHAPTER II

THE TRANCE

THE STATE of cataleptic rigour into which this man had fallen, lasted for an unprecedented length of time, and then he passed slowly to the flaccid state, to a lax attitude suggestive of profound repose. Then it was his eyes could be closed.

He was removed from the hotel to the Boscastle surgery, and from the surgery, after some weeks, to London. But he still resisted every attempt at reanimation. After a time, for reasons that will appear later, these attempts were discontinued. For a great space he lay in that strange condition, inert and still—neither dead nor living but, as it were, suspended, hanging midway between nothingness and existence. His was a darkness unbroken by a ray of thought or sensation, a dreamless inanition, a vast space of peace. The tumult of his mind had swelled and risen to an abrupt climax of silence. Where was the man? Where is any man when insensibility takes hold of him?

"It seems only yesterday," said Isbister. "I remember it all as though it happened yesterday—clearer perhaps, than if it had happened yesterday."

It was the Isbister of the last chapter, but he was no longer a young man. The hair that had been brown and a trifle in excess of the fashionable length, was iron grey and clipped close, and the face that had been pink and white was buff and ruddy. He had a pointed beard shot with grey. He talked to an elderly man who wore a summer suit of drill (the summer of that year was unusually hot). This was Warming, a London solicitor and next of kin to Graham, the man who had fallen into the trance. And the two men stood side by side in a room in a house in London regarding his recumbent figure.

It was a yellow figure lying lax upon a water-bed and clad in a flowing shirt, a figure with a shrunken face and a stubby beard, lean limbs and lank nails, and about it was a case of thin glass. This glass seemed to mark off the sleeper from the reality of life about him, he was a thing apart, a strange, isolated abnormality. The two men stood close to the glass, peering in.

"The thing gave me a shock," said Isbister. "I feel a queer sort of surprise even now when I think of his white eyes. They were white, you know, rolled up. Coming here again brings it all back to me."

"Have you never seen him since that time?" asked Warming.

"Often wanted to come," said Isbister; "but business nowadays is too serious a thing for much holiday keeping. I've been in America most of the time."

"If I remember rightly," said Warming, "you were an artist?"

"Was. And then I became a married man. I saw it was all up with black and white, very soon—at least for a mediocre man, and I jumped on to process. Those posters on the Cliffs at Dover are by my people."

"Good posters," admitted the solicitor, "though I was sorry to see them there."

"Last as long as the cliffs, if necessary," exclaimed Isbister with satisfaction. "The world changes. When he fell asleep, twenty years ago, I was down at Boscastle with a box of water-colours and a noble, old-fashioned ambition. I didn't expect that some day my pigments would glorify the whole blessed coast of England, from Land's End round again to the Lizard. Luck comes to a man very often when he's not looking."

Warming seemed to doubt the quality of the luck. "I just missed seeing you, if I recollect aright."

"You came back by the trap that took me to Camelford railway station. It was close on the Jubilee, Victoria's Jubilee, because I remember the seats and flags in Westminster, and the row with the cabman at Chelsea."

"The Diamond Jubilee, it was," said Warming; "the second one."

"Ah, yes! At the proper Jubilee—the Fifty Year affair—I was down at Wookey—a boy. I missed all that. . . . What a fuss we had with him! My landlady wouldn't take him in, wouldn't let him stay—he looked so queer when he was rigid. We had to carry him in a chair up to the hotel. And the Boscastle doctor—it wasn't the present chap, but the G.P. before him—was at him until nearly two, with me and the landlord holding lights and so forth."

"It was a cataleptic rigour at first, wasn't it?"

"Stiff!—wherever you bent him he stuck. You might have stood him on his head and he'd have stopped. I never saw such stiffness. Of course this"—he indicated the prostrate figure by a movement of his head—"is quite different. And, of course, the little doctor—what was his name?"

"Smithers?"

"Smithers it was—was quite wrong in trying to fetch him round too soon, according to all accounts. The things he did. Even now it makes me feel all—ugh! Mustard, snuff, pricking. And one of those beastly little things, not dynamos——"

"Induction coils."

"Yes. You could see his muscles throb and jump, and he twisted about. There was just two flaring yellow candles, and all the shadows were shivering, and the little doctor nervous and putting on side, and *him*— stark and squirming in the most unnatural ways. Well, it made me dream."

Pause.

"It's a strange state," said Warming.

"It's a sort of complete absence," said Isbister. "Here's the body, empty. Not dead a bit, and yet not alive. It's like a seat vacant and marked 'engaged'. No feeling, no digestion, no beating of the heart— not a flutter. *That* doesn't make me feel as if there was a man present. In a sense it's more dead than death, for these doctors tell me that even the hair has stopped growing. Now with the proper dead, the hair will go on growing——"

"I know," said Warming, with a flash of pain in his expression.

They peered through the glass again. Graham was indeed in a strange state, in the flaccid phase of a trance, but a trance unprecedented in medical history. Trances had lasted for as much as a year before—but at the end of that time it had ever been a waking or a death; sometimes first one and then the other. Isbister noted the marks the physicians had made in injecting nourishment, for that device had been resorted to to postpone collapse; he pointed them out to Warming, who had been trying not to see them.

"And while he has been lying here," said Isbister, with the zest of a life freely spent, "I have changed my plans in life; married, raised a family, my eldest lad—I hadn't begun to think of sons then—is an American citizen, and looking forward to leaving Harvard. There's a touch of grey in my hair. And this man, not a day older nor wiser (practically) than I was in my downy days. It's curious to think of."

Warming turned. "And I have grown old too. I played cricket with him when I was still only a lad. And he looks a young man still. Yellow perhaps. But that *is* a young man nevertheless."

"And there's been the War," said Isbister.

"From beginning to end."

"And these Martians."

"I've understood," said Isbister after a pause, "that he had some moderate property of his own?"

"That is so," said Warming. He coughed primly. "As it happens—I have charge of it."

"Ah!" Isbister thought, hesitated and spoke: "No doubt—his keep here is not expensive—no doubt it will have improved—accumulated?"

"It has. He will wake up very much better off—if he wakes—than when he slept."

"As a business man," said Isbister, "that thought has naturally been in my mind. I have, indeed, sometimes thought that, speaking commercially, of course, this sleep may be a very good thing for him. That he knows what he is about, so to speak, in being insensible so long. If he had lived straight on——"

"I doubt if he would have premeditated as much," said Warming. "He was not a far-sighted man. In fact——"

"Yes?"

"We differed on that point. I stood to him somewhat in the relation of a guardian. You have probably seen enough of affairs to recognise that occasionally a certain friction——. But even if that was the case, there is a doubt whether he will ever wake. This sleep exhausts slowly, but it exhausts. Apparently he is sliding slowly, very slowly and tediously, down a long slope, if you can understand me?"

"It will be a pity to lose his surprise. There's been a lot of change these twenty years. It's Rip Van Winkle come real."

"It's Bellamy," said Warming. "There has been a lot of change certainly. And, among other changes, I have changed. I am an old man."

Isbister hesitated, and then feigned a belated surprise. "I shouldn't have thought it."

"I was forty-three when his bankers—you remember you wired to his bankers—sent on to me."

"I got their address from the cheque book in his pocket," said Isbister.

"Well, the addition is not difficult," said Warming.

There was another pause, and then Isbister gave way to an unavoidable curiosity. "He may go on for years yet," he said, and had a moment of hesitation. "We have to consider that. His affairs, you know, may fall some day into the hands of—someone else, you know."

"That, if you will believe me, Mr. Isbister, is one of the problems most constantly before my mind. We happen to be—as a matter of fact, there are no very trustworthy connexions of ours. It is a grotesque and unprecedented position."

"It is," said Isbister. "As a matter of fact, it's a case for a public trustee, if only we had such a functionary."

"It seems to me it's a case for some public body, some practically undying guardian. If he really is going on living—as the doctors, some of them, think. As a matter of fact, I have gone to one or two public men about it. But, so far, nothing has been done."

"It wouldn't be a bad idea to hand him over to some public body—the British Museum Trustees, or the Royal College of Physicians. Sounds a bit odd, of course, but the whole situation is odd."

"The difficulty is to induce them to take him."

"Red tape, I suppose?"

"Partly."

Pause. "It's a curious business, certainly," said Isbister. "And compound interest has a way of mounting up."

"It has," said Warming. "And now the gold supplies are running short there is a tendency towards . . . appreciation."

"I've felt that," said Isbister with a grimace. "But it makes it better for *him*."

"*If* he wakes."

"If he wakes," echoed Isbister. "Do you notice the pinched-in look of his nose, and the way in which his eyelids sink?"

Warming looked and thought for a space. "I doubt if he will wake," he said at last.

"I never properly understood," said Isbister, "what it was brought this on. He told me something about overstudy. I've often been curious."

"He was a man of considerable gifts, but spasmodic, emotional. He had grave domestic troubles, divorced his wife, in fact, and it was as a relief from that, I think, that he took up politics of the rabid sort. He was a fanatical Radical—a Socialist—or typical Liberal, as they used to call themselves, of the advanced school. Energetic—flighty—undisciplined. Overwork upon a controversy did this for him. I remember the pamphlet he wrote—a curious production. Wild, whirling stuff. There were one or two prophecies. Some of them are already exploded, some of them are established facts. But for the most part to read such a thesis is to realise how full the world is of unanticipated things. He will have much to learn, much to unlearn, when he wakes. If ever a waking comes."

"I'd give anything to be there," said Isbister, "just to hear what he would say to it all."

"So would I," said Warming. "Aye! so would I," with an old man's sudden turn to self pity. "But I shall never see him wake."

He stood looking thoughtfully at the waxen figure. "He will never wake," he said at last. He sighed. "He will never wake again."

<hr />

CHAPTER III

THE AWAKENING

BUT WARMING was wrong in that. An awakening came.

What a wonderfully complex thing! this simple seeming unity—the self! Who can trace its reintegration as morning after morning we awaken, the flux and confluence of its countless factors interweaving, rebuilding, the dim first stirrings of the soul, the growth and synthesis of the unconscious to the sub-conscious, the sub-conscious to dawning consciousness, until at last we recognise ourselves again. And as it happens to most of us after the night's sleep, so it was with Graham at the end of his vast slumber. A dim cloud of sensation taking shape, a cloudy dreariness, and he found himself vaguely somewhere, recumbent, faint, but alive.

The pilgrimage towards a personal being seemed to traverse vast gulfs, to occupy epochs. Gigantic dreams that were terrible realities at the time, left vague perplexing memories, strange creatures, strange scenery, as if from another planet. There was a distinct impression, too, of a momentous conversation, of a name—he could not tell what name—that was subsequently to recur, of some queer long-forgotten sensation of vein and muscle, of a feeling of vast hopeless effort, the effort of a man near drowning in darkness. Then came a panorama of dazzling unstable confluent scenes.

Graham became aware his eyes were open and regarding some unfamiliar thing.

It was something white, the edge of something, a frame of wood. He moved his head slightly, following the contour of this shape. It went up beyond the top of his eyes. He tried to think where he might be. Did it matter, seeing he was so wretched? The colour of his thoughts was a dark depression. He felt the featureless misery of one who wakes towards the hour of dawn. He had an uncertain sense of whispers and footsteps hastily receding.

The movement of his head involved a perception of extreme physical weakness. He supposed he was in bed in the hotel at the place in the valley—but he could not recall that white edge. He must have slept. He remembered now that he had wanted to sleep. He recalled the cliff and waterfall again, and then recollected something about talking to a passer-by. . . .

How long had he slept? What was that sound of pattering feet? And that rise and fall, like the murmur of breakers on pebbles? He put out a languid hand to reach his watch from the chair whereon it was his habit to place it, and touched some smooth hard surface like glass. This was so unexpected that it startled him extremely. Quite suddenly he rolled over, stared for a moment, and struggled into a sitting position. The effort was unexpectedly difficult, and it left him giddy and weak—and amazed.

He rubbed his eyes. The riddle of his surroundings was confusing but his mind was quite clear—evidently his sleep had benefitted him. He was not in a bed at all as he understood the word, but lying naked on a very soft and yielding mattress, in a trough of dark glass. The mattress was partly transparent, a fact he observed with a strange sense of insecurity, and below it was a mirror reflecting him greyly. About his arm—and he saw with a shock that his skin was strangely dry and yellow—was bound a curious apparatus of rubber, bound so cunningly that it seemed to pass into his skin above and below. And this strange bed was placed in a case of greenish coloured glass (as it seemed to him), a bar in the white framework of which had first arrested his attention. In the corner of the case was a stand of glittering and delicately made apparatus, for the most part quite strange appliances, though a maximum and minimum thermometer was recognisable.

The slightly greenish tint of the glass-like substance which surrounded him on every hand obscured what lay behind, but he perceived it was a vast apartment of splendid appearance, and with a very large and simple white archway facing him. Close to the walls of the cage were articles of furniture, a table covered with a silvery cloth, silvery like the side of a fish, a couple of graceful chairs, and on the table a number of dishes with substances piled on them, a bottle and two glasses. He realised that he was intensely hungry.

He could see no human being, and after a period of hesitation scrambled off the translucent mattress and tried to stand on the clean white floor of his little apartment. He had miscalculated his strength, however, and staggered and put his hand against the glass-like pane before him to steady himself. For a moment it resisted his hand, bending outward like a distended bladder, then it broke with a slight report and vanished—a pricked bubble. He reeled out into the general space of the hall, greatly astonished. He caught at the table to save himself, knocking one of the glasses to the floor—it rang but did not break—and sat down in one of the armchairs.

When he had a little recovered he filled the remaining glass from the bottle and drank—a colourless liquid it was, but not water, with a pleasing faint aroma and taste and a quality of immediate support and stimulus. He put down the vessel and looked about him.

The apartment lost none of its size and magnificence now that the greenish transparency that had intervened was removed. The archway he saw led to a flight of steps, going downward without the intermediation of a door, to a spacious transverse passage. This passage ran between polished pillars of some white-veined substance of deep ultramarine, and along it came the sound of human movements and voices and a deep undeviating droning note. He sat, now fully awake, listening alertly, forgetting the viands in his attention.

Then with a shock he remembered that he was naked, and casting about him for covering, saw a long black robe thrown on one of the chairs beside him. This he wrapped about him and sat down again, trembling.

His mind was still a surging perplexity. Clearly he had slept, and had been removed in his sleep. But where? And who were those people, the distant crowd beyond the deep blue pillars? Boscastle? He poured out and partially drank another glass of the colourless fluid.

What was this place?—this place that to his senses seemed subtly quivering like a thing alive? He looked about him at the clean and beautiful form of the apartment, unstained by ornament, and saw that the roof was broken in one place by a circular shaft full of light, and, as he looked, a steady, sweeping shadow blotted it out and passed, and came again and passed. "Beat, beat," that sweeping shadow had a note of its own in the subdued tumult that filled the air.

He would have called out, but only a little sound came into his throat. Then he stood up, and, with the uncertain steps of a drunkard, made his way towards the archway. He staggered down the steps, tripped on the corner of the black cloak he had wrapped about himself, and saved himself by catching at one of the blue pillars.

The passage ran down a cool vista of blue and purple, and ended remotely in a railed space like a balcony, brightly lit and projecting into a space of haze, a space like the interior of some gigantic building. Beyond and remote were vast and vague architectural forms. The tumult of voices rose now loud and clear, and on the balcony and with their backs to him, gesticulating and apparently in animated conversation, were three figures, richly dressed in loose and easy garments of bright soft colourings. The noise of a great multitude of people poured up over the balcony, and once it seemed the top of a banner passed, and once some brightly coloured object, a pale blue cap or garment thrown up into the air perhaps, flashed athwart the space and fell. The shouts sounded like English, there was a reiteration of "Wake!" He heard some indistinct shrill cry, and abruptly these three men began laughing.

"Ha, ha, ha!" laughed one—a red-haired man in a short purple robe. "When the Sleeper wakes—*When!*"

He turned his eyes full of merriment along the passage. His face changed, the whole man changed, became rigid. The other two turned swiftly at his exclamation and stood motionless. Their faces assumed an expression of consternation, an expression that deepened into awe.

Suddenly Graham's knees bent beneath him, his arm against the pillar collapsed limply, he staggered forward and fell upon his face.

CHAPTER IV

THE SOUND OF A TUMULT

GRAHAM'S LAST IMPRESSION before he fainted was of a clamorous ringing of bells. He learnt afterwards that he was insensible, hanging between life and death, for the better part of an hour. When he recovered his senses, he was back on his translucent couch, and there was a stirring warmth at heart and throat. The dark apparatus, he perceived, had been removed from his arm, which was bandaged. The white framework was still about him, but the greenish transparent substance that had filled it was altogether gone. A man in a deep violet robe, one of those who had been on the balcony, was looking keenly into his face.

Remote but insistent was a clamour of bells and confused sounds, that suggested to his mind the picture of a great number of people shouting together. Something seemed to fall across this tumult, a door suddenly closed.

Graham moved his head. "What does this all mean?" he said slowly. "Where am I?"

He saw the red-haired man who had been first to discover him. A voice seemed to be asking what he had said, and was abruptly stilled.

The man in violet answered in a soft voice, speaking English with a slightly foreign accent, or so at least it seemed to the Sleeper's ears, "You are quite safe. You were brought hither from where you fell asleep. It is quite safe. You have been here some time—sleeping. In a trance."

He said something further that Graham could not hear, and a little phial was handed across to him. Graham felt a cooling spray, a fragrant mist played over his forehead for a moment, and his sense of refreshment increased. He closed his eyes in satisfaction.

"Better?" asked the man in violet, as Graham's eyes reopened. He was a pleasant-faced man of thirty, perhaps, with a pointed flaxen beard, and a clasp of gold at the neck of his violet robe.

"Yes," said Graham.

"You have been asleep some time. In a cataleptic trance. You have heard? Catalepsy? It may seem strange to you at first, but I can assure you everything is well."

Graham did not answer, but these words served their reassuring purpose. His eyes went from face to face of the three people about him. They were regarding him strangely. He knew he ought to be somewhere in Cornwall, but he could not square these things with that impression.

A matter that had been in his mind during his last waking moments at Boscastle recurred, a thing resolved upon and somehow neglected. He cleared his throat.

"Have you wired my cousin?" he asked. "E. Warming, 27, Chancery Lane?"

They were all assiduous to hear. But he had to repeat it. "What an odd *blurr* in his accent!" whispered the red-haired man. "Wire, sir?" said the young man with the flaxen beard, evidently puzzled.

"He means send an electric telegram," volunteered the third, a pleasant-faced youth of nineteen or twenty. The flaxen-bearded man gave a cry of comprehension. "How stupid of me! You may be sure everything shall be done, sir," he said to Graham. "I am afraid it would be difficult to—*wire* to your cousin. He is not in London now. But don't trouble about arrangements yet; you have been asleep a very long time and the important thing is to get over that, sir." (Graham concluded the word was sir, but this man pronounced it "*Sire*.")

"Oh!" said Graham, and became quiet.

It was all very puzzling, but apparently these people in unfamiliar dress knew what they were about. Yet they were odd and the room was odd. It seemed he was in some newly established place. He had a sudden flash of suspicion. Surely this wasn't some hall of public exhibition! If it was he would give Warming a piece of his mind. But it scarcely had that character. And in a place of public exhibition he would not have discovered himself naked.

Then suddenly, quite abruptly, he realised what had happened. There was no perceptible interval of suspicion, no dawn to his knowledge. Abruptly he knew that his trance had lasted for a vast interval; as if by some processes of thought reading he interpreted the awe in the faces that peered into his. He looked at them strangely, full of intense emotion. It seemed they read his eyes. He framed his lips to speak and could not. A queer impulse to hide his knowledge came into his mind almost at the moment of his discovery. He looked at his bare feet, regarding them silently. His impulse to speak passed. He was trembling exceedingly.

They gave him some pink fluid with a greenish fluorescence and a meaty taste, and the assurance of returning strength grew.

"That—that makes me feel better," he said hoarsely, and there were murmurs of respectful approval. He knew now quite clearly. He made to speak again, and again he could not.

He pressed his throat and tried a third time. "How long?" he asked in a level voice. "How long have I been asleep?"

"Some considerable time," said the flaxen-bearded man, glancing quickly at the others.

"How long?"

"A very long time."

"Yes—yes," said Graham, suddenly testy. "But I want—— Is it—it is—some years? Many years? There was something—I forget what. I feel—confused. But you——" He sobbed. "You need not fence with me. How long——?"

He stopped, breathing irregularly. He squeezed his eyes with his knuckles and sat waiting for an answer.

They spoke in undertones.

"Five or six?" he asked faintly. "More?"

"Very much more than that."

"More!"

"More."

He looked at them and it seemed as though imps were twitching the muscles of his face. He looked his question.

"Many years," said the man with the red beard.

Graham struggled into a sitting position. He wiped a rheumy tear from his face with a lean hand. "Many years!" he repeated. He shut his eyes tight, opened them, and sat looking about him from one unfamiliar thing to another.

"How many years?" he asked.

"You must be prepared to be surprised."

"Well?"

"More than a gross of years."

He was irritated at the strange word. "More than a *what*?"

Two of them spoke together. Some quick remarks that were made about "decimal" he did not catch.

"How long did you say?" asked Graham. "How long? Don't look like that. Tell me."

Among the remarks in an undertone, his ear caught six words: "More than a couple of centuries."

"*What?*" he cried, turning on the youth who he thought had spoken. "Who says——? What was that? A couple of *centuries*!"

"Yes," said the man with the red beard. "Two hundred years."

Graham repeated the words. He had been prepared to hear of a vast repose, and yet these concrete centuries defeated him.

"Two hundred years," he said again, with the figure of a great gulf opening very slowly in his mind; and then, "Oh, but——!"

They said nothing.

"You—did you say——?"

"Two hundred years. Two centuries of years," said the man with the red beard.

There was a pause. Graham looked at their faces and saw that what he had heard was indeed true.

"But it can't be," he said querulously. "I am dreaming. Trances. Trances don't last. That is not right—this is a joke you have played upon me! Tell me—some days ago, perhaps, I was walking along the coast of Cornwall——?"

His voice failed him.

The man with the flaxen beard hesitated. "I'm not very strong in history, sir," he said weakly, and glanced at the others.

"That was it, sir," said the youngster. "Boscastle, in the old Duchy of Cornwall—it's in the southwest country beyond the dairy meadows. There is a house there still. I have been there."

"Boscastle!" Graham turned his eyes to the youngster. "That was it —Boscastle. Little Boscastle. I fell asleep—somewhere there. I don't exactly remember. I don't exactly remember."

He pressed his brows and whispered, "More than *two hundred years*!"

He began to speak quickly with a twitching face, but his heart was cold within him. "But if it *is* two hundred years, every soul I know, every human being that ever I saw or spoke to before I went to sleep, must be dead."

They did not answer him.

"The Queen and the Royal Family, her Ministers, Church and State. High and low, rich and poor, one with another——"

"Is there England still?"

"That's a comfort! Is there London?"

"This *is* London, eh? And you are my assistant-custodian; assistant-custodian. And these——? Eh? Assistant-custodians too!"

He sat with a gaunt stare on his face. "But why am I here? No! Don't talk. Be quiet. Let me——"

He sat silent, rubbed his eyes, and, uncovering them, found another little glass of pinkish fluid held towards him. He took the dose. It was almost immediately sustaining. Directly he had taken it he began to weep naturally and refreshingly.

Presently he looked at their faces, suddenly laughed through his tears, a little foolishly. "But—two—hun—dred—years!" he said. He grimaced hysterically and covered up his face again.

After a space he grew calm. He sat up, his hands hanging over his knees in almost precisely the same attitude in which Isbister had found him on the cliff at Pentargen. His attention was attracted by a thick domineering voice, the footsteps of an advancing personage. "What are you doing? Why was I not warned? Surely you could tell? Someone will suffer for this. The man must be kept quiet. Are the doorways closed? All the doorways? He must be kept perfectly quiet. He must not be told. Has he been told anything?"

The man with the fair beard made some inaudible remark, and Graham looking over his shoulder saw approaching a very short, fat, and thickset beardless man, with aquiline nose and heavy neck and chin. Very thick black and slightly sloping eyebrows that almost met over his nose and overhung deep grey eyes, gave his face an oddly formidable expression. He scowled momentarily at Graham and then his regard returned to the man with the flaxen beard. "These others," he said in a voice of extreme irritation. "You had better go."

"Go?" said the red-bearded man.

"Certainly—go now. But see the doorways are closed as you go."

The two men addressed turned obediently, after one reluctant glance at Graham, and instead of going through the archway as he expected, walked straight to the dead wall of the apartment opposite the archway. And then came a strange thing; a long strip of this apparently solid wall rolled up with a snap, hung over the two retreating men and fell again, and immediately Graham was alone with the new comer and the purple-robed man with the flaxen beard.

For a space the thickset man took not the slightest notice of Graham, but proceeded to interrogate the other—obviously his subordinate—upon the treatment of their charge. He spoke clearly, but in phrases only partially intelligible to Graham. The awakening seemed not only a matter of surprise but of consternation and annoyance to him. He was evidently profoundly excited.

"You must not confuse his mind by telling him things," he repeated again and again. "You must not confuse his mind."

His questions answered, he turned quickly and eyed the awakened sleeper with an ambiguous expression.

"Feel queer?" he asked.

"Very."

"The world, what you see of it, seems strange to you?"

"I suppose I have to live in it, strange as it seems."

"I suppose so, now."

"In the first place, hadn't I better have some clothes?"

"They——" said the thickset man and stopped, and the flaxen-bearded man met his eye and went away. "You will very speedily have clothes," said the thickset man.

"Is it true indeed, that I have been asleep two hundred——?" asked Graham.

"They have told you that, have they? Two hundred and three, as a matter of fact."

Graham accepted the indisputable now with raised eyebrows and depressed mouth. He sat silent for a moment, and then asked a question, "Is there a mill or dynamo near here?" He did not wait for an answer. "Things have changed tremendously, I suppose?" he said.

"What is that shouting?" he asked abruptly.

"Nothing," said the thickset man impatiently. "It's people. You'll understand better later—perhaps. As you say, things have changed." He spoke shortly, his brows were knit, and he glanced about him like a man trying to decide in an emergency. "We must get you clothes and so forth, at any rate. Better wait here until some can come. No one will come near you. You want shaving."

Graham rubbed his chin.

The man with the flaxen beard came back towards them, turned suddenly, listened for a moment, lifted his eyebrows at the older man, and hurried off through the archway towards the balcony. The tumult of shouting grew louder, and the thickset man turned and listened also. He cursed suddenly under his breath, and turned his eyes upon Graham with an unfriendly expression. It was a surge of many voices, rising and falling, shouting and screaming, and once came a sound like blows and sharp cries, and then a snapping like the crackling of dry sticks. Graham strained his ears to draw some single thread of sound from the woven tumult.

Then he perceived, repeated again and again, a certain formula. For a time he doubted his ears. But surely these were the words: "Show us the Sleeper! Show us the Sleeper!"

The thickset man rushed suddenly to the archway.

"Wild!" he cried, "How do they know? Do they know? Or is it guessing?"

There was perhaps an answer.

"I can't come," said the thickset man; "I have *him* to see to. But shout from the balcony."

There was an inaudible reply.

"Say he is not awake. Anything! I leave it to you."

He came hurrying back to Graham. "You must have clothes at once," he said. "You cannot stop here—and it will be impossible to——"

He rushed away, Graham shouting unanswered questions after him. In a moment he was back.

"I can't tell you what is happening. It is too complex to explain. In a moment you shall have your clothes made. Yes—in a moment. And then I can take you away from here. You will find out our troubles soon enough."

"But those voices. They were shouting——?"

"Something about the Sleeper—that's you. They have some twisted idea. I don't know what it is. I know nothing."

A shrill bell jetted acutely across the indistinct mingling of remote noises, and this brusque person sprang to a little group of appliances in the corner of the room. He listened for a moment, regarding a ball of crystal, nodded, and said a few indistinct words; then he walked to the wall through which the two men had vanished. It rolled up again like a curtain, and he stood waiting.

Graham lifted his arm and was astonished to find what strength the restoratives had given him. He thrust one leg over the side of the couch and then the other. His head no longer swam. He could scarcely credit his rapid recovery. He sat feeling his limbs.

The man with the flaxen beard re-entered from the archway, and as he did so the cage of a lift came sliding down in front of the thickset man, and a lean, grey-bearded man, carrying a roll, and wearing a tightly-fitting costume of dark green, appeared therein.

"This is the tailor," said the thickset man with an introductory gesture. "It will never do for you to wear that black. I cannot understand how it got here. But I shall. I shall. You will be as rapid as possible?" he said to the tailor.

The man in green bowed, and, advancing, seated himself by Graham on the bed. His manner was calm, but his eyes were full of curiosity. "You will find the fashions altered, Sire," he said. He glanced from under his brows at the thickset man.

He opened the roller with a quick movement, and a confusion of brilliant fabrics poured out over his knees. "You lived, Sire, in a period essentially cylindrical—the Victorian. With a tendency to the hemisphere in hats. Circular curves always. Now——" He flicked out a little appliance the size and appearance of a keyless watch, whirled the knob, and behold—a little figure in white appeared kinetoscope fashion on the dial, walking and turning. The tailor caught up a pattern of bluish white satin. "That is my conception of your immediate treatment," he said.

The thickset man came and stood by the shoulder of Graham.

"We have very little time," he said.

"Trust me," said the tailor. "My machine follows. What do you think of this?"

"What is that?" asked the man from the nineteenth century.

"In your days they showed you a fashion-plate," said the tailor, "but this is our modern development. See here." The little figure repeated its evolutions, but in a different costume. "Or this," and with a click another small figure in a more voluminous type of robe marched on to the dial. The tailor was very quick in his movements, and glanced twice towards the lift as he did these things.

It rumbled again, and a crop-haired anaemic lad with features of the Chinese type, clad in coarse pale blue canvas, appeared together with a complicated machine, which he pushed noiselessly on little castors into the room. Incontinently the little kinetoscope was dropped, Graham was invited to stand in front of the machine and the tailor muttered some instructions to the crop-haired lad, who answered in guttural tones and with words Graham did not recognise. The boy then went to conduct an incomprehensible monologue in the corner, and the tailor pulled out a number of slotted arms terminating in little discs, pulling them out until the discs were flat against the body of Graham, one at each shoulder blade, one at the elbows, one at the neck and so forth, so that at last there were, perhaps, two score of them upon his body and limbs. At the same time, some other person entered the room by the lift, behind Graham. The tailor set moving a mechanism that initiated a faint-sounding rhythmic movement of parts in the machine, and in another moment he was knocking up the levers and Graham was released. The tailor replaced his cloak of black, and the man with the flaxen beard proffered him a little glass of some refreshing fluid. Graham saw over the rim of the glass a pale-faced young man regarding him with a singular fixity.

The thickset man had been pacing the room fretfully, and now turned and went through the archway towards the balcony, from which the noise of a distant crowd still came in gusts and cadences. The crop-headed lad handed the tailor a roll of the bluish satin and the two began fixing this in the mechanism in a manner reminiscent of a roll of paper in a nineteenth century printing machine. Then they ran the entire thing on its easy, noiseless bearings across the room to a remote corner where a twisted cable looped rather gracefully from the wall. They made some connexion and the machine became energetic and swift.

"What is that doing?" asked Graham, pointing with the empty glass to the busy figures and trying to ignore the scrutiny of the new comer. "Is that—some sort of force—laid on?"

"Yes," said the man with the flaxen beard.

"Who is *that*?" He indicated the archway behind him.

The man in purple stroked his little beard, hesitated, and answered in an undertone, "He is Howard, your chief guardian. You see, Sire—it's a little difficult to explain. The Council appoints a guardian and assistants. This hall has under certain restrictions been public. In order that people might satisfy themselves. We have barred the doorways for the first time. But I think—if you don't mind, I will leave him to explain."

"Odd!" said Graham. "Guardian? Council?" Then turning his back on the new comer, he asked in an undertone, "Why is this man *glaring* at me? Is he a mesmerist?"

"Mesmerist! He is a capillotomist."

"Capillotomist!"

"Yes—one of the chief. His yearly fee is sixdoz lions."

It sounded sheer nonsense. Graham snatched at the last phrase with an unsteady mind. "Sixdoz lions?" he said.

"Didn't you have lions? I suppose not. You had the old pounds? They are our monetary units."

"But what was that you said—sixdoz?"

"Yes. Six dozen, Sire. Of course things, even these little things, have altered. You lived in the days of the decimal system, the Arab system—tens, and little hundreds and thousands. We have eleven numerals now. We have single figures for both ten and eleven, two figures for a dozen, and a dozen dozen makes a gross, a great hundred, you know, a dozen gross a dozand, and a dozand dozand a myriad. Very simple?"

"I suppose so," said Graham. "But about this cap—what was it?"

The man with the flaxen beard glanced over his shoulder.

"Here are your clothes!" he said. Graham turned round sharply and saw the tailor standing at his elbow smiling, and holding some palpably new garments over his arm. The crop-headed boy, by means of one finger, was impelling the complicated machine towards the lift by which he had arrived. Graham stared at the completed suit. "You don't mean to say——!"

"Just made," said the tailor. He dropped the garments at the feet of Graham, walked to the bed on which Graham had so recently been lying, flung out the translucent mattress, and turned up the looking-glass. As he did so a furious bell summoned the thickset man to the corner. The man with the flaxen beard rushed across to him and then hurried out by the archway.

The tailor was assisting Graham into a dark purple combination garment, stockings, vest, and pants in one, as the thickset man came back from the corner to meet the man with the flaxen beard returning from the balcony. They began speaking quickly in an undertone, their bearing had an unmistakable quality of anxiety. Over the purple under-garment came a complex but graceful garment of bluish white, and Graham was clothed in the fashion once more and saw himself, sallow-faced, unshaven and shaggy still, but at least naked no longer, and in some indefinable unprecedented way graceful.

"I must shave," he said regarding himself in the glass.

"In a moment," said Howard.

The persistent stare ceased. The young man closed his eyes, reopened them, and with a lean hand extended, advanced on Graham. Then he stopped, with his hand slowly gesticulating, and looked about him.

"A seat," said Howard impatiently, and in a moment the flaxen-bearded man had a chair behind Graham. "Sit down, please," said Howard.

Graham hesitated, and in the other hand of the wild-eyed man he saw the glint of steel.

"Don't you understand, Sire?" cried the flaxen-bearded man with hurried politeness. "He is going to cut your hair."

"Oh!" cried Graham enlightened. "But you called him——"

"A capillotomist—precisely! He is one of the finest artists in the world."

Graham sat down abruptly. The flaxen-bearded man disappeared. The capillotomist came forward with graceful gestures, examined Graham's ears and surveyed him, felt the back of his head, and would have sat down again to regard him but for Howard's audible impatience. Forthwith with rapid movements and a succession of deftly handled implements he shaved Graham's chin, clipped his moustache, and cut and arranged his hair. All this he did without a word, with something of the rapt air of a poet inspired. And as soon as he had finished Graham was handed a pair of shoes.

Suddenly a loud voice shouted—it seemed from a piece of machinery in the corner—"At once—at once. The people know all over the city. Work is being stopped. Work is being stopped. Wait for nothing, but come."

This shout appeared to perturb Howard exceedingly. By his gestures it seemed to Graham that he hesitated between two directions. Abruptly he went towards the corner where the apparatus stood about the little crystal ball. As he did so the undertone of tumultuous shouting from the archway that had continued during all these occurrences rose to a mighty sound, roared as if it were sweeping past, and fell again as if receding swiftly. It drew Graham after it with an irresistible attraction. He glanced at the thickset man, and then obeyed his impulse. In two strides he was down the steps and in the passage, and in a score he was out upon the balcony upon which the three men had been standing.

CHAPTER V

THE MOVING WAYS

HE WENT to the railings of the balcony and stared upward. An exclamation of surprise at his appearance, and the movements of a number of people came from the spacious area below.

His first impression was of overwhelming architecture. The place into which he looked was an aisle of Titanic buildings, curving spaciously in either direction. Overhead mighty cantilevers sprang together across the huge width of the place, and a tracery of translucent material shut out the sky. Gigantic globes of cool white light shamed the pale sunbeams that filtered down through the girders and wires. Here and there a gossamer suspension bridge dotted with foot passengers flung across the chasm and the air was webbed with slender cables. A cliff of edifice hung above him, he perceived as he glanced upward, and the opposite façade was grey and dim and broken by great archings, circular perforations, balconies, buttresses, turret projections, myriads of vast windows, and an intricate scheme of architectural relief. Athwart these ran inscriptions horizontally and obliquely in an unfamiliar lettering. Here and there close to the roof cables of a peculiar stoutness were fastened, and drooped in a steep curve to circular openings on the opposite side of the space, and even as Graham noted these a remote and tiny figure of a man clad in pale blue arrested his attention. This little figure was far overhead across the space beside the higher fastening of one of these festoons, hanging forward from a little ledge of masonry and handling some well-nigh invisible strings dependent from the line. Then suddenly, with a swoop that sent Graham's heart into his mouth, this man had rushed down the curve and vanished through a round opening on the hither side of the way. Graham had been looking up as he came out upon the balcony, and the things he saw above and opposed to him at at first seized his attention to the exclusion of anything else. Then suddenly he discovered the roadway! It was not a roadway at all, as Graham understood such things, for in the nineteenth century the only roads and streets were beaten tracks of motionless earth, jostling rivulets of vehicles between narrow footways. But this roadway was three hundred feet across, and it moved; it moved, all save the middle, the lowest part. For a moment, the motion dazzled his mind. Then he understood.

Under the balcony this extraordinary roadway ran swiftly to Graham's right, an endless flow rushing along as fast as a nineteenth century express train, an endless platform of narrow transverse overlapping slats with little interspaces that permitted it to follow the curvatures of the street. Upon it were seats, and here and there little kiosks, but they swept by too swiftly for him to see what might be therein. From this nearest and swiftest platform a series of others descended to the centre of the space. Each moved to the right, each perceptibly slower than the one above it, but the difference in pace was small enough to permit anyone to step from any platform to the one adjacent, and so walk uninterruptedly from the swiftest to the motionless middle way. Beyond this middle way was another series of endless platforms rushing with varying pace to Graham's left. And seated in crowds upon the two widest and swiftest platforms, or stepping from one to another down the steps, or swarming over the central space, was an innumerable and wonderfully diversified multitude of people.

"You must not stop here," shouted Howard suddenly at his side. "You must come away at once."

Graham made no answer. He heard without hearing. The platforms ran with a roar and the people were shouting. He perceived women and girls with flowing hair, beautifully robed, with bands crossing between the breasts. These first came out of the confusion. Then he perceived that the dominant note in that kaleidoscope of costume was the pale blue that the tailor's boy had worn. He became aware of cries of "The Sleeper. What has happened to the Sleeper?" and it seemed as though the rushing platforms before him were suddenly spattered with the pale buff of human faces, and then still more thickly. He saw pointing fingers. He perceived that the motionless central area of this huge arcade just opposite to the balcony was densely crowded with blue-clad people. Some sort of struggle had sprung into life. People seemed to be pushed up the running platforms on either side, and carried away against their will. They would spring off so soon as they were beyond the thick of the confusion, and run back towards the conflict.

"It is the Sleeper. Verily it is the Sleeper," shouted voices. "That is never the Sleeper," shouted others. More and more faces were turned to him. At the intervals along this central area Graham noted openings, pits, apparently the heads of staircases going down with people ascending out of them and descending into them. The struggle it seemed centred about the one of these nearest to him. People were running down the moving platforms to this, leaping dexterously from platform to platform. The clustering people on the higher platforms seemed to divide their interest between this point and the balcony. A number of sturdy little figures clad in a uniform of bright red, and working methodically together, were employed it seemed in preventing access to this descending staircase. About them a crowd was rapidly accumulating. Their brilliant colour contrasted vividly with the whitish-blue of their antagonists, for the struggle was indisputable.

He saw these things with Howard shouting in his ear and shaking his arm. And then suddenly Howard was gone and he stood alone.

He perceived that the cries of "The Sleeper!" grew in volume, and that the people on the nearer platform were standing up. The nearer swifter platform he perceived was empty to the right of him, and far across the space the platform running in the opposite direction was coming crowded and passing away bare. With incredible swiftness a vast crowd had gathered in the central space before his eyes; a dense swaying mass of people, and the shouts grew from a fitful crying to a voluminous incessant clamour: "The Sleeper! The Sleeper!" and yells and cheers, a waving of garments and cries of "Stop the ways!" They were also crying another name strange to Graham. It sounded like "Ostrog." The slower platforms were soon thick with active people, running against the movement so as to keep themselves opposite to him.

"Stop the ways," they cried. Agile figures ran up swiftly from the centre to the swift road nearest to him, were borne rapidly past him, shouting strange, unintelligible things, and ran back obliquely to the central way. One thing he distinguished: "It is indeed the Sleeper. It is indeed the Sleeper," they testified.

For a space Graham stood without a movement. Then he became

vividly aware that all this concerned him. He was pleased at his wonderful popularity, he bowed, and, seeking a gesture of longer range, waved his arm. He was astonished at the violence of uproar that this provoked. The tumult about the descending stairway rose to furious violence. He became aware of crowded balconies, of men sliding along ropes, of men in trapeze-like seats hurling athwart the space. He heard voices behind him, a number of people descending the steps through the archway; he suddenly perceived that his guardian Howard was back again and gripping his arm painfully, and shouting inaudibly in his ear.

He turned, and Howard's face was white. "Come back," he heard. "They will stop the ways. The whole city will be in confusion."

He perceived a number of men hurrying along the passage of blue pillars behind Howard, the red-haired man, the man with the flaxen beard, a tall man in vivid vermilion, a crowd of others in red carrying staves, and all these people had anxious eager faces.

"Get him away," cried Howard.

"But why?" said Graham. "I don't see——"

"You must come away!" said the man in red in a resolute voice. His face and eyes were resolute, too. Graham's glances went from face to face, and he was suddenly aware of that most disagreeable flavour in life, compulsion. Some one gripped his arm. . . . He was being dragged away. It seemed as though the tumult suddenly became two, as if half the shouts that had come in from this wonderful roadway had sprung into the passages of the great building behind him. Marvelling and confused, feeling an impotent desire to resist, Graham was half led, half thrust, along the passage of blue pillars, and suddenly he found himself alone with Howard in a lift and moving swiftly upward.

———

CHAPTER VI

THE HALL OF THE ATLAS

FROM THE MOMENT when the tailor had bowed his farewell to the moment when Graham found himself in the lift, was altogether barely five minutes. And as yet the haze of his vast interval of sleep hung about him, as yet the initial strangeness of his being alive at all in this remote age touched everything with wonder, with a sense of the irrational, with something of the quality of a realistic dream. He was still detached, an astonished spectator, still but half involved in life. What he had seen, and especially the last crowded tumult, framed in the setting of the balcony, had a spectacular turn, like a thing witnessed from the box of a theatre. "I don't understand," he said. "What was the trouble? My mind is in a whirl. Why were they shouting? What is the danger?"

"We have our troubles," said Howard. His eyes avoided Graham's enquiry. "This is a time of unrest. And, in fact, your appearance, your waking just now, has a sort of connexion——"

He spoke jerkily, like a man not quite sure of his breathing. He stopped abruptly.

"I don't understand," said Graham.

"It will be clearer later," said Howard.

He glanced uneasily upward, as though he found the progress of the lift slow.

"I shall understand better, no doubt, when I have seen my way about a little," said Graham puzzled. "It will be—it is bound to be perplexing. At present it is all so strange. Anything seems possible. Anything. In the details even. Your counting, I understand, is different."

The lift stopped, and they stepped out into a narrow but very long passage between high walls, along which ran an extraordinary number of tubes and big cables.

"What a huge place this is!" said Graham. "Is it all one building? What place is it?"

"This is one of the city ways for various public services. Light and so forth."

"Was it a social trouble—that—in the great roadway place? How are you governed? Have you still a police?"

"Several," said Howard.

"Several?"

"About fourteen."

"I don't understand."

"Very probably not. Our social order will probably seem very complex to you. To tell you the truth, I don't understand it myself very clearly. Nobody does. You will, perhaps—bye and bye. We have to go to the Council."

Graham's attention was divided between the urgent necessity of his inquiries and the people in the passages and halls they were traversing. For a moment his mind would be concentrated upon Howard and the halting answers he made, and then he would lose the thread in response to some vivid unexpected impression. Along the passages, in the halls, half the people seemed to be men in the red uniform. The pale blue canvas that had been so abundant in the aisle of moving ways did not appear. Invariably these men looked at him, and saluted him and Howard as they passed.

He had a clear vision of entering a long corridor, and there were a number of girls sitting on low seats, and as though in a class. He saw no teacher, but only a novel apparatus from which he fancied a voice proceeded. The girls regarded him and his conductor, he thought, with curiosity and astonishment. But he was hurried on before he could form a clear idea of the gathering. He judged they knew Howard and not himself, and that they wondered who he was. This Howard, it seemed, was a person of importance. But then he was also merely Graham's guardian. That was odd.

There came a passage in twilight, and into this passage a footway hung so that he could see the feet and ankles of people going to and fro thereon, but no more of them. Then vague impressions of galleries and of casual astonished passers-by turning round to stare after the two of them with their red-clad guard.

The stimulus of the restoratives he had taken was only temporary. He was speedily fatigued by this excessive haste. He asked Howard to slacken his speed. Presently he was in a lift that had a window upon the great street space, but this was glazed and did not open, and they were too high for him to see the moving platforms below. But he saw people going to and fro along cables and along strange, frail-looking bridges.

And thence they passed across the street and at a vast height above it. They crossed by means of a narrow bridge closed in with glass, so clear that it made him giddy even to remember it. The floor of it also was of glass. From his memory of the cliffs between New Quay and Boscastle, so remote in time, and so recent in his experience, it seemed to him that they must be near four hundred feet above the moving ways. He stopped, looked down between his legs upon the swarming blue and red multitudes, minute and foreshortened, struggling and gesticulating still towards the little balcony far below, a little toy balcony, it seemed, where he had so recently been standing. A thin haze and the glare of the mighty globes of light obscured everything. A man seated in a little openwork cradle shot by from some point still higher than the little narrow bridge, rushing down a cable as swiftly almost as if he were falling. Graham stopped involuntarily to watch this strange passenger vanish in a great circular opening below, and then his eyes went back to the tumultuous struggle.

Along one of the swifter ways rushed a thick crowd of red spots. This broke up into individuals as it approached the balcony, and went pouring down the slower ways towards the dense struggling crowd on the central area. These men in red appeared to be armed with sticks or truncheons; they seemed to be striking and thrusting. A great shouting, cries of wrath, screaming, burst out and came up to Graham, faint and thin. "Go on," cried Howard, laying hands on him.

Another man rushed down a cable. Graham suddenly glanced up to see whence he came, and beheld through the glassy roof and the network of cables and girders, dim rhythmically passing forms like the vans of windmills, and between them glimpses of a remote and pallid sky. Then Howard had thrust him forward across the bridge, and he was in a little narrow passage decorated with geometrical patterns.

"I want to see more of that," cried Graham, resisting.

"No, no," cried Howard, still gripping his arm. "This way. You must go this way." And the men in red following them seemed ready to enforce his orders.

Some negroes in a curious wasp-like uniform of black and yellow appeared down the passage, and one hastened to throw up a sliding shutter that had seemed a door to Graham, and led the way through it. Graham found himself in a gallery overhanging the end of a great chamber. The attendant in black and yellow crossed this, thrust up a second shutter and stood waiting.

This place had the appearance of an ante-room. He saw a number of people in the central space, and at the opposite end a large and imposing doorway at the top of a flight of steps, heavily curtained but giving a glimpse of some still larger hall beyond. He perceived white men in red and other negroes in black and yellow standing stiffly about those portals.

As they crossed the gallery he heard a whisper from below, "The Sleeper," and was aware of a turning of heads, a hum of observation. They entered another little passage in the wall of this ante-chamber, and then he found himself on an iron-railed gallery of metal that passed round the side of the great hall he had already seen through the curtains. He entered the place at the corner, so that he received the fullest impression of its huge proportions. The black in the wasp uniform stood aside like a well-trained servant, and closed the valve behind him.

Compared with any of the places Graham had seen thus far, this second hall appeared to be decorated with extreme richness. On a pedestal at the remoter end, and more brilliantly lit than any other object, was a gigantic white figure of Atlas, strong and strenuous, the globe upon his bowed shoulders. It was the first thing to strike his attention, it was so vast, so patiently and painfully real, so white and simple. Save for this figure and for a dais in the centre, the wide floor of the place was a shining vacancy. The dais was remote in the greatness of the area; it would have looked a mere slab of metal had it not been for the group of seven men who stood about a table on it, and gave an inkling of its proportions. They were all dressed in white robes, they seemed to have arisen that moment from their seats, and they were regarding Graham steadfastly. At the end of the table he perceived the glitter of some mechanical appliances.

Howard led him along the end gallery until they were opposite this mighty labouring figure. Then he stopped. The two men in red who had followed them into the gallery came and stood on either hand of Graham.

"You must remain here," murmured Howard, "for a few moments," and, without waiting for a reply, hurried away along the gallery.

"But, *why*——?" began Graham.

He moved as if to follow Howard, and found his path obstructed by one of the men in red. "You have to wait here, Sire," said the man in red.

"*Why?*"

"Orders, Sire."

"Whose orders?"

"Our orders, Sire."

Graham looked his exasperation.

"What place is this?" he said presently. "Who are those men?"

"They are the lords of the Council, Sire."

"What Council?"

"*The* Council."

"Oh!" said Graham, and after an equally ineffectual attempt at the other man, went to the railing and stared at the distant men in white, who stood watching him and whispering together.

The Council? He perceived there were now eight, though how the newcomer had arrived he had not observed. They made no gestures of greeting; they stood regarding him as in the nineteenth century a group of men might have stood in the street regarding a distant balloon that had suddenly floated into view. What council could it be that gathered there, that little body of men beneath the significant white Atlas, secluded from every eavesdropper in this impressive spaciousness? And why should he be brought to them, and be looked at strangely and spoken of inaudibly? Howard appeared beneath, walking quickly across the polished floor towards them. As he drew near he bowed and performed certain peculiar movements, apparently of a ceremonious nature. Then he ascended the steps of the dais, and stood by the apparatus at the end of the table.

Graham watched that visible inaudible conversation. Occasionally, one of the white-robed men would glance towards him. He strained his ears in vain. The gesticulation of two of the speakers became animated. He glanced from them to the passive faces of his attendants. . . . When he looked again Howard was extending his hands and moving his head like a man who protests. He was interrupted, it seemed, by one of the white-robed men rapping the table.

The conversation lasted an interminable time to Graham's sense. His eyes rose to the still giant at whose feet the Council sat. Thence they wandered at last to the walls of the hall. It was decorated in long painted panels of a quasi-Japanese type, many of them very beautiful. These panels were grouped in a great and elaborate framing of dark metal, which passed into the metallic caryatidae of the galleries, and the great structural lines of the interior. The facile grace of these panels enhanced the mighty white effort that laboured in the centre of the scheme. Graham's eyes came back to the Council, and Howard was descending the steps. As he drew nearer his features could be distinguished, and Graham saw that he was flushed and blowing out his cheeks. His countenance was still disturbed when presently he reappeared along the gallery.

"This way," he said concisely, and they went on in silence to a little door that opened at their approach. The two men in red stopped on either side of this door. Howard and Graham passed in, and Graham, glancing back, saw the white-robed Council still standing in a close group and looking at him. Then the door closed behind him with a heavy thud, and for the first time since his awakening he was in silence. The floor, even, was noiseless to his feet.

Howard opened another door, and they were in the first of two contiguous chambers furnished in white and green. "What Council was that?" began Graham. "What were they discussing? What have they to do with me?" Howard closed the door carefully, heaved a huge sigh, and said something in an undertone. He walked slantingways across the room and turned, blowing out his cheeks again. "Ugh!" he grunted, a man relieved.

Graham stood regarding him.

"You must understand," began Howard abruptly, avoiding Graham's eyes, "that our social order is very complex. A half explanation, a bare unqualified statement would give you false impressions. As a matter of fact—it is a case of compound interest partly—your small fortune, and the fortune of your cousin Warming which was left to you—and certain other beginnings—have become very considerable. And in other ways that will be hard for you to understand, you have become a person of significance—of very considerable significance—involved in the world's affairs."

He stopped.

"Yes?" said Graham.

"We have grave social troubles."

"Yes?"

"Things have come to such a pass that, in fact, it is advisable to seclude you here."

"Keep me prisoner!" exclaimed Graham.

"Well—to ask you to keep in seclusion."

Graham turned on him. "This is strange!" he said.

"No harm will be done you."

"No harm!"

"But you must be kept here——"

"While I learn my position, I presume."

"Precisely."

"Very well then. Begin. Why *harm*?"

"Not now."

"Why not?"

"It is too long a story, Sire."

"All the more reason I should begin at once. You say I am a person of importance. What was that shouting I heard? Why is a great multitude shouting and excited because my trance is over, and who are the men in white in that huge council chamber?"

"All in good time, Sire," said Howard. "But not crudely, not crudely. This is one of those flimsy times when no man has a settled mind. Your awakening. No one expected your awakening. The Council is consulting."

"What council?"

"The Council you saw."

Graham made a petulant movement. "This is not right," he said. "I should be told what is happening."

"You must wait. Really you must wait."

Graham sat down abruptly. "I suppose since I have waited so long to resume life," he said, "that I must wait a little longer."

"That is better," said Howard. "Yes, that is much better. And I must leave you alone. For a space. While I attend the discussion in the Council. . . . I am sorry."

He went towards the noiseless door, hesitated and vanished.

Graham walked to the door, tried it, found it securely fastened in some way he never came to understand, turned about, paced the room restlessly, made the circuit of the room, and sat down. He remained sitting for some time with folded arms and knitted brow, biting his finger nails and trying to piece together the kaleidoscopic impressions of this first hour of awakened life; the vast mechanical spaces, the endless series of chambers and passages, the great struggle that roared and splashed through these strange ways, the little group of remote unsympathetic men beneath the colossal Atlas, Howard's mysterious behaviour. There was an inkling of some vast inheritance already in his mind—a vast inheritance perhaps misapplied—of some unprecedented importance and opportunity. What had he to do? And this room's secluded silence was eloquent of imprisonment!

It came into Graham's mind with irresistible conviction that this series of magnificent impressions was a dream. He tried to shut his eyes and succeeded, but that time-honoured device led to no awakening.

Presently he began to touch and examine all the unfamiliar appointments of the two small rooms in which he found himself.

In a long oval panel of mirror he saw himself and stopped astonished. He was clad in a graceful costume of purple and bluish white, with a little greyshot beard trimmed to a point, and his hair, its blackness streaked now with bands of grey, arranged over his forehead in an unfamiliar but graceful manner. He seemed a man of five-and-forty perhaps. For a moment he did not perceive this was himself.

A flash of laughter came with the recognition. "To call on old Warming like this!" he exclaimed, "and make him take me out to lunch!"

Then he thought of meeting first one and then another of the few familiar acquaintances of his early manhood, and in the midst of his amusement realised that every soul with whom he might jest had died many score of years ago. The thought smote him abruptly and keenly; he stopped short, the expression of his face changed to a white consternation.

The tumultuous memory of the moving platforms and the huge façade of that wonderful street reasserted itself. The shouting multitudes came back clear and vivid, and those remote, inaudible, unfriendly councillors in white. He felt himself a little figure, very small and ineffectual, pitifully conspicuous. And all about him the world was—*strange*.

CHAPTER VII

IN THE SILENT ROOMS

PRESENTLY GRAHAM resumed his examination of his apartments. Curiosity kept him moving in spite of his fatigue. The inner room, he perceived, was high, and its ceiling dome shaped, with an oblong aperture in the centre, opening into a funnel in which a wheel of broad vans seemed to be rotating, apparently driving the air up the shaft. The faint humming note of its easy motion was the only clear sound in that quiet place. As these vans sprang up one after the other, Graham could get transient glimpses of the sky. He was surprised to see a star.

This drew his attention to the fact that the bright lighting of these rooms was due to a multitude of very faint glow lamps set about the cornices. There were no windows. And he began to recall that along all the vast chambers and passages he had traversed with Howard he had observed no windows at all. Had there been windows? There were windows on the street indeed, but were they for light? Or was the whole city lit day and night for evermore, so that there was no night there?

And another thing dawned upon him. There was no fireplace in either room. Was the season summer, and were these merely summer apartments, or was the whole city uniformly heated or cooled? He became interested in these questions, began examining the smooth texture of the walls, the simply constructed bed, the ingenious arrangements by which the labour of bedroom service was practically abolished. And over everything was a curious absence of deliberate ornament, a bare grace of form and colour, that he found very pleasing to the eye. There were several very comfortable chairs, a light table on silent runners carrying several bottles of fluids and glasses, and two plates bearing a clear substance like jelly. Then he noticed there were no books, no newspapers, no writing materials. "The world has changed indeed," he said.

He observed one entire side of the outer room was set with rows of peculiar double cylinders inscribed with green lettering on white that harmonised with the decorative scheme of the room, and in the centre of this side projected a little apparatus about a yard square and having a white smooth face to the room. A chair faced this. He had a transitory idea that these cylinders might be books, or a modern substitute for books, but at first it did not seem so.

The lettering on the cylinders puzzled him. At first sight it seemed like Russian. Then he noticed a suggestion of mutilated English about certain of the words.

"Θi Man huwdbi Kiη,"

forced itself on him as "The Man who would be King." "Phonetic spelling." he said. He remembered reading a story with that title, then he recalled the story vividly, one of the best stories in the world. But this thing before him was not a book as he understood it. He puzzled out the titles of two adjacent cylinders. "The Heart of Darkness," he had never heard of before nor "The Madonna of the Future"—no doubt if they were indeed stories, they were by post Victorian authors.

He puzzled over this peculiar cylinder for some time and replaced it. Then he turned to the square apparatus and examined that. He opened a

First ed. Harper's 1899

sort of lid and found one of the double cylinders within, and on the upper edge a little stud like the stud of an electric bell. He pressed this and a rapid clicking began and ceased. He became aware of voices and music, and noticed a play of colour on the smooth front face. He suddenly realised what this might be, and stepped back to regard it.

On the flat surface was now a little picture, very vividly coloured, and in this picture were figures that moved. Not only did they move, but they were conversing in clear small voices. It was exactly like reality viewed through an inverted opera glass and heard through a long tube. His interest was seized at once by the situation, which presented a man pacing up and down and vociferating angry things to a pretty but petulant woman. Both were in the picturesque costume that seemed so strange to Graham. "I have worked," said the man, "but what have you been doing?"

"Ah!" said Graham. He forgot everything else, and sat down in the chair. Within five minutes he heard himself named, heard "when the Sleeper wakes," used jestingly as a proverb for remote postponement, and passed himself by, a thing remote and incredible. But in a little while he knew those two people like intimate friends.

At last the miniature drama came to an end, and the square face of the apparatus was blank again.

It was a strange world into which he had been permitted to see, un-scrupulous, pleasure seeking, energetic, subtle, a world too of dire economic struggle; there were allusions he did not understand, incidents that conveyed strange suggestions of altered moral ideals, flashes of dubious enlightenment. The blue canvas that bulked so largely in his first impression of the city ways appeared again and again as the costume of the common people. He had no doubt the story was contemporary, and its intense realism was undeniable. And the end had been a tragedy that oppressed him. He sat staring at the blankness.

He started and rubbed his eyes. He had been so absorbed in the latter-day substitute for a novel, that he awoke to the little green and white room with more than a touch of the surprise of his first awakening.

He stood up, and abruptly he was back in his own wonderland. The clearness of the kinetoscope drama passed, and the struggle in the vast place of streets, the ambiguous Council, the swift phases of his waking hour, came back. These people had spoken of the Council with suggestions of a vague universality of power. And they had spoken of the Sleeper; it had not really struck him vividly at the time that he was the Sleeper. He had to recall precisely what they had said. . . .

He walked into the bedroom and peered up through the quick intervals of the revolving fan. As the fan swept round, a dim turmoil like the noise of machinery came in rhythmic eddies. All else was silence. Though the perpetual day still irradiated his apartments, he perceived the little inter-mittent strip of sky was now deep blue—black almost, with a dust of little stars. . . .

He resumed his examination of the rooms. He could find no way of opening the padded door, no bell nor other means of calling for attend-ance. His feeling of wonder was in abeyance; but he was curious, anxious for information. He wanted to know exactly how he stood to these new things. He tried to compose himself to wait until someone came to him. Presently he became restless and eager for information, for distraction, for fresh sensations.

He went back to the apparatus in the other room, and had soon puzzled out the method of replacing the cylinders by others. As he did so, it came into his mind that it must be these little appliances had fixed the language so that it was still clear and understandable after two hun-dred years. The haphazard cylinders he substituted displayed a musical fantasia. At first it was beautiful, and then it was sensuous. He presently recognised what appeared to him to be an altered version of the story of Tannhauser. The music was unfamiliar. But the rendering was realistic, and with a contemporary unfamiliarity. Tannhauser did not go to a Venusberg, but to a Pleasure City. What was a Pleasure City? A dream, surely, the fancy of a fantastic, voluptuous writer.

He became interested, curious. The story developed with a flavour of strangely twisted sentimentality. Suddenly he did not like it. He liked it less as it proceeded.

He had a revulsion of feeling. These were no pictures, no idealisations, but photographed realities. He wanted no more of the twenty-second century Venusberg. He forgot the part played by the model in nineteenth century art, and gave way to an archaic indignation. He rose, angry and half ashamed at himself for witnessing this thing even in solitude. He pulled forward the apparatus, and with some violence sought for a means of stopping its action. Something snapped. A violet spark stung and con-vulsed his arm and the thing was still. When he attempted next day to replace these Tannhauser cylinders by another pair, he found the apparatus broken. . . .

He struck out a path oblique to the room and paced to and fro, strug-gling with intolerable vast impressions. The things he had derived from the cylinders and the things he had seen, conflicted, confused him. It seemed to him the most amazing thing of all that in his thirty years of life he had never tried to shape a picture of these coming times. "We were making the future," he said, "and hardly any of us troubled to think what future we were making. And here it is!"

"What have they got to, what has been done? How do I come into the midst of it all?" The vastness of street and house he was prepared for, the multitudes of people. But conflicts in the city ways! And the systematised sensuality of a class of rich men!

He thought of Bellamy, the hero of whose Socialistic Utopia had so oddly anticipated this actual experience. But here was no Utopia, no Socialistic state. He had already seen enough to realise that the ancient antithesis of luxury, waste and sensuality on the one hand and abject poverty on the other, still prevailed. He knew enough of the essential factors of life to understand that correlation. And not only were the buildings of the city gigantic and the crowds in the street gigantic, but the voices he had heard in the ways, the uneasiness of Howard, the very atmosphere spoke of gigantic discontent. What country was he in? Still England it seemed, and yet strangely "un-English." His mind glanced at the rest of the world, and saw only an enigmatical veil.

He prowled about his apartment, examining everything as a caged animal might do. He felt very tired, felt that feverish exhaustion that does not admit of rest. He listened for long spaces under the ventilator to catch some distant echo of the tumults he felt must be proceeding in the city.

He began to talk to himself. "Two hundred and three years!" he said to himself over and over again, laughing stupidly. "Then I am two hundred and thirty-three years old! The oldest inhabitant. Surely they haven't reversed the tendency of our time and gone back to the rule of the oldest. My claims are indisputable. Mumble, mumble. I remember the Bulgarian atrocities as though it was yesterday. 'Tis a great age! Ha ha!" He was surprised at first to hear himself laughing, and then laughed again deliberately and louder. Then he realised that he was behaving foolishly. "Steady," he said. "Steady!"

His pacing became more regular. "This new world," he said. "I don't understand it. *Why?* . . . But it is all *why*!"

"I suppose they can fly and do all sorts of things. Let me try and remember just how it began."

He was surprised at first to find how vague the memories of his first thirty years had become. He remembered fragments, for the most part trivial moments, things of no great importance that he had observed. His boyhood seemed the most accessible at first, he recalled school books and certain lessons in mensuration. Then he revived the more salient features of his life, memories of the wife long since dead, her magic influence now gone beyond corruption, of his rivals and friends and betrayers, of the swift decision of this issue and that, and then of his last years of misery, of fluctuating resolves, and at last of his strenuous studies. In a little while he perceived he had it all again; dim perhaps, like metal long laid aside, but in no way defective or injured, capable of re-polishing. And the hue of it was a deepening misery. Was it worth re-polishing? By a miracle he had been lifted out of a life that had become intolerable. . . .

He reverted to his present condition. He wrestled with the facts in vain. It became an inextricable tangle. He saw the sky through the ventilator pink with dawn. An old persuasion came out of the dark recesses of his memory. "I must sleep," he said. It appeared as a delightful relief from this mental distress and from the growing pain and heaviness of his limbs. He went to the strange little bed, lay down and was presently asleep. . . .

He was destined to become very familiar indeed with these apartments before he left them, for he remained imprisoned for three days. During that time no one, except Howard, entered his prison. The marvel of his fate mingled with and in some way minimised the marvel of his survival. He had awakened to mankind it seemed only to be snatched away into this unaccountable solitude. Howard came regularly with subtly sustaining and nutritive fluids, and light and pleasant foods, quite strange to Graham. He always closed the door carefully as he entered. On matters of detail he was increasingly obliging, but the bearing of Graham on the great issues that were evidently being contested so closely beyond the soundproof walls that enclosed him, he would not elucidate. He evaded, as politely as possible, every question on the position of affairs in the outer world.

And in those three days Graham's incessant thoughts went far and wide. All that he had seen, all this elaborate contrivance to prevent him seeing, worked together in his mind. Almost every possible interpretation of his position he debated—even as it chanced, the right interpretation. Things that presently happened to him, came to him at last credible, by virtue of this seclusion. When at length the moment of his release arrived, it found him prepared. . . .

Howard's bearing went far to deepen Graham's impression of his own strange importance; the door between its opening and closing seemed to admit with him a breath of momentous happening. His enquiries became more definite and searching. Howard retreated through protests and difficulties. The awakening was unforeseen, he repeated; it happened to have fallen in with the trend of a social convulsion. "To explain it I must tell you the history of a gross and a half of years," protested Howard.

"The thing is this," said Graham. "You are afraid of something I shall do. In some way I am arbitrator—I might be arbitrator."

"It is not that. But you have—I may tell you this much—the automatic increase of your property puts great possibilities of interference in your hands. And in certain other ways you have influence, with your eighteenth century notions."

"Nineteenth century," corrected Graham.

"With your old world notions, anyhow, ignorant as you are of every feature of our State."

"Am I a fool?"

"Certainly not."

"Do I seem to be the sort of man who would act rashly?"

"You were never expected to act at all. No one counted on your awakening. No one dreamt you would ever awake. The Council had surrounded you with antiseptic conditions. As a matter of fact, we thought that you were dead—a mere arrest of decay. And—but it is too complex. We dare not suddenly—while you are still half awake."

"It won't do," said Graham. "Suppose it is as you say—why am I not being crammed night and day with facts and warnings and all the wisdom of the time to fit me for my responsibilities? Am I any wiser now than two days ago, if it is two days, when I awoke?"

Howard pulled his lip.

"I am beginning to feel—every hour I feel more clearly—a sense of complex concealment of which you are the salient point. Is this Council, or committee, or whatever they are, cooking the accounts of my estate? Is that it?"

"That note of suspicion——" said Howard.

"Ugh!" said Graham. "Now, mark my words, it will be ill for those who have put me here. It will be ill. I am alive. Make no doubt of it, I am alive. Every day my pulse is stronger and my mind clearer and more vigorous. No more quiescence. I am a man come back to life. And I want to *live*——"

"*Live!*"

Howard's face lit with an idea. He came towards Graham and spoke in an easy confidential tone.

"The Council secludes you here for your good. You are restless. Naturally—an energetic man! You find it dull here. But we are anxious that everything you may desire—every desire—every sort of desire . . . There may be something. Is there any sort of company?"

He paused meaningly.

"Yes," said Graham thoughtfully. "There is."

"Ah! *Now!* We have treated you neglectfully."

"The crowds in yonder streets of yours."

"That," said Howard, "I am afraid——. But——"

Graham began pacing the room. Howard stood near the door watching him. The implication of Howard's suggestion was only half evident to Graham. Company? Suppose he were to accept the proposal, demand some sort of *company*? Would there be any possibilities of gathering from the conversation of this additional person some vague inkling of the struggle that had broken out so vividly at his waking moment? He meditated again, and the suggestion took colour. He turned on Howard abruptly.

"What do you mean by company?"

Howard raised his eyes and shrugged his shoulders. "Human beings," he said, with a curious smile on his heavy face.

"Our social ideas," he said, "have a certain increased liberality, perhaps, in comparison with your times. If a man wishes to relieve such a tedium as this—by feminine society, for instance. We think it no scandal. We have cleared our minds of formulæ. There is in our city a class, a necessary class, no longer despised—discreet——"

Graham stopped dead.

"It would pass the time," said Howard. "It is a thing I should perhaps have thought of before, but, as a matter of fact, so much is happening——"

He indicated the exterior world.

Graham hesitated. For a moment the figure of a possible woman that his imagination suddenly created dominated his mind with an intense attraction. Then he flashed into anger.

"No!" he shouted.

He began striding up and down the room. "Everything you say, everything you do, convinces me—of some great issue in which I am concerned. I do not want to pass the time, as you call it. Yes, I know. Desire and indulgence are life in a sense—and Death! Extinction! In my life before I slept I had worked out that pitiful question. I will not begin again. There is a city, a multitude—— And meanwhile I am here like a rabbit in a bag."

His rage surged high. He choked for a moment and began to wave his clenched fists. He gave way to an anger fit, he swore archaic curses. His gestures had the quality of physical threats.

"I do not know who your party may be. I am in the dark, and you keep me in the dark. But I know this, that I am secluded here for no good purpose. For no good purpose. I warn you, I warn you of the consequences. Once I come at my power——"

He realised that to threaten thus might be a danger to himself. He stopped. Howard stood regarding him with a curious expression.

"I take it this is a message to the Council," said Howard.

Graham had a momentary impulse to leap upon the man, fell or stun him. It must have shown upon his face; at any rate Howard's movement was quick. In a second the noiseless door had closed again, and the man from the nineteenth century was alone.

For a moment he stood rigid, with clenched hands half raised. Then he flung them down. "What a fool I have been!" he said, and gave way to his anger again, stamping about the room and shouting curses. . . . For a long time he kept himself in a sort of frenzy, raging at his position, at his own folly, at the knaves who had imprisoned him. He did this because he did not want to look calmly at his position. He clung to his anger—because he was afraid of Fear.

Presently he found himself reasoning with himself. This imprisonment was unaccountable, but no doubt the legal forms—new legal forms—of the time permitted it. It must, of course, be legal. These people were two hundred years further on in the march of civilisation than the Victorian generation. It was not likely they would be less—humane. Yet they had cleared their minds of formulæ! Was humanity a formula as well as chastity?

His imagination set to work to suggest things that might be done to him. The attempts of his reason to dispose of these suggestions, though for the most part logically valid, were quite unavailing. "Why should anything be done to me?"

"If the worst comes to the worst," he found himself saying at last, "I can give up what they want. But what do they want? And why don't they ask me for it instead of cooping me up?"

He returned to his former preoccupation with the Council's possible intentions. He began to reconsider the details of Howard's behaviour, sinister glances, inexplicable hesitations. Then, for a time, his mind circled about the idea of escaping from these rooms; but whither could he escape into this vast, crowded world? He would be worse off than a Saxon yeoman suddenly dropped into nineteenth century London. And besides, how could anyone escape from these rooms?

"How can it benefit anyone if harm should happen to me?"

He thought of the tumult, the great social trouble of which he was so unaccountably the axis. A text, irrelevant enough and yet curiously insistent, came floating up out of the darkness of his memory. This also a Council had said:

"It is expedient for us that one man should die for the people."

CHAPTER VIII

THE ROOF SPACES

AS THE FANS in the circular aperture of the inner room rotated and permitted glimpses of the night, dim sounds drifted in thereby. And Graham, standing underneath, wrestling darkly with the unknown powers that imprisoned him, and which he had now deliberately challenged, was startled by the sound of a voice.

He peered up and saw in the intervals of the rotation, dark and dim, the face and shoulders of a man regarding him. Then a dark hand was extended, the swift van struck it, swung round and beat on with a little brownish patch on the edge of its thin blade, and something began to fall therefrom upon the floor, dripping silently.

Graham looked down, and there were spots of blood at his feet. He looked up again in a strange excitement. The figure had gone.

He remained motionless—his every sense intent upon the flickering patch of darkness, for outside it was high night. He became aware of some faint, remote, dark specks floating lightly through the outer air. They came down towards him, fitfully, eddyingly, and passed aside out of the uprush from the fan. A gleam of light flickered, the specks flashed white, and then the darkness came again. Warmed and lit as he was, he perceived that it was snowing within a few feet of him.

Graham walked across the room and came back to the ventilator again. He saw the head of a man pass near. There was a sound of whispering. Then a smart blow on some metallic substance, effort, voices, and the vans stopped. A gust of snowflakes whirled into the room, and vanished before they touched the floor. "Don't be afraid," said a voice.

Graham stood under the van. "Who are you?" he whispered.

For a moment there was nothing but a swaying of the fan, and then the head of a man was thrust cautiously into the opening. His face appeared nearly inverted to Graham; his dark hair was wet with dissolving flakes of snow upon it. His arm went up into the darkness holding something unseen. He had a youthful face and bright eyes, and the veins of his forehead were swollen. He seemed to be exerting himself to maintain his position.

For several seconds neither he nor Graham spoke.

"You were the Sleeper?" said the stranger at last.

"Yes," said Graham. "What do you want with me?"

"I come from Ostrog, Sire."

"Ostrog?"

The man in the ventilator twisted his head round so that his profile was towards Graham. He appeared to be listening. Suddenly there was a hasty exclamation, and the intruder sprang back just in time to escape the sweep of the released fan. And when Graham peered up there was nothing visible but the slowly falling snow.

It was perhaps a quarter of an hour before anything returned to the ventilator. But at last came the same metallic interference again; the fans stopped and the face reappeared. Graham had remained all this time in the same place, alert and tremulously excited.

"Who are you? What do you want?" he said.

"We want to speak to you, Sire," said the intruder. "We want—I can't hold the thing. We have been trying to find a way to you—these three days."

"Is it rescue?" whispered Graham. "Escape?"

"Yes, Sire. If you will."

"You are my party—the party of the Sleeper?"

"Yes, Sire."

"What am I to do?" said Graham.

There was a struggle. The stranger's arm appeared, and his hand was bleeding. His knees came into view over the edge of the funnel. "Stand away from me," he said, and he dropped rather heavily on his hands and one shoulder at Graham's feet. The released ventilator whirled noisily. The stranger rolled over, sprang up nimbly and stood panting, hand to a bruised shoulder, and with his bright eyes on Graham.

"You are indeed the Sleeper," he said. "I saw you asleep. When it was the law that anyone might see you."

"I am the man who was in the trance," said Graham. "They have imprisoned me here. I have been here since I awoke—at least three days."

The intruder seemed about to speak, heard something, glanced swiftly at the door, and suddenly left Graham and ran towards it, shouting quick incoherent words. A bright wedge of steel flashed in his hand, and he began tap, tap, a quick succession of blows upon the hinges. "Mind!" cried a voice. "Oh!" The voice came from above.

Graham glanced up, saw the soles of two feet, ducked, was struck on the shoulder by one of them, and a heavy weight bore him to the earth. He fell on his knees and forward, and the weight went over his head. He knelt up and saw a second man from above seated before him.

"I did not see you, Sire," panted the man. He rose and assisted Graham to arise. "Are you hurt, Sire?" he panted. A succession of heavy blows on the ventilator began, something fell close to Graham's face, and a shivering edge of white metal danced, fell over, and lay flat upon the floor.

"What is this?" cried Graham, confused and looking at the ventilator. "Who are you? What are you going to do? Remember, I understand nothing."

"Stand back," said the stranger, and drew him from under the ventilator as another fragment of metal fell heavily.

"We want you to come, Sire," panted the newcomer, and Graham glancing at his face again, saw a new cut had changed from white to red on his forehead, and a couple of little trickles of blood starting therefrom. "Your people call for you."

"Come where? My people?"

"To the hall about the markets. Your life is in danger here. We have spies. We learned but just in time. The Council has decided—this very day—either to drug or kill you. And everything is ready. The people are drilled, the wind-vane police, the engineers, and half the way-gearers are with us. We have the halls crowded—shouting. The whole city shouts against the Council. We have arms." He wiped the blood with his hand. "Your life here is not worth——"

"But why arms?"

"The people have risen to protect you, Sire. What?"

He turned quickly as the man who had first come down made a hissing with his teeth. Graham saw the latter start back, gesticulate to them to conceal themselves, and move as if to hide behind the opening door.

As he did so Howard appeared, a little tray in one hand and his heavy face downcast. He started, looked up, the door slammed behind him, the tray tilted sideways, and the steel wedge struck him behind the ear. He went down like a felled tree, and lay as he fell athwart the floor of the outer room. The man who had struck him bent hastily, studied his face for a moment, rose, and returned to his work at the door.

"Your poison!" said a voice in Graham's ear.

Then abruptly they were in darkness. The innumerable cornice lights had been extinguished. Graham saw the aperture of the ventilator with ghostly snow whirling above it and dark figures moving hastily. Three knelt on the van. Some dim thing—a ladder—was being lowered through the opening, and a hand appeared holding a fitful yellow light.

He had a moment of hesitation. But the manner of these men, their swift alacrity, their words, marched so completely with his own fears of the Council, with his idea and hope of a rescue, that it lasted not a moment. And his people awaited him!

"I do not understand," he said, "I trust. Tell me what to do."

The man with the cut brow gripped Graham's arm. "Clamber up the ladder," he whispered. "Quick. They will have heard——"

Graham felt for the ladder with extended hands, put his foot on the lower rung, and, turning his head, saw over the shoulder of the nearest man, in the yellow flicker of the light, the first-comer astride over Howard and still working at the door. Graham turned to the ladder again, and was thrust by his conductor and helped up by those above, and then he was standing on something hard and cold and slippery outside the ventilating funnel.

He shivered. He was aware of a great difference in the temperature. Half a dozen men stood about him, and light flakes of snow touched hands and face and melted. For a moment it was dark, then for a flash a ghastly violet white, and then everything was dark again.

He saw he had come out upon the roof of the vast city structure which had replaced the miscellaneous houses, streets and open spaces of Victorian London. The place upon which he stood was level, with huge serpentine cables lying athwart it in every direction. The circular wheels of a number of windmills loomed indistinct and gigantic through the darkness and snowfall, and roared with a varying loudness as the fitful wind rose and fell. Some way off an intermittent white light smote up from below, touched the snow eddies with a transient glitter, and made an evanescent spectre in the night; and here and there, low down, some vaguely outlined wind-driven mechanism flickered with livid sparks.

All this he appreciated in a fragmentary manner as his rescuers stood about him. Someone threw a thick soft cloak of fur-like texture about him, and fastened it by buckled straps at waist and shoulders. Things were said briefly, decisively. Someone thrust him forward.

Before his mind was yet clear a dark shape gripped his arm. "This way," said this shape, urging him along, and pointed Graham across the flat roof in the direction of a dim semicircular haze of light. Graham obeyed.

"Mind!" said a voice, as Graham stumbled against a cable. "Between them and not across them," said the voice. And, "We must hurry."

"Where are the people?" said Graham. "The people you said awaited me?"

The stranger did not answer. He left Graham's arm as the path grew narrower, and led the way with rapid strides. Graham followed blindly. In a minute he found himself running. "Are the others coming?" he panted, but received no reply. His companion glanced back and ran on. They came to a sort of pathway of open metal-work, transverse to the direction they had come, and they turned aside to follow this. Graham looked back, but the snowstorm had hidden the others.

"Come on!" said his guide. Running now, they drew near a little windmill spinning high in the air. "Stoop," said Graham's guide, and they avoided an endless band running roaring up to the shaft of the vane. "This way!" and they were ankle deep in a gutter full of drifted thawing snow, between two low walls of metal that presently rose waist high. "I will go first," said the guide. Graham drew his cloak about him and followed. Then suddenly came a narrow abyss across which the gutter leapt to the snowy darkness of the further side. Graham peeped over the side once and the gulf was black. For a moment he regretted his flight. He dared not look again, and his brain spun as he waded through the half liquid snow.

Then out of the gutter they clambered and hurried across a wide flat space damp with thawing snow, and for half its extent dimly translucent to lights that went to and fro underneath. He hesitated at this unstable looking substance, but his guide ran on unheeding, and so they came to and clambered up slippery steps to the rim of a great dome of glass. Round this they went. Far below a number of people seemed to be dancing, and music filtered through the dome. . . . Graham fancied he heard a shouting through the snowstorm, and his guide hurried him on with a new spurt of haste. They clambered panting to a space of huge windmills, one so vast that only the lower edge of its vans came rushing into sight and rushed up again and was lost in the night and the snow. They hurried for a time through the colossal metallic tracery of its supports, and came at last above a place of moving platforms like the place into which Graham had looked from the balcony. They crawled across the sloping transparency that covered this street of platforms, crawling on hands and knees because of the slipperiness of the snowfall.

For the most part the glass was bedewed, and Graham saw only hazy suggestions of the forms below, but near the pitch of the transparent roof the glass was clear, and he found himself looking sheerly down upon it all. For awhile, in spite of the urgency of his guide, he gave way to vertigo and lay spread-eagled on the glass, sick and paralysed. Far below, mere stirring specks and dots, went the people of the unsleeping city in their perpetual daylight, and the moving platforms ran on their incessant journey. Messengers and men on unknown businesses shot along the drooping cables and the frail bridges were crowded with men. It was like peering into a gigantic glass hive, and it lay vertically below him with only a tough glass of unknown thickness to save him from a fall. The street showed warm and lit, and Graham was wet now to the skin with thawing snow, and his feet were numbed with cold. For a space he could not move. "Come on!" cried his guide, with terror in his voice. "Come on!"

Graham reached the pitch of the roof by an effort.

Over the ridge, following his guide's example, he turned about and

slid backward down the opposite slope very swiftly, amid a little ava-
lanche of snow. While he was sliding he thought of what would happen
if some broken gap should come in his way. At the edge he stumbled to
his feet ankle deep in slush, thanking heaven for an opaque footing again.
His guide was already clambering up a metal screen to a level expanse.

Through the spare snowflakes above this loomed another line of vast
windmills, and then suddenly the amorphous tumult of the rotating
wheels was pierced with a deafening sound. It was a mechanical shrilling
of extraordinary intensity that seemed to come simultaneously from
every point of the compass.

"They have missed us already!" cried Graham's guide in an accent of
terror, and suddenly, with a blinding flash, the night became day.

Above the driving snow, from the summits of the wind-wheels,
appeared vast masts carrying globes of livid light. They receded in
illimitable vistas in every direction. As far as his eye could penetrate the
snowfall they glared.

"Get on this," cried Graham's conductor, and thrust him forward to
a long grating of snowless metal that ran like a band between two slightly
sloping expanses of snow. It felt warm to Graham's benumbed feet, and
a faint eddy of steam rose from it.

"Come on!" shouted his guide ten yards off, and, without waiting,
ran swiftly through the incandescent glare towards the iron supports of
the next range of wind-wheels. Graham, recovering from his astonishment, followed as fast, convinced of his imminent capture. . . .

In a score of seconds they were within a tracery of glare and black
shadows shot with moving bars beneath the monstrous wheels. Graham's
conductor ran on for some time, and suddenly darted sideways and
vanished into a black shadow in the corner of the foot of a huge support.
In another moment Graham was beside him.

They cowered panting and stared out.

The scene upon which Graham looked was very wild and strange. The
snow had now almost ceased; only a belated flake passed now and again
across the picture. But the broad stretch of level before them was a
ghastly white, broken only by gigantic masses and moving shapes and
lengthy strips of impenetrable darkness, vast ungainly Titans of shadow.
All about them, huge metallic structures, iron girders, inhumanly vast as
it seemed to him, interlaced, and the edges of wind-wheels, scarcely
moving in the lull, passed in great shining curves steeper and steeper up
into a luminous haze. Wherever the snow-spangled light struck down,
beams and girders, and incessant bands running with a halting, indomit-
able resolution, passed upward and downward into the black. And with
all that mighty activity, with an omnipresent sense of motive and design,

this snow-clad desolation of mechanism seemed void of all human presence save themselves, seemed as trackless and deserted and unfrequented by men as some inaccessible Alpine snowfield.

"They will be chasing us," cried the leader. "We are scarcely halfway there yet. Cold as it is we must hide here for a space—at least until it snows more thickly again."

His teeth chattered in his head.

"Where are the markets?" asked Graham staring out. "Where are all the people?"

The other made no answer.

"*Look!*" whispered Graham, crouched close, and became very still.

The snow had suddenly become thick again, and sliding with the whirling eddies out of the black pit of the sky came something, vague and large and very swift. It came down in a steep curve and swept round, wide wings extended and a trail of white condensing steam behind it, rose with an easy swiftness and went gliding up the air, swept horizontally forward in a wide curve, and vanished again in the steaming specks of snow. And, through the ribs of its body, Graham saw two little men, very minute and active, searching the snowy areas about him, as it seemed to him, with field glasses. For a second they were clear, then hazy through a thick whirl of snow, then small and distant, and in a minute they were gone.

"*Now!*" cried his companion. "Come!"

He pulled Graham's sleeve, and incontinently the two were running headlong down the arcade of ironwork beneath the wind-wheels. Graham, running blindly, collided with his leader, who had turned back on him suddenly. He found himself within a dozen yards of a black chasm. It extended as far as he could see right and left. It seemed to cut off their progress in either direction.

"Do as I do," whispered his guide. He lay down and crawled to the edge, thrust his head over and twisted until one leg hung. He seemed to feel for something with his foot, found it, and went sliding over the edge into the gulf. His head reappeared. "It is a ledge," he whispered. "In the dark all the way along. Do as I did."

Graham hesitated, went down upon all fours, crawled to the edge, and peered into a velvety blackness. For a sickly moment he had courage neither to go on nor retreat, then he sat and hung his leg down, felt his guide's hands pulling at him, had a horrible sensation of sliding over the edge into the unfathomable, splashed, and felt himself in a slushy gutter, impenetrably dark.

"This way," whispered the voice, and he began crawling along the gutter through the trickling thaw, pressing himself against the wall. They continued along it for some minutes. He seemed to pass through a hundred stages of misery, to pass minute after minute through a hundred degrees of cold, damp, and exhaustion. In a little while he ceased to feel his hands and feet.

The gutter sloped downwards. He observed that they were now many feet below the edge of the buildings. Rows of spectral white shapes like the ghosts of blind-drawn windows rose above them. They came to the end of a cable fastened above one of these white windows, dimly visible and dropping into impenetrable shadows. Suddenly his hand came against his guide's. "*Still!*" whispered the latter very softly.

He looked up with a start and saw the huge wings of the flying machine gliding slowly and noiselessly overhead athwart the broad band of snow-flecked grey-blue sky. In a moment it was hidden again.

"Keep still; they were just turning."

For awhile both were motionless, then Graham's companion stood up, and reaching towards the fastenings of the cable fumbled with some indistinct tackle.

"What is that?" asked Graham.

The only answer was a faint cry. The man crouched motionless. Graham peered and saw his face dimly. He was staring down the long ribbon of sky, and Graham, following his eyes, saw the flying machine small and faint and remote. Then he saw that the wings spread on either side, that it headed towards them, that every moment it grew larger. It was following the edge of the chasm towards them.

The man's movements became convulsive. He thrust two cross bars into Graham's hand. Graham could not see them, he ascertained their form by feeling. They were slung by thin cords to the cable. On the cord were hand grips of some soft elastic substance. "Put the cross between your legs," whispered the guide hysterically, "and grip the holdfasts. Grip tightly, grip!"

Graham did as he was told.

"Jump," said the voice. "In heaven's name, jump!"

For one momentous second Graham could not speak. He was glad afterwards that darkness hid his face. He said nothing. He began to tremble violently. He looked sideways at the swift shadow that swallowed up the sky as it rushed upon him.

"Jump! Jump—in God's name! Or they will have us," cried Graham's guide, and in the violence of his passion thrust him forward.

Graham tottered convulsively, gave a sobbing cry, a cry in spite of himself, and then, as the flying machine swept over them, fell forward into the pit of that darkness, seated on the cross wood and holding the ropes with the clutch of death. Something cracked, something rapped smartly against a wall. He heard the pulley of the cradle hum on its rope. He heard the aeronauts shout. He felt a pair of knees digging into his back. . . . He was sweeping headlong through the air, falling through the air. All his strength was in his hands. He would have screamed but he had no breath.

He shot into a blinding light that made him grip the tighter. He recognised the great passage with the running ways, the hanging lights and interlacing girders. They rushed upward and by him. He had a momentary impression of a great circular aperture yawning to swallow him up.

He was in the dark again, falling, falling, gripping with aching hands, and behold! a clap of sound, a burst of light, and he was in a brightly lit hall with a roaring multitude of people beneath his feet. The people! His people! A proscenium, a stage rushed up towards him, and his cable swept down to a circular aperture to the right of this. He felt he was travelling slower, and suddenly very much slower. He distinguished shouts of "Saved! The Master. He is safe!" The stage rushed up towards him with rapidly diminishing swiftness. Then——

He heard the man clinging behind him shout as if suddenly terrified, and this shout was echoed by a shout from below. He felt that he was no longer gliding along the cable but falling with it. There was a tumult of yells, screams and cries. He felt something soft against his extended hand, and the impact of a broken fall quivering through his arm. . . .

He wanted to be still and the people were lifting him. He believed afterwards he was carried to the platform and given some drink, but he was never sure. He did not notice what became of his guide. When his mind was clear again he was on his feet; eager hands were assisting him to stand. He was in a big alcove, occupying the position that in his previous experience had been devoted to the lower boxes. If this was indeed a theatre.

A mighty tumult was in his ears, a thunderous roar, the shouting of a countless multitude. "It is the Sleeper! The Sleeper is with us!"

"The Sleeper is with us! The Master—the Owner! The Master is with us. He is safe."

Graham had a surging vision of a great hall crowded with people. He saw no individuals, he was conscious of a froth of pink faces, of waving arms and garments, he felt the occult influence of a vast crowd pouring over him, buoying him up. There were balconies, galleries, great archways giving remoter perspectives, and everywhere people, a vast arena of people, densely packed and cheering. Across the nearer space lay the collapsed cable like a huge snake. It had been cut by the men of the flying machine at its upper end, and had crumpled down into the hall. Men seemed to be hauling this out of the way. But the whole effect was vague, the very buildings throbbed and leapt with the roar of the voices.

He stood unsteadily and looked at those about him. Someone supported him by one arm. "Let me go into a little room," he said, weeping; "a little room," and could say no more. A man in black stepped forward, took his disengaged arm. He was aware of officious men opening a door before him. Someone guided him to a seat. He staggered. He sat down heavily and covered his face with his hands; he was trembling violently, his nervous control was at an end. He was relieved of his cloak, he could not remember how; his purple hose he saw were black with wet. People were running about him, things were happening, but for some time he gave no heed to them.

He had escaped. A myriad of cries told him that. He was safe. These were the people who were on his side. For a space he sobbed for breath, and then he sat still with his face covered. The air was full of the shouting of innumerable men.

CHAPTER IX

THE PEOPLE MARCH

HE BECAME aware of someone urging a glass of clear fluid upon his attention, looked up and discovered this was a dark young man in a yellow garment. He took the dose forthwith, and in a moment he was glowing. A tall man in a black robe stood by his shoulder, and pointed to the half open door into the hall. This man was shouting close to his ear and yet what was said was indistinct because of the tremendous uproar from the great theatre. Behind the man was a girl in a silvery grey robe, whom Graham, even in this confusion, perceived to be beautiful. Her dark eyes, full of wonder and curiosity, were fixed on him, her lips trembled apart. A partially opened door gave a glimpse of the crowded hall, and admitted a vast uneven tumult, a hammering, clapping and shouting that died away and began again, and rose to a thunderous pitch, and so continued intermittently all the time that Graham remained in the little room. He watched the lips of the man in black and gathered that he was making some clumsy explanation.

He stared stupidly for some moments at these things and then stood up abruptly; he grasped the arm of this shouting person.

"Tell me!" he cried. "Who am I? Who am I?"

The others came nearer to hear his words. "Who am I?" His eyes searched their faces.

"They have told him nothing!" cried the girl.

"Tell me, tell me!" cried Graham.

"You are the Master of the Earth. You are owner of half the world."

He did not believe he heard aright. He resisted the persuasion. He pretended not to understand, not to hear. He lifted his voice again. "I have been awake three days—a prisoner three days. I judge there is some struggle between a number of people in this city—it is London?"

"Yes," said the younger man.

"And those who meet in the great hall with the white Atlas? How does it concern me? In some way it has to do with me. *Why*, I don't know. Drugs? It seems to me that while I have slept the world has gone mad. I have gone mad."

"Who are those Councillors under the Atlas? Why should they try to drug me?"

"To keep you insensible," said the man in yellow. "To prevent your interference."

"But *why*?"

"Because *you* are the Atlas, Sire," said the man in yellow. "The world is on your shoulders. They rule it in your name."

The sounds from the hall had died into a silence threaded by one monotonous voice. Now suddenly, trampling on these last words, came a deafening tumult, a roaring and thundering, cheer crowded on cheer, voices hoarse and shrill, beating, overlapping, and while it lasted the people in the little room could not hear each other shout.

Graham stood, his intelligence clinging helplessly to the thing he had just heard. "The Council," he repeated blankly, and then snatched at a name that had struck him. "But who is Ostrog?" he said.

"He is the organiser—the organiser of the revolt. Our Leader—in your name."

"In my name?—— And you? Why is he not here?"

"He—has deputed us. I am his brother—his half-brother, Lincoln. He wants you to show yourself to these people and then come on to him. That is why he has sent. He is at the wind-vane offices directing. The people are marching."

"In your name," shouted the younger man. "They have ruled, crushed, tyrannised. At last even——"

"In my name! My name! Master?"

The younger man suddenly became audible in a pause of the outer thunder, indignant and vociferous, a high penetrating voice under his red aquiline nose and bushy moustache. "No one expected you to wake. No one expected you to wake. They were cunning. Damned tyrants! But they were taken by surprise. They did not know whether to drug you, hypnotise you, kill you."

Again the hall dominated everything.

"Ostrog is at the wind-vane offices ready—— Even now there is a rumour of fighting beginning."

The man who had called himself Lincoln came close to him. "Ostrog has it planned. Trust him. We have our organisations ready. We shall seize the flying stages—— Even now he may be doing that. Then——"

"This public theatre," bawled the man in yellow, "is only a contingent. We have five myriads of drilled men——"

"We have arms," cried Lincoln. "We have plans. A leader. Their police have gone from the streets and are massed in the——" (inaudible). "It is now or never. The Council is rocking—— They cannot trust even their drilled men——"

"Hear the people calling to you!"

Graham's mind was like a night of moon and swift clouds, now dark and hopeless, now clear and ghastly. He was Master of the Earth, he was a man sodden with thawing snow. Of all his fluctuating impressions the dominant ones presented an antagonism; on the one hand was the White Council, powerful, disciplined, few, the White Council from which he had just escaped; and on the other, monstrous crowds, packed masses of indistinguishable people clamouring his name, hailing him Master. The other side had imprisoned him, debated his death. These shouting thousands beyond the little doorway had rescued him. But why these things should be so he could not understand.

The door opened, Lincoln's voice was swept away and drowned, and a rush of people followed on the heels of the tumult. These intruders came towards him and Lincoln gesticulating. The voices without explained their soundless lips. "Show us the Sleeper, show us the Sleeper!" was the burden of the uproar. Men were bawling for "Order! Silence!"

Graham glanced towards the open doorway, and saw a tall, oblong picture of the hall beyond, a waving, incessant confusion of crowded, shouting faces, men and women together, waving pale blue garments, extended hands. Many were standing, one man in rags of dark brown, a gaunt figure, stood on the seat and waved a black cloth. He met the wonder and expectation of the girl's eyes. What did these people expect from him. He was dimly aware that the tumult outside had changed its character, was in some way beating, marching. His own mind, too, changed.

For a space he did not recognise the influence that was transforming him. But a moment that was near to panic passed. He tried to make audible inquiries of what was required of him.

Lincoln was shouting in his ear, but Graham was deafened to that. All the others save the woman gesticulated towards the hall. He perceived what had happened to the uproar. The whole mass of people was chanting together. It was not simply a song, the voices were gathered together and upborne by a torrent of instrumental music, music like the music of an organ, a woven texture of sounds, full of trumpets, full of flaunting banners, full of the march and pageantry of opening war. And the feet of the people were beating time—tramp, tramp.

He was urged towards the door. He obeyed mechanically. The strength of that chant took hold of him, stirred him, emboldened him. The hall opened to him, a vast welter of fluttering colour swaying to the music.

"Wave your arm to them," said Lincoln. "Wave your arm to them."

"This," said a voice on the other side, "he must have this." Arms were about his neck detaining him in the doorway, and a black subtly-folding mantle hung from his shoulders. He threw his arm free of this and followed Lincoln. He perceived the girl in grey close to him, her face lit, her gesture onward. For the instant she became to him, flushed and eager as she was, an embodiment of the song. He emerged in the alcove again. Incontinently the mounting waves of the song broke upon his appearing, and flashed up into a foam of shouting. Guided by Lincoln's hand he marched obliquely across the centre of the stage facing the people.

The hall was a vast and intricate space—galleries, balconies, broad spaces of amphitheatral steps, and great archways. Far away, high up, seemed the mouth of a huge passage full of struggling humanity. The whole multitude was swaying in congested masses. Individual figures sprang out of the tumult, impressed him momentarily, and lost definition again. Close to the platform swayed a beautiful fair woman, carried by three men, her hair across her face and brandishing a green staff. Next this group an old careworn man in blue canvas maintained his place in the crush with difficulty, and behind shouted a hairless face, a great cavity of toothless mouth. A voice called that enigmatical word "Ostrog." All his impressions were vague save the massive emotion of that trampling song. The multitude were beating time with their feet—marking time, tramp, tramp, tramp, tramp. The green weapons waved, flashed and slanted. Then he saw those nearest to him on a level space before the stage were marching in front of him, passing towards a great archway, shouting "To the Council!" Tramp, tramp, tramp, tramp. He raised his arm, and the roaring was redoubled. He remembered he had to shout "March!" His mouth shaped inaudible heroic words. He waved his arm again and pointed to the archway, shouting "Onward!" They were no longer marking time, they were marching; tramp, tramp, tramp, tramp. In that host were bearded men, old men, youths, fluttering robed bare-armed women, girls. Men and women of the new age! Rich robes, grey rags fluttered together in the whirl of their movement amidst the dominant blue. A monstrous black banner jerked its way to the right. He perceived a blue-clad negro, a shrivelled woman in yellow, then a group of tall fair-haired, white-faced, blue-clad men pushed theatrically past him. He noted two Chinamen. A tall, sallow, dark-haired, shining-eyed youth, white clad from top to toe, clambered up towards the platform shouting loyally, and sprang down again and receded, looking backward. Heads, shoulders, hands clutching weapons, all were swinging with those marching cadences.

Faces came out of the confusion to him as he stood there, eyes met his and passed and vanished. Men gesticulated to him, shouted inaudible personal things. Most of the faces were flushed, but many were ghastly white. And disease was there, and many a hand that waved to him was gaunt and lean. Men and women of the new age! Strange and incredible meeting! As the broad stream passed before him to the right, tributary gangways from the remote uplands of the hall thrust downward in an incessant replacement of people; tramp, tramp, tramp. The unison of the song was enriched and complicated by the massive echoes of arches and passages. Men and women mingled in the ranks; tramp, tramp, tramp, tramp. The whole world seemed marching. Tramp, tramp, tramp, tramp; his brain was tramping. The garments waved onward, the faces poured by more abundantly.

Tramp, tramp, tramp, tramp; at Lincoln's pressure he turned towards the archway, walking unconsciously in that rhythm, scarcely noticing his movement for the melody and stir of it. The multitude, the gesture and song, all moved in that direction, the flow of people smote downward until the upturned faces were below the level of his feet. He was aware of a path before him, of a suite about him, of guards and dignities, and Lincoln on his right hand. Attendants intervened, and ever and again blotted out the sight of the multitude to the left. Before him went the backs of the guards in black—three and three and three. He was marched along a little railed way, and crossed above the archway, with the torrent dipping to flow beneath, and shouting up to him. He did not know whither he went; he did not want to know. He glanced back across a flaming spaciousness of hall. Tramp, tramp, tramp, tramp.

CHAPTER X

THE BATTLE OF THE DARKNESS

HE WAS no longer in the hall. He was marching along a gallery overhanging one of the great streets of the moving platforms that traversed the city. Before him and behind him tramped his guards. The whole concave of the moving ways below was a congested mass of people marching, tramping to the left, shouting, waving hands and arms, pouring along a huge vista, shouting as they came into view, shouting as they passed, shouting as they receded, until the globes of electric light receding in perspective dropped down it seemed and hid the swarming bare heads. Tramp, tramp, tramp, tramp.

The song roared up to Graham now, no longer upborne by music, but coarse and noisy, and the beating of the marching feet, tramp, tramp, tramp, tramp, interwove with a thunderous irregularity of footsteps from the undisciplined rabble that poured along the higher ways.

Abruptly he noted a contrast. The buildings on the opposite side of the way seemed deserted, the cables and bridges that laced across the aisle were empty and shadowy. It came into Graham's mind that these also should have swarmed with people.

He felt a curious emotion—throbbing—very fast! He stopped again. The guards before him marched on; those about him stopped as he did. He saw the direction of their faces. The throbbing had something to do with the lights. He too looked up.

At first it seemed to him a thing that affected the lights simply, an isolated phenomenon, having no bearing on the things below. Each huge globe of blinding whiteness was as it were clutched, compressed in a systole that was followed by a transitory diastole, and again a systole like a tightening grip, darkness, light, darkness, in rapid alternation.

Graham became aware that this strange behaviour of the lights had to do with the people below. The appearance of the houses and ways, the appearance of the packed masses changed, became a confusion of vivid lights and leaping shadows. He saw a multitude of shadows had sprung into aggressive existence, seemed rushing up, broadening, widening, growing with steady swiftness—to leap suddenly back and return reinforced. The song and the tramping had ceased. The unanimous march, he discovered, was arrested, there were eddies, a flow sideways, shouts of "The lights!" Voices were crying together one thing. "The lights!" cried these voices. "The lights!" He looked down. In this dancing death of the lights the area of the street had suddenly become a monstrous struggle. The huge white globes became purple-white, purple with a reddish glow, flickered, flickered faster and faster, fluttered between light and extinction, ceased to flicker and became mere fading specks of glowing red in a vast obscurity. In ten seconds the extinction was accomplished, and there was only this roaring darkness, a black monstrosity that had suddenly swallowed up those glittering myriads of men.

He felt invisible forms about him; his arms were gripped. Something rapped sharply against his shin. A voice bawled in his ear, "It is all right —all right."

Graham shook off the paralysis of his first astonishment. He struck his forehead against Lincoln's and bawled, "What is this darkness?"

"The Council has cut the currents that light the city. We must wait— stop. The people will go on. They will——"

His voice was drowned. Voices were shouting, "Save the Sleeper. Take care of the Sleeper." A guard stumbled against Graham and hurt his hand by an inadvertent blow of his weapon. A wild tumult tossed and whirled about him, growing, as it seemed, louder, denser, more furious each moment. Fragments of recognisable sounds drove towards him, were whirled away from him as his mind reached out to grasp them. Voices seemed to be shouting conflicting orders, other voices answered. There were suddenly a succession of piercing screams close beneath them.

A voice bawled in his ear, "The red police," and receded forthwith beyond his questions.

A crackling sound grew to distinctness, and therewith a leaping of faint flashes along the edge of the further ways. By their light Graham saw the heads and bodies of a number of men, armed with weapons like those of his guards, leap into an instant's dim visibility. The whole area began to crackle, to flash with little instantaneous streaks of light, and abruptly the darkness rolled back like a curtain.

A glare of light dazzled his eyes, a vast seething expanse of struggling men confused his mind. A shout, a burst of cheering, came across the ways. He looked up to see the source of the light. A man hung far over-head from the upper part of a cable, holding by a rope the blinding star that had driven the darkness back. He wore a red uniform.

Graham's eyes fell to the ways again. A wedge of red a little way along the vista caught his eye. He saw it was a dense mass of red-clad men jammed on the higher further way, their backs against the pitiless cliff of building, and surrounded by a dense crowd of antagonists. They were fighting. Weapons flashed and rose and fell, heads vanished at the edge of the contest, and other heads replaced them, the little flashes from the green weapons became little jets of smoky grey while the light lasted.

Abruptly the flare was extinguished and the ways were an inky darkness once more, a tumultuous mystery.

He felt something thrusting against him. He was being pushed along the gallery. Someone was shouting—it might be at him. He was too confused to hear. He was thrust against the wall, and a number of people blundered past him. It seemed to him that his guards were struggling with one another.

Suddenly the cable-hung star-holder appeared again, and the whole scene was white and dazzling. The band of red-coats seemed broader and nearer; its apex was half-way down the ways towards the central aisle. And raising his eyes Graham saw that a number of these men had also appeared now in the darkened lower galleries of the opposite building, and were firing over the heads of their fellows below at the boiling confusion of people on the lower ways. The meaning of these things dawned upon him. The march of the people had come upon an ambush at the very outset. Thrown into confusion by the extinction of the lights they were now being attacked by the red police. Then he became aware that he was standing alone, that his guards and Lincoln were along the gallery in the direction along which he had come before the darkness fell. He saw they were gesticulating to him wildly, running back towards him. A great shouting came from across the ways. Then it seemed as though the whole face of the darkened building opposite was lined and speckled with red-clad men. And they were pointing over to him and shouting. "The Sleeper! Save the Sleeper!" shouted a multitude of throats.

Something struck the wall above his head. He looked up at the impact and saw a star-shaped splash of silvery metal. He saw Lincoln near him. Felt his arm gripped. Then, pat, pat; he had been missed twice.

For a moment he did not understand this. The street was hidden, everything was hidden, as he looked. The second flare had burned out.

Lincoln had gripped Graham by the arm, was lugging him along the gallery. "Before the next light!" he cried. His haste was contagious. Graham's instinct of self-preservation overcame the paralysis of his incredulous astonishment. He became for a time the blind creature of the fear of death. He ran, stumbling because of the uncertainty of the darkness, blundered into his guards as they turned to run with him. Haste was his one desire, to escape this perilous gallery upon which he was exposed. A third glare came close on its predecessors. With it came a great shouting across the ways, an answering tumult from the ways. The red-coats below, he saw, had now almost gained the central passage. Their countless faces turned towards him, and they shouted. The white façade opposite was densely stippled with red. All these wonderful things concerned him, turned upon him as a pivot. These were the guards of the Council attempting to recapture him.

Lucky it was for him that these shots were the first fired in anger for a hundred and fifty years. He heard bullets whacking over his head, felt a splash of molten metal sting his ear, and perceived without looking that the whole opposite façade, an unmasked ambuscade of red police, was crowded and bawling and firing at him.

Down went one of his guards before him, and Graham, unable to stop, leapt the writhing body.

In another second he had plunged, unhurt, into a black passage, and incontinently someone, coming, it may be, in a transverse direction, blundered violently into him. He was hurling down a staircase in absolute darkness. He reeled, and was struck again, and came against a wall with his hands. He was crushed by a weight of struggling bodies, whirled round, and thrust to the right. A vast pressure pinned him. He could not breathe, his ribs seemed cracking. He felt a momentary relaxation, and then the whole mass of people moving together, bore him back towards the great theatre from which he had so recently come. There were moments when his feet did not touch the ground. Then he was staggering and shoving. He heard shouts of "They are coming!" and a muffled cry close to him. His foot blundered against something soft, he heard a hoarse scream under foot. He heard shouts of "The Sleeper!" but he was too confused to speak. He heard the green weapons crackling. For a space he lost his individual will, became an atom in a panic, blind, unthinking, mechanical. He thrust and pressed back and writhed in the pressure, kicked presently against a step, and found himself ascending a slope. And abruptly the faces all about him leapt out of the black, visible, ghastly-white and astonished, terrified, perspiring, in a livid glare. One face, a young man's, was very near to him, not twenty inches away. At the time it was but a passing incident of no emotional value, but afterwards it came back to him in his dreams. For this young man, wedged upright in the crowd for a time, had been shot and was already dead.

A fourth white star must have been lit by the man on the cable. Its light came glaring in through vast windows and arches and showed Graham that he was now one of a dense mass of flying black figures pressed back across the lower area of the great theatre. This time the picture was livid and fragmentary, slashed and barred with black shadows. He saw that quite near to him the red guards were fighting their way through the people. He could not tell whether they saw him. He looked for Lincoln and his guards. He saw Lincoln near the stage of the theatre surrounded in a crowd of black-badged revolutionaries, lifted up and staring to and fro as if seeking him. Graham perceived that he himself was near the opposite edge of the crowd, that behind him, separated by a barrier, sloped the now vacant seats of the theatre. A sudden idea came to him, and he began fighting his way towards the barrier. As he reached it the glare came to an end.

In a moment he had thrown off the great cloak that not only impeded his movements but made him conspicuous, and had slipped it from his shoulders. He heard someone trip in its folds. In another he was scaling the barrier and had dropped into the blackness on the further side. Then feeling his way he came to the lower end of an ascending gangway. In the darkness the sound of firing ceased and the roar of feet and voices lulled. Then suddenly he came to an unexpected step and tripped and fell. As he did so pools and islands amidst the darkness about him leapt to vivid light again, the uproar surged louder and the glare of the fifth white star shone through the vast fenestrations of the theatre walls.

He rolled over among some seats, heard a shouting and the whirring rattle of weapons, struggled up and was knocked back again, perceived that a number of black-badged men were all about him firing at the reds below, leaping from seat to seat, crouching among the seats to reload. Instinctively he crouched amidst the seats, as stray shots ripped the pneumatic cushions and cut bright slashes on their soft metal frames. Instinctively he marked the direction of the gangways, the most plausible way of escape for him so soon as the veil of darkness fell again.

A young man in faded blue garments came vaulting over the seats. "Hullo!" he said, with his flying feet within six inches of the crouching Sleeper's face.

He stared without any sign of recognition, turned to fire, fired, and, shouting, "To hell with the Council!" was about to fire again. Then it seemed to Graham that the half of this man's neck had vanished. A drop of moisture fell on Graham's cheek. The green weapon stopped half raised. For a moment the man stood still with his face suddenly expressionless, then he began to slant forward. His knees bent. Man and darkness fell together. At the sound of his fall Graham rose up and ran for his life until a step down to the gangway tripped him. He scrambled to his feet, turned up the gangway and ran on.

When the sixth star glared he was already close to the yawning throat of a passage. He ran on the swifter for the light, entered the passage and turned a corner into absolute night again. He was knocked sideways, rolled over, and recovered his feet. He found himself one of a crowd of invisible fugitives pressing in one direction. His one thought now was their thought also; to escape out of this fighting. He thrust and struck, staggered, ran, was wedged tightly, lost ground and then was clear again.

For some minutes he was running through the darkness along a winding passage, and then he crossed some wide and open space, passed down a long incline, and came at last down a flight of steps to a level place. Many people were shouting, "They are coming! The guards are coming. They are firing. Get out of the fighting. The guards are firing. It will be safe in Seventh Way. Along here to Seventh Way!" There were women and children in the crowd as well as men. Men called names to him. The crowd converged on an archway, passed through a short throat and emerged on a wider space again, lit dimly. The black figures about him spread out and ran up what seemed in the twilight to be a gigantic series of steps. He followed. The people dispersed to the right and left. . . . He perceived that he was no longer in a crowd. He stopped near the highest step. Before him, on that level, were groups of seats and a little kiosk. He went up to this and, stopping in the shadow of its eaves, looked about him panting.

Everything was vague and gray, but he recognised that these great steps were a series of platforms of the "ways", now motionless again. The platform slanted up on either side, and the tall buildings rose beyond, vast dim ghosts, their inscriptions and advertisements indistinctly seen, and up through the girders and cables was a faint interrupted ribbon of pallid sky. A number of people hurried by. From their shouts and voices, it seemed they were hurrying to join the fighting. Other less noisy figures flitted timidly among the shadows.

From very far away down the street he could hear the sound of a struggle. But it was evident to him that this was not the street into which the theatre opened. That former fight, it seemed, had suddenly dropped out of sound and hearing. And—grotesque thought!—they were fighting for him!

For a space he was like a man who pauses in the reading of a vivid book, and suddenly doubts what he has been taking unquestioningly. At that time he had little mind for details; the whole effect was a huge astonishment. Oddly enough, while the flight from the Council prison, the great crowd in the hall, and the attack of the red police upon the swarming people were clearly present in his mind, it cost him an effort to piece in his awakening and to revive the meditative interval of the Silent Rooms. At first his memory leapt these things and took him back to the cascade at Pentargen quivering in the wind, and all the sombre splendours of the sunlit Cornish coast. The contrast touched everything with unreality. And then the gap filled, and he began to comprehend his position.

It was no longer absolutely a riddle, as it had been in the Silent Rooms. At least he had the strange, bare outline now. He was in some way the owner of half the world, and great political parties were fighting to possess him. On the one hand was the White Council, with its red police, set resolutely, it seemed, on the usurpation of his property and perhaps his murder; on the other, the revolution that had liberated him, with this unseen "Ostrog" as its leader. And the whole of this gigantic city was convulsed by their struggle. Frantic development of his world! "I do not understand," he cried. "I do not understand!"

He had slipped out between the contending parties into this liberty of the twilight. What would happen next? What was happening? He figured the red-clad men as busily hunting him, driving the black-badged revolutionists before them.

At any rate chance had given him a breathing space. He could lurk unchallenged by the passers-by, and watch the course of things. His eye followed up the intricate dim immensity of the twilight buildings, and it came to him as a thing infinitely wonderful, that above there the sun was rising, and the world was lit and glowing with the old familiar light of day. In a little while he had recovered his breath. His clothing had already dried upon him from the snow.

He wandered for miles along these twilight ways, speaking to no one, accosted by no one—a dark figure among dark figures—the coveted man out of the past, the inestimable unintentional owner of half the world. Wherever there were lights or dense crowds, or exceptional excitement he was afraid of recognition, and watched and turned back or went up and down by the middle stairways, into some transverse system of ways at a lower or higher level. And though he came on no more fighting, the whole city stirred with battle. Once he had to run to avoid a marching multitude of men that swept the street. Everyone abroad seemed involved. For the most part they were men, and they carried what he judged were weapons. It seemed as though the struggle was concentrated mainly in the quarter of the city from which he came. Ever and again a distant roaring, the remote suggestion of that conflict, reached his ears. Then his caution and his curiosity struggled together. But his caution prevailed, and he continued wandering away from the fighting—so far as he could judge. He went unmolested, unsuspected through the dark. After a time he ceased to hear even a remote echo of the battle, fewer and fewer people passed him, until at last the Titanic streets became deserted. The frontages of the buildings grew plain and harsh; he seemed to have come to a district of vacant warehouses. Solitude crept upon him—his pace slackened.

He became aware of a growing fatigue. At times he would turn aside and seat himself on one of the numerous seats of the upper ways. But a feverish restlessness, the knowledge of his vital implication in this struggle, would not let him rest in any place for long. Was the struggle on his behalf alone?

And then in a desolate place came the shock of an earthquake—a roaring and thundering—a mighty wind of cold air pouring through the city, the smash of glass, the slip and thud of falling masonry—a series of gigantic concussions. A mass of glass and ironwork fell from the remote roofs into the middle gallery, not a hundred yards away from him, and in the distance were shouts and running. He, too, was startled to an aimless activity, and ran first one way and then as aimlessly back.

A man came running towards him. His self-control returned. "What have they blown up?" asked the man breathlessly. "That was an explosion," and before Graham could speak he had hurried on.

The great buildings rose dimly, veiled by a perplexing twilight, albeit the rivulet of sky above was now bright with day. He noted many strange features, understanding none at the time; he even spelt out many of the inscriptions in Phonetic lettering. But what profits it to decipher a confusion of odd-looking letters resolving itself, after painful strain of eye and mind, into "Here is Eadhamite," or, "Labour Bureau—Little Side?" Grotesque thought, that in all probability some or all of these cliff-like houses were his!

The perversity of his experience came to him vividly. In actual fact he had made such a leap in time as romancers have imagined again and again. And that fact realised, he had been prepared, his mind had, as it were, seated itself for a spectacle. And no spectacle, but a great vague danger, unsympathetic shadows and veils of darkness. Somewhere through the labyrinthine obscurity his death sought him. Would he, after all, be killed before he saw? It might be that even at the next shadowy corner his destruction ambushed. A great desire to see, a great longing to know, arose in him.

He became fearful of corners. It seemed to him that there was safety in concealment. Where could he hide to be inconspicuous when the lights returned? At last he sat down upon a seat in a recess on one of the higher ways, conceiving he was alone there.

He squeezed his knuckles into his weary eyes. Suppose when he looked again he found the dark trough of parallel ways and that intolerable altitude of edifice, gone? Suppose he were to discover the whole story of these last few days, the awakening, the shouting multitudes, the darkness and the fighting, a phantasmagoria, a new and more vivid sort of dream. It must be a dream; it was so inconsecutive, so reasonless. Why were the people fighting for him? Why should this saner world regard him as Owner and Master?

So he thought, sitting blinded, and then he looked again, half hoping in spite of his ears to see some familiar aspect of the life of the nineteenth century, to see, perhaps, the little harbour of Boscastle about him, the cliffs of Pentargen, or the bedroom of his home. But fact takes no heed of human hopes. A squad of men with a black banner tramped athwart the nearer shadows, intent on conflict, and beyond rose that giddy wall of frontage, vast and dark, with the dim incomprehensible lettering showing faintly on its face.

"It is no dream," he said, "no dream." And he bowed his face upon his hands.

CHAPTER XI

THE OLD MAN WHO KNEW EVERYTHING

HE WAS startled by a cough close at hand.

He turned sharply, and peering, saw a small, hunched-up figure sitting a couple of yards off in the shadow of the enclosure.

"Have ye any news?" asked the high-pitched wheezy voice of a very old man.

Graham hesitated. "None," he said.

"I stay here till the lights come again," said the old man. "These blue scoundrels are everywhere—everywhere."

Graham's answer was inarticulate assent. He tried to see the old man but the darkness hid his face. He wanted very much to respond, to talk, but he did not know how to begin.

"Dark and damnable," said the old man suddenly. "Dark and damnable. Turned out of my room among all these dangers."

"That's hard," ventured Graham. "That's hard on you."

"Darkness. An old man lost in the darkness. And all the world gone mad. War and fighting. The police beaten and rogues abroad. Why don't they bring some negroes to protect us?... No more dark passages for me. I fell over a dead man."

"You're safer with company," said the old man, "if it's company of the right sort," and peered frankly. He rose suddenly and came towards Graham.

Apparently the scrutiny was satisfactory. The old man sat down as if relieved to be no longer alone. "Eh!" he said, "but this is a terrible time! War and fighting, and the dead lying there—men, strong men, dying in the dark. Sons! I have three sons. God knows where they are tonight."

The voice ceased. Then repeated quavering: "God knows where they are tonight."

Graham stood revolving a question that should not betray his ignorance. Again the old man's voice ended the pause.

"This Ostrog will win," he said. "He will win. And what the world will be like under him no one can tell. My sons are under the wind-vanes, all three. One of my daughters-in-law was his mistress for a while. His mistress! We're not common people. Though they've sent me to wander tonight and take my chance. . . . I knew what was going on. Before most people. But this darkness! And to fall over a dead body suddenly in the dark!"

His wheezy breathing could be heard.

"Ostrog!" said Graham.

"The greatest Boss the world has ever seen," said the voice.

Graham ransacked his mind. "The Council has few friends among the people," he hazarded.

"Few friends. And poor ones at that. They've had their time. Eh! They should have kept to the clever ones. But twice they held election. And Ostrog—— And now it has burst out and nothing can stay it, nothing can stay it. Twice they rejected Ostrog—Ostrog the Boss. I heard of his rages at the time—he was terrible. Heaven save them! For nothing on earth can now, he has raised the Labour Companies upon them. No one else would have dared. All the blue canvas armed and marching! He will go through with it. He will go through."

He was silent for a little while. "This Sleeper," he said, and stopped.

"Yes," said Graham. "Well?"

The senile voice sank to a confidential whisper, the dim, pale face came close. "The real Sleeper——"

"Yes," said Graham.

"Died years ago."

"What?" said Graham, sharply.

"Years ago. Died. Years ago."

"You don't say so!" said Graham.

"I do. I do say so. He died. This Sleeper who's woke up—they changed in the night. A poor, drugged insensible creature. But I mustn't tell all I know. I mustn't tell all I know."

For a little while he muttered inaudibly. His secret was too much for him. "I don't know the ones that put him to sleep—that was before my time—but I know the man who injected the stimulants and woke him again. It was ten to one—wake or kill. Wake or kill. Ostrog's way."

Graham was so astonished at these things that he had to interrupt, to make the old man repeat his words, to re-question vaguely, before he was sure of the meaning and folly of what he heard. And his awakening had not been natural! Was that an old man's senile superstition, too, or had it any truth in it? Feeling in the dark corners of his memory, he presently came on something that might conceivably be an impression of some such stimulating effect. It dawned upon him that he had happened upon a lucky encounter, that at last he might learn something of the new age. The old man wheezed a while and spat, and then the piping, reminiscent voice resumed:

"The first time they rejected him. I've followed it all."

"Rejected whom?" said Graham. "The Sleeper?"

"Sleeper? *No.* Ostrog. He was terrible—terrible! And he was promised then, promised certainly the next time. Fools they were—not to be more afraid of him. Now all the city's his millstone, and such as we dust ground upon it. Dust ground upon it. Until he set to work—the workers cut each other's throats, and murdered a Chinaman or a Labour policeman at times, and left the rest of us in peace. Dead bodies! Robbing! Darkness! Such a thing hasn't been this gross of years. Eh!—but 'tis ill on small folks when the great fall out! It's ill."

"Did you say—there had not been—what?—for a gross of years?"

"Eh?" said the old man.

The old man said something about clipping his words, and made him repeat this a third time. "Fighting and slaying, and weapons in hand, and fools bawling freedom and the like," said the old man. "Not in all my life has there been that. These are like the old days—for sure—when the Paris people broke out—three gross of years ago. That's what I mean hasn't been. But it's the world's way. It had to come back. I know. I know. This five years Ostrog has been working, and there has been trouble and trouble, and hunger and threats and high talk and arms. Blue canvas and murmurs. No one safe. Everything sliding and slipping. And now here we are! Revolt and fighting, and the Council come to its end."

"You are rather well-informed on these things," said Graham.

"I know what I hear. It isn't all Babble Machine with me."

"No," said Graham, wondering what Babble Machine might be. "And you are certain this Ostrog—you are certain Ostrog organised this rebellion and arranged for the waking of the Sleeper? Just to assert himself—because he was not elected to the Council?"

"Everyone knows that, I should think," said the old man. "Except—just fools. He meant to be master somehow. In the Council or not. Everyone who knows anything knows that. And here we are with dead bodies lying in the dark! Why, where have you been if you haven't heard all about the trouble between Ostrog and the Verneys? And what do you think the troubles are about? The Sleeper? Eh? You think the Sleeper's real and woke of his own accord—eh?"

"I'm a dull man, older than I look, and forgetful," said Graham. "Lots of things that have happened—especially of late years—— If I was the Sleeper, to tell you the truth, I couldn't know less about them."

"Eh!" said the voice. "Old, are you? You don't sound so very old! But it's not everyone keeps his memory to my time of life—truly. But these notorious things! But you're not so old as me—not nearly so old as me. Well! I ought not to judge other men by myself, perhaps. I'm young—for so old a man. Maybe you're old for so young."

"That's it," said Graham. "And I've a queer history. I know very little. And history! Practically I know no history. The Sleeper and Julius Caesar are all the same to me. It's interesting to hear you talk of these things."

"I know· a few things," said the old man. "I know a thing or two. But—— Hark!"

The two men became silent, listening. There was a heavy thud, a concussion that made their seat shiver. The passers-by stopped, shouted to one another. The old man was full of questions; he shouted to a man who passed near. Graham, emboldened by his example, got up and accosted others. None knew what had happened.

He returned to the seat and found the old man muttering vague interrogations in an undertone. For a while they said nothing to one another.

The sense of this gigantic struggle, so near and yet so remote oppressed Graham's imagination. Was this old man right, was the report of the people right, and were the revolutionaries winning? Or were they all in error, and were the red guards driving all before them? At any time the flood of warfare might pour into this silent quarter of the city and seize upon him again. It behoved him to learn all he could while there was time. He turned suddenly to the old man with a question and left it unsaid. But his motion moved the old man to speech again.

"Eh! but how things work together!" said the old man. "This Sleeper that all the fools put their trust in! I've the whole history of it—I was always a good one for histories. When I was a boy—I'm that old—I used to read printed books. You'd hardly think it. Likely you've seen none—they rot and dust so—and the Sanitary Company burns them to make ashlarite. But they were convenient in their dirty way. One learnt a lot. These new-fangled Babble Machines—they don't seem new-fangled to you, eh?—they're easy to hear, easy to forget. But I've traced all the Sleeper business from the first."

"You will scarcely believe it," said Graham slowly, "I'm so ignorant —I've been so preoccupied in my own little affairs, my circumstances have been so odd—I know nothing of this Sleeper's history. Who was he?"

"Eh!" said the old man. "I know. I know. He was a poor nobody, and set on a playful woman, poor soul! And he fell into a trance. There's the old things they had, those brown things—silver photographs—still showing him as he lay, a gross and a half years ago—a gross and a half of years."

"Set on a playful woman, poor soul," said Graham softly to himself, and then aloud, "Yes—well! go on."

"You must know he had a cousin named Warming, a solitary man without children, who made a big fortune speculating in roads—the first Eadhamite roads. But surely you've heard? No? Why? He bought all the patent rights and made a big company. In those days there were grosses of grosses of separate businesses and business companies. Grosses of grosses! His roads killed the railroads—the old things—in two dozen years; he bought up and Eadhamited the tracks. And because he didn't want to break up his great property or let in shareholders, he left it all to the Sleeper, and put it under a Board of Trustees that he had picked and trained. He knew then the Sleeper wouldn't wake, that he would go on sleeping, sleeping till he died. He knew that quite well! And plump! a man in the United States, who had lost two sons in a boat accident, followed that up with another great bequest. His trustees found themselves with a dozen myriads of lions'-worth or more of property at the very beginning."

"What was his name?"

"Graham."

"No—I mean—that American's."

"Isbister."

"Isbister!" cried Graham. "Why, I don't even know the name."

"Of course not," said the old man. "Of course not. People don't learn much in the schools nowadays. But I know all about him. He was a rich American who went from England, and he left the Sleeper even more than Warming. How he made it? That I don't know. Something about pictures by machinery. But he made it and left it, and so the Council had its start. It was just a council of trustees at first."

"And how did it grow?"

"Eh!—but you're not up to things. Money attracts money—and twelve brains are better than one. They played it cleverly. They worked politics with money, and kept on adding to the money by working currency and tariffs. They grew—they grew. And for years the twelve trustees hid the growing of the Sleeper's estate, under double names and company titles and all that. The Council spread by title deed, mortgage, share, every political party, every newspaper, they bought. If you listen to the old stories you will see the Council growing and growing. Billions and billions of lions at last—the Sleeper's estate. And all growing out of a whim—out of this Warming's will, and an accident to Isbister's sons.

"Men are strange," said the old man. "The strange thing to me is how the Council worked together so long. As many as twelve. But they worked in cliques from the first. And they've slipped back. In my young days speaking of the Council was like an ignorant man speaking of God. We didn't think they could do wrong. We didn't know of their women and all that! Or else I've got wiser.

"Men are strange," said the old man. "Here are you, young and ignorant, and me—sevendy years old, and I might reasonably be forgetting—explaining it all to you short and clear.

"Sevendy," he said, "sevendy, and I hear and see—hear better than I see. And reason clearly, and keep myself up to all the happenings of things. Sevendy!

"Life is strange. I was twaindy before Ostrog was a baby. I remember him long before he'd pushed his way to the head of the Wind Vanes Control. I've seen many changes. Eh! I've worn the blue. And at last I've come to see this crush and darkness and tumult and dead men carried by in heaps on the ways. And all his doing! All his doing!"

His voice died away in scarcely articulate praises of Ostrog.

Graham thought. "Let me see," he said, "if I have it right."

He extended a hand and ticked off points upon his fingers. "The Sleeper has been asleep——"

"Changed," said the old man.

"Perhaps. And meanwhile the Sleeper's property grew in the hands of Twelve Trustees, until it swallowed up nearly all the great ownership of the world. The Twelve Trustees—by virtue of this property have become virtually masters of the world. Because they are the paying power—just as the old English Parliament used to be——"

"Eh!" said the old man. "That's so—that's a good comparison. You're not so——"

"And now this Ostrog—has suddenly revolutionised the world by waking the Sleeper—whom no one but the superstitious, common people had ever dreamt would wake again—raising the Sleeper to claim his property from the Council, after all these years."

The old man endorsed this statement with a cough. "It's strange," he said, "to meet a man who learns these things for the first time tonight."

"Aye," said Graham, "it's strange."

"Have you been in a Pleasure City?" said the old man. "All my life

I've longed——" He laughed. "Even now," he said, "I could enjoy a little fun. Enjoy seeing things, anyhow." He mumbled a sentence Graham did not understand.

"The Sleeper—when did he awake?" said Graham suddenly.

"Three days ago."

"Where is he?"

"Ostrog has him. He escaped from the Council not four hours ago. My dear sir, where were you at the time? He was in the hall of the markets —where the fighting has been. All the city was screaming about it. All the Babble Machines. Everywhere it was shouted. Even the fools who speak for the Council were admitting it. Everyone was rushing off to see him—everyone was getting arms. Were you drunk or asleep? And even then! But you're joking! Surely you're pretending. It was to stop the shouting of the Babble Machines and prevent the people gathering that they turned off the electricity—and put this damned darkness upon us. Do you mean to say——?"

"I had heard the Sleeper was rescued," said Graham. "But—to come back a minute. Are you sure Ostrog has him?"

"He won't let him go," said the old man.

"And the Sleeper. Are you sure he is not genuine? I have never heard——"

"So all the fools think. So they think. As if there wasn't a thousand things that were never heard. I know Ostrog too well for that. Did I tell you? In a way I'm a sort of relation of Ostrog's. A sort of relation. Through my daughter-in-law."

"I suppose——"

"Well?"

"I suppose there's no chance of this Sleeper asserting himself. I suppose he's certain to be a puppet—in Ostrog's hands or the Council's, as soon as the struggle is over."

"In Ostrog's hands—certainly. Why shouldn't he be a puppet? Look at his position. Everything done for him, every pleasure possible. Why should he want to assert himself?"

"What are these Pleasure Cities?" said Graham, abruptly.

The old man made him repeat the question. When at last he was assured of Graham's words, he nudged him violently. "That's *too* much," said he. "You're poking fun at an old man. I've been suspecting you know more than you pretend."

"Perhaps I do," said Graham. "But no! why should I go on acting? No, I do not know what a Pleasure City is."

The old man laughed in an intimate way.

"What is more, I do not know how to read your letters, I do not know what money you use, I do not know what foreign countries there are. I do not know where I am. I cannot count. I do not know where to get food, nor drink, nor shelter."

"Come, come," said the old man, "if you had a glass of drink, now, would you put it in your ear or your eye?"

"I want you to tell me all these things."

"He, he! Well, gentlemen who dress in silk must have their fun." A withered hand caressed Graham's arm for a moment. "Silk. Well, well! But, all the same, I wish I was the man who was put up as the Sleeper. He'll have a fine time of it. All the pomp and pleasure. He's a queer looking face. When they used to let anyone go to see him, I've got tickets and been. The image of the real one, as the photographs show, this substitute used to be. Yellow. But he'll get fed up. It's a queer world. Think of the luck of it. The luck of it. I expect he'll be sent to Capri. It's the best fun for a greener."

His cough overtook him again. Then he began mumbling enviously of pleasures and strange delights. "The luck of it, the luck of it! All my life I've been in London, hoping to get my chance."

"But you don't know that the Sleeper died," said Graham, suddenly.

The old man made him repeat his words.

"Men don't live beyond ten dozen. It's not in the order of things," said the old man. "I'm not a fool. Fools may believe it, but not me."

Graham became angry with the old man's assurance. "Whether you are a fool or not," he said, "it happens you are wrong about the Sleeper."

"Eh?"

"You are wrong about the Sleeper. I haven't told you before, but I will tell you now. You are wrong about the Sleeper."

"How do you know? I thought you didn't know anything—not even about Pleasure Cities."

Graham paused.

"You don't know," said the old man. "How are you to know? It's very few men——"

"I *am* the Sleeper."

He had to repeat it.

There was a brief pause. "There's a silly thing to say, sir, if you'll excuse me. It might get you into trouble in a time like this," said the old man.

Graham, slightly dashed, repeated his assertion.

"I was saying I was the Sleeper. That years and years ago I did, indeed, fall asleep, in a little stone-built village, in the days when there were hedgerows, and villages, and inns, and all the countryside cut up into little pieces, little fields. Have you never heard of those days? And it is I —I who speak to you—who awakened again these four days since."

"Four days since!—the Sleeper! But they've *got* the Sleeper. They have him and they won't let him go. Nonsense! You've been talking sensibly enough up to now. I can see it as though I was there. There will be Lincoln like a keeper just behind him; they won't let him go about alone. Trust them. You're a queer fellow. One of these fun pokers. I see now why you have been clipping your words so oddly, but——"

He stopped abruptly, and Graham could see his gesture.

"As if Ostrog would let the Sleeper run about alone! No, you're telling that to the wrong man altogether. Eh! as if I should believe. What's your game? And besides, we've been talking of the Sleeper."

Graham stood up. "Listen," he said. "I am the Sleeper."

"You're an odd man," said the old man, "to sit here in the dark, talking clipped, and telling a lie of that sort. But——"

Graham's exasperation fell to laughter. "It is preposterous," he cried. "Preposterous. The dream must end. It gets wilder and wilder. Here am I—in this damned twilight—I never knew a dream in twilight before—an anachronism by two hundred years and trying to persuade an old fool that I am myself, and meanwhile—— Ugh!"

He moved in gusty irritation and went striding. In a moment the old man was pursuing him. "Eh! but don't go!" cried the old man. "I'm an old fool, I know. Don't go. Don't leave me in all this darkness."

Graham hesitated, stopped. Suddenly the folly of telling his secret flashed into his mind.

"I didn't mean to offend you—disbelieving you," said the old man coming near. "It's no manner of harm. Call yourself the Sleeper if it pleases you. 'Tis a foolish trick——"

Graham hesitated, turned abruptly and went on his way.

For a time he heard the old man's hobbling pursuit and his wheezy cries receding. But at last the darkness swallowed him, and Graham saw him no more.

CHAPTER XII

OSTROG

GRAHAM COULD now take a clearer view of his position. For a long time yet he wandered, bui after the talk of the old man his discovery of this Ostrog was clear in his mind as the final inevitable decision. One thing was evident, those who were at the headquarters of the revolt had succeeded very admirably in suppressing the fact of his disappearance. But every moment he expected to hear the report of his death or of his recapture by the Council.

Presently a man stopped before him. "Have you heard?" he said.

"No!" said Graham starting.

"Near a dozand," said the man, "a dozand men!" and hurried on.

A number of men and a girl passed in the darkness, gesticulating and shouting: "Capitulated! Given up!" "A dozand of men." "Two dozand of men." "Ostrog, Hurrah! Ostrog, Hurrah!" These cries receded, became indistinct.

Other shouting men followed. For a time his attention was absorbed in the fragments of speech he heard. He had a doubt whether all were speaking English. Scraps floated to him, scraps like Pigeon English, like dialect, blurred and mangled distortions. He dared accost no one with questions. The impression the people gave him jarred altogether with his preconceptions of the struggle and confirmed the old man's faith in Ostrog. It was only slowly he could bring himself to believe that all these people were rejoicing at the defeat of the Council, that the Council which had pursued him with such power and vigour was after all the weaker of the two sides in conflict. And if that was so, how did it affect him? Several times he hesitated on the verge of fundamental questions. Once he turned and walked for a long way after a little man of rotund inviting outline, but he was unable to master confidence to address him.

It was only slowly that it came to him that he might ask for the "wind-vane offices," whatever the "wind-vane offices" might be. His first enquiry simply resulted in a direction to go on towards Westminster. His second led to the discovery of a short cut in which he was speedily lost. He was told to leave the ways to which he had hitherto confined himself—knowing no other means of transit—and to plunge down one of the middle staircases into the blackness of a crossway. Thereupon came some trivial adventures; chief of these an ambiguous encounter with a gruff-voiced invisible creature speaking in a strange dialect that seemed at first a strange tongue, a thick flow of speech with the drifting corpses of English words therein, the dialect of the latter-day vile. Then another voice drew near, a girl's voice singing, "tralala tralala." She spoke to Graham, her English touched with something of the same quality. She professed to have lost her sister, she blundered needlessly into him he thought, caught hold of him and laughed. But a word of vague remonstrance sent her into the unseen again.

The sounds about him increased. Stumbling people passed him, speaking excitedly. "They have surrendered!" "The Council! Surely not the Council!" "They are saying so in the Ways." The passage seemed wider. Suddenly the wall fell away. He was in a great space and people were stirring remotely. He inquired his way of an indistinct figure. "Strike straight across," said a woman's voice. He left his guiding wall, and in a moment had stumbled against a little table on which were utensils of glass. Graham's eyes, now attuned to darkness, made out a long vista with pallid tables on either side. He went down this. At one or two of the tables he heard a clang of glass and a sound of eating. There were people then cool enough to dine, or daring enough to steal a meal in spite of social convulsion and darkness. Far off and high up he presently saw a pallid light of a semi-circular shape. As he approached this, a black edge came up and hid it. He stumbled at steps and found himself in a gallery. He heard a sobbing, and found two scared little girls crouched by a railing. These children became silent at the near sound of feet. He tried to console them, but they were very still until he left them. Then as he receded he could hear them sobbing again.

Presently he found himself at the foot of a staircase and near a wide opening. He saw a dim twilight above this and ascended out of the blackness into a street of moving Ways again. Along this a disorderly swarm of people marched shouting. They were singing snatches of the song of the revolt, most of them out of tune. Here and there torches flared creating brief hysterical shadows. He asked his way and was twice puzzled by that same thick dialect. His third attempt won an answer he could understand. He was two miles from the wind-vane offices in Westminster, but the way was easy to follow.

When at last he did approach the district of the wind-vane offices it seemed to him, from the cheering processions that came marching along the Ways, from the tumult of rejoicing, and finally from the restoration of the lighting of the city, that the overthrow of the Council must already be accomplished. And still no news of his absence came to his ears.

The re-illumination of the city came with startling abruptness. Suddenly he stood blinking, all about him men halted dazzled, and the world was incandescent. The light found him already upon the outskirts of the excited crowds that choked the Ways near the wind-vane offices, and the sense of visibility and exposure that came with it turned his colourless intention of joining Ostrog to a keen anxiety.

For a time he was jostled, obstructed, and endangered by men hoarse and weary with cheering his name, some of them bandaged and bloody in his cause. The frontage of the wind-vane offices was illuminated by some moving picture, but what it was he could not see, because in spite of his strenuous attempts the density of the crowd prevented his approaching it. From the fragments of speech he caught, he judged it conveyed news of the fighting about the Council House. Ignorance and indecision made him slow and ineffective in his movements. For a time he could not conceive how he was to get within the unbroken façade of this place. He made his way slowly into the midst of this mass of people, until he realised that the descending staircase of the central Way led to the interior of the buildings. This gave him a goal, but the crowding in the central path was so dense that it was long before he could reach it. And even then he encountered intricate obstruction, and had an hour of vivid argument first in this guard room and then in that before he could get a note taken to the one man of all men who was most eager to see him. His story was laughed to scorn at one place, and wiser for that, when at last he reached a second stairway he professed simply to have news of extraordinary importance for Ostrog. What it was he would not say. They sent his note reluctantly. For a long time he waited in a little room at the foot of the lift shaft, and thither at last came Lincoln, eager, apologetic, astonished. He stopped in the doorway scrutinising Graham, then rushed forward effusively.

"Yes," he cried. "It is you. And you are not dead!"

Graham made a brief explanation.

"My brother is waiting," explained Lincoln. "He is alone in the wind-vane offices. We feared you had been killed in the theatre. He doubted—and things are very urgent still in spite of what we are telling them *there*—or he would have come to you."

They ascended a lift, passed along a narrow passage, crossed a great hall, empty save for two hurrying messengers, and entered a comparatively little room, whose only furniture was a long settee and a large oval disc of cloudy, shifting grey, hung by cables from the wall. There Lincoln left Graham for a space, and he remained alone without understanding the shifting smoky shapes that drove slowly across this disc.

His attention was arrested by a sound that began abruptly. It was cheering, the frantic cheering of a vast but very remote crowd, a roaring exultation. This ended as sharply as it had begun, like a sound heard between the opening and shutting of a door. In the outer room was a noise of hurrying steps and a melodious clinking as if a loose chain was running over the teeth of a wheel.

Then he heard the voice of a woman, the rustle of unseen garments. "It is Ostrog!" he heard her say. A little bell rang fitfully, and then everything was still again.

Presently came voices, footsteps and movement without. The footsteps of some one person detached itself from the other sounds and drew near, firm, evenly measured steps. The curtain lifted slowly. A tall, white-haired man, clad in garments of cream-coloured silk, appeared, regarding Graham from under his raised arm.

For a moment the white form remained holding the curtain, then dropped it and stood before it. Graham's first impression was of a very broad forehead, very pale blue eyes deep sunken under white brows, an aquiline nose, and a heavily-lined resolute mouth. The folds of flesh over the eyes, the drooping of the corners of the mouth contradicted the upright bearing, and said the man was old. Graham rose to his feet instinctively, and for a moment the two men stood in silence, regarding each other.

"You are Ostrog?" said Graham.

"I am Ostrog."

"The Boss?"

"So I am called."

Graham felt the inconvenience of the silence. "I have to thank you chiefly, I understand, for my safety," he said presently.

"We were afraid you were killed," said Ostrog. "Or sent to sleep again—for ever. We have been doing everything to keep our secret—the secret of your disappearance. Where have you been? How did you get here?"

Graham told him briefly.

Ostrog listened in silence.

He smiled faintly. "Do you know what I was doing when they came to tell me you had come?"

"How can I guess?"

"Preparing your double."

"My double?"

"A man as like you as we could find. We were going to hypnotise him, to save him the difficulty of acting. It was imperative. The whole of this revolt depends on the idea that you are awake, alive, and with us. Even now a great multitude of people has gathered in the theatre clamouring to see you. They do not trust . . . You know, of course—something of your position?"

"Very little," said Graham.

"It is like this." Ostrog walked a pace or two into the room and turned. "You are absolute owner," he said, "of more than half the world. As a result of that you are practically King. Your powers are limited in many intricate ways, but you are the figurehead, the popular symbol of government. This White Council, the Council of Trustees as it is called——"

"I have heard the vague outline of these things."

"I wondered."

"I came upon a garrulous old man."

"I see . . . Our masses—the word comes from your days—you know of course, that we still have masses—regard you as our actual ruler. Just as a great number of people in your days regarded the Crown as the ruler. They are discontented—the masses all over the earth—with the rule of your Trustees. For the most part it is the old discontent, the old quarrel of the common man with his commonness—the misery of work and discipline and unfitness. But your Trustees have ruled ill. In certain matters, in the administration of the Labour Companies, for example, they have been unwise. They have given endless opportunities. Already we of the popular party were agitating for reforms—when your waking came. Came! If it had been contrived it could not have come more opportunely." He smiled. "The public mind, making no allowance for your years of quiescence, had already hit on the thought of waking you and appealing to you, and—Flash!"

He indicated the outbreak by a gesture, and Graham moved his head to show that he understood.

"The Council muddled—quarrelled. They always do. They could not decide what to do with you. You know how they imprisoned you?"

"I see. I see. And now—we win?"

"We win. Indeed we win. Tonight, in five swift hours. Suddenly we struck everywhere. The wind-vane people, the Labour Company and its millions, burst the bonds. We got the pull of the aëropiles."

He paused. "Yes," said Graham, guessing that aëropile meant flying machine.

"That was, of course, essential. Or they could have got away. All the city rose, every third man almost was in it! All the blue, all the public services, save only just a few aëronauts and about half the red police. You were rescued, and their own police of the Ways—not half of them could be massed at the Council House—have been broken up, disarmed or killed. All London is ours—now. Only the Council House remains.

"Half of those who remain to them of the red police were lost in that foolish attempt to recapture you. They lost their heads when they lost you. They flung all they had at the theatre. We cut them off from the Council House there. Truly tonight has been a night of victory. Everywhere your star has blazed. A day ago—the White Council ruled as it has ruled for a gross of years, for a century and a half of years, and then, with only a little whispering, a covert arming here and there, suddenly —So!"

"I am very ignorant," said Graham. "I suppose—— I do not clearly understand the conditions of this fighting. If you could explain. Where is the Council? Where is the fight?"

Ostrog stepped across the room, something clicked, and suddenly, save for an oval glow, they were in darkness. For a moment Graham was puzzled.

Then he saw that the cloudy grey disc had taken depth and colour, had assumed the appearance of an oval window looking out upon a strange unfamiliar scene.

At the first glance he was unable to guess what this scene might be. It was a daylight scene, the daylight of a wintry day, grey and clear. Across the picture and halfway as it seemed between him and the remoter view, a stout cable of twisted white wire stretched vertically. Then he perceived that the rows of great wind-wheels he saw, the wide intervals, the occasional gulfs of darkness, were akin to those through which he had fled from the Council House. He distinguished an orderly file of red figures marching across an open space between files of men in black, and realised before Ostrog spoke that he was looking down on the upper surface of latter-day London. The overnight snows had gone. He judged that this mirror was some modern replacement of the camera obscura, but that matter was not explained to him. He saw that though the file of red figures was trotting from left to right, yet they were passing out of the picture to the left. He wondered momentarily, and then saw that the picture was passing slowly, panorama fashion, across the oval.

"In a moment you will see the fighting," said Ostrog at his elbow. "Those fellows in red you notice are prisoners. This is the roof space of London—all the houses are practically continuous now. The streets and public squares are covered in. The gaps and chasms of your time have disappeared."

Something out of focus obliterated half the picture. Its form suggested a man. There was a gleam of metal, a flash, something that swept across the oval, as the eyelid of a bird sweeps across its eye, and the picture was clear again. And now Graham beheld men running down among the wind-wheels, pointing weapons from which jetted out little smoky flashes. They swarmed thicker and thicker to the right, gesticulating—it might be they were shouting, but of that the picture told nothing. They and the wind-wheels passed slowly and steadily across the field of the mirror.

"Now," said Ostrog, "comes the Council House," and slowly a black edge crept into view and gathered Graham's attention. Soon it was no longer an edge but a cavity, a huge blackened space amidst the clustering edifices, and from it thin spires of smoke rose into the pallid winter sky. Gaunt ruinous masses of the building, mighty truncated piers and girders, rose dismally out of this cavernous darkness. And over these vestiges of some splendid place, countless minute men were clambering, leaping, swarming.

"This is the Council House," said Ostrog. "Their last stronghold. And the fools wasted enough ammunition to hold out for a month in blowing up the buildings all about them—to stop our attack. You heard the smash? It shattered half the brittle glass in the city."

And while he spoke, Graham saw that beyond this area of ruins, over-hanging it and rising to a great height, was a ragged mass of white build-ing. This mass had been isolated by the ruthless destruction of its sur-roundings. Black gaps marked the passages the disaster had torn apart; big halls had been slashed open and the decoration of their interiors showed dismally in the wintry dawn, and down the jagged walls hung festoons of divided cables and twisted ends of lines and metallic rods. And amidst all the vast details moved little red specks, the red-clothed defenders of the Council. Every now and then faint flashes illuminated the bleak shadows. At the first sight it seemed to Graham that an attack upon this isolated white building was in progress, but then he perceived that the party of the revolt was not advancing, but sheltered amidst the colossal wreckage that encircled this last ragged stronghold of the red-garbed men, was keeping up a fitful firing.

And not ten hours ago he had stood beneath the ventilating fans in a little chamber within that remote building wondering what was happen-ing in the world!

Looking more attentively as this warlike episode moved silently across the centre of the mirror, Graham saw that the white building was sur-rounded on every side by ruins, and Ostrog proceeded to describe in con-cise phrases how its defenders had sought by such destruction to isolate themselves from a storm. He spoke of the loss of men that huge downfall had entailed in an indifferent tone. He indicated an improvised mortuary among the wreckage, showed ambulances swarming like cheese-mites along a ruinous groove that had once been a street of moving ways. He was more interested in pointing out the parts of the Council House, the distribution of the besiegers. In a little while the civil contest that had convulsed London was no longer a mystery to Graham. It was no tumultuous revolt had occurred that night, no equal warfare, but a splendidly organised *coup d'état*. Ostrog's grasp of details was astonish-ing; he seemed to know the business of even the smallest knot of black and red specks that crawled amidst these places.

He stretched a huge black arm across the luminous picture, and showed the room whence Graham had escaped, and across the chasm of ruins the course of his flight. Graham recognised the gulf across which the gutter ran, and the wind-wheels where he had crouched from the flying machine. The rest of his path had succumbed to the explosion. He looked again at the Council House, and it was already half hidden, and on the right a hillside with a cluster of domes and pinnacles, hazy, dim and distant, was gliding into view.

"And the Council is really overthrown?" he said.

"Overthrown," said Ostrog.

"And I——— Is it indeed true that I———?"

"You are Master of the World."

"But that white flag———"

"That is the flag of the Council—the flag of the Rule of the World. It will fall. The fight is over. Their attack on the theatre was their last frantic struggle. They have only a thousand men or so, and some of these men will be disloyal. They have little ammunition. And we are reviving the ancient arts. We are casting guns."

"But—help. Is this city the world?"

"Practically this is all they have left to them of their empire. Abroad the cities have either revolted with us or wait the issue. Your awakening has perplexed them, paralysed them."

"But haven't the Council flying machines? Why is there no fighting with them?"

"They had. But the greater part of the aëronauts were in the revolt with us. They wouldn't take the risk of fighting on our side, but they would not stir against us. We *had* to get a pull with the aëronauts. Quite half were with us, and the others knew it. Directly they knew you had got away, those looking for you dropped. We killed the man who shot at you—an hour ago. And we occupied the flying stages at the outset in every city we could, and so stopped and captured the aëroplanes, and as for the little flying machines that turned out—for some did—we kept up too straight and steady a fire for them to get near the Council House. If they dropped they couldn't rise again, because there's no clear space about there for them to get up. Several we have smashed, several others have dropped and surrendered, the rest have gone off to the Continent to find a friendly city if they can before their fuel runs out. Most of these men were only too glad to be taken prisoner and kept out of harm's way. Upsetting in a flying machine isn't a very attractive prospect. There's no chance for the Council that way. Its days are done."

He laughed and turned to the oval reflection again to show Graham what he meant by flying stages. Even the four nearer ones were remote and obscured by a thin morning haze. But Graham could perceive they were very vast structures, judged even by the standard of the things about them.

And then as these dim shapes passed to the left there came again the sight of the expanse across which the disarmed men in red had been marching. And then the black ruins, and then again the beleaguered

* 23 years before the Wright brothers at Kitty Hawk

white fastness of the Council. It appeared no longer a ghostly pile, but glowing amber in the sunlight, for a cloud shadow had passed. About it the pigmy struggle still hung in suspense, but now the red defenders were no longer firing.

So, in a dusky stillness, the man from the nineteenth century saw the closing scene of the great revolt, the forcible establishment of his rule. With a quality of startling discovery it came to him that this was his world, and not that other he had left behind; that this was no spectacle to culminate and cease; that in this world lay whatever life was still before him, lay all his duties and dangers and responsibilities. He turned with fresh questions. Ostrog began to answer them, and then broke off abruptly. "But these things I must explain more fully later. At present there are—duties. The people are coming by the moving ways towards this ward from every part of the city—the markets and theatres are densely crowded. You are just in time for them. They are clamouring to see you. And abroad they want to see you. Paris, New York, Chicago, Denver, Capri—thousands of cities are up and in a tumult, undecided, and clamouring to see you. They have clamoured that you should be awakened for years, and now it is done they will scarcely believe——"

"But surely—I can't go . . ."

Ostrog answered from the other side of the room, and the picture on the oval disc paled and vanished as the light jerked back again. "There are kineto-tele-photographs," he said. "As you bow to the people here —all over the world myriads of myriads of people, packed and still in darkened halls, will see you also. In black and white, of course—not like this. And you will hear their shouts reinforcing the shouting in the hall.

"And there is an optical contrivance we shall use," said Ostrog, "used by some of the posturers and women dancers. It may be novel to you. You stand in a very bright light, and they see not you but a magnified image of you thrown on a screen—so that even the furtherest man in the remotest gallery can, if he chooses, count your eyelashes."

Graham clutched desperately at one of the questions in his mind. "What is the population of London?" he said.

"Eight and twaindy myriads."

"Eight and what?"

"More than thirty-three millions."

These figures went beyond Graham's imagination.

"You will be expected to say something," said Ostrog. "Not what you used to call a Speech, but what our people call a Word—just one sentence, six or seven words. Something formal. If I might suggest—'I have awakened and my heart is with you.' That is the sort of thing they want."

"What was that?" asked Graham.

" 'I am awakened and my heart is with you.' And bow—bow royally. But first we must get you black robes—for black is your colour. Do you mind? And then they will disperse to their homes."

Graham hesitated. "I am in your hands," he said.

Ostrog was clearly of that opinion. He thought for a moment, turned to the curtain and called brief directions to some unseen attendants. Almost immediately a black robe, the very fellow of the black robe Graham had worn in the theatre, was brought. And as he threw it about his shoulders there came from the room without the shrilling of a high-pitched bell. Ostrog turned in interrogation to the attendant, then suddenly seemed to change his mind, pulled the curtain aside and disappeared.

For a moment Graham stood with the deferential attendant listening to Ostrog's retreating steps. There was a sound of quick question and answer and of men running. The curtain was snatched back and Ostrog reappeared, his massive face glowing with excitement. He crossed the room in a stride, clicked the room into darkness, gripped Graham's arm and pointed to the mirror.

"Even as we turned away," he said.

Graham saw his index finger, black and colossal, above the mirrored Council House. For a moment he did not understand. And then he perceived that the flagstaff that had carried the white banner was bare.

"Do you mean——?" he began.

"The Council has surrendered. Its rule is at an end for evermore."

"Look!" and Ostrog pointed to a coil of black that crept in little jerks up the vacant flagstaff, unfolding as it rose.

The oval picture paled as Lincoln pulled the curtain aside and entered.

"They are clamourous," he said.

Ostrog kept his grip of Graham's arm.

"We have raised the people," he said. "We have given them arms. For today at least their wishes must be law."

Lincoln held the curtain open for Graham and Ostrog to pass through. . . .

On his way to the markets Graham had a transitory glance of a long narrow white-walled room in which men in the universal blue canvas were carrying covered things like biers, and about which men in medical purple hurried to and fro. From this room came groans and wailing. He had an impression of an empty blood-stained couch, of men on other couches, bandaged and blood-stained. It was just a glimpse from a railed footway and then a buttress hid the place and they were going on towards the markets. . . .

The roar of the multitude was near now: it leapt to thunder. And, arresting his attention, a fluttering of black banners, the waving of blue canvas and brown rags, and the swarming vastness of the theatre near the public markets came into view down a long passage. The picture opened out. He perceived they were entering the great theatre of his first appearance, the great theatre he had last seen as a chequer-work of glare and blackness in his flight from the red police. This time he entered it along a gallery at a level high above the stage. The place was now brilliantly lit again. He sought the gangway up which he had fled, but he could not tell it from among its dozens of fellows; nor could he see anything of the smashed seats, deflated cushions, and such like traces of the fight because of the density of the people. Except the stage the whole place was closely packed. Looking down, the effect was a vast area of stippled pink, each dot a still upturned face regarding him. At his appearance with Ostrog the cheering died away, the singing died away, a common interest stilled and unified the disorder. It seemed as though every individual of those myriads was watching him.

CHAPTER XIII

THE END OF THE OLD ORDER

SO FAR as Graham was able to judge, it was near midday when the white banner of the Council fell. But some hours had to elapse before it was possible to effect the formal capitulation, and so after he had spoken his "Word" he retired to his new apartments in the wind-vane offices. The continuous excitement of the last twelve hours had left him inordinately fatigued, even his curiosity was exhausted; for a space he sat inert and passive with open eyes, and for a space he slept. He was roused by two medical attendants, come prepared with stimulants to sustain him through the next occasion. After he had taken their drugs and bathed by their advice in cold water, he felt a rapid return of interest and energy, and was presently able and willing to accompany Ostrog through several miles (as it seemed) of passages, lifts, and slides to the closing scene of the White Council's rule.

The way ran deviously through a maze of buildings. They came at last to a passage that curved about, and showed broadening before him an oblong opening, clouds hot with sunset, and the ragged skyline of the ruinous Council House. A tumult of shouts came drifting up to him. In another moment they had come out high up on the brow of the cliff of torn buildings that overhung the wreckage. The vast area opened to Graham's eyes, none the less strange and wonderful for the remote view he had had of it in the oval mirror.

This rudely amphitheatral space seemed now the better part of a mile to its outer edge. It was gold lit on the left hand, catching the sunlight, and below and to the right clear and cold in the shadow. Above the shadowy grey Council House that stood in the midst of it, the great black banner of the surrender still hung in sluggish folds against the blazing sunset. Severed rooms, halls and passages gaped strangely, broken masses of metal projected dismally from the complex wreckage, vast masses of twisted cable dropped like tangled seaweed, and from its base came a tumult of innumerable voices, violent concussions, and the sound of trumpets. All about this great white pile was a ring of desolation; the smashed and blackened masses, the gaunt foundations and ruinous lumber of the fabric that had been destroyed by the Council's orders, skeletons of girders, Titanic masses of wall, forests of stout pillars. Amongst the sombre wreckage beneath, running water flashed and glistened, and far away across the space, out of the midst of a vague vast mass of buildings, there thrust the twisted end of a water-main, two hundred feet in the air, thunderously spouting a shining cascade. And everywhere great multitudes of people.

Wherever there was space and foothold, people swarmed, little people, small and minutely clear, except where the sunset touched them to indistinguishable gold. They clambered up the tottering walls, they clung in wreaths and groups about the high-standing pillars. They swarmed along the edges of the circle of ruins. The air was full of their shouting, and they were pressing and swaying towards the central space.

The upper storeys of the Council House seemed deserted, not a human being was visible. Only the drooping banner of the surrender hung heavily against the light. The dead were within the Council House, or hidden by the swarming people, or carried away. Graham could see only a few neglected bodies in gaps and corners of the ruins, and amidst the flowing water.

"Will you let them see you, Sire?" said Ostrog. "They are very anxious to see you."

Graham hesitated, and then walked forward to where the broken verge of wall dropped sheer. He stood looking down, a lonely, tall, black figure against the sky.

Very slowly the swarming ruins became aware of him. And as they did so little bands of black-uniformed men appeared remotely, thrusting through the crowds towards the Council House. He saw little black heads become pink, looking at him, saw by that means a wave of recognition sweep across the space. It occurred to him that he should accord them some recognition. He held up his arm, then pointed to the Council House and dropped his hand. The voices below became unanimous, gathered volume, came up to him as multitudinous wavelets of cheering.

The western sky was a pallid bluish green, and Jupiter shone high in the south, before the capitulation was accomplished. Above was a slow insensible change, the advance of night serene and beautiful; below was hurry, excitement, conflicting orders, pauses, spasmodic developments of organisation, a vast ascending clamour and confusion. Before the Council came out, toiling perspiring men, directed by a conflict of shouts, carried forth hundreds of those who had perished in the hand-to-hand conflict within those long passages and chambers. . . .

Guards in black lined the way that the Council would come, and as far as the eye could reach into the hazy blue twilight of the ruins, and swarming now at every possible point in the captured Council House and along the shattered cliff of its circumadjacent buildings, were innumerable people, and their voices even when they were not cheering, were as the soughing of the sea upon a pebble beach. Ostrog had chosen a huge commanding pile of crushed and overthrown masonry, and on this a stage of timbers and metal girders was being hastily constructed. Its essential parts were complete, but humming and clangorous machinery still glared fitfully in the shadows beneath this temporary edifice.

The stage had a small higher portion on which Graham stood with Ostrog and Lincoln close beside him, a little in advance of a group of minor officers. A broader lower stage surrounded this quarter deck, and on this were the black-uniformed guards of the revolt armed with the little green weapons whose very names Graham still did not know. Those standing about him perceived that his eyes wandered perpetually from the swarming people in the twilight ruins about him to the darkling mass of the White Council House, whence the Trustees would presently come, and to the gaunt cliffs of ruin that encircled him, and so back to the people. The voices of the crowd swelled to a deafening tumult.

He saw the Councillors first afar off in the glare of one of the temporary lights that marked their path, a little group of white figures blinking in a black archway. In the Council House they had been in darkness. He watched them approaching, drawing nearer past first this blazing electric star and then that; the minatory roar of the crowd over whom their power had lasted for a hundred and fifty years marched along beside them. As they drew still nearer their faces came out weary, white and anxious. He saw them blinking up through the glare about him and

Ostrog. He contrasted their strange cold looks in the Hall of Atlas. . . . Presently he could recognise several of them; the man who had rapped the table at Howard, a burly man with a red beard, and one delicate-featured, short, dark man with a peculiarly long skull. He noted that two were whispering together and looking behind him at Ostrog. Next there came a tall, dark and handsome man, walking downcast. Abruptly he glanced up, his eyes touched Graham for a moment, and passed beyond him to Ostrog. The way that had been made for them was so contrived that they had to march past and curve about before they came to the sloping path of planks that ascended to the stage where their surrender was to be made.

"The Master, the Master! God and the Master," shouted the people. "To hell with the Council!" Graham looked at their multitudes, receding beyond counting into a shouting haze, and then at Ostrog beside him, white and steadfast and still. His eye went again to the little group of White Councillors. And then he looked up at the familiar quiet stars overhead. The marvellous element in his fate was suddenly vivid. Could that be his indeed, that little life in his memory two hundred years gone by—and this as well?

CHAPTER XIV

FROM THE CROW'S NEST

AND SO after strange delays and through an avenue of doubt and battle, this man from the nineteenth century came at last to his position at the head of that complex world.

At first when he rose from the long deep sleep that followed his rescue and the surrender of the Council, he did not recognise his surroundings. By an effort he gained a clue in his mind, and all that had happened came back to him, at first with a quality of insincerity like a story heard, like something read out of a book. And even before his memories were clear, the exultation of his escape, the wonder of his prominence were back in his mind. He was owner of half the world; Master of the Earth. This new great age was in the completest sense his. He no longer hoped to discover his experiences a dream; he became anxious now to convince himself that they were real.

An obsequious valet assisted him to dress under the direction of a dignified chief attendant, a little man whose face proclaimed him Japanese, albeit he spoke English like an Englishman. From the latter he learnt something of the state of affairs. Already the revolution was an accepted fact; already business was being resumed throughout the city. Abroad the downfall of the Council had been received for the most part with delight. Nowhere was the Council popular, and the thousand cities of Western America, after two hundred years still jealous of New York, London, and the East, had risen almost unanimously two days before at the news of Graham's imprisonment. Paris was fighting within itself. The rest of the world hung in suspense.

While he was breaking his fast, the sound of a telephone bell jetted from a corner, and his chief attendant called his attention to the voice of Ostrog making polite enquiries. Graham interrupted his refreshment to reply. Very shortly Lincoln arrived, and Graham at once expressed a strong desire to talk to people and to be shown more of the new life that was opening before him. Lincoln informed him that in three hours' time a representative gathering of officials and their wives would be held in the state apartments of the wind-vane Chief. Graham's desire to traverse the ways of the city was, however, at present impossible, because of the enormous excitement of the people. It was, however, quite possible for him to take a bird's-eye view of the city from the crow's nest of the wind-vane keeper. To this accordingly Graham was conducted by his attendant. Lincoln, with a graceful compliment to the attendant, apologised for not accompanying them, on account of the present pressure of administrative work.

Higher even than the most gigantic wind-wheels hung this crow's nest, a clear thousand feet above the roofs, a little disc-shaped speck on a spear of metallic filigree, cable stayed. To its summit Graham was drawn in a little wire-hung cradle. Halfway down the frail-seeming stem was a light gallery about which hung a cluster of tubes—minute they looked from above—rotating slowly on the ring of its outer rail. These were the specula, *en rapport* with the wind-vane keeper's mirrors, in one of which Ostrog had shown him the coming of his rule. His Japanese attendant ascended before him and they spent nearly an hour asking and answering questions.

It was a day full of the promise and quality of spring. The touch of the wind warmed. The sky was an intense blue and the vast expanse of London shone dazzling under the morning sun. The air was clear of smoke and haze, sweet as the air of a mountain glen.

Save for the irregular oval of ruins about the House of the Council and the black flag of the surrender that fluttered there, the mighty city seen from above showed few signs of the swift revolution that had, to his imagination, in one night and one day, changed the destinies of the world. A multitude of people still swarmed over these ruins, and the huge openwork stagings in the distance from which started in times of peace the service of aeroplanes to the various great cities of Europe and America, were also black with the victors. Across a narrow way of planking raised on trestles that crossed the ruins a crowd of workmen were busy restoring the connection between the cables and wires of the Council House and the rest of the city, preparatory to the transfer thither of Ostrog's headquarters from the Wind-Vane buildings.

For the rest the luminous expanse was undisturbed. So vast was its serenity in comparison with the areas of disturbance, that presently Graham, looking beyond them, could almost forget the thousands of men lying out of sight in the artificial glare within the quasi-subterranean labyrinth, dead or dying of the overnight wounds, forget the improvised wards with the hosts of surgeons, nurses, and bearers feverishly busy, forget, indeed, all the wonder, consternation and novelty under the electric lights. Down there in the hidden ways of the anthill he knew that the revolution triumphed, that black everywhere carried the day, black favours, black banners, black festoons across the streets. And out here, under the fresh sunlight, beyond the crater of the fight, as if nothing had happened to the earth, the forest of Wind Vanes that had grown from one or two while the Council had ruled, roared peacefully upon their incessant duty.

Far away, spiked, jagged and indented by the wind vanes, the Surrey Hills rose blue and faint; to the north and nearer, the sharp contours of Highgate and Muswell Hill were similarly jagged. And all over the countryside, he knew, on every crest and hill, where once the hedges had interlaced, and cottages, churches, inns, and farmhouses had nestled among their trees, wind wheels similar to those he saw and bearing like them vast advertisements, gaunt and distinctive symbols of the new age, cast their whirling shadows and stored incessantly the energy that flowed away incessantly through all the arteries of the city. And underneath these wandered the countless flocks and herds of the British Food Trust with their lonely guards and keepers.

Not a familiar outline anywhere broke the cluster of gigantic shapes below. St. Paul's he knew survived, and many of the old buildings in Westminster, embedded out of sight, arched over and covered in among the giant growths of this great age. The Thames, too, made no fall and gleam of silver to break the wilderness of the city; the thirsty water mains drank up every drop of its waters before they reached the walls. Its bed and estuary, scoured and sunken, was now a canal of sea water and a race of grimy bargemen brought the heavy materials of trade from the Pool thereby beneath the very feet of the workers. Faint and dim in the east-ward between earth and sky hung the clustering masts of the colossal shipping in the Pool. For all the heavy traffic, for which there was no need of haste, came in gigantic sailing ships from the ends of the earth, and the heavy goods for which there was urgency in mechanical ships of a smaller swifter sort.

And to the south over the hills, came vast aqueducts with sea water for the sewers and in three separate directions, ran pallid lines—the roads, stippled with moving grey specks. On the first occasion that offered he was determined to go out and see these roads. That would come after the flying ship he was presently to try. His attendant officer described them as a pair of gently curving surfaces a hundred yards wide, each one for the traffic going in one direction, and made of a substance called Ead-hamite—an artificial substance, so far as he could gather, resembling toughened glass. Along this shot a strange traffic of narrow rubber-shod vehicles, great single wheels, two and four wheeled vehicles, sweeping along at velocities of from one to six miles a minute. Railroads had vanished; a few embankments remained as rust-crowned trenches here and there. Some few formed the cores of Eadhamite ways.

Among the first things to strike his attention had been the great fleets of advertisement balloons and kites that receded in irregular vistas north-ward and southward along the lines of the aëroplane journeys. No aëro-planes were to be seen. Their passages had ceased, and only one little-seeming aëropile circled high in the blue distance above the Surrey Hills, an unimpressive soaring speck.

A thing Graham had already learnt, and which he found very hard to imagine, was that nearly all the towns in the country, and almost all the villages, had disappeared. Here and there only, he understood, some gigantic hotel-like edifice stood amid square miles of some single cultiva-tion and preserved the name of a town—as Bournemouth, Wareham, or Swanage. Yet the officer had speedily convinced him how inevitable such a change had been. The old order had dotted the country with farm-houses, and every two or three miles was the ruling landlord's estate, and the place of the inn and cobbler, the grocer's shop and church—the vil-lage. Every eight miles or so was the country town, where lawyer, corn merchant, wool-stapler, saddler, veterinary surgeon, doctor, draper, milliner and so forth lived. Every eight miles—simply because that eight mile marketing journey, four there and back, was as much as was com-fortable for the farmer. But directly the railways came into play, and after them the light railways, and all the swift new motor cars that had replaced waggons and horses, and so soon as the high roads began to be made of wood, and rubber, and Eadhamite, and all sorts of elastic durable substances—the necessity of having such frequent market towns disappeared. And the big towns grew. They drew the worker with the gravitational force of seemingly endless work, the employer with their suggestions of an infinite ocean of labour.

And as the standard of comfort rose, as the complexity of the mechanism of living increased, life in the country had become more and more costly, or narrow and impossible. The disappearance of vicar and squire, the extinction of the general practitioner by the city specialist, had robbed the village of its last touch of culture. After telephone, kinematograph and phonograph had replaced newspaper, book, schoolmaster, and letter, to live outside the range of the electric cables was to live an isolated savage. In the country were neither means of being clothed nor fed (according to the refined conceptions of the time), no efficient doctors for an emergency, no company and no pursuits.

Moreover, mechanical appliances in agriculture made one engineer the equivalent of thirty labourers. So, inverting the condition of the city clerk in the days when London was scarce inhabitable because of the coaly foulness of its air, the labourers now came hurrying by road or air to the city and its life and delights at night to leave it again in the morning. The city had swallowed up humanity; man had entered upon a new stage in his development. First had come the nomad, the hunter, then had followed the agriculturist of the agricultural state, whose towns and cities and ports were but the headquarters and markets of the countryside. And now, logical consequence of an epoch of invention, was this huge new aggregation of men. Save London, there were only four other cities in Britain—Edinburgh, Portsmouth, Manchester and Shrewsbury. Such things as these, simple statements of fact though they were to contemporary men, strained Graham's imagination to picture. And when he glanced "over beyond there" at the strange things that existed on the Continent, it failed him altogether.

He had a vision of city beyond city, cities on great plains, cities beside great rivers, vast cities along the sea margin, cities girdled by snowy mountains. Over a great part of the earth the English tongue was spoken; taken together with its Spanish American and Hindoo and Negro and "Pidgin" dialects, it was the everyday language of two-thirds of the people of the earth. On the Continent, save as remote and curious survivals, three other languages alone held sway—German, which reached to Antioch and Genoa and jostled Spanish-English at Cadiz, a Gallicised Russian which met the Indian English in Persia and Kurdistan and the "Pidgin" English in Pekin, and French still clear and brilliant, the language of lucidity, which shared the Mediterranean with the Indian

English and German and reached through a negro dialect to the Congo.

And everywhere now, through the city-set earth, save in the administered "black belt" territories of the tropics, the same cosmopolitan social organisation prevailed, and everywhere from Pole to Equator his property and his responsibilities extended. The whole world was civilised; the whole world dwelt in cities; the whole world was property. Over the British Empire and throughout America his ownership was scarcely disguised, Congress and Parliament were usually regarded as antique, curious gatherings. And even in the two Empires of Russia and Germany, the influence of his wealth was conceivably of enormous weight. There, of course, came problems—possibilities, but, uplifted as he was, even Russia and Germany seemed sufficiently remote. And of the quality of the black belt administration, and of what that might mean for him he thought, after the fashion of his former days, not at all. That it should hang like a threat over the spacious vision before him could not enter his nineteenth century mind. But his mind turned at once from the scenery to the thought of a vanished dread. "What of the yellow peril?" he asked and Asano made him explain. The Chinese spectre had vanished. Chinaman and European were at peace. The twentieth century had discovered with reluctant certainty that the average Chinaman was as civilised, more moral, and far more intelligent than the average European serf, and had repeated on a gigantic scale the fraternisation of Scot and Englishman that happened in the seventeenth century. As Asano put it; "They thought it over. They found we were white men after all." Graham turned again to the view and his thoughts took a new direction.

Out of the dim south-west, glittering and strange, voluptuous, and in some way terrible, shone those Pleasure Cities, of which the kinematograph-phonograph and the old man in the street had spoken. Strange places reminiscent of the legendary Sybaris, cities of art and beauty, mercenary art and mercenary beauty, sterile wonderful cities of motion and music, whither repaired all who profited by the fierce, inglorious, economic struggle that went on in the glaring labyrinth below.

Fierce he knew it was. How fierce he could judge from the fact that these latter-day people referred back to the England of the nineteenth century as the figure of an idyllic easy-going life. He turned his eyes to the scene immediately before him again, trying to conceive the big factories of that intricate maze.

Northward he knew were the potters, makers not only of earthenware and china, but of the kindred pastes and compounds a subtler mineralogical chemistry had devised; there were the makers of statuettes and wall ornaments and much intricate furniture; there too were the factories where feverishly competitive authors devised their phonograph discourses and advertisements and arranged the groupings and developments for their perpetually startling and novel kinematographic dramatic works. Thence, too, flashed the world-wide messages, the world-wide falsehoods of the news-tellers, the chargers of the telephonic machines that had replaced the newspapers of the past.

To the westward beyond the smashed Council House were the voluminous offices of municipal control and government; and to the eastward, towards the port, the trading quarters, the huge public markets, the theatres, houses of resort, betting palaces, miles of billiard saloons, baseball and football circuses, wild beast rings and the innumerable temples of the Christian and quasi-Christian sects, the Mahomedans, Buddhists, Gnostics, Spook Worshippers, the Incubus Worshippers, the Furniture Worshippers, and so forth; and to the south again a vast manufacture of textiles, pickles, wines and condiments. And from point to point tore the countless multitudes along the roaring mechanical ways. A gigantic hive, of which the winds were tireless servants, and the ceaseless wind-vanes an appropriate crown and symbol.

He thought of the unprecedented population that had been sucked up by this sponge of halls and galleries—the thirty-three million lives that were playing out each of its own brief ineffectual drama below him, and the complacency that the brightness of the day and the space and splendour of the view, and above all the sense of his own importance had begotten, dwindled and perished. Looking down from this height over the city it became at last possible to conceive this overwhelming multitude of thirty-three millions, the reality of the responsibility he would take upon himself, the vastness of the human Maelstrom over which his slender kingship hung.

He tried to figure the individual life. It astonished him to realise how little the common man had changed in spite of the visible change in his conditions. Life and property, indeed, were secure from violence almost all over the world, zymotic diseases, bacterial diseases of all sorts had practically vanished, everyone had a sufficiency of food and clothing, was warmed in the city ways and sheltered from the weather—so much the almost mechanical progress of science and the physical organisation of society had accomplished. But the crowd, he was already beginning to discover, was a crowd still, helpless in the hands of demagogue and organiser, individually cowardly, individually swayed by appetite, collectively incalculable. The memory of countless figures in pale blue canvas came before his mind. Millions of such men and women below him, he knew, had never been out of the city, had never seen beyond the little round of unintelligent grudging participation in the world's business, and unintelligent dissatisfied sharing in its tawdrier pleasures. He thought of the hopes of his vanished contemporaries, and for a moment the dream of London in Morris's quaint old *News from Nowhere*, and the perfect land of Hudson's beautiful *Crystal Age* appeared before him in an atmosphere of infinite loss. He thought of his own hopes.

For in the latter days of that passionate life that lay now so far behind him, the conception of a free and equal manhood had become a very real thing to him. He had hoped, as indeed his age had hoped, rashly taking it for granted, that the sacrifice of the many to the few would some day cease, that a day was near when every child born of woman should have a fair and assured chance of happiness. And here, after two hundred years, the same hope, still unfulfilled, cried passionately through the city. After two hundred years, he knew, greater than ever, grown with the city to gigantic proportions, were poverty and helpless labour and all the sorrows of his time.

Already he knew something of the history of the intervening years. He had heard now of the moral decay that had followed the collapse of supernatural religion in the minds of ignoble man, the decline of public honour, the ascendency of wealth. For men who had lost their belief in God had still kept their faith in property, and wealth ruled a venial world.

His Japanese attendant, Asano, in expounding the political history of the intervening two centuries, drew an apt image from a seed eaten by insect parasites. First there is the original seed, ripening vigorously enough. And then comes some insect and lays an egg under the skin, and behold! in a little while the seed is a hollow shape with an active grub inside that has eaten out its substance. And then comes some secondary parasite, some ichneumon fly, and lays an egg within this grub, and behold! that, too, is a hollow shape, and the new living thing is inside its predecessor's skin which itself is snug within the seed coat. And the seed coat still keeps its shape, most people think it a seed still, and for all one knows it may still think itself a seed, vigorous and alive. "Your Victorian kingdom," said Asano, "was like that—kingship with the heart eaten out." The landowners—the barons and gentry—began ages ago with King John; there were lapses, but they beheaded King Charles, and ended practically with King George, a mere husk of a king . . . the real power in the hands of their parliament. But the Parliament—the organ of the land-holding tenant-ruling gentry—did not keep its power long. The change had already come in the nineteenth century. The franchises had been broadened until it included masses of ignorant men, "urban myriads," who went in their featureless thousands to vote together. And the natural consequence of a swarming constituency is the rule of the party organisation. Power was passing even in the Victorian time to the party machinery, secret, complex, and corrupt. Very speedily power was in the hands of great men of business who financed the machines. A time came when the real power and interest of the Empire rested visibly between the two party councils, ruling by newspapers and electoral organisations—two small groups of rich and able men, working at first in opposition, then presently together.

There was a reaction of a genteel ineffectual sort. There were numberless books in existence, Asano said, to prove that—the publication of some of them was as early as Graham's sleep—a whole literature of reaction in fact. The party of the reaction seems to have locked itself into its study and rebelled with unflinching determination—on paper. The urgent necessity of either capturing or depriving the party councils of power is a common suggestion underlying all the thoughtful work of the early twentieth century, both in America and England. In most of these things America was a little earlier than England, though both countries drove the same way.

That counter-revolution never came. It could never organise and keep pure. There was not enough of the old sentimentality, the old faith in righteousness, left among men. Any organisation that became big enough to influence the polls became complex enough to be undermined, broken up, or bought outright by capable rich men. Socialistic and Popular, Reactionary and Purity Parties were all at last mere Stock Exchange counters, selling their principles to pay for their electioneering. And the great concern of the rich was naturally to keep property intact, the board clear for the game of trade. Just as the feudal concern had been to keep the board clear for hunting and war. The whole world was exploited, a battlefield of businesses; and financial convulsions, the scourge of currency manipulation, tariff wars, made more human misery during the twentieth century—because the wretchedness was dreary life instead of speedy death—than had war, pestilence and famine, in the darkest hours of earlier history.

His own part in the development of this time he now knew clearly enough. Through the successive phases in the development of this mechanical civilisation, aiding and presently directing its development, there had grown a new power, the Council, the board of his trustees. At first it had been a mere chance union of the millions of Isbister and Warming, a mere property holding company, the creation of two childless testators' whims, but the collective talent of its first constitution had speedily guided it to a vast influence, until by title deed, loan and share, under a hundred disguises and pseudonyms it had ramified through the fabric of the American and English States.

Wielding an enormous influence and patronage, the Council had early assumed a political aspect; and in its development it had continually used its wealth to tip the beam of political decisions and its political advantages to grasp yet more and more wealth. At last the party organisations of two hemispheres were in its hands; it became an inner council of political control. Its last struggle was with the tacit alliance of the great Jewish families. But these families were linked only by a feeble sentiment, at any time inheritance might fling a huge fragment of their resources to a minor, a woman or a fool, marriages and legacies alienated hundreds of thousands at one blow. The Council had no such breach in its continuity. Steadily, steadfastly it grew.

The original Council was not simply twelve men of exceptional ability; they fused, it was a council of genius. It struck boldly for riches, for political influence, and the two subserved each other. With amazing foresight it spent great sums of money on the art of flying, holding that invention back against an hour foreseen. It used the patent laws, and a thousand half-legal expedients, to hamper all investigators who refused to work with it. In the old days it never missed a capable man. It paid his price. Its policy in those days was vigorous—unerring, and against it as it grew steadily and incessantly was only the chaotic selfish rule of the casually rich. In a hundred years Graham had become almost exclusive owner of Africa, of South America, of France, of London, of England and all its influence—for all practical purposes, that is—a power in North America —then the dominant power in America. The Council bought and organised China, drilled Asia, crippled the Old World empires, undermined them financially, fought and defeated them.

And this spreading usurpation of the world was so dexterously performed—a proteus—hundreds of banks, companies, syndicates, masked the Council's operations—that it was already far advanced before common men suspected the tyranny that had come. The Council never hesitated, never faltered. Means of communication, land, buildings, governments, municipalities, the territorial companies of the tropics, every human enterprise, it gathered greedily. And it drilled and marshalled its men, its railway police, its roadway police, its house guards, and drain and cable guards, its hosts of land-workers. Their unions it did not fight, but it undermined and betrayed and bought them. It bought the world at last. And, finally, its culminating stroke was the introduction of flying.

When the Council, in conflict with the workers in some of its huge monopolies, did something flagrantly illegal and that without even the ordinary civility of bribery, the old Law, alarmed for the profits of its complaisance, looked about it for weapons. But there were no more armies, no fighting navies; the age of Peace had come. The only possible war ships were the great steam vessels of the Council's Navigation Trust. The police forces they controlled; the police of the railways, of the ships, of their agricultural estates, their time-keepers and order-keepers, outnumbered the neglected little forces of the old country and municipal organisations ten to one. And they produced flying machines. There were men alive still who could remember the last great debate in the London House of Commons—the legal party, the party against the Council was in a minority, but it made a desperate fight—and how the members came crowding out upon the terrace to see these great unfamiliar winged shapes circling quietly overhead. The Council had soared to its power. The last sham of a democracy that had permitted unlimited irresponsible property was at an end.

Within one hundred and fifty years of Graham's falling asleep, his Council had thrown off its disguises and ruled openly, supreme in his name. Elections had become a cheerful formality, a septennial folly, an ancient unmeaning custom; a social Parliament as ineffectual as the convocation of the Established Church in Victorian times assembled now and then; and a legitimate King of England, disinherited, drunken and witless, played foolishly in a second-rate music-hall. So the magnificent dream of the nineteenth century, the noble project of universal individual liberty and universal happiness, touched by a disease of honour, crippled by a superstition of absolute property, crippled by the religious feuds that had robbed the common citizens of education, robbed men of standards of conduct, and brought the sanctions of morality to utter contempt, had worked itself out in the face of invention and ignoble enterprise, first to a warring plutocracy, and finally to the rule of a supreme plutocrat. His Council at last had ceased even to trouble to have its decrees endorsed by the constitutional authorities, and he a motionless, sunken, yellow-skinned figure had lain, neither dead nor living, recognisably and immediately Master of the Earth. And awoke at last to find himself—Master of that inheritance! Awoke to stand under the cloudless empty sky and gaze down upon the greatness of his dominion.

To what end had he awakened? Was this city, this hive of hopeless toilers, the final refutation of his ancient hopes? Or was the fire of liberty, the fire that had blazed and waned in the years of his past life, still smouldering below there? He thought of the stir and impulse of the song of the revolution. Was that song merely the trick of a demagogue, to be forgotten when its purpose was served? Was the hope that still stirred within him only the memory of abandoned things, the vestige of a creed outworn?

Or had it a wider meaning, an import interwoven with the destiny of man? To what end had he awakened, what was there for him to do? Humanity was spread below him like a map. He thought of the millions and millions of humanity following each other unceasingly for ever out of the darkness of non-existence into the darkness of death. To what end? Aim there must be, but it transcended his power of thought. He saw for the first time clearly his own infinite littleness, saw stark and terrible the tragic contrast of human strength and the craving of the human heart. For that little while he knew himself for the petty accident he was, and knew therewith the greatness of his desire. And suddenly his littleness was intolerable, his aspiration was intolerable, and there came to him an irresistible impulse to pray. And he prayed. He prayed vague, incoherent, contradictory things, his soul strained up through time and space and all the fleeting multitudinous confusion of being, towards something—he scarcely knew what—towards something that could comprehend his striving and endure.

A man and a woman were far below on a roof space to the southward enjoying the freshness of the morning air. The man had brought out a per-spective glass to spy upon the Council House and he was showing her how to use it. Presently their curiosity was satisfied, they could see no traces of bloodshed from their position, and after a survey of the empty sky she came round to the crow's nest. And there she saw two little black figures, so small it was hard to believe they were men, one who watched and one who gesticulated with hands outstretched to the silent emptiness of Heaven.

She handed the glass to the man. He looked and exclaimed:

"I believe it is the Master. Yes. I am sure. It *is* the Master!"

He lowered the glass and looked at her. "Waving his hands about almost as if he was praying. I wonder what he is up to. Worship-ping the sun? There weren't Parsees in this country in *his* time, were there?"

He looked again. "He's stopped it now. It was a chance attitude, I suppose." He put down the glass and became meditative. "He won't have anything to do but enjoy himself—just enjoy himself. Ostrog will boss the show of course. Ostrog will have to, because of keeping all these Labourer fools in bounds. Them and their song! And got it all by sleep-ing, dear eyes—just sleeping. It's a wonderful world."

CHAPTER XV

PROMINENT PEOPLE

THE STATE apartments of the Wind Vane Keeper would have seemed astonishingly intricate to Graham had he entered them fresh from his nineteenth century life, but already he was growing accustomed to the scale of the new time. They can scarcely be described as halls and rooms, seeing that a complicated system of arches, bridges, passages and galleries divided and united every part of the great space. He came out through one of the now familiar sliding panels upon a plateau of landing at the head of a flight of very broad and gentle steps, with men and women far more brilliantly dressed than any he had hitherto seen ascending and descending. From this position he looked down a vista of intricate ornament in lustreless white and mauve and purple, spanned by bridges that seemed wrought of porcelain and filigree, and terminating far off in a cloudy mystery of perforated screens.

Glancing upward, he saw tier above tier of ascending galleries with faces looking down upon him. The air was full of the babble of innumerable voices and of a music that descended from above, a gay and exhilarating music whose source he never discovered.

The central aisle was thick with people, but by no means uncomfortably crowded; altogether that assembly must have numbered many thousands. They were brilliantly, even fantastically dressed, the men as fancifully as the women, for the sobering influence of the Puritan conception of dignity upon masculine dress had long since passed away. The hair of the men, too, though it was rarely worn long, was commonly curled in a manner that suggested the barber, and baldness had vanished from the earth. Frizzy straight-cut masses that would have charmed Rossetti abounded, and one gentleman, who was pointed out to Graham under the mysterious title of an "amorist", wore his hair in two becoming plaits *a la* Marguerite. The pigtail was in evidence; it would seem that citizens of Chinese extraction were no longer ashamed of their race. There was little uniformity of fashion apparent in the forms of clothing worn. The more shapely men displayed their symmetry in trunk hose, and here were puffs and slashes, and there a cloak and there a robe. The fashions of the days of Leo the Tenth were perhaps the prevailing influence, but the aesthetic conceptions of the far east were also patent. Masculine embonpoint, which, in Victorian times, would have been subjected to the tightly buttoned perils, the ruthless exaggeration of tight-legged tight-armed evening dress, now formed but the basis of a wealth of dignity and drooping folds. Graceful slenderness abounded also. To Graham, a typically stiff man from a typically stiff period, not only did these men seem altogether too graceful in person, but altogether too expressive in their vividly expressive faces. They gesticulated, they expressed surprise, interest, amusement, above all, they expressed the emotions excited in their minds by the ladies about them with astonishing frankness. Even at the first glance it was evident that women were in a great majority.

The ladies in the company of these gentlemen displayed in dress, bearing and manner alike, less emphasis and more intricacy. Some affected a classical simplicity of robing and subtlety of fold, after the fashion of the First French Empire, and flashed conquering arms and shoulders as Graham passed. Others had closely-fitting dresses without seam or belt at the waist, sometimes with long folds falling from the shoulders. The delightful confidences of evening dress had not been diminished by the passage of two centuries.

Everyone's movements seemed graceful. Graham remarked to Lincoln that he saw men as Raphael's cartoons walking, and Lincoln told him that the attainment of an appropriate set of gestures was part of every rich person's education. The Master's entry was greeted with a sort of tittering applause, but these people showed their distinguished manners by not crowding upon him nor annoying him by any persistent scrutiny, as he descended the steps towards the floor of the aisle.

He had already learnt from Lincoln that these were the leaders of existing London society; almost every person there that night was either a powerful official or the immediate connexion of a powerful official. Many had returned from the European Pleasure Cities expressly to welcome him. The aëronautic authorities, whose defection had played a part in the overthrow of the Council only second to Graham's, were very prominent, and so, too, was the Wind Vane Control. Amongst others there were several of the more prominent officers of the Food Trust; the controller of the European Piggeries had a particularly melancholy and interesting countenance and a daintily cynical manner. A bishop in full canonicals passed athwart Graham's vision, conversing with a gentleman dressed exactly like the traditional Chaucer, including even the laurel wreath.

"Who is that?" he asked almost involuntarily.

"The Bishop of London," said Lincoln.

"No—the other, I mean."

"Poet Laureate."

"You still——?"

"He doesn't make poetry, of course. He's a cousin of Wotton—one of the Councillors. But he's one of the Red Rose Royalists—a delightful club—and they keep up the tradition of these things."

"Asano told me there was a King."

"The King doesn't belong. They had to expel him. It's the Stuart blood I suppose; but really——"

"Too much?"

"Far too much."

Graham did not quite follow all this, but it seemed part of the general inversion of the new age. He bowed condescendingly to his first introduction. It was evident that subtle distinctions of class prevailed even in this assembly, that only to a small proportion of the guests, to an inner group, did Lincoln consider it appropriate to introduce him. This first introduction was the Master Aëronaut, a man whose sun-tanned face contrasted oddly with the delicate complexions about him. Just at present his critical defection from the Council made him a very important person indeed.

His manner contrasted very favourably, according to Graham's ideas, with the general bearing. He made a few commonplace remarks, assurances of loyalty and frank inquiries about the Master's health. His manner was breezy, his accent lacked the easy staccato of latter-day English. He made it admirably clear to Graham that he was a bluff "aerial dog"—he used that phrase—that there was no nonsense about him, that he was a thoroughly manly fellow and old-fashioned at that, that he didn't profess to know much, and that what he did not know was not worth knowing. He made a manly bow, ostentatiously free from obsequiousness, and passed.

"I am glad to see that type endures," said Graham.

"Phonographs and kinematographs," said Lincoln, a little spitefully. "He has studied from the life." Graham glanced at the burly form again. It was oddly reminiscent.

"As a matter of fact we bought him," said Lincoln. "Partly. And partly he was afraid of Ostrog. Everything rested with him."

He turned sharply to introduce the Surveyor-General of the Public School Trust. This person was a willowy figure in a blue-grey academic gown, he beamed down upon Graham through *pince-nez* of a Victorian pattern, and illustrated his remarks by gestures of a beautifully manicured hand. Graham was immediately interested in this gentleman's functions, and asked him a number of singularly direct questions. The Surveyor-General seemed quietly amused at the Master's fundamental bluntness. He was a little vague as to the monopoly of education his Company possessed; it was done by contract with the syndicate that ran the numerous London Municipalities, but he waxed enthusiastic over educational progress since the Victorian times. "We have conquered Cram," he said, "completely conquered Cram—there is not an examination left in the world. Aren't you glad?"

"How do you get the work done?" asked Graham.

"We make it attractive—as attractive as possible. And if it does not attract then—we let it go. We cover an immense field."

He proceeded to details, and they had a lengthy conversation. The Surveyor-General mentioned the names of Pestalozzi and Froebel with profound respect, although he displayed no intimacy with their epoch-making works. Graham learnt that University Extension still existed in a modified form. "There is a certain type of girl, for example," said the Surveyor-General, dilating with a sense of his usefulness, "with a perfect passion for severe studies—when they are not too difficult you know. We cater for them by the thousand. At this moment," he said with a Napoleonic touch, "nearly five hundred phonographs are lecturing in different parts of London on the influence exercised by Plato and Swift on the love affairs of Shelley, Hazlitt, and Burns. And afterwards they write essays on the lectures, and the names in order of merit are put in conspicuous places. You see how your little germ has grown? The illiterate middle-class of your days has quite passed away."

"About the public elementary schools," said Graham. "Do you control them?"

The Surveyor-General did, "entirely." Now, Graham, in his later democratic days, had taken a keen interest in these and his questioning quickened. Certain casual phrases that had fallen from the old man with whom he had talked in the darkness recurred to him. The Surveyor-General, in effect, endorsed the old man's words. "We have abolished Cram," he said, a phrase Graham was beginning to interpret as the abolition of all sustained work. The Surveyor-General became sentimental. "We try and make the elementary schools very pleasant for the little children. They will have to work so soon. Just a few simple principles—obedience—industry."

"You teach them very little?"

"Why should we? It only leads to trouble and discontent. We amuse them. Even as it is—there are troubles—agitations. Where the labourers get the ideas, one cannot tell. They tell one another. There are socialistic dreams—anarchy even! Agitators *will* get to work among them. I take it—I have always taken it—that my foremost duty is to fight against popular discontent. Why should people be made unhappy?"

"I wonder," said Graham thoughtfully. "But there are a great many things I want to know."

Lincoln, who had stood watching Graham's face throughout the conversation, intervened. "There are others," he said in an undertone.

The Surveyor-General of schools gesticulated himself away. "Perhaps," said Lincoln, intercepting a casual glance, "you would like to know some of these ladies?"

The daughter of the Manager of the Piggeries of the European Food Trust was a particularly charming little person with red hair and animated blue eyes. Lincoln left him awhile to converse with her, and she displayed herself as quite an enthusiast for the "dear old times," as she called them, that had seen the beginning of his trance. As she talked she smiled, and her eyes smiled in a manner that demanded reciprocity.

"I have tried," she said, "countless times—to imagine those old romantic days. And to you—they are memories. How strange and crowded the world must seem to you! I have seen photographs and pictures of the old times, the little isolated houses built of bricks made out of burnt mud and all black with soot from your fires, the railway bridges, the simple advertisements, the solemn savage Puritanical men in strange black coats and those tall hats of theirs, iron railway trains on iron bridges overhead, horses and cattle, and even dogs running half wild about the streets. And suddenly, you have come into this!"

"Into this," said Graham.

"Out of your life—out of all that was familiar."

"The old life was not a happy one," said Graham. "I do not regret that."

She looked at him quickly. There was a brief pause. She sighed encouragingly. "No?"

"No," said Graham. "It was a little life—and unmeaning. But this——
We thought the world complex and crowded and civilised enough. Yet I see—although in this world I am barely four days old—looking back on my own time, that it was a queer, barbaric time—the mere beginning of this new order. The mere beginning of this new order. You will find it hard to understand how little I know."

"You may ask me what you like," she said, smiling at him.

"Then tell me who these people are. I'm still very much in the dark about them. It's puzzling. Are there any Generals?"

"Men in hats and feathers?"

"Of course not. No. I suppose they are the men who control the great public businesses. Who is that distinguished looking man?"

"That? He's a most important officer. That is Morden. He is managing director of the Antibilious Pill Company. I have heard that his workers sometimes turn out a myriad myriad pills a day in the twenty-four hours. Fancy a myriad myriad!"

"A myriad myriad. No wonder he looks proud," said Graham. "Pills! What a wonderful time it is! That man in purple?"

"He is not quite one of the inner circle, you know. But we like him. He is really clever and very amusing. He is one of the heads of the Medical Faculty of our London University. All medical men, you know, are shareholders in the Medical Faculty Company, and wear that purple. You have to be—to be qualified. But of course, people who are paid by fees for *doing* something——" She smiled away the social pretensions of all such people.

"Are any of your great artists or authors here?"

"No authors. They are mostly such queer people—and so preoccupied about themselves. And they quarrel so dreadfully! They will fight, some of them, for precedence on staircases! Dreadful isn't it? But I think Wraysbury, the fashionable capillotomist, is here. From Capri."

"Capillotomist," said Graham. "Ah! I remember. An artist! Why not?"

"We have to cultivate him," she said apologetically. "Our heads are in his hands." She smiled.

Graham hesitated at the invited compliment, but his glance was expressive. "Have the arts grown with the rest of civilised things?" he said. "Who are your great painters?"

She looked at him doubtfully. Then laughed. "For a moment," she said, "I thought you meant——" She laughed again. "You mean, of course, those good men you used to think so much of because they could cover great spaces of canvas with oil-colours? Great oblongs. And people used to put the things in gilt frames and hang them up in rows in their square rooms. We haven't any. People grew tired of that sort of thing."

"But what did you think I meant?"

She put a finger significantly on a cheek whose glow was above suspicion, and smiled and looked very arch and pretty and inviting. "And here," and she indicated her eyelid.

Graham had an adventurous moment. Then a grotesque memory of a picture he had somewhere seen of Uncle Toby and the Widow flashed across his mind. An archaic shame came upon him. He became acutely aware that he was visible to a great number of interested people. "I see," he remarked inadequately. He turned awkwardly away from her fascinating facility. He looked about him to meet a number of eyes that immediately occupied themselves with other things. Possibly he coloured a little. "Who is that talking with the lady in saffron?" he asked, avoiding her eyes.

The person in question he learnt was one of the great organisers of the

American theatres just fresh from a gigantic production at Mexico. His face reminded Graham of a bust of Caligula. Another striking looking man was the Black Labour Master. The phrase at the time made no deep impression, but afterwards it recurred—the Black Labour Master? The little lady, in no degree embarrassed, pointed out to him a charming little woman as one of the subsidiary wives of the Anglican Bishop of London. She added encomiums of the episcopal courage—hitherto there had been a rule of clerical monogamy—"neither a natural nor an expedient condition of things. Why should the natural development of the affections be dwarfed and restricted because a man is a priest?"

"And, bye the bye," she added, "are you an Anglican?" Graham was on the verge of hesitating inquiries about the status of a "subsidiary wife," apparently an euphemistic phrase, when Lincoln's return broke off this very suggestive and interesting conversation. They crossed the aisle to where a tall man in crimson, and two charming persons in Burmese costume (as it seemed to him) awaited him diffidently. From their civilities he passed to other presentations.

In a little while his multitudinous impressions began to organise themselves into a general effect. At first the glitter of the gathering had raised all the democrat in Graham; he had felt hostile and satirical. But it is not in human nature to resist an atmosphere of courteous regard. Soon the music, the light, the play of colours, the shining arms and shoulders about him, the touch of hands, the transient interest of smiling faces, the frothing sound of skilfully modulated voices, the atmosphere of compliment, interest and respect, had woven together into a fabric of indisputable pleasure. Graham for a time forgot his spacious resolutions. He gave way insensibly to the intoxication of the position that was conceded him, his manner became less conscious, more convincingly regal, his feet walked assuredly, the black robe fell with a bolder fold and pride ennobled his voice. After all this was a brilliant interesting world.

His glance went approvingly over the shifting colours of the people, it rested here and there in kindly criticism upon a face. Presently it occurred to him that he owed some apology to the charming little person with the red hair and blue eyes. He felt guilty of a clumsy snub. It was not princely to ignore her advances, even if his policy necessitated their rejection. He wondered if he should see her again. And suddenly a little thing touched all the glamour of this brilliant gathering and changed its quality.

He looked up and saw passing across a bridge of porcelain and looking down upon him, a face that was almost immediately hidden, the face of the girl he had seen overnight in the little room beyond the theatre after his escape from the Council. And she was looking with much the same

expression of curious expectation, of uncertain intentness, upon his proceedings. For the moment he did not remember when he had seen her,
and then with recognition came a vague memory of the stirring emotions
of their first encounter. But the dancing web of melody about him kept
the air of that great marching song from his memory.

The lady to whom he was talking repeated her remark, and Graham
recalled himself to the quasi-regal flirtation upon which he was engaged.

But from that moment a vague restlessness, a feeling that grew to dis-
satisfaction, came into his mind. He was troubled as if by some half forgotten duty, by the sense of things important slipping from him amidst
this light and brilliance. The attraction that these bright ladies who
crowded about him were beginning to exercise ceased. He no longer
made vague and clumsy responses to the subtly amorous advances that
he was now assured were being made to him, and his eyes wandered for
another sight of that face that had appealed so strongly to his sense of
beauty. But he did not see her again until he was awaiting Lincoln's
return to leave this assembly. In answer to his request Lincoln had
promised that an attempt should be made to fly that afternoon, if the
weather permitted. He had gone to make certain necessary arrangements.

Graham was in one of the upper galleries in conversation with a bright-
eyed lady on the subject of Eadhamite—the subject was his choice and
not hers. He had interrupted her warm assurances of personal devotion
with a matter-of-fact inquiry. He found her, as he had already found
several other latter-day women that night, less well informed than
charming. Suddenly, struggling against the eddying drift of nearer
melody, the song of the Revolt, the great song he had heard in the Hall,
hoarse and massive, came beating down to him.

He glanced up startled, and perceived above him an *oeil de boeuf*
through which this song had come, and beyond, the upper courses of
cable, the blue haze, and the pendant fabric of the lights of the public
ways. He heard the song break into a tumult of voices and cease. But
now he perceived quite clearly the drone and tumult of the moving platforms and a murmur of many people. He had a vague persuasion that
he could not account for, a sort of instinctive feeling that outside in the
ways a huge crowd must be watching this place in which their Master
amused himself. He wondered what they might be thinking.

Though the song had stopped so abruptly, though the special music
of this gathering reasserted itself, the *motif* of the marching song, once
it had begun, lingered in his mind.

The bright-eyed lady was still struggling with the mysteries of Eadhamite when he perceived the girl he had seen in the theatre again. She
was coming now along the gallery towards him; he saw her first before

she saw him. She was dressed in a faintly luminous grey, her dark hair about her brows was like a cloud, and as he saw her the cold light from the circular opening into the ways fell upon her downcast face.

The lady in trouble about the Eadhamite saw the change in his expression, and grasped her opportunity to escape. "Would you care to know that girl, Sire?" she asked boldly. "She is Helen Wotton—a niece of Ostrog's. She knows a great many serious things. She is one of the most serious persons alive. I am sure you will like her."

In another moment Graham was talking to the girl, and the bright-eyed lady had fluttered away.

"I remember you quite well," said Graham. "You were in that little room. When all the people were singing and beating time with their feet. Before I walked across the Hall."

Her momentary embarrassment passed. She looked up at him, and her face was steady. "It was wonderful," she said, hesitated, and spoke with a sudden effort. "All those people would have died for you, Sire. Countless people did die for you that night."

Her face glowed. She glanced swiftly aside to see that no other heard her words.

Lincoln appeared some way off along the gallery, making his way through the press towards them. She saw him and turned to Graham strangely eager, with a swift change to confidence and intimacy. "Sire," she said quickly, "I cannot tell you now and here. But the common people are very unhappy; they are oppressed—they are misgoverned. Do not forget the people, who faced death—death that you might live."

"I know nothing——" began Graham.

"I cannot tell you now."

Lincoln's face appeared close to them. He bowed an apology to the girl.

"You find the new world pleasant, Sire?" asked Lincoln, with smiling deference, and indicating the space and splendour of the gathering by one comprehensive gesture. "At any rate, you find it changed."

"Yes," said Graham, "changed. And yet, after all, not so greatly changed."

"Wait till you are in the air," said Lincoln. "The wind has fallen; even now an aëropile awaits you."

The girl's attitude awaited dismissal.

Graham glanced at her face, was on the verge of a question, found a warning in her expression, bowed to her and turned to accompany Lincoln.

CHAPTER XVI

THE AËROPILE

FOR A WHILE, as Graham went through the passages of the Wind-Vane offices with Lincoln, he was preoccupied. But, by an effort, he attended to the things which Lincoln was saying. Soon his preoccupation vanished. Lincoln was talking of flying. Graham had a strong desire to know more of this new human attainment. He began to ply Lincoln with questions. He had followed the crude beginnings of aërial navigation very keenly in his previous life; he was delighted to find the familiar names of Maxim and Pilcher, Langley and Chanute, and, above all, of the aërial proto-martyr Lillienthal, still honoured by men.

Even during his previous life two lines of investigation had pointed clearly to two distinct types of contrivance as possible, and both of these had been realised. On the one hand was the great engine-driven aëroplane, a double row of horizontal floats with a big aërial screw behind, and on the other the nimbler aëropile. The aëroplanes flew safely only in a calm or moderate wind, and sudden storms, occurrences that were now accurately predictable, rendered them for all practical purposes useless. They were built of enormous size—the usual stretch of wing being six hundred feet or more, and the length of the fabric a thousand feet. They were for passenger traffic alone. The lightly swung car they carried was from a hundred to a hundred and fifty feet in length. It was hung in a peculiar manner in order to minimise the complex vibration that even a moderate wind produced, and for the same reason the little seats within the car—each passenger remained seated during the voyage—were slung with great freedom of movement. The starting of the mechanism was only possible from a gigantic car on the rail of a specially constructed stage. Graham had seen these vast stages, the flying stages, from the crow's nest very well. Six huge blank areas they were, with a giant "carrier" stage on each.

The choice of descent was equally circumscribed, an accurately plane surface being needed for safe grounding. Apart from the destruction that would have been caused by the descent of this great expanse of sail and metal, and the impossibility of its rising again, the concussion of an irregular surface, a tree-set hillside, for instance, or an embankment, would be sufficient to pierce or damage the framework, to smash the ribs of the body, and perhaps kill those aboard.

At first Graham felt disappointed with these cumbersome contrivances, but he speedily grasped the fact that smaller machines would have been unremunerative, for the simple reason that their carrying power would be disproportionately diminished with diminished size. Moreover, the huge size of these things enabled them—and it was a consideration of primary importance—to traverse the air at enormous speeds, and so run no risks of unanticipated weather. The briefest journey performed, that from London to Paris, took about three-quarters of an hour, but the velocity attained was not high; the leap to New York occupied about two hours, and by timing oneself carefully at the intermediate stations it was possible in quiet weather to go around the world in a day.

The little aëropiles (as for no particular reason they were distinctively called) were of an altogether different type. Several of these were going to and fro in the air. They were designed to carry only one or two persons, and their manufacture and maintenance was so costly as to render them the monopoly of the richer sort of people. Their sails, which were brilliantly coloured, consisted only of two pairs of lateral air floats in the same plane, and of a screw behind. Their small size rendered a descent in any open space neither difficult nor disagreeable, and it was possible to attach pneumatic wheels or even the ordinary motors for terrestrial traffic to them, and so carry them to a convenient starting place. They required a special sort of swift car to throw them into the air, but such a car was efficient in any open place clear of high buildings or trees. Human aëronautics, Graham perceived, were evidently still a long way behind the instinctive gift of the albatross or the fly-catcher. One great influence that might have brought the aëropile to a more rapid perfection had been withheld; these inventions had never been used in warfare. The last great international struggle had occurred before the usurpation of the Council.

The Flying Stages of London were collected together in an irregular crescent on the southern side of the river. They formed three groups of two each and retained the names of ancient suburban hills or villages. They were named in order, Roehampton, Wimbledon Park, Streatham, Norwood, Blackheath, and Shooter's Hill. They were uniform structures rising high above the general roof surfaces. Each was about four thousand yards long and a thousand broad, and constructed of the compound of aluminium and iron that had replaced iron in architecture. Their higher tiers formed an openwork of girders through which lifts and staircases ascended. The upper surface was a uniform expanse, with portions—the starting carriers—that could be raised and were then able to run on very slightly inclined rails to the end of the fabric. Save for any aëropiles or aëroplanes that were in port these open surfaces were kept clear for arrivals.

During the adjustment of the aëroplanes it was the custom for passengers to wait in the system of theatres, restaurants, news-rooms, and places of pleasure and indulgence of various sorts that interwove with the prosperous shops below. This portion of London was in consequence commonly the gayest of all its districts, with something of the meretricious gaiety of a seaport or city of hotels. And for those who took a more serious view of aëronautics, the religious quarters had flung out an attractive colony of devotional chapels, while a host of brilliant medical establishments competed to supply physical preparatives for the journey. At various levels through the mass of chambers and passages beneath these, ran, in addition to the main moving ways of the city which laced and gathered here, a complex system of special passages and lifts and slides, for the convenient interchange of people and luggage between stage and stage. And a distinctive feature of the architecture of this section was the ostentatious massiveness of the metal piers and girders that everywhere broke the vistas and spanned the halls and passages, crowding and twining up to meet the weight of the stages and the weighty impact of the aëroplanes overhead.

Graham went to the flying stages by the public ways. He was accompanied by Asano, his Japanese attendant. Lincoln was called away by Ostrog, who was busy with his administrative concerns. A strong guard of the Wind-Vane police awaited the Master outside the Wind-Vane offices, and they cleared a space for him on the upper moving platform. His passage to the flying stages was unexpected, nevertheless a considerable crowd gathered and followed him to his destination. As he went along, he could hear the people shouting his name, and saw numberless men and women and children in blue come swarming up the staircases in the central path, gesticulating and shouting. He could not hear what they shouted. He was struck again by the evident existence of a vulgar dialect among the poor of the city. When at last he descended, his guards were immediately surrounded by a dense excited crowd. Afterwards it occurred to him that some had attempted to reach him with petitions. His guards cleared a passage for him with difficulty.

He found an aëropile in charge of an aëronaut awaiting him on the westward stage. Seen close this mechanism was no longer small. As it lay on its launching carrier upon the wide expanse of the flying stage, its aluminium body skeleton was as big as the hull of a twenty-ton yacht. Its lateral supporting sails braced and stayed with metal nerves almost like the nerves of a bee's wing, and made of some sort of glassy artificial membrane, cast their shadow over many hundreds of square yards. The chairs for the engineer and his passenger hung free to swing by a complex tackle, within the protecting ribs of the frame and well abaft the middle.

The passenger's chair was protected by a wind-guard and guarded about with metallic rods carrying air cushions. It could, if desired, be completely closed in, but Graham was anxious for novel experiences, and desired that it should be left open. The aëronaut sat behind a glass that sheltered his face. The passenger could secure himself firmly in his seat, and this was almost unavoidable on landing, or he could move along by means of a little rail and rod to a locker at the stem of the machine, where his personal luggage, his wraps and restoratives were placed, and which also with the seats, served as a makeweight to the parts of the central engine that projected to the propeller at the stern.

The engine was very simple in appearance. Asano, pointing out the parts of this apparatus to him, told him that, like the gas-engine of Victorian days, it was of the explosive type, burning a small drop of a substance called "fomile" at each stroke. It consisted simply of reservoir and piston about the long fluted crank of the propeller shaft. So much Graham saw of the machine.

The flying stage about him was empty save for Asano and their suite of attendants. Directed by the aëronaut he placed himself in his seat. He then drank a mixture containing ergot—a dose, he learnt, invariably administered to those about to fly, and designed to counteract the possible effect of diminished air pressure upon the system. Having done so, he declared himself ready for the journey. Asano took the empty glass from him, stepped through the bars of the hull, and stood below on the stage waving his hand. Suddenly he seemed to slide along the stage to the right and vanish.

The engine was beating, the propeller spinning, and for a second the stage and the buildings beyond were gliding swiftly and horizontally past Graham's eye; then these things seemed to tilt up abruptly. He gripped the little rods on either side of him instinctively. He felt himself moving upward, heard the air whistle over the top of the wind screen. The propeller screw moved round with powerful rhythmic impulses—one, two, three, pause; one, two, three—which the engineer controlled very delicately. The machine began a quivering vibration that continued throughout the flight, and the roof areas seemed running away to starboard very quickly and growing rapidly smaller. He looked from the face of the engineer through the ribs of the machine. Looking sideways, there was nothing very startling in what he saw—a rapid funicular railway might have given the same sensations. He recognised the Council House and the Highgate Ridge. And then he looked straight down between his feet.

For a moment physical terror possessed him, a passionate sense of insecurity. He held tight. For a second or so he could not lift his eyes.

Some hundred feet or more sheer below him was one of the big wind-vanes of south-west London, and beyond it the southernmost flying stage crowded with little black dots. These things seemed to be falling away from him. For a second he had an impulse to pursue the earth. He set his teeth, he lifted his eyes by a muscular effort, and the moment of panic passed.

He remained for a space with his teeth set hard, his eyes staring into the sky. Throb, throb, throb—beat, went the engine; throb, throb, throb—beat. He gripped his bars tightly, glanced at the aëronaut, and saw a smile upon his sun-tanned face. He smiled in return—perhaps a little artificially. "A little strange at first," he shouted before he recalled his dignity. But he dared not look down again for some time. He stared over the aëronaut's head to where a rim of vague blue horizon crept up the sky. For a little while he could not banish the thought of possible accidents from his mind. Throb, throb, throb—beat; suppose some trivial screw went wrong in that supporting engine! Suppose——! He made a grim effort to dismiss all such suppositions. After a while they did at least abandon the foreground of his thoughts. And up he went steadily, higher and higher into the clear air.

Once the mental shock of moving unsupported through the air was over, his sensations ceased to be unpleasant, became very speedily pleasurable. He had been warned of air sickness. But he found the pulsating movement of the aëropile as it drove up the faint south-west breeze was very little in excess of the pitching of a boat head on to broad rollers in a moderate gale, and he was constitutionally a good sailor. And the keenness of the more rarefied air into which they ascended produced a sense of lightness and exhilaration. He looked up and saw the blue sky above fretted with cirrus clouds. His eye came cautiously down through the ribs and bars to a shining flight of white birds that hung in the lower sky. For a space he watched these. Then going lower and less apprehensively, he saw the slender figure of the Wind-Vane keeper's crow's nest shining golden in the sunlight and growing smaller every moment. As his eye fell with more confidence now, there came a blue line of hills, and then London, already to leeward, an intricate space of roofing. Its near edge came sharp and clear, and banished his last apprehensions in a shock of surprise. For the boundary of London was like a wall, like a cliff, a steep fall of three or four hundred feet, a frontage broken only by terraces here and there, a complex decorative façade.

That gradual passage of town into country through an extensive sponge of suburbs, which was so characteristic a feature of the great cities of the nineteenth century, existed no longer. Nothing remained of it but a waste of ruins here, variegated and dense with thickets of the heterogeneous growths that had once adorned the gardens of the belt, interspersed among levelled brown patches of sown ground, and verdant stretches of winter greens. The latter even spread among the vestiges of houses. But for the most part the reefs and skerries of ruins, the wreckage of suburban villas, stood among their streets and roads, queer islands amidst the levelled expanses of green and brown, abandoned indeed by the inhabitants years since, but too substantial, it seemed, to be cleared out of the way of the wholesale horticultural mechanisms of the time.

The vegetation of this waste undulated and frothed amidst the countless cells of crumbling house walls, and broke along the foot of the city wall in a surf of bramble and holly and ivy and teazle and tall grasses. Here and there gaudy pleasure palaces towered amidst the puny remains of Victorian times, and cable ways slanted to them from the city. That winter day they seemed deserted. Deserted, too, were the artificial gardens among the ruins. The city limits were indeed as sharply defined as in the ancient days when the gates were shut at nightfall and the robber foeman prowled to the very walls. A huge semi-circular throat poured out a vigorous traffic upon the Eadhamite Bath Road. So the first prospect of the world beyond the city flashed on Graham, and dwindled. And when at last he could look vertically downward again, he saw below him the vegetable fields of the Thames valley—innumerable minute oblongs of ruddy brown, intersected by shining threads, the sewage ditches.

His exhilaration increased rapidly, became a sort of intoxication. He found himself drawing deep breaths of air, laughing aloud, desiring to shout. After a time that desire became too strong for him, and he shouted.

The machine had now risen as high as was customary with aëropiles, and they began to curve about towards the south. Steering, Graham perceived, was effected by the opening or closing of one or two thin strips of membrane in one or other of the otherwise rigid wings, and by the movement of the whole engine backward or forward along its supports. The aëronaut set the engine gliding slowly forward along its rail and opened the valve of the leeward wing until the stem of the aëropile was horizontal and pointing southward. And in that direction they drove with a slight list to leeward, and with a slow alternation of moveemnt, first a short, sharp ascent and then a long downward glide that was very swift and pleasing. During these downward glides the propellor was inactive altogether. These ascents gave Graham a glorious sense of successful effort; the descents through the rarefied air were beyond all experience. He wanted never to leave the upper air again.

For a time he was intent upon the minute details of the landscape that ran swiftly northward beneath him. Its minute, clear detail pleased him exceedingly. He was impressed by the ruin of the houses that had once dotted the country, by the vast treeless expanse of country from which all farms and villages had gone, save for crumbling ruins. He had known the thing was so, but seeing it so was an altogether different matter. He tried to make out places he had known within the hollow basin of the world below, but at first he could distinguish no data now that the Thames valley was left behind. Soon, however, they were driving over a sharp chalk hill that he recognised as the Guildford Hog's Back, because of the familiar outline of the gorge at its eastward end, and because of the ruins of the town that rose steeply on either lip of this gorge. And from that he made out other points, Leith Hill, the sandy wastes of Aldershot, and so forth. The Downs escarpment was set with gigantic slow-moving wind-wheels. Save where the broad Eadhamite Portsmouth Road, thickly dotted with rushing shapes, followed the course of the old railway, the gorge of the Wey was choked with thickets.

The whole expanse of the Downs escarpment, so far as the grey haze permitted him to see, was set with wind-wheels to which the largest of the city was but a younger brother. They stirred with a stately motion before the south-west wind. And here and there were patches dotted with the sheep of the British Food Trust, and here and there a mounted shepherd made a spot of black. Then rushing under the stern of the aëropile came the Wealden Heights, the line of Hindhead, Pitch Hill, and Leith Hill, with a second row of wind-wheels that seemed striving to rob the downland whirlers of their share of breeze. The purple heather was speckled with yellow gorse, and on the further side a drove of black oxen stampeded before a couple of mounted men. Swiftly these swept behind, and dwindled and lost colour, and became scarce moving specks that were swallowed up in haze.

And when these had vanished in the distance Graham heard a peewit wailing close at hand. He perceived he was now above the South Downs, and staring over his shoulder saw the battlements of Portsmouth Landing Stage towering over the ridge of Portsdown Hill. In another moment there came into sight a spread of shipping like floating cities, the little white cliffs of the Needles dwarfed and sunlit, and the grey and glittering waters of the narrow sea. They seemed to leap the Solent in a moment, and in a few seconds the Isle of Wight was running past, and then beneath him spread a wider and wider extent of sea, here purple with the shadow of a cloud, here grey, here a burnished mirror, and here a spread of cloudy greenish blue. The Isle of Wight grew smaller and smaller. In a few more minutes a strip of grey haze detached itself from other strips that were clouds, descended out of the sky and became a coastline—sunlit and pleasant—the coast of northern France. It rose, it took colour, became definite and detailed, and the counterpart of the Downland of England was speeding by below.

In a little time, as it seemed, Paris came above the horizon, and hung there for a space, and sank out of sight again as the aëropile circled about to the north again. But he perceived the Eiffel Tower still standing, and beside it a huge dome surmounted by a pin-point Colossus. And he perceived, too, though he did not understand it at the time, a slanting drift of smoke. The aëronaut said something about "trouble in the under-ways," that Graham did not heed at the time. But he marked the minarets and towers and slender masses that streamed skyward above the city wind-vanes, and knew that in the matter of grace at least Paris still kept in front of her larger rival. And even as he looked a pale blue shape ascended very swiftly from the city like a dead leaf driving up before a gale. It curved round and soared towards them growing rapidly larger and larger. The aëronaut was saying something. "What?" said Graham, loth to take his eyes from this. "Aëroplane, Sire," bawled the aëronaut pointing.

They rose and curved about northward as it drew nearer. Nearer it came and nearer, larger and larger. The throb, throb, throb—beat, of the aëropile's flight, that had seemed so potent and so swift, suddenly appeared slow by comparison with this tremendous rush. How great the monster seemed, how swift and steady! It passed quite closely beneath them, driving along silently, a vast spread of wire-netted translucent wings, a thing alive. Graham had a momentary glimpse of the rows and rows of wrapped-up passengers, slung in their little cradles behind wind-screens, of a white-clothed engineer crawling against the gale along a ladder way, of spouting engines beating together, of the whirling wind screw, and of a wide waste of wing. He exulted in the sight. And in an instant the thing had passed.

It rose slightly and their own little wings swayed in the rush of its flight. It fell and grew smaller. Scarcely had they moved, as it seemed, before it was again only a flat blue thing that dwindled in the sky. This was the aëroplane that went to and fro between London and Paris. In fair weather and in peaceful times it came and went four times a day.

They beat across the Channel, slowly as it seemed now, to Graham's enlarged ideas, and Beachy Head rose greyly to the left of them.

"Land," called the aëronaut, his voice small against the whistling of the air over the wind-screen.

"Not yet," bawled Graham, laughing. "Not land yet. I want to learn more of this machine."

"I meant——" said the aëronaut.

"I want to learn more of this machine," repeated Graham.

"I'm coming to you," he said, and had flung himself free of his chair and taken a step along the guarded rail between them. He stopped for a moment, and his colour changed and his hands tightened. Another step and he was clinging close to the aëronaut. He felt a weight on his shoulder, the pressure of the air. His hat was a whirling speck behind. The wind came in gusts over his wind-screen and blew his hair in streamers past his cheek. The aëronaut made some hasty adjustments for the shifting of the centres of gravity and pressure.

"I want to have these things explained," said Graham. "What do you do when you move that engine forward?"

The aëronaut hesitated. Then he answered, "They are complex, Sire."

"I don't mind," shouted Graham. "I don't mind."

There was a moment's pause. "Aëronautics is the secret—the privilege——"

"I know. But I'm the Master, and I mean to know." He laughed, full of this novel realisation of power that was his gift from the upper air.

The aëropile curved about, and the keen fresh wind cut across Graham's face and his garment lugged at his body as the stem pointed round to the west. The two men looked into each other's eyes.

"Sire, there are rules——"

"Not where I am concerned," said Graham. "You seem to forget."

The aëronaut scrutinised his face. "No," he said. "I do not forget, Sire. But in all the earth—no man who is not a sworn aëronaut—has ever a chance. They come as passengers——"

"I have heard something of the sort. But I'm not going to argue these points. Do you know why I have slept two hundred years? To fly!"

"Sire," said the aëronaut, "the rules—if I break the rules——"

Graham waved the penalties aside.

"Then if you will watch me——"

"No," said Graham, swaying and gripping tight as the machine lifted its nose again for an ascent. "That's not my game. I want to do it myself. Do it myself if I smash for it! No! I will. See. I am going to clamber by this—to come and share your seat. Steady! I mean to fly of my own accord if I smash at the end of it. I will have something to pay for my sleep. Of all other things—— In my past it was my dream to fly. Now—keep your balance."

"A dozen spies are watching me, Sire!"

Graham's temper was at end. Perhaps he chose it should be. He swore. He swung himself round the intervening mass of levers and the aëropile swayed.

"Am I Master of the earth?" he said. "Or is your Society? Now. Take your hands off those levers, and hold my wrists. Yes—so. And now, how do we turn her nose down to the glide?"

"Sire," said the aëronaut.

"What is it?"

"You will protect me?"

"Lord! Yes! If I have to burn London. Now!"

And with that promise Graham bought his first lesson in aërial navigation. "It's clearly to your advantage, this journey," he said with a loud laugh—for the air was like strong wine—"to teach me quickly and well. Do I pull this? Ah! So! Hullo!"

"Back, Sire! Back!"

"Back—right. One—two—three—good God! Ah! Up she goes! But this is living!"

And now the machine began to dance the strangest figures in the air. Now it would sweep round a spiral of scarcely a hundred yards diameter, now it would rush up into the air and swoop down again, steeply, swiftly, falling like a hawk, to recover in a rushing loop that swept it high again. In one of these descents it seemed driving straight at the drifting park of balloons in the south-east, and only curved about and cleared them by a sudden recovery of dexterity. The extraordinary swiftness and smoothness of the motion, the extraordinary effect of the rarefied air upon his constitution, threw Graham into a careless fury.

But at last a queer incident came to sober him, to send him flying down once more to the crowded life below with all its dark insoluble riddles. As he swooped, came a tap and something flying past, and a drop like a drop of rain. Then as he went on down he saw something like a white rag whirling down in his wake. "What was that?" he asked. "I did not see."

The aëronaut glanced, and then clutched at the lever to recover, for they were sweeping down. When the aëropile was rising again he drew a deep breath and replied. "That," and he indicated the white thing still fluttering down, "was a swan."

"I never saw it," said Graham.

The aëronaut made no answer, and Graham saw little drops upon his forehead.

They drove horizontally while Graham clambered back to the passenger's place out of the lash of the wind. And then came a swift rush down, with the wind-screw whirling to check their fall, and the flying stage growing broad and dark before them. The sun, sinking over the chalk hills in the west, fell with them, and left the sky a blaze of gold.

Soon men could be seen as little specks. He heard a noise coming up to meet him, a noise like the sound of waves upon a pebbly beach, and saw that the roofs about the flying stage were dark with his people rejoicing over his safe return. A dark mass was crushed together under the stage, a darkness stippled with innumerable faces, and quivering with the minute oscillation of waved white handkerchiefs and waving hands.

———————

CHAPTER XVII

THREE DAYS

LINCOLN AWAITED Graham in an apartment beneath the flying stages. He seemed curious to learn all that had happened, pleased to hear of the extraordinary delight and interest which Graham took in flying. Graham was in a mood of enthusiasm. "I must learn to fly," he cried. "I must master that. I pity all poor souls who have died without this opportunity. The sweet swift air! It is the most wonderful experience in the world."

"You will find our new times full of wonderful experiences," said Lincoln. "I do not know what you will care to do now. We have music that may seem novel."

"For the present," said Graham, "flying holds me. Let me learn more of that. Your aëronaut was saying there is some trades union objection to one's learning."

"There is, I believe," said Lincoln. "But for you——! If you would like to occupy yourself with that, we can make you a sworn aëronaut tomorrow."

Graham expressed his wishes vividly and talked of his sensations for a while. "And as for affairs," he asked abruptly. "How are things going on?"

Lincoln waved affairs aside. "Ostrog will tell you that tomorrow," he said. "Everything is settling down. The Revolution accomplishes itself all over the world. Friction is inevitable here and there, of course; but your rule is assured. You may rest secure with things in Ostrog's hands."

"Would it be possible for me to be made a sworn aëronaut, as you call it, forthwith—before I sleep?" said Graham, pacing. "Then I could be at it the very first thing tomorrow again. . . ."

"It would be possible," said Lincoln thoughtfully. "Quite possible. Indeed, it shall be done." He laughed. "I came prepared to suggest amusements, but you have found one for yourself. I will telephone to the aëronautical offices from here and we will return to your apartments in the Wind-Vane Control. By the time you have dined the aëronauts will be able to come. You don't think that after you have dined, you might prefer——?" He paused.

"Yes," said Graham.

"We had prepared a show of dancers—they have been brought from the Capri theatre."

"I hate ballets," said Graham, shortly. "Always did. That other—— That's not what I want to see. We had dancers in the old days. For the matter of that, they had them in ancient Egypt. But flying——"

"True," said Lincoln. "Though our dancers——"

"They can afford to wait," said Graham; "they can afford to wait. I know. I'm not a Latin. There's questions I want to ask some expert— about your machinery. I'm keen. I want no distractions."

"You have the world to choose from," said Lincoln; "whatever you want is yours."

Asano appeared, and under the escort of a strong guard they returned through the city streets to Graham's apartments. Far larger crowds had assembled to witness his return than his departure had gathered, and the shouts and cheering of these masses of people sometimes drowned Lincoln's answers to the endless questions Graham's aërial journey had suggested. At first Graham had acknowledged the cheering and cries of the crowd by bows and gestures, but Lincoln warned him that such a recognition would be considered incorrect behaviour. Graham, already a little wearied by rhythmic civilities, ignored his subjects for the remainder of his public progress.

Directly they arrived at his apartments Asano departed in search of kinematographic renderings of machinery in motion, and Lincoln despatched Graham's commands for models of machines and small machines to illustrate the various mechanical advances of the last two centuries. The little group of appliances for telegraphic communication attracted the Master so strongly that his delightfully prepared dinner, served by a number of charmingly dexterous girls, waited for a space. The habit of smoking had almost ceased from the face of the earth, but when he expressed a wish for that indulgence, inquiries were made and some excellent cigars were discovered in Florida, and sent to him by pneumatic despatch while the dinner was still in progress. Afterwards came the aëronauts, and a feast of ingenious wonders in the hands of a latter-day engineer. For the time, at any rate, the neat dexterity of counting and numbering machines, building machines, spinning engines, patent doorways, explosive motors, grain and water elevators, slaughter-house machines and harvesting appliances, was more fascinating to Graham than any bayadere. "We were savages," was his refrain, "we were savages. We were in the stone age—compared with this. . . . And what else have you?"

There came also practical psychologists with some very interesting developments in the art of hypnotism. The names of Milne Bramwell, Fechner, Liebault, William James, Myers and Gurney, he found, bore a value now that would have astonished their contemporaries. Several practical applications of psychology were now in general use; it had largely superseded drugs, antiseptics and anaesthetics in medicine; was employed by almost all who had any need of mental concentration. A real enlargement of human faculty seemed to have been effected in this direction. The feats of "calculating boys," the wonders, as Graham had been wont to regard them, of mesmerisers, were now within the range of anyone who could afford the services of a skilled hypnotist. Long ago the old examination methods in education had been destroyed by these expedients. Instead of years of study, candidates had substituted a few weeks of trances, and during the trances expert coaches had simply to repeat all the points necessary for adequate answering, adding a suggestion of the post hypnotic recollection of these points. In process mathematics particularly, this aid had been of singular service, and it was now invariably invoked by such players of chess and games of manual dexterity as were still to be found. In fact, all operations conducted under finite rules, of a quasi-mechanical sort that is, were now systematically relieved from the wanderings of imagination and emotion, and brought to an unexampled pitch of accuracy. Little children of the labouring classes, so soon as they were of sufficient age to be hypnotised, were thus converted into beautifully punctual and trustworthy machine minders, and released forthwith from the long, long thoughts of youth. Aëronautical pupils, who gave way to giddiness, could be relieved from their imaginary terrors. In every street were hypnotists ready to print permanent memories upon the mind. If anyone desired to remember a name, a series of numbers, a song or a speech, it could be done by this method, and conversely memories could be effaced, habits removed, and desires eradicated—a sort of psychic surgery was, in fact, in general use. Indignities, humbling experiences, were thus forgotten, amorous widows would obliterate their previous husbands, angry lovers release themselves from their slavery. To graft desires, however, was still impossible, and the facts of thought transference were yet unsystematised. The psychologists illustrated their expositions with some astounding experiments in mnemonics made through the agency of a troupe of pale-faced children in blue.

Graham, like most of the people of his former time, distrusted the hypnotist, or he might then and there have eased his mind of many painful preoccupations. But in spite of Lincoln's assurances he held to the old theory that to be hypnotised was in some way the surrender of his personality, the abdication of his will. At the banquet of wonderful experiences that was beginning, he wanted very keenly to remain absolutely himself.

The next day, and another day, and yet another day passed in such interests as these. Each day Graham spent many hours in the glorious entertainment of flying. On the third day he soared across middle France, and within sight of the snow-clad Alps. These vigorous exercises gave him restful sleep, and each day saw a great stride in his health from the spiritless anaemia of his first awakening. And whenever he was not in the air, and awake, Lincoln was assiduous in the cause of his amusement; all that was novel and curious in contemporary invention was brought to him, until at last his appetite for novelty was well-nigh glutted. One might fill a dozen inconsecutive volumes with the strange things they exhibited. Each afternoon he held his court for an hour or so. He speedily found his interest in his contemporaries becoming personal and intimate. At first he had been alert chiefly for unfamiliarity and peculiarity; any foppishness in their dress, any discordance with his preconceptions of nobility in their status and manners had jarred upon him, and it was remarkable to him how soon that strangeness and the faint hostility that arose from it, disappeared; how soon he came to appreciate the true perspective of his position, and see the old Victorian days remote and quaint. He found himself particularly amused by the red-haired daughter of the Manager of the European Piggeries. On the second day after dinner he made the acquaintance of a latter-day dancing girl, and found her an astonishing artist. And after that, more hypnotic wonders. On the third day Lincoln was moved to suggest that the Master should repair to a Pleasure City, but this Graham declined, nor would he accept the services of the hypnotists in his aëronautical experiments. The link of locality held him to London; he found a perpetual wonder in topographical identifications that he would have missed abroad. "Here—or a hundred feet below here," he could say, "I used to eat my midday cutlets during my London University days. Underneath here was Waterloo and the perpetual hunt for confusing trains. Often have I stood waiting down there, bag in hand, and stared up into the sky above the forest of signals, little thinking I should walk some day a hundred yards in the air. And now in that very sky that was once a grey smoke canopy, I circle in an aëropile."

During those three days Graham was so occupied with such distractions that the vast political movements in progress outside his quarters had but a small share of his attention. Those about him told him little. Daily came Ostrog, the Boss, his Grand Vizier, his mayor of the palace, to report in vague terms the steady establishment of his rule; "a little trouble" soon to be settled in this city, "a slight disturbance" in that. The song of the social revolt came to him no more; he never learned that it had been forbidden in the municipal limits; and all the great emotions of the crow's nest slumbered in his mind.

But on the second and third of the three days he found himself, in spite of his interest in the daughter of the Pig Manager, or it may be by reason of the thoughts her conversation suggested, remembering the girl Helen Wotton, who had spoken to him so oddly at the Wind-Vane Keeper's gathering. The impression she had made was a deep one, albeit the incessant surprise of novel circumstances had kept him from brooding upon it for a space. But now her memory was coming to its own. He wondered what she had meant by those broken half-forgotten sentences; the picture of her eyes and the earnest passion of her face became more vivid as his mechanical interests faded. Her beauty came compellingly between him and certain immediate temptations of ignoble passion. But he did not see her again until three full days were past.

CHAPTER XVIII

GRAHAM REMEMBERS

SHE CAME upon him at last in a little gallery that ran from the Wind Vane Offices toward his state apartments. The gallery was long and narrow, with a series of recesses, each with an arched fenestration that looked upon a court of palms. He came upon her suddenly in one of these recesses. She was seated. She turned her head at the sound of his footsteps and started at the sight of him. Every touch of colour vanished from her face. She rose instantly, made a step toward him as if to address him, and hesitated. He stopped and stood still, expectant. Then he perceived that a nervous tumult silenced her, perceived too, that she must have sought speech with him to be waiting for him in this place.

He felt a regal impulse to assist her. "I have wanted to see you," he said. "A few days ago you wanted to tell me something—you wanted to tell me of the people. What was it you had to tell me?"

She looked at him with troubled eyes.

"You said the people were unhappy?"

For a moment she was silent still.

"It must have seemed strange to you," she said abruptly.

"It did. And yet——"

"It was an impulse."

"Well?"

"That is all."

She looked at him with a face of hesitation. She spoke with an effort. "You forget," she said, drawing a deep breath.

"What?"

"The people——"

"Do you mean——?"

"You forget the people."

He looked interrogative.

"Yes. I know you are surprised. For you do not understand what you are. You do not know the things that are happening."

"Well?"

"You do not understand."

"Not clearly, perhaps. But—tell me."

She turned to him with sudden resolution. "It is so hard to explain. I have meant to, I have wanted to. And now—I cannot. I am not ready with words. But about you—there is something. It is Wonder. Your sleep—your awakening. These things are miracles. To me at least—and to all the common people. You who lived and suffered and died, you who were a common citizen, wake again, live again, to find yourself Master almost of the earth."

"Master of the earth," he said. "So they tell me. But try and imagine how little I know of it."

"Cities—Trusts—the Labour Company——"

"Principalities, powers, dominions—the power and the glory. Yes, I have heard them shout. I know. I am Master. King, if you wish. With Ostrog, the Boss——"

He paused.

She turned upon him and surveyed his face with a curious scrutiny. "Well?"

He smiled. "To take the responsibility."

"That is what we have begun to fear." For a moment she said no more. "No," she said slowly. " *You* will take the responsibility. You will take the responsibility. The people look to you."

She spoke softly. "Listen! For at least half the years of your sleep—in every generation—multitudes of people, in every generation greater multitudes of people, have prayed that you might awake—*prayed*."

Graham moved to speak and did not.

She hesitated, and a faint colour crept back to her cheek. "Do you know that you have been to myriads—King Arthur, Barbarossa—the King who would come in his own good time and put the world right for them?"

"I suppose the imagination of the people——"

"Have you not heard our proverb, 'When the Sleeper wakes?' While you lay insensible and motionless there—thousands came. Thousands. Every first of the month you lay in state with a white robe upon you and the people filed by you. When I was a little girl I saw you like that, with your face white and calm."

She turned her face from him and looked steadfastly at the painted wall before her. Her voice fell. "When I was a little girl I used to look at your face . . . it seemed to me fixed and waiting, like the patience of God."

"That is what we thought of you," she said. "That is how you seemed to us."

She turned shining eyes to him, her voice was clear and strong. "In the city, in the earth, a myriad myriad men and women are waiting to see what you will do, full of strange incredible expectations."

"Yes?"

"Ostrog—no one—can take that responsibility."

Graham looked at her in surprise, at her face lit with emotion. She seemed at first to have spoken with an effort, and to have fired herself by speaking.

"Do you think," she said, "that you who have lived that little life so far away in the past, you who have fallen into and risen out of this miracle of sleep—do you think that the wonder and reverence and hope of half the world has gathered about you only that you may live another little life? . . . That you may shift the responsibility to any other man?"

"I know how great this kingship of mine is," he said haltingly. "I know how great it seems. But is it real? It is incredible—dreamlike. Is it real, or is it only a great delusion?"

"It is real," she said; "if you dare."

"After all, like all kingship, my kingship is Belief. It is an illusion in the minds of men."

"If you dare!" she said.

"But——"

"Countless men," she said, "and while it is in their minds—they will obey."

"But I know nothing. That is what I had in mind. I know nothing. And these others—the Councillors, Ostrog. They are wiser, cooler, they know so much, every detail. And, indeed, what are these miseries of which you speak? What am I to know? Do you mean———"

He stopped blankly.

"I am still hardly more than a girl," she said. "But to me the world seems full of wretchedness. The world has altered since your day, altered very strangely. I have prayed that I might see you and tell you these things. The world has changed. As if a canker had seized it—and robbed life of—everything worth having."

She turned a flushed face upon him, moving suddenly. "Your days were the days of freedom. Yes—I have thought. I have been made to think, for my life—has not been happy. Men are no longer free—no greater, no better than the men of your time. That is not all. This city— is a prison. Every city now is a prison. Mammon grips the key in his hand. Myriads, countless myriads, toil from the cradle to the grave. Is that right? Is that to be—for ever? Yes, far worse than in your time. All about us, beneath us, sorrow and pain. All the shallow delight of such life as you find about you, is separated by just a little from a life of wretchedness beyond any telling. Yes, the poor know it—they know they suffer. These countless multitudes who faced death for you two nights since——! You owe your life to them."

"Yes," said Graham, slowly. "Yes. I owe my life to them."

"You come," she said, "from the days when this new tyranny of the cities was scarcely beginning. It is a tyranny—a tyranny. In your days the feudal war lords had gone, and the new lordship of wealth had still to come. Half the men in the world still lived out upon the free countryside. The cities had still to devour them. I have heard the stories out of the old books—there was nobility! Common men led lives of love and faithfulness then—they did a thousand things. And you—you come from that time."

"It was not—— But never mind. How is it now——?"

"Gain and the Pleasure Cities! Or slavery—unthanked, unhonoured, slavery."

"Slavery!" he said.

"Slavery."

"You don't mean to say that human beings are chattels."

"Worse. That is what I want you to know, what I want you to see. I know you do not know. They will keep things from you, they will take you presently to a Pleasure City. But you have noticed men and women and children in pale blue canvas, with thin yellow faces and dull eyes?"

"Everywhere."

"Speaking a horrible dialect, coarse and weak."

"I have heard it."

"They are the slaves—your slaves. They are the slaves of the Labour Company you own."

"The Labour Company! In some way—that is familiar. Ah! now I remember. I saw it when I was wandering about the city, after the lights returned, great fronts of buildings coloured pale blue. Do you really mean——?"

"Yes. How can I explain it to you? Of course the blue uniform struck you. Nearly a third of our people wear it—more assume it now every day. This Labour Company has grown imperceptibly."

"What *is* this Labour Company?" asked Graham.

"In the old times, how did you manage with starving people?"

"There was the workhouse—which the parishes maintained."

"Workhouse! Yes—there was something. In our history lessons. I remember now. The Labour Company ousted the workhouse. It grew—partly—out of something—you, perhaps, may remember it—an emotional religious organisation called the Salvation Army—that became a business company. In the first place it was almost a charity. To save people from workhouse rigours. Now I come to think of it, it was one of the earliest properties your Trustees acquired. They bought the Salvation Army and reconstructed it as this. The idea in the first place was to give work to starving homeless people."

"Yes."

"Nowadays there are no workhouses, no refuges and charities, nothing but that Company. Its offices are everywhere. That blue is its colour. And any man, woman or child who comes to be hungry and weary and with neither home nor friend nor resort, must go to the Company in the end—or seek some way of death. The Euthanasy is beyond their means—for the poor there is no easy death. And at any hour in the day or night there is food, shelter and a blue uniform for all comers—that is the first condition of the Company's incorporation—and in return for a day's shelter the Company extracts a day's work, and then returns the visitor's proper clothing and sends him or her out again."

"Yes?"

"Perhaps that does not seem so terrible to you. In your days men starved in your streets. That was bad. But they died—men. These people in blue—— The proverb runs: 'Blue canvas once and ever.' The Company trades in their labour, and it has taken care to assure itself of the supply. People come to it starving and helpless—they eat and sleep for a night and day, they work for a day, and at the end of the day they go out again. If they have worked well they have a penny or so—enough for a theatre or a cheap dancing place, or a kinematograph story, or a dinner or a bet. They wander about after that is spent. Begging is prevented by the police of the ways. Besides, no one gives. They come back again the next day or the day after—brought back by the same incapacity that brought them first. At last their proper clothing wears out, or their rags get so shabby that they are ashamed. Then they must work for months to get fresh. If they want fresh. A great number of children are born under the Company's care. The mother owes them a month thereafter—the children they cherish and educate until they are fourteen, and they pay two years' service. You may be sure these children are educated for the blue canvas. And so it is the Company works."

"And none are destitute in the city?"

"None. They are either in blue canvas or in prison."

"If they will not work?"

"Most people will work at that pitch, and the Company has powers. There are stages of unpleasantness in the work—stoppage of food—and a man or woman who has refused to work once is known by a thumb-marking system in the Company's offices all over the world. Besides, who can leave the city poor? To go to Paris costs two Lions. And for in-subordination there are the prisons—dark and miserable—out of sight below. There are prisons now for many things."

"And a third of the people wear this blue canvas?"

"More than a third. Toilers, living without pride or delight or hope, with the stories of Pleasure Cities ringing in their ears, mocking their shameful lives, their privations and hardships. Too poor even for the Euthanasy, the rich man's refuge from life. Dumb, crippled millions, countless millions, all the world about, ignorant of anything but limita-tions and unsatisfied desires. They are born, they are thwarted and they die. That is the state to which we have come."

For a space Graham sat downcast.

"But there has been a revolution," he said. "All these things will be changed. Ostrog——"

"That is our hope. That is the hope of the world. But Ostrog will not do it. He is a politician. To him it seems things must be like this. He does not mind. He takes it for granted. All the rich, all the influential, all who are happy, come at last to take these miseries for granted. They use the people in their politics, they live in ease by their degradation. But you— you who come from a happier age—it is to you the people look. To you."

He looked at her face. Her eyes were bright with unshed tears. He felt a rush of emotion. For a moment he forgot this city, he forgot the race, and all those vague remote voices, in the immediate humanity of her beauty.

"But what am I to do?" he said with his eyes upon her.

"Rule," she answered, bending towards him and speaking in a low tone. "Rule the world as it has never been ruled, for the good and happiness of men. For you might rule it—you could rule it.

"The people are stirring. All over the world the people are stirring. It wants but a word—but a word from you—to bring them all together. Even the middle sort of people are restless—unhappy.

"They are not telling you the things that are happening. The people will not go back to their drudgery—they refuse to be disarmed. Ostrog has awakened something greater than he dreamt of—he has awakened hopes."

His heart was beating fast. He tried to seem judicial, to weigh considerations.

"They only want their leader," she said.

"And then?"

"You could do what you would—the world is yours."

He sat, no longer regarding her. Presently he spoke. "The old dreams, and the thing I have dreamt, liberty, happiness. Are they dreams? Could one man—*one man*—?" His voice sank and ceased.

"Not one man, but all men—give them only a leader to speak the desire of their hearts."

He shook his head, and for a time there was silence.

He looked up suddenly, and their eyes met. "I have not your faith," he said. "I have not your youth. I am here with power that mocks me. No—let me speak. I want to do—not right—I have not the strength for that—but something rather right than wrong. It will bring no millennium, but I am resolved now that I will rule. What you have said has awakened me. . . . You are right. Ostrog must know his place. And I will learn——. . . . One thing I promise you. This Labour slavery shall end."

"And you will rule?"

"Yes. Provided—— There is one thing."

"Yes?"

"That you will help me."

"*I!*—a girl!"

"Yes. Does it not occur to you I am absolutely alone?"

She started and for an instant her eyes had pity. "Need you ask whether I will help you?" she said.

She stood before him, beautiful, worshipful, and her enthusiasm and the greatness of their theme was like a great gulf fixed between them. To touch her, to clasp her hand, was a thing beyond hope. "Then I will rule indeed," he said slowly. "I will rule——" He paused. "With you."

There came a tense silence, and then the beating of a clock striking the hour. She made him no answer. Graham rose.

"Even now," he said, "Ostrog will be waiting." He hesitated, facing her. "When I have asked him certain questions—— There is much I do not know. It may be, that I will go to see with my own eyes the things of which you have spoken. And when I return——?"

"I shall know of your going and coming. I will wait for you here again."

He stood for a moment regarding her.

"I knew," she said, and stopped.

He waited, but she said no more. They regarded one another steadfastly, questioningly, and then he turned from her towards the Wind Vane office.

<hr />

CHAPTER XIX

OSTROG'S POINT OF VIEW

GRAHAM FOUND Ostrog waiting to give a formal account of his day's stewardship. On previous occasions he had passed over this ceremony as speedily as possible, in order to resume his aërial experiences, but now he began to ask quick short questions. He was very anxious to take up his empire forthwith. Ostrog brought flattering reports of the development of affairs abroad. In Paris and Berlin, Graham perceived that he was saying, there had been trouble, not organised resistance indeed, but insubordinate proceedings. "After all these years," said Ostrog, when Graham pressed enquiries; "the Commune has lifted its head again. That is the real nature of the struggle, to be explicit." But order had been restored in these cities. Graham, the more deliberately judicial for the stirring emotions he felt, asked if there had been any fighting. "A little," said Ostrog. "In one quarter only. But the Senegalese division of our African agricultural police—the Consolidated African Companies have a very well drilled police—was ready, and so were the aëroplanes. We expected a little trouble in the continental cities, and in America. But things are very quiet in America. They are satisfied with the overthrow of the Council. For the time."

"Why should you expect trouble?" asked Graham abruptly.

"There is a lot of discontent—social discontent."

"The Labour Company?"

"You are learning," said Ostrog with a touch of surprise. "Yes. It is chiefly the discontent with the Labour Company. It was that discontent supplied the motive force of this overthrow—that and your awakening."

"Yes?"

Ostrog smiled. He became explicit. "We had to stir up their discontent, we had to revive the old ideals of universal happiness—all men equal—all men happy—no luxury that everyone may not share—ideas that have slumbered for two hundred years. You know that? We had to revive these ideals, impossible as they are—in order to overthrow the Council. And now——"

"Well?"

"Our revolution is accomplished, and the Council is overthrown, and people whom we have stirred up—remain surging. There was scarcely enough fighting. . . . We made promises, of course. It is extraordinary how violently and rapidly this vague out-of-date humanitarianism has revived and spread. We who sowed the seed even, have been astonished. In Paris, as I say—we have had to call in a little external help."

"And here?"

"There is trouble. Multitudes will not go back to work. There is a general strike. Half the factories are empty and the people are swarming in the Ways. They are talking of a Commune. Men in silk and satin have been insulted in the streets. The blue canvas is expecting all sorts of things from you. . . . Of course there is no need for you to trouble. We are setting the Babble Machines to work with counter suggestions in the cause of law and order. We must keep the grip tight; that is all."

Graham thought. He perceived a way of asserting himself. But he spoke with restraint.

"Even to the pitch of bringing a foreign police," he said.

"They are useful," said Ostrog. "They are loyal, with no wash of ideas in their heads—such as our rabble has. The Council should have had them as police of the Ways, and things might have been different. Of course, there is nothing to fear except rioting and wreckage. You can manage your own wings now, and you can soar away to Capri if there is any smoke or fuss. We have the pull of all the great things; the aëronauts are privileged and rich, the closest trades union in the world, and so are the engineers of the wind vanes. We have the air, and the mastery of the air is the mastery of the earth. No one of any ability is organising against us. They have no leaders—only the sectional leaders of the secret society we organised before your very opportune awakening. Mere busybodies and sentimentalists they are and bitterly jealous of each other. None of them is man enough for a central figure. The only trouble will be a disorganised upheaval. To be frank—that may happen. But it won't interrupt your aëronautics. The days when the People could make revolutions are past."

"I suppose they are," said Graham. "I suppose they are." He mused. "This world of yours has been full of surprises to me. In the old days we dreamt of a wonderful democratic life, of a time when all men would be equal and happy."

Ostrog looked at him steadfastly. "The day of democracy is past," he said. "Past for ever. That day began with the bowmen of Creçy, it ended when marching infantry, when common men in masses ceased to win the battles of the world, when costly cannon, great ironclads, and strategic railways became the means of power. To-day is the day of wealth. Wealth now is power as it never was power before—it commands earth and sea and sky. All power is for those who can handle wealth. . . . You must accept facts, and these are facts. The world for the Crowd! The Crowd as Ruler! Even in your days that creed had been tried and condemned. To-day it has only one believer—a multiplex, silly one—the man in the Crowd."

Graham did not answer immediately. He stood lost in sombre preoccupations.

"No," said Ostrog. "The day of the common man is past. On the open countryside one man is as good as another, or nearly as good. The earlier aristocracy had a precarious tenure of strength and audacity. They were tempered—tempered. There were insurrections, duels, riots. The first real aristocracy, the first permanent aristocracy, came in with castles and armour, and vanished before the musket and bow. But this is the second aristocracy. The real one. Those days of gunpowder and democracy were only an eddy in the stream. The common man now is a helpless unit. In these days we have this great machine of the city, and an organisation complex beyond his understanding."

"Yet," said Graham, "there is something resists, something you are holding down—something that stirs and presses."

"You will see," said Ostrog, with a forced smile that would brush these difficult questions aside. "I have not roused the force to destroy myself—trust me."

"I wonder," said Graham.

Ostrog stared.

"*Must* the world go this way?" said Graham, with his emotions at the speaking point. "Must it indeed go in this way? Have all our hopes been vain?"

"What do you mean?" said Ostrog. "Hopes?"

"I came from a democratic age. And I find an aristocratic tyranny!"

"Well—but you are the chief tyrant."

Graham shook his head.

"Well," said Ostrog, "take the general question. It is the way that change has always travelled. Aristocracy, the prevalence of the best—the suffering and extinction of the unfit, and so to better things."

"But aristocracy! those people I met——"

"Oh! not *those*!" said Ostrog. "But for the most part they go to their death. Vice and pleasure! They have no children. That sort of stuff will die out. If the world keeps to one road, that is, if there is no turning back. An easy road to excess, convenient Euthanasia for the pleasure seekers singed in the flame, that is the way to improve the race!"

"Pleasant extinction," said Graham. "Yet——" He thought for an instant. "There is that other thing—the Crowd, the great mass of poor men. Will that die out? That will not die out. And it suffers, its suffering is a force that even you——"

Ostrog moved impatiently, and when he spoke, he spoke rather less evenly than before.

"Don't you trouble about these things," he said. "Everything will be settled in a few days now. The Crowd is a huge foolish beast. What if it does not die out? Even if it does not die, it can still be tamed and driven. I have no sympathy with servile men. You heard those people shouting and singing two nights ago. They were taught that song. If you had taken any man there in cold blood and asked why he shouted, he could not have told you. They think they are shouting for you, that they are loyal and devoted to you. Just then they were ready to slaughter the Council. To-day—they are already murmuring against those who have over-thrown the Council."

"No, no," said Graham. "They shouted because their lives were dreary, without joy or pride, and because in me—in me—they hoped."

"And what was their hope? What is their hope? What right have they to hope? They work ill and they want the reward of those who work well. The hope of mankind—what is it? That some day the Over-man may come, that some day the inferior, the weak and the bestial may be sub-dued or eliminated. Subdued if not eliminated. The world is no place for the bad, the stupid, the enervated. Their duty—it's a fine duty too!—is to die. The death of the failure! That is the path by which the beast rose to manhood, by which man goes on to higher things."

Ostrog took a pace, seemed to think, and turned on Graham. "I can imagine how this great world state of ours seems to a Victorian Englishman. You regret all the old forms of representative government—their spectres still haunt the world, the voting councils and parliaments and all that eighteenth century tomfoolery. You feel moved against our Pleasure Cities. I might have thought of that—had I not been busy. But you will learn better. The people are mad with envy—they would be in sympathy with you. Even in the streets now, they clamour to destroy the Pleasure Cities. But the Pleasure Cities are the excretory organs of the State, attractive places that year after year draw together all that is weak and vicious, all that is lascivious and lazy, all the easy roguery of the world, to a graceful destruction. They go there, they have their time, they die childless, all the pretty silly lascivious women die childless, and mankind is the better. If the people were sane they would not envy the rich their way of death. And you would emancipate the silly brainless workers that we have enslaved, and try to make their lives easy and pleasant again. Just as they have sunk to what they are fit for." He smiled a smile that irritated Graham oddly. "You will learn better. I know those ideas; in my boyhood I read your Shelley and dreamt of Liberty. There is no liberty, save wisdom and self-control. Liberty is within—not without. It is each man's own affair. Suppose—which is impossible—that these swarming yelping fools in blue get the upper hand of us, what then? They will only fall to other masters. So long as there are sheep Nature will insist on beasts of prey. It would mean but a few hundred years' delay. The coming of the aristocrat is fatal and assured. The end will be the Over-man—for all the mad protests of humanity. Let them revolt, let them win and kill me and my like. Others will arise—other masters. The end will be the same."

"I wonder," said Graham doggedly.

For a moment he stood downcast.

"But I must see these things for myself," he said, suddenly assuming a tone of confident mastery. "Only by seeing can I understand. I must learn. That is what I want to tell you, Ostrog. I do not want to be King in a Pleasure City; that is not my pleasure. I have spent enough time with aëronautics—and those other things. I must learn how people live now, how the common life has developed. Then I shall understand these things better. I must learn how common people live—the labour people more especially—how they work, marry, bear children, die——"

"You get that from our realistic novelists," suggested Ostrog, suddenly preoccupied.

"I want reality," said Graham, "not realism."

"There are difficulties," said Ostrog, and thought. "On the whole perhaps——

"I did not expect——

"I had thought—— And yet, perhaps—— You say you want to go through the Ways of the city and see the common people."

Suddenly he came to some conclusion. "You would need to go disguised," he said. "The city is intensely excited, and the discovery of your presence among them might create a fearful tumult. Still this wish of yours to go into this city—this idea of yours—— Yes, now I think the thing over it seems to me not altogether—— It can be contrived. If you would really find an interest in that! You are, of course, Master. You can go soon if you like. A disguise for this excursion Asano will be able to manage. He would go with you. After all it is not a bad idea of yours."

"You will not want to consult me in any matter?" asked Graham suddenly, struck by an odd suspicion.

"Oh, dear no! No! I think you may trust affairs to me for a time, at any rate," said Ostrog, smiling. "Even if we differ——"

Graham glanced at him sharply.

"There is no fighting likely to happen soon?" he asked abruptly.

"Certainly not."

"I have been thinking about these foreign troops. I don't believe the people intend any hostility to me, and, after all, I am the Master. I do not want them brought to London. It is an archaic prejudice perhaps, but I have peculiar feelings about it. Even about Paris——"

Ostrog stood watching him from under his drooping brows. "I am not bringing foreign troops to London," he said slowly. "But if——"

"You are not to bring them to London, whatever happens," said Graham. "In that matter I am quite decided."

Ostrog, after a pause, decided not to speak, and bowed deferentially.

———◆———

CHAPTER XX

IN THE CITY WAYS

AND THAT night, unknown and unsuspected, Graham, dressed in the costume of an inferior wind-vane official keeping holiday, and accompanied by Asano in Labour Company canvas, surveyed the city through which he had wandered when it was veiled in darkness. But now he saw it lit and waking, a whirlpool of life. In spite of the surging and swaying of the forces of revolution, in spite of the unusual discontent, the mutterings of the greater struggle of which the first revolt was but the prelude, the myriad streams of commerce still flowed wide and strong. He knew now something of the dimensions and quality of the new age, but he was not prepared for the infinite surprise of the detailed view, for the torrent of colour and vivid impressions that poured past him.

This was his first real contact with the people of these latter days. He realised that all that had gone before, saving his glimpses of the public theatres and markets, had had its element of seclusion, had been a movement within the comparatively narrow political quarter, that all his previous experiences had revolved immediately about the question of his own position. But here was the city at the busiest hours of night, the people to a large extent returned to their own immediate interests, the resumption of the real informal life, the common habits of the new time.

They emerged at first into a street whose opposite ways were crowded with the blue canvas liveries. This swarm Graham saw was a portion of a procession—it was odd to see a procession parading the city *seated*. They carried banners of coarse red stuff with red letters. "No disarmament," said the banners, for the most part in crudely daubed letters and with variant spelling, and "Why should we disarm?" "No disarming." "No disarming." Banner after banner went by, a stream of banners flowing past, and at last at the end, the song of the revolt and a noisy band of strange instruments. "They all ought to be at work," said Asano. "They have had no food these two days, or they have stolen it."

Presently Asano made a detour to avoid the congested crowd that gaped upon the occasional passage of dead bodies from hospital to a mortuary, the gleanings after death's harvest of the first revolt.

That night few people were sleeping, everyone was abroad. A vast excitement, perpetual crowds perpetually changing, surrounded Graham; his mind was confused and darkened by an incessant tumult, by the cries and enigmatical fragments of the social struggle that was as yet only beginning. Everywhere festoons and banners of black and strange decorations, intensified the quality of his popularity. Everywhere he caught snatches of that crude thick dialect that served the illiterate class, the class, that is, beyond the reach of phonograph culture, in their common-place intercourse. Everywhere this trouble of disarmament was in the air, with a quality of immediate stress of which he had no inkling during his seclusion in the Wind-Vane quarter. He perceived that as soon as he returned he must discuss this with Ostrog, this and the greater issues of which it was the expression, in a far more conclusive way than he had so far done. Perpetually that night, even in the earlier hours of their wanderings about the city, the spirit of unrest and revolt swamped his attention, to the exclusion of countless strange things he might otherwise have observed.

This preoccupation made his impressions fragmentary. Yet amidst so much that was strange and vivid, no subject, however personal and insistent, could exert undivided sway. There were spaces when the revolutionary movement passed clean out of his mind, was drawn aside like a curtain from before some startling new aspect of the time. Helen had swayed his mind to this intense earnestness of enquiry, but there came times when she, even, receded beyond his conscious thoughts. At one moment, for example, he found they were traversing the religious quarter, for the easy transit about the city afforded by the moving ways rendered sporadic churches and chapels no longer necessary—and his attention was vividly arrested by the façade of one of the Christian sects.

They were travelling seated on one of the swift upper ways, the place leapt upon them at a bend and advanced rapidly towards them. It was covered with inscriptions from top to base, in vivid white and blue, save where a vast and glaring kinematograph transparency presented a realistic New Testament scene, and where a vast festoon of black to show that the popular religion followed the popular politics, hung across the lettering. Graham had already become familiar with the phonotype writing and these inscriptions arrested him, being to his sense for the most part almost incredible blasphemy. Among the less offensive were "Salvation on the First Floor and turn to the Right." "Put your Money on your Maker." "The Sharpest Conversion in London, Expert Operators! Look Slippy!" "What Christ would say to the Sleeper—Join the Up-to-date Saints!" "Be a Christian—without hindrance to your present Occupation." "All the Brightest Bishops on the Bench to-night and Prices as Usual." "Brisk Blessings for Busy Business Men."

"But this is appalling!" said Graham, as that deafening scream of mercantile piety towered above them.

"What is appalling?" asked his little officer, apparently seeking vainly for anything unusual in this shrieking enamel.

"*This!* Surely the essence of religion is reverence."

"Oh *that*!" Asano looked at Graham. "Does it shock you?" he said in the tone of one who makes a discovery. "I suppose it would, of course. I had forgotten. Nowadays the competition for attention is so keen, and people simply haven't the leisure to attend to their souls, you know, as they used to do." He smiled. "In the old days you had quiet Sabbaths and the countryside. Though somewhere I've read of Sunday afternoons that——"

"But, *that*," said Graham, glancing back at the receding blue and white. "That is surely not the only——"

"There are hundreds of different ways. But, of course, if a sect doesn't *tell* it doesn't pay. Worship has moved with the times. There are high class sects with quieter ways—costly incense and personal attentions and all that. These people are extremely popular and prosperous. They pay several dozen lions for those apartments to the Council—to you, I should say."

Graham still felt a difficulty with the coinage, and this mention of a dozen lions brought him abruptly to that matter. In a moment the screaming temples and their swarming touts were forgotten in this new interest. A turn of a phrase suggested, and an answer confirmed the idea that gold and silver were both demonetised, that stamped gold which had begun its reign amidst the merchants of Phoenicia was at last dethroned. The change had been graduated but swift, brought about by an extension of the system of cheques that had even in his previous life already practically superseded gold in all the larger business transactions. The common traffic of the city, the common currency indeed of all the world, was conducted by means of the little brown, green and pink council cheques for small amounts, printed with a blank payee. Asano had several with him, and at the first opportunity he supplied the gaps in his set. They were printed not on tearable paper, but on a semi-transparent fabric of silken flexibility, interwoven with silk. Across them all sprawled a fac-simile of Graham's signature, his first encounter with the curves and turns of that familiar autograph for two hundred and three years.

Some intermediary experiences made no impression sufficiently vivid to prevent the matter of the disarmament claiming his thoughts again; a blurred picture of a Theosophist temple that promised MIRACLES in enormous letters of unsteady fire was least submerged perhaps, but then came the view of the dining hall in Northumberland Avenue. That interested him very greatly.

By the energy and thought of Asano he was able to view this place from a little screened gallery reserved for the attendants of the tables. The building was pervaded by a distant muffled hooting, piping and bawling, of which he did not at first understand the import, but which recalled a certain mysterious leathery voice he had heard after the resumption of the lights on the night of his solitary wandering.

He had grown accustomed now to vastness and great numbers of people, nevertheless this spectacle held him for a long time. It was as he watched the table service more immediately beneath, and interspersed with many questions and answers concerning details, that the realisation of the full significance of the feast of several thousand people came to him.

It was his constant surprise to find that points that one might have expected to strike vividly at the very outset never occurred to him until some trivial detail suddenly shaped as a riddle and pointed to the obvious thing he had overlooked. In this matter, for instance, it had not occurred to him that this continuity of the city, this exclusion of weather, these vast halls and ways, involved the disappearance of the household; that the typical Victorian "Home," the little brick cell containing kitchen and scullery, living rooms and bedrooms, had, save for the ruins that diversified the countryside, vanished as surely as the wattle hut. But now he saw what had indeed been manifest from the first, that London, regarded as a living place, was no longer an aggregation of houses but a prodigious hotel, an hotel with a thousand classes of accommodation, thousands of dining halls, chapels, theatres, markets and places of assembly, a synthesis of enterprises, of which he chiefly was the owner. People had their sleeping rooms, with, it might be, antechambers, rooms that were always sanitary at least whatever the degree of comfort and privacy, and for the rest they lived much as many people had lived in the new-made giant hotels of the Victorian days, eating, reading, thinking, playing, conversing, all in places of public resort, going to their work in the industrial quarters of the city or doing business in their offices in the trading section.

He perceived at once how necessarily this state of affairs had developed from the Victorian city. The fundamental reason for the modern city had ever been the economy of co-operation. The chief thing to prevent the merging of the separate households in his own generation was simply the still imperfect civilisation of the people, the strong barbaric pride, passions, and prejudices, the jealousies, rivalries, and violence of the middle and lower classes, which had necessitated the entire separation of contiguous households. But the change, the taming of the people, had been in rapid progress even then. In his brief thirty years of previous life he had seen an enormous extension of the habit of consuming meals from home, the casually patronised horse-box coffee-house had given place to the open and crowded Aërated Bread Shop for instance, women's clubs had had their beginning, and an immense development of reading rooms, lounges and libraries had witnessed to the growth of social confidence. These promises had by this time attained to their complete fulfilment. The locked and barred household had passed away.

These people below him belonged, he learnt, to the lower middle class, the class just above the blue labourers, a class so accustomed in the Victorian period to feed with every precaution of privacy that its members, when occasion confronted them with a public meal, would usually hide their embarrassment under horseplay or a markedly militant demeanour. But these gaily, if lightly dressed people below, albeit vivacious, hurried and uncommunicative, were dexterously mannered and certainly quite at their ease with regard to one another.

He noted a slight significant thing; the table, as far as he could see, was and remained delightfully neat, there was nothing to parallel the confusion, the broadcast crumbs, the splashes of viand and condiment, the overturned drink and displaced ornaments, which would have marked the stormy progress of the Victorian meal. The table furniture was very different. There were no ornaments, no flowers, and the table was without a cloth, being made, he learnt, of a solid substance having the texture and appearance of damask. He discerned that this damask substance was patterned with gracefully designed trade advertisements.

In a sort of recess before each diner was a complex apparatus of porcelain and metal. There was one plate of white porcelain, and by means of taps for hot and cold volatile fluids the diner washed this himself between the courses; he also washed his elegant white metal knife and fork and spoon as occasion required.

Soup and the chemical wine that was the common drink were delivered by similar taps, and the remaining covers travelled automatically in tastefully arranged dishes down the table along silver rails. The diner stopped these and helped himself at his discretion. They appeared at a little door at one end of the table, and vanished at the other. That turn of democratic sentiment in decay, that ugly pride of menial souls, which renders equals loth to wait on one another, was very strong he found among these people. He was so preoccupied with these details that it was only just as he was leaving the place that he remarked the huge advertisement dioramas that marched majestically along the upper walls and proclaimed the most remarkable commodities.

Beyond this place they came into a crowded hall, and he discovered the cause of the noise that had perplexed him. They paused at a turnstile at which a payment was made.

Graham's attention was immediately arrested by a violent, loud hoot, followed by a vast leathery voice. "The Master is sleeping peacefully," it vociferated. "He is in excellent health. He is going to devote the rest of his life to aëronautics. He says women are more beautiful than ever. Galloop! Wow! Our wonderful civilisation astonishes him beyond measure. Beyond all measure. Galloop. He puts great trust in Boss Ostrog, absolute confidence in Boss Ostrog. Ostrog is to be his chief minister; is authorised to remove or reinstate public officers—all patronage will be in his hands. All patronage in the hands of Boss Ostrog! The Councillors have been sent back to their own prison above the Council House."

Graham stopped at the first sentence, and, looking up, beheld a foolish trumpet face from which this was brayed. This was the General Intelligence Machine. For a space it seemed to be gathering breath, and a regular throbbing from its cylindrical body was audible. Then it trumpeted "Galloop, Galloop," and broke out again.

"Paris is now pacified. All resistance is over. Galloop! The police hold every position of importance in the city. They fought with great bravery, singing songs written in praise of their ancestors by the poet Kipling. Once or twice they got out of hand, and tortured and mutilated wounded and captured insurgents, men and women. Moral—don't go rebelling. Haha! Galloop, Galloop! They are lively fellows. Lively brave fellows. Let this be a lesson to the disorderly banderlog of this city. Yah! Banderlog! Filth of the earth! Galloop, Galloop!"

The voice ceased. There was a confused murmur of disapproval among the crowd. A man began to harangue near them. "Is this the Master's doing, brothers? Is this the Master's doing?"

"Police!" said Graham. "What is that? You don't mean——"

Asano touched his arm and gave him a warning look, and forthwith another of these mechanisms screamed deafeningly and gave tongue in a shrill voice. "Yahaha, Yahah, Yap! Hear a live paper yelp! Live paper. Yaha! Shocking outrage in Paris. Yahahah! The Parisians exasperated by the police to the pitch of assassination. Dreadful reprisals. Savage times come again. Blood! Blood! Yaha!" The nearer Babble Machine hooted stupendously, "Galloop, Galloop," drowned the end of the sentence, and proceeded in a rather flatter note than before with novel comments on the horrors of disorder. "Law and order must be maintained," said the nearer Babble Machine.

"But," began Graham.

"Don't ask questions here," said Asano, "or you will be involved in an argument."

"Then let us go on," said Graham, "for I want to know more of this."

As he and his companion pushed their way through the excited crowd that swarmed beneath these voices, towards the exit, Graham conceived more clearly the proportion and features of this room. Altogether, great and small, there must have been nearly a thousand of these erections, piping, hooting, bawling and gabbling in that great space, each with its crowd of excited listeners, the majority of them men dressed in blue canvas. There were all sizes of machines, from the little gossiping mechanisms that chuckled out mechanical sarcasm in odd corners, through a number of grades to such fifty-foot giants as that which had first hooted over Graham.

This place was unusually crowded, because of the intense public interest in the course of affairs in Paris. Evidently the struggle had been much more savage than Ostrog had represented it. All the mechanisms were discoursing upon that topic, and the repetition of the people made the huge hive buzz with such phrases as "Lynched policemen," "Women burnt alive." "But does the Master allow such things?" asked a man near him. "Is *this* the beginning of the Master's rule?"

Is *this* the beginning of the Master's rule? For a long time after he had left the place, the hooting, whistling and braying of the machines pursued him; "Galloop, Galloop," "Yahahah, Yaha, Yap! Yaha!" Is *this* the beginning of the Master's rule?

Directly they were out upon the ways he began to question Asano closely on the nature of the Parisian struggle. "This disarmament! What was their trouble? What does it all mean?" Asano seemed chiefly anxious to reassure him that it was "all right." "But these outrages!" "You cannot have an omelette," said Asano, "without breaking eggs. It is only the rough people. Only in one part of the city. All the rest is all right. The Parisian labourers are the wildest in the world, except ours."

"What! the Londoners?"

"No, the Japanese. They have to be kept in order."

"But burning women alive!"

"A Commune!" said Asano. "They would rob you of your property. They would do away with property and give the world over to mob rule. You are Master, the world is yours. But there will be no Commune here. There is no need for foreign police here.

"And every consideration has been shown. They are French speaking. Senegal regiments, and Niger and Timbuctoo."

"Regiments?" said Graham, "I thought there was only one——"

"No," said Asano, and glanced at him. "There is more than one."

Graham felt unpleasantly helpless.

"I did not think," he began and stopped abruptly. He went off at a tangent to ask for information about these Babble Machines. For the most part, the crowd present had been shabbily or even raggedly dressed, and Graham learnt that so far as the more prosperous classes were concerned, in all the more comfortable private apartments of the city were fixed Babble Machines that would speak directly a lever was pulled. The tenant of the apartment could connect this with the cables of any of the great News Syndicates that he preferred. When he learnt this presently, he demanded the reason of their absence from his own suite of apartments. Asano stared. "I never thought," he said. "Ostrog must have had them removed."

Graham stared. "How was I to know?" he exclaimed.

"Perhaps he thought they would annoy you," said Asano.

"They must be replaced directly I return," said Graham after an interval.

He found a difficulty in understanding that this news room and the dining hall were not great central places, that such establishments were repeated almost beyond counting all over the city. But ever and again during the night's expedition his ears, in some new quarter would pick out from the tumult of the ways the peculiar hooting of the organ of Boss

Ostrog, "Galloop, Galloop!" or the shrill "Yahaha, Yaha, Yap!—Hear a live paper yelp!" of its chief rival.

Repeated, too, everywhere, were such *crèches* as the one he now entered. It was reached by a lift, and by a glass bridge that flung across the dining hall and traversed the ways at a slight upward angle. To enter the first section of the place necessitated the use of his solvent signature under Asano's direction. They were immediately attended to by a man in a violet robe and gold clasp, the insignia of practising medical men. He perceived from this man's manner that his identity was known, and proceeded to ask questions on the strange arrangements of the place without reserve.

On either side of the passage, which was silent and padded, as if to deaden the footfall, were narrow little doors, their size and arrangement suggestive of the cells of a Victorian prison. But the upper portion of each door was of the same greenish transparent stuff that had enclosed him at his awakening, and within, dimly seen, lay, in every case, a very young baby in a little nest of wadding. Elaborate apparatus watched the atmosphere and rang a bell far away in the central office at the slightest departure from the optimum of temperature and moisture. A system of such *crèches* had almost entirely replaced the hazardous adventures of the old-world nursing. The attendant presently called Graham's attention to the wet nurses, a vista of mechanical figures, with arms, shoulders and breasts of astonishingly realistic modelling, articulation, and texture, but mere brass tripods below, and having in the place of features a flat disc bearing advertisements likely to be of interest to mothers.

Of all the strange things that Graham came upon that night, none jarred more upon his habits of thought than this place. The spectacle of the little pink creatures, their feeble limbs swaying uncertainly in vague first movements, left alone, without embrace or endearment, was wholly repugnant to him. The attendant doctor was of a different opinion. His statistical evidence showed beyond dispute that in the Victorian times the most dangerous passage of life was the arms of the mother, that there human mortality had ever been most terrible. On the other hand this *crèche* company, the International Crèche Syndicate, lost not one-half per cent of the million babies or so that formed its peculiar care. But Graham's prejudice was too strong even for those figures.

Along one of the many passages of the place they presently came upon a young couple in the usual blue canvas peering through the transparency and laughing hysterically at the bald head of their first-born. Graham's face must have showed his estimate of them, for their merriment ceased and they looked abashed. But this little incident accentuated his sudden realisation of the gulf between his habits of thought and the ways of the new age. He passed on to the crawling rooms and the Kindergarten, perplexed and distressed. He found the endless long playrooms were empty! the latter-day children at least still spent their nights in sleep. As they went through these, the little officer pointed out the nature of the toys, developments of those devised by that inspired sentimentalist Froebel. There were nurses here, but much was done by machines that sang and danced and dandled.

Graham was still not clear upon many points. "But so many orphans," he said perplexed, reverting to a first misconception, and learnt again that they were not orphans.

So soon as they had left the *crèche* he began to speak of the horror the babies in their incubating cases had caused him. "Is motherhood gone?" he said. "Was it a cant? Surely it was an instinct. This seems so unnatural —abominable almost."

"Along here we shall come to the dancing place," said Asano by way of reply. "It is sure to be crowded. In spite of all the political unrest it will be crowded. The women take no great interest in politics—except a few here and there. You will see the mothers—most young women in London are mothers. In that class it is considered a creditable thing to have one child—a proof of animation. Few middle class people have more than one. With the Labour Company it is different. As for motherhood! They still take an immense pride in the children. They come here to look at them quite often."

"Then do you mean that the population of the world——?"

"Is falling? Yes. Except among the people under the Labour Company. They are reckless——"

The air was suddenly dancing with music, and down a way they approached obliquely, set with gorgeous pillars as it seemed of clear amethyst, flowed a concourse of gay people and a tumult of merry cries and laughter. He saw curled heads, wreathed brows, and a happy intricate flutter of gamboge pass triumphant across the picture.

"You will see," said Asano with a faint smile. "The world has changed. In a moment you will see the mothers of the new age. Come this way. We shall see those yonder again very soon."

They ascended a certain height in a swift lift, and changed to a slower one. As they went on the music grew upon them, until it was near and full and splendid, and, moving with its glorious intricacies they could distinguish the beat of innumerable dancing feet. They made a payment at a turnstile, and emerged upon the wide gallery that overlooked the dancing place, and upon the full enchantment of sound and sight.

"Here," said Asano, "are the fathers and mothers of the little ones you saw."

The hall was not so richly decorated as that of the Atlas, but saving that, it was, for its size, the most splendid Graham had seen. The beautiful white-limbed figures that supported the galleries reminded him once more of the restored magnificence of sculpture; they seemed to writhe in engaging attitudes, their faces laughed. The source of the music that filled the place was hidden, and the whole vast shining floor was thick with dancing couples. "Look at them," said the little officer, "see how much they show of motherhood."

The gallery they stood upon ran along the upper edge of a huge screen that cut the dancing hall on one side from a sort of outer hall that showed through broad arches the incessant onward rush of the city ways. In this outer hall was a great crowd of less brilliantly dressed people, as numerous almost as those who danced within, the great majority wearing the blue uniform of the Labour Company that was now so familiar to Graham. Too poor to pass the turnstiles to the festival, they were yet unable to keep away from the sound of its seductions. Some of them even had cleared spaces, and were dancing also, fluttering their rags in the air. Some shouted as they danced, jests and odd allusions Graham did not understand. Once someone began whistling the refrain of the revolutionary song, but it seemed as though that beginning was promptly suppressed. The corner was dark and Graham could not see. He turned to the hall again. Above the caryatidæ were marble busts of men whom that age esteemed great moral emancipators and pioneers; for the most part their names were strange to Graham, though he recognised Grant Allen, Le Gallienne, Nietzsche, Shelley and Godwin. Great black festoons and eloquent sentiments reinforced the huge inscription that partially defaced the upper end of the dancing place, and asserted that "The Festival of the Awakening" was in progress.

"Myriads are taking holiday or staying from work because of that, quite apart from the labourers who refuse to go back," said Asano. "These people are always ready for holidays."

Graham walked to the parapet and stood leaning over, looking down at the dancers. Save for two or three remote whispering couples, who had stolen apart, he and his guide had the gallery to themselves. A warm breath of scent and vitality came up to him. Both men and women below were lightly clad, bare-armed, open-necked, as the universal warmth of the city permitted. The hair of the men was often a mass of effeminate curls, their chins were always shaven, and many of them had flushed or coloured cheeks. Many of the women were very pretty, and all were dressed with elaborate coquetry. As they swept by beneath, he saw ecstatic faces with eyes half closed in pleasure.

"What sort of people are these?" he asked abruptly.

"Workers—prosperous workers. What you would have called the

middle class. Independent tradesmen with little separate businesses have vanished long ago, but there are store servers, managers, engineers of a hundred sorts. Tonight is a holiday of course, and every dancing place in the city will be crowded, and every place of worship."

"But—the women?"

"The same. There's a thousand forms of work for women now. But you had the beginning of the independent working-woman in your days. Most women are independent now. Most of these are married more or less—there are a number of methods of contract—and that gives them more money, and enables them to enjoy themselves."

"I see," said Graham looking at the flushed faces, the flash and swirl of movement, and still thinking of that nightmare of pink helpless limbs. "And these are—mothers."

"Most of them."

"The more I see of these things the more complex I find your problems. This, for instance, is a surprise. That news from Paris was a surprise."

In a little while he spoke again:

"These are mothers. Presently, I suppose, I shall get into the modern way of seeing things. I have old habits of mind clinging about me—habits based, I suppose, on needs that are over and done with. Of course, in our time, a woman was supposed not only to bear children, but to cherish them, to devote herself to them, to educate them—all the essentials of moral and mental education a child owed its mother. Or went without. Quite a number, I admit, went without. Nowadays, clearly, there is no more need for such care than if they were butterflies. I see that! Only there was an ideal—that figure of a grave, patient woman, silently and serenely mistress of a home, mother and maker of men—to love her was a sort of worship——"

He stopped and repeated, "A sort of worship."

"Ideals change," said the little man, "as needs change."

Graham awoke from an instant reverie and Asano repeated his words. Graham's mind returned to the thing at hand.

"Of course I see the perfect reasonableness of this. Restraint, soberness, the matured thought, the unselfish act, they are necessities of the barbarous state, the life of dangers. Dourness is man's tribute to unconquered nature. But man has conquered nature now for all practical purposes—his political affairs are managed by Bosses with African police—and life is joyous."

He looked at the dancers again. "Joyous," he said.

"There are weary moments," said the little officer, reflectively.

"They all look young. Down there I should be visibly the oldest man. And in my own time I should have passed as middle-aged."

"They are young. There are few old people in this class in the work cities."

"How is that?"

"Old people's lives are not so pleasant as they used to be, unless they are rich to hire lovers and helpers. And we have an institution called Euthanasy."

"Ah! that Euthanasy!" said Graham. "The easy death?"

"The easy death. It is the last pleasure. The Euthanasy Company does it well. People will pay the sum—it is a costly thing—long beforehand, go off to some pleasure city and return impoverished and weary, very weary."

"There is a lot left for me to understand," said Graham after a pause. "Yet I see the logic of it all. Our array of angry virtues and sour restraints was the consequence of danger and insecurity. The Stoic, the Puritan, even in my time, were vanishing types. In the old days man was armed against Pain, now he is eager for Pleasure. There lies the difference. Civilisation has driven pain and danger so far off—for well-to-do people. And only well-to-do people matter now. I have been asleep two hundred years."

For a minute they leant on the balustrading, following the intricate evolution of the dance. Indeed the scene was very beautiful.

"Before God," said Graham, suddenly, "I would rather be a wounded sentinel freezing in the snow than one of these painted fools!"

"In the snow," said Asano, "one might think differently."

"I am uncivilised," said Graham, not heeding him. "That is the trouble. I am primitive—Palæolithic. *Their* fountain of rage and fear and anger is sealed and closed, the habits of a lifetime make them cheerful and easy and delightful. You must bear with my nineteenth century shocks and disgusts. These people, you say, are skilled workers and so forth. And while these dance, men are fighting—men are dying in Paris to keep the world—that they may dance."

Asano smiled faintly. "For that matter, men are dying in London," he said.

There was a moment's silence.

"Where do these sleep?" asked Graham.

"Above and below—an intricate warren."

"And where do they work? This is—the domestic life."

"You will see little work to-night. Half the workers are out or under arms. Half these people are keeping holiday. But we will go to the work places if you wish it."

For a time Graham watched the dancers, then suddenly turned away. "I want to see the workers. I have seen enough of these," he said.

Asano led the way along the gallery across the dancing hall. Presently they came to a transverse passage that brought a breath of fresher, colder air.

Asano glanced at this passage as they went past, stopped, went back to it, and turned to Graham with a smile. "Here, Sire," he said, "is something—will be familiar to you at least—and yet—— But I will not tell you. Come!"

He led the way along a closed passage that presently became cold. The reverberation of their feet told that this passage was a bridge. They came into a circular gallery that was glazed in from the outer weather, and so reached a circular chamber which seemed familiar, though Graham could not recall distinctly when he had entered it before. In this was a ladder—the first ladder he had seen since his awakening—up which they went, and came into a high, dark, cold place in which was another almost vertical ladder. This they ascended, Graham still perplexed.

But at the top he understood, and recognized the metallic bars to which he clung. He was in the cage under the ball of St. Paul's. The dome rose but a little way above the general contour of the city, into the still twilight, and sloped away, shining greasily under a few distant lights, into a circumambient ditch of darkness.

Out between the bars he looked upon the wind-clear northern sky and saw the starry constellations all unchanged. Capella hung in the west, Vega was rising, and the seven glittering points of the Great Bear swept overhead in their stately circle about the Pole.

He saw these stars in a clear gap of sky. To the east and south the great circular shapes of complaining wind-wheels blotted out the heavens, so that the glare about the Council House was hidden. To the south-west hung Orion, showing like a pallid ghost through a tracery of iron-work and interlacing shapes above a dazzling coruscation of lights. A bellowing and siren screaming that came from the flying stages warned the world that one of the aëroplanes was ready to start. He remained for a space gazing towards the glaring stage. Then his eyes went back to the northward constellations.

For a long time he was silent. "This," he said at last, smiling in the shadow, "seems the strangest thing of all. To stand in the dome of Saint Paul's and look once more upon these familiar, silent stars!"

Thence Graham was taken by Asano along devious ways to the great gambling and business quarters where the bulk of the fortunes in the city were lost and made. It impressed him as a well-nigh interminable series of very high halls, surrounded by tiers upon tiers of galleries into which opened thousands of offices, and traversed by a complicated multitude of bridges, footways, aërial motor rails, and trapeze and cable leaps. And here more than anywhere the note of vehement vitality, of uncontrollable, hasty activity, rose high. Everywhere was violent advertisement, until his brain swam at the tumult of light and colour. And Babble Machines of a peculiarly rancid tone were abundant and filled the air with strenuous squealing and an idiotic slang. "Skin your eyes and slide," "Gewhoop, Bonanza," "Gollipers come and hark!"

The place seemed to him to be dense with people either profoundly agitated or swelling with obscure cunning, yet he learnt that the place was comparatively empty, that the great political convulsion of the last few days had reduced transactions to an unprecedented minimum. In one huge place were long avenues of roulette tables, each with an excited, undignified crowd about it; in another a yelping Babel of white-faced women and red-necked leathery-lunged men bought and sold the shares of an absolutely fictitious business undertaking which, every five minutes, paid a dividend of ten per cent and cancelled a certain proportion of its shares by means of a lottery wheel.

These business activities were prosecuted with an energy that readily passed into violence, and Graham approaching a dense crowd found at its centre a couple of prominent merchants in violent controversy with teeth and nails on some delicate point of business etiquette. Something still remained in life to be fought for. Further he had a shock at a vehement announcement in phonetic letters of scarlet flame, each twice the height of a man, that "WE ASSURE THE PROPRAIET'R. WE ASSURE THE PROPRAIET'R."

"Who's the proprietor?" he asked.

"You."

"But what do they assure me?" he asked. "What do they assure me?"

"Didn't you have assurance?"

Graham thought. "Insurance?"

"Yes—Insurance. I remember that was the older word. They are insuring your life. Dozands of people are taking out policies, myriads of lions are being put on you. And further on other people are buying annuities. They do that on everybody who is at all prominent. Look there!"

A crowd of people surged and roared, and Graham saw a vast black screen suddenly illuminated in still larger letters of burning purple. "Anuetes on the Propraiet'r—x 5 pr. G." The people began to boo and shout at this, a number of hard breathing, wild-eyed men came running past, clawing with hooked fingers at the air. There was a furious crush about a little doorway.

Asano did a brief calculation. "Seventeen per cent per annum is their annuity on you. They would not pay so much per cent if they could see you now, Sire. But they do not know. Your own annuities used to be a very safe investment, but now you are sheer gambling, of course. This is probably a desperate bid. I doubt if people will get their money."

The crowd of would-be annuitants grew so thick about them that for some time they could move neither forward nor backward. Graham noticed what appeared to him to be a high proportion of women among the speculators, and was reminded again of the economical independence of their sex. They seemed remarkably well able to take care of themselves in the crowd, using their elbows with particular skill, as he learnt to his cost. One curly-headed person caught in the pressure for a space, looked steadfastly at him several times, almost as if she recognized him, and then, edging deliberately towards him, touched his hand with her arm in a scarcely accidental manner, and made it plain by a look as ancient as Chaldea that he had found favour in her eyes. And then a lank, grey-bearded man, perspiring copiously in a noble passion of self-help, blind to all earthly things save that glaring bait, thrust between them in a cataclysmal rush towards that alluring "x 5 pr. G."

"I want to get out of this," said Graham to Asano. "This is not what I came to see. Show me the workers. I want to see the people in blue. These parasitic lunatics——"

He found himself wedged in a struggling mass of people, and this hopeful sentence went unfinished.

CHAPTER XXI

THE UNDER SIDE

FROM THE Business Quarter they presently passed by the running ways into a remote quarter of the city, where the bulk of the manufactures was done. On their way the platforms crossed the Thames twice, and passed in a broad viaduct across one of the great roads that entered the city from the North. In both cases his impression was swift and in both very vivid. The river was a broad wrinkled glitter of black sea water, over-arched by buildings, and vanishing either way into a blackness starred with receding lights. A string of black barges passed seaward, manned by blue-clad men. The road was a long and very broad and high tunnel, along which big-wheeled machines drove noiselessly and swiftly. Here, too, the distinctive blue of the Labour Company was in abundance. The smoothness

of the double tracks, the largeness and the lightness of the big pneumatic wheels in proportion to the vehicular body, struck Graham most
vividly. One lank and very high carriage with longitudinal metallic rods
hung with the dripping carcasses of many hundred sheep arrested his
attention unduly. Abruptly the edge of the archway cut and blotted out
the picture.

Presently they left the way and descended by a lift and traversed a
passage that sloped downward, and so came to a descending lift again.
The appearance of things changed. Even the pretence of architectural
ornament disappeared, the lights diminished in number and size, the
architecture became more and more massive in proportion to the spaces
as the factory quarters were reached. And in the dusty biscuit-making
place of the potters, among the felspar mills, in the furnace rooms of the
metal workers, among the incandescent lakes of crude Eadhamite, the
blue canvas clothing was on man, woman and child.

Many of these great and dusty galleries were silent avenues of
machinery, endless raked out ashen furnaces testified to the revolutionary
dislocation, but wherever there was work it was being done by slow-
moving workers in blue canvas. The only people not in blue canvas were
the overlookers of the work-places and the orange-clad Labour Police.
And fresh from the flushed faces of the dancing halls, the voluntary
vigours of the business quarter, Graham could note the pinched faces,
the feeble muscles, and weary eyes of many of the latter-day workers.
Such as he saw at work were noticeably inferior in physique to the few
gaily dressed managers and forewomen who were directing their labours.
The burly labourers of the old Victorian times had followed the dray
horse and all such living force producers, to extinction; the place of his
costly muscles was taken by some dexterous machine. The latter-day
labourer, male as well as female, was essentially a machine-minder and
feeder, a servant and attendant, or an artist under direction.

The women, in comparison with those Graham remembered, were as a
class distinctly plain and flat-chested. Two hundred years of emancipation from the moral restraints of Puritanical religion, two hundred years
of city life, had done their work in eliminating the strain of feminine
beauty and vigour from the blue canvas myriads. To be brilliant physically or mentally, to be in any way attractive or exceptional, had been and
was still a certain way of emancipation to the drudge, a line of escape to
the Pleasure City and its splendours and delights, and at last to the
Euthanasy and peace. To be steadfast against such inducements was
scarcely to be expected of meanly nourished souls. In the young cities of
Graham's former life, the newly aggregated labouring mass had been a
diverse multitude, still stirred by the tradition of personal honour and a

high morality; now it was differentiating into a distinct class, with a moral and physical difference of its own—even with a dialect of its own.

They penetrated downward, ever downward, towards the working places. Presently they passed underneath one of the streets of the moving ways, and saw its platforms running on their rails far overhead, and chinks of white lights between the transverse slits. The factories that were not working were sparsely lighted; to Graham they and their shrouded aisles of giant machines seemed plunged in gloom, and even where work was going on the illumination was far less brilliant than upon the public ways.

Beyond the blazing lakes of Eadhamite he came to the warren of the jewellers, and, with some difficulty and by using his signature, obtained admission to these galleries. They were high and dark, and rather cold. In the first a few men were making ornaments of gold filigree, each man at a little bench by himself, and with a little shaded light. The long vista of light patches, with the nimble fingers brightly lit and moving among the gleaming yellow coils, and the intent face like the face of a ghost, in each shadow, had the oddest effect.

The work was beautifully executed, but without any strength of modelling or drawing, for the most part intricate grotesques or the ringing of the changes on a geometrical *motif*. These workers wore a peculiar white uniform without pockets or sleeves. They assumed this on coming to work, but at night they were stripped and examined before they left the premises of the Company. In spite of every precaution, the Labour policeman told them in a depressed tone, the Company was not infrequently robbed.

Beyond was a gallery of women busied in cutting and setting slabs of artificial ruby, and next these were men and women busied together upon the slabs of copper net that formed the basis of *cloisonné* tiles. Many of these workers had lips and nostrils a livid white, due to a disease caused by a peculiar purple enamel that chanced to be much in fashion. Asano apologised to Graham for the offence of their faces, but excused himself on the score of the convenience of this route. "This is what I wanted to see," said Graham; "this is what I wanted to see," trying to avoid a start at a particularly striking disfigurement that suddenly stared him in the face.

"She might have done better with herself than that," said Asano.

Graham made some indignant comments.

"But, Sire, we simply could not stand that stuff without the purple," said Asano. "In your days people could stand such crudities, they were nearer the barbaric by two hundred years."

They continued along one of the lower galleries of this *cloisonné* factory, and came to a little bridge that spanned a vault. Looking over the parapet, Graham saw that beneath was a wharf under yet more tremendous archings than any he had seen. Three barges, smothered in floury dust, were being unloaded of their cargoes of powdered felspar by a multitude of coughing men, each guiding a little truck; the dust filled the place with a choking mist, and turned the electric glare yellow. The vague shadows of these workers gesticulated about their feet, and rushed to and fro against a long stretch of white-washed wall. Every now and then one would stop to cough.

A shadowy, huge mass of masonry rising out of the inky water, brought to Graham's mind the thought of the multitude of ways and galleries and lifts, that rose floor above floor overhead between him and the sky. The men worked in silence under the supervision of two of the Labour Police; their feet made a hollow thunder on the planks along which they went to and fro. And as he looked at this scene, some hidden voice in the darkness began to sing.

"Stop that!" shouted one of the policemen, but the order was disobeyed, and first one and then all the white-stained men who were working there had taken up the beating refrain, singing it defiantly, the Song of the Revolt. The feet upon the planks thundered now to the rhythm of the song, tramp, tramp, tramp. The policeman who had shouted glanced at his fellow, and Graham saw him shrug his shoulders. He made no further effort to stop the singing.

And so they went through these factories and places of toil, seeing many painful and grim things. But why should the gentle reader be depressed? Surely to a refined nature our present world is distressing enough without bothering ourselves about these miseries to come. We shall not suffer anyhow. Our children may, but what is that to us? That walk left on Graham's mind a maze of memories, fluctuating pictures of swathed halls, and crowded vaults seen through clouds of dust, of intricate machines, the racing threads of looms, the heavy beat of stamping machinery, the roar and rattle of belt and armature, of ill-lit subterranean aisles of sleeping places, illimitable vistas of pin-point lights. And here the smell of tanning, and here the reek of a brewery and here, unprecedented reeks. And everywhere were pillars and cross archings of such a massiveness as Graham had never before seen, thick Titans of greasy, shining brickwork crushed beneath the vast weight of that complex city world, even as these anæmic millions were crushed by its complexity. And everywhere were pale features, lean limbs, disfigurement and degradation.

Once and again, and again a third time, Graham heard the song of the revolt during his long, unpleasant research in these places, and once he saw a confused struggle down a passage, and learnt that a number of these serfs had seized their bread before their work was done. Graham was ascending towards the ways again when he saw a number of blue-clad children running down a transverse passage, and presently perceived the reason of their panic in a company of the Labour Police armed with clubs, trotting towards some unknown disturbance. And then came a remote disorder. But for the most part this remnant that worked, worked hopelessly. All the spirit that was left in fallen humanity was above in the streets that night, calling for the Master, and valiantly and noisily keeping its arms.

They emerged from these wanderings and stood blinking in the bright light of the middle passage of the platforms again. They became aware of the remote hooting and yelping of the machines of one of the General Intelligence Offices, and suddenly came men running, and along the platforms and about the ways everywhere was a shouting and crying. Then a woman with a face of mute white terror, and another who gasped and shrieked as she ran.

"What has happened now?" said Graham, puzzled, for he could not understand their thick speech. Then he heard it in English and perceived that the thing that everyone was shouting, that men yelled to one another, that women took up screaming, that was passing like the first breeze of a thunderstorm, chill and sudden through the city, was this: "Ostrog has ordered the Police to London. The Police are coming from South Africa. . . . The African Police. The African Police."

Asano's face was white and astonished; he hesitated, looked at Graham's face, and told him the thing he already knew. "But how can they know?" asked Asano.

Graham heard someone shouting. "Stop all work. Stop all work," and a swarthy hunchback, ridiculously gay in green and gold, came leaping down the platforms toward him, bawling again and again in good English, "This is Ostrog's doing, Ostrog, the Knave! The Master is betrayed." His voice was hoarse and a thin foam dropped from his ugly shouting mouth. He yelled an unspeakable horror that the police had done in Paris, and so passed shrieking, "Ostrog the Knave!"

For a moment Graham stood still, for it had come upon him again that these things were a dream. He looked up at the great cliff of buildings on either side, vanishing into blue haze at last above the lights, and down to the roaring tiers of platforms, and the shouting, running people who were gesticulating past. "The Master is betrayed!" they cried. "The Master is betrayed!"

Suddenly the situation shaped itself in his mind real and urgent. His heart began to beat fast and strong.

"It has come," he said. "I might have known. The hour has come."
He thought swiftly. "What am I to do?"

"Go back to the Council House," said Asano.

"Why should I not appeal——? The people are here."

"You will lose time. They will doubt if it is you. But they will mass about the Council House. There you will find their leaders. Your strength is there—with them."

"Suppose this is only a rumour?"

"It sounds true," said Asano.

"Let us have the facts," said Graham.

Asano shrugged his shoulders. "We had better get towards the Council House," he cried. "That is where they will swarm. Even now the ruins may be impassable."

Graham regarded him doubtfully and followed him.

They went up the stepped platforms to the swiftest one, and there Asano accosted a labourer. The answers to his questions were in the thick, vulgar speech.

"What did he say?" asked Graham.

"He knows little, but he told me that the African Police would have arrived here before the people knew—had not someone in the Wind-Vane Offices learnt. He said a girl."

"A girl? Not——?"

"He said a girl—he did not know who she was. Who came out from the Council House crying aloud, and told the men at work among the ruins."

And then another thing was shouted, something that turned an aimless tumult into determinate movements, it came like a wind along the street. "To your Wards, to your Wards. Every man get arms. Every man to his Ward!"

CHAPTER XXII

THE STRUGGLE IN THE COUNCIL HOUSE

AS ASANO and Graham hurried along to the ruins about the Council House, they saw everywhere the excitement of the people rising. "To your Wards! To your Wards!" Everywhere men and women in blue were hurrying from unknown subterranean employments, up the staircases of the middle path; at one place Graham saw an arsenal of the revolutionary committee besieged by a crowd of shouting men, at another a couple of men in the hated yellow uniform of the Labour Police, pursued by a gathering crowd, fled precipitately along the swift way that went in the opposite direction.

The cries of "To your Wards!" became at last a continuous shouting as they drew near the Government quarter. Many of the shouts were unintelligible. "Ostrog has betrayed us," one man bawled in a hoarse voice, again and again, dinning that refrain into Graham's ear until it haunted him. This person stayed close beside Graham and Asano on the swift way, shouting to the people who swarmed on the lower platforms as he rushed past them. His cry about Ostrog alternated with some incomprehensible orders. Presently he went leaping down and disappeared.

Graham's mind was filled with the din. His plans were vague and unformed. He had one picture of some commanding position from which he could address the multitudes, another of meeting Ostrog face to face. He was full of rage, of tense muscular excitement, his hands gripped, his lips were pressed together.

The way to the Council House across the ruins was impassable, but Asano met that difficulty and took Graham into the premises of the central post-office. The post-office was nominally at work, but the blue-clothed porters moved sluggishly or had stopped to stare through the arches of their galleries at the shouting men who were going by outside. "Every man to his Ward! Every man to his Ward!" Here, by Asano's advice, Graham revealed his identity.

They crossed to the Council House by a cable cradle. Already in the brief interval since the capitulation of the Councillors a great change had been wrought in the appearance of the ruins. The spurting cascades of the ruptured sea water-mains had been captured and tamed, and huge temporary pipes ran overhead along a flimsy looking fabric of girders. The sky was laced with restored cables and wires that served the Council House, and a mass of new fabric with cranes and other building machines going to and fro upon it, projected to the left of the white pile.

The moving ways that ran across this area had been restored, albeit for once running under the open sky. These were the ways that Graham had seen from the little balcony in the hour of his awakening, not nine days since, and the hall of his Trance had been on the further side, where now shapeless piles of smashed and shattered masonry were heaped together.

It was already high day and the sun was shining brightly. Out of their tall caverns of blue electric light came the swift ways crowded with multitudes of people, who poured off them and gathered ever denser over the wreckage and confusion of the ruins. The air was full of their shouting, and they were pressing and swaying towards the central building. For the most part that shouting mass consisted of shapeless swarms, but here and there Graham could see that a rude discipline struggled to establish itself. And every voice clamoured for order in the chaos. "To your Wards! Every man to his Ward!"

The cable carried them into a hall which Graham recognised as the ante-chamber to the Hall of the Atlas, about the gallery of which he had walked days ago with Howard to show himself to the vanished Council, an hour from his awakening. Now the place was empty except for two cable attendants. These men seemed hugely astonished to recognise the Sleeper in the man who swung down from the cross seat.

"Where is Helen Wotton?" he demanded. "Where is Helen Wotton?" They did not know.

"Then where is Ostrog? I must see Ostrog forthwith. He has disobeyed me. I have come back to take things out of his hands." Without waiting for Asano, he went straight across the place, ascended the steps at the further end, and, pulling the curtain aside, found himself facing the perpetually labouring Titan.

The hall was empty. Its appearance had changed very greatly since his first sight of it. It had suffered serious injury in the violent struggle of the first outbreak. On the right hand side of the great figure the upper half of the wall had been torn away for nearly two hundred feet of its length, and a sheet of the same glassy film that had enclosed Graham at his awakening had been drawn across the gap. This deadened, but did not altogether exclude the roar of the people outside. "Wards! Wards! Wards!" they seemed to be saying. Through it there were visible the beams and supports of metal scaffoldings that rose and fell according to the requirements of a great crowd of workmen. An idle building machine, with lank arms of red painted metal that caught the still plastic blocks of mineral paste and swung them neatly into position, stretched gauntly across this green tinted picture. On it were still a number of workmen staring at the crowd below. For a moment he stood regarding these things, and Asano overtook him.

"Ostrog," said Asano, "will be in the small offices beyond there." The little man looked livid now and his eyes searched Graham's face.

They had scarcely advanced ten paces from the curtain before a little panel to the left of the Atlas rolled up, and Ostrog, accompanied by Lincoln and followed by two black and yellow clad negroes, appeared crossing the remote corner of the hall, towards a second panel that was raised and open. "Ostrog," shouted Graham, and at the sound of his voice the little party turned astonished.

Ostrog said something to Lincoln and advanced alone.

Graham was the first to speak. His voice was loud and dictatorial. "What is this I hear?" he asked. "Are you bringing troops here—to keep the people down?"

"It is none too soon," said Ostrog. "They have been getting out of hand more and more, since the revolt. I under-estimated——"

"Do you mean that they are on the way?"

"On the way. As it is, you have seen the people—outside?"

"No wonder! But—after what was said. You have taken too much on yourself, Ostrog."

Ostrog said nothing, but drew nearer.

"They must not come to London," said Graham. "I am Master and they shall not come."

Ostrog glanced at Lincoln, who at once came towards them with his two attendants close behind him. "Why not?" asked Ostrog.

"That is not the question. I am the Master. I mean to be the Master. And I tell you they shall not come."

"The people——"

"I believe in the people."

"Because you are an anachronism. You are a man out of the Past—an accident. You are Owner perhaps of half the property in the world. But you are not Master. You do not know enough to be Master."

He glanced at Lincoln again. "I know now what you think—I can guess something of what you mean to do. Even now it is not too late to warn you. You dream of human equality—of a socialistic order—you have all those worn-out dreams of the nineteenth century fresh and vivid in your mind, and you would rule this age that you do not understand."

"Listen!" said Graham. "You can hear it—a sound like the sea. Not voices—but a voice. Do *you* altogether understand?"

"We taught them that," said Ostrog.

"Perhaps. Can you teach them to forget it? But enough of this! They must not come."

There was a pause and Ostrog looked him in the eyes.

"They will," he said.

"I forbid it," said Graham.

"They have started."

"I will not have it."

"No," said Ostrog. "Sorry as I am to follow the method of the Council—— For your own good—you must not side with—Disorder. And now that you are here—— It was kind of you to come here."

Lincoln laid his hand on Graham's shoulder. Abruptly Graham realised the enormity of his blunder in coming to the Council House. He

turned towards the curtains that separated the hall from the ante-
chamber. The clutching hand of Asano intervened. In another moment
Lincoln had grasped Graham's cloak.

He turned and struck at Lincoln's face, and incontinently a negro had
him by collar and arm. He wrenched himself away, his sleeve tore noisily,
and he stumbled back, to be tripped by the other attendant. Then he
struck the ground heavily and he was staring at the distant ceiling of the
hall.

He shouted, rolled over, struggling fiercely, clutched an attendant's leg
and threw him headlong, and struggled to his feet.

Lincoln appeared before him, went down heavily again with a blow
under the point of the jaw and lay still. Graham made two strides, stumbled. And then Ostrog's arm was round his neck, he was pulled over
backward, fell heavily, and his arms were pinned to the ground. After a
few violent efforts he ceased to struggle and lay staring at Ostrog's
heaving throat.

"You—are—a prisoner," panted Ostrog, exulting. "You—were
rather a fool—to come back."

Graham turned his head about and perceived through the irregular
green window in the walls of the hall the men who had been working the
building cranes gesticulating excitedly to the people below them. They
had seen!

Ostrog followed his eyes and started. He shouted something to Lincoln, but Lincoln did not move. A bullet smashed among the mouldings
above the Atlas. The two sheets of transparent matter that had been
stretched across this gap were rent, the edges of the torn aperture darkened, curved, ran rapidly towards the framework, and in a moment the
Council chamber stood open to the air. A chilly gust blew in by the gap,
bringing with it a war of voices from the ruinous spaces without, an elvish
babblement, "Save the Master!" "What are they doing to the Master?"
"The Master is betrayed!"

And then he realised that Ostrog's attention was distracted, that
Ostrog's grip had relaxed, and, wrenching his arms free, he struggled to
his knees. In another moment he had thrust Ostrog back, and he was on
one foot, his hand gripping Ostrog's throat, and Ostrog's hands clutching
the silk about his neck.

But now men were coming towards them from the dais—men whose
intentions he misunderstood. He had a glimpse of someone running in
the distance towards the curtains of the antechamber, and then Ostrog
had slipped from him and these newcomers were upon him. To his infinite
astonishment, they seized him. They obeyed the shouts of Ostrog.

He was lugged a dozen yards before he realised that they were not friends—that they were dragging him towards the open panel. When he saw this he pulled back, he tried to fling himself down, he shouted for help with all his strength. And this time there were answering cries.

The grip upon his neck relaxed, and behold! in the lower corner of the rent upon the wall, first one and then a number of little black figures appeared shouting and waving arms. They came leaping down from the gap into the light gallery that had led to the Silent Rooms. They ran along it, so near were they that Graham could see the weapons in their hands. Then Ostrog was shouting in his ear to the men who held him, and once more he was struggling with all his strength against their endeavours to thrust him towards the opening that yawned to receive him. "They can't come down," panted Ostrog. "They daren't fire. It's all right." "We'll save him from them yet."

For long minutes as it seemed to Graham that inglorious struggle continued. His clothes were rent in a dozen places, he was covered in dust, one hand had been trodden upon. He could hear the shouts of his supporters, and once he heard shots. He could feel his strength giving way, feel his efforts wild and aimless. But no help came, and surely, irresistibly, that black, yawning opening came nearer.

The pressure upon him relaxed and he struggled up. He saw Ostrog's grey head receding and perceived that he was no longer held. He turned about and came full into a man in black. One of the green weapons cracked close to him, a drift of pungent smoke came into his face, and a steel blade flashed. The huge chamber span about him.

He saw a man in pale blue stabbing one of the black and yellow attendants not three yards from his face. Then hands were upon him again.

He was being pulled in two directions now. It seemed as though people were shouting to him. He wanted to understand and could not. Someone was clutching about his thighs, he was being hoisted in spite of his vigorous efforts. He understood suddenly, he ceased to struggle. He was lifted up on men's shoulders and carried away from that devouring panel. Ten thousand throats were cheering.

He saw men in blue and black hurrying after the retreating Ostrogites and firing. Lifted up, he saw now across the whole expanse of the hall beneath the Atlas image, saw that he was being carried towards the raised platform in the centre of the place. The far end of the hall was already full of people running towards him. They were looking at him and cheering.

He became aware that a sort of body-guard surrounded him. Active men about him shouted vague orders. He saw close at hand the black moustached man in yellow who had been among those who had greeted him in the public theatre, shouting directions. The hall was already densely packed with swaying people, the little metal gallery sagged with a shouting load, the curtains at the end had been torn away, and the ante-chamber was revealed densely crowded. He could scarcely make the man near him hear for the tumult about them. "Where has Ostrog gone?" he asked.

The man he questioned pointed over the heads towards the lower panels about the hall on the side opposite the gap. They stood open and armed men, blue clad with black sashes, were running through them and vanishing into the chambers and passages beyond. It seemed to Graham that a sound of firing drifted through the riot. He was carried in a staggering curve across the great hall towards an opening beneath the gap.

He perceived men working with a sort of rude discipline to keep the crowd off him, to make a space clear about him. He passed out of the hall, and saw a crude, new wall rising blankly before him topped by blue sky. He was swung down to his feet; someone gripped his arm and guided him. He found the man in yellow close at hand. They were taking him up a narrow stairway of brick, and close at hand rose the great red painted masses, the cranes and levers and the still engines of the big building machine.

He was at the top of the steps. He was hurried across a narrow railed footway, and suddenly with a vast shouting the amphitheatre of ruins opened again before him. "The Master is with us! The Master! The Master!" The shout swept athwart the lake of faces like a wave, broke against the distant cliff of ruins, and came back in a welter of cries. "The Master is on our side!"

Graham perceived that he was no longer encompassed by people, that he was standing upon a little temporary platform of white metal, part of a flimsy seeming scaffolding that laced about the great mass of the Council House. Over all the huge expanse of the ruins, swayed and eddied the shouting people; and here and there the black banners of the revolutionary societies ducked and swayed and formed rare nuclei of organisation in the chaos. Up the steep stairs of wall and scaffolding by which his rescuers had reached the opening in the Atlas Chamber, clung a solid crowd, and little energetic black figures clinging to pillars and projections were strenuous to induce these congested masses to stir. Be-hind him at a higher point on the scaffolding, a number of men struggled upwards with the flapping folds of a huge black standard. Through the yawning gap in the walls below him he could look down upon the packed attentive multitudes in the Hall of the Atlas. The distant flying stages to the south came out bright and vivid, brought nearer as it seemed by an unusual translucency of the air. A solitary aëropile beat up from the central stage as if to meet the coming aëroplanes.

"What had become of Ostrog?" asked Graham, and even as he spoke he saw that all eyes were turned from him towards the crest of the Council House building. He looked also in this direction of universal attention. For a moment he saw nothing but the jagged corner of a wall, hard and clear against the sky. Then in the shadow he perceived the interior of a room and recognised with a start the green and white decorations of his former prison. And coming quickly across this opened room and up to the very verge of the cliff of the ruins came a little white clad figure followed by two other smaller seeming figures in black and yellow. He heard the man beside him exclaim "Ostrog," and turned to ask a question. But he never did, because of the startled exclamation of another of those who were with him and a lank finger suddenly pointing. He looked, and behold the aëropile that had been rising from the flying stage when last he had looked in that direction, was driving towards them. The swift steady flight was still novel enough to hold his attention.

Nearer it came, growing rapidly larger and larger, until it had swept over the further edge of the ruins and into view of the dense multitudes below. It drooped across the space and rose and passed overhead, rising to clear the mass of the Council House, a filmy translucent shape with the solitary aëronaut peering down through its ribs. It vanished beyond the skyline of the ruins.

Graham transferred his attention to Ostrog. He was signalling with his hands, and his attendants busy breaking down the wall beside him. In another moment the aëropile came into view again, a little thing far away, coming round in a wide curve and going slower.

Then suddenly the man in yellow shouted: "What are they doing? What are the people doing? Why is Ostrog left there? Why is he not captured? They will lift him—the aëropile will lift him! Ah!"

The exclamation was echoed by a shout from the ruins. The rattling sound of the green weapons drifted across the intervening gulf to Graham, and, looking down, he saw a number of black and yellow uniforms running along one of the galleries that lay open to the air below the promontory upon which Ostrog stood. They fired as they ran at men unseen, and then emerged a number of pale blue figures in pursuit. These minute fighting figures had the oddest effect; they seemed as they ran like little model soldiers in a toy. This queer appearance of a house cut open gave that struggle amidst furniture and passages a quality of unreality. It was perhaps two hundred yards away from him, and very nearly fifty above the heads in the ruins below. The black and yellow men ran into an open archway, and turned and fired a volley. One of the blue pursuers striding forward close to the edge, flung up his arms, staggered sideways, seemed to Graham's sense to hang over the edge for several seconds, and fell headlong down. Graham saw him strike a projecting corner, fly out, head over heels, head over heels, and vanish behind the red arm of the building machine.

And then a shadow came between Graham and the sun. He looked up and the sky was clear, but he knew the aëropile had passed. Ostrog had vanished. The man in yellow thrust before him, zealous and perspiring, pointing and blatant.

"They are grounding!" cried the man in yellow. "They are grounding. Tell the people to fire at him. Tell them to fire at him!"

Graham could not understand. He heard loud voices repeating these enigmatical orders.

Suddenly over the edge of the ruins he saw the prow of the aëropile come gliding and stop with a jerk. In a moment Graham understood that the thing had grounded in order that Ostrog might escape by it. He saw a blue haze climbing out of the gulf, perceived that the people below him were now firing up at the projecting stem.

A man beside him cheered hoarsely, and he saw that the blue rebels had gained the archway that had been contested by the men in black and yellow a moment before, and were running in a continual stream along the open passage.

And suddenly the aëropile slipped over the edge of the Council House and fell. It dropped, tilting at an angle of forty-five degrees, and dropping so steeply that it seemed to Graham, it seemed perhaps to most of those below, that it could not possibly rise again.

It fell so closely past him that he could see Ostrog clutching the guides of the seat, with his grey hair streaming; see the white-faced aëronaut wrenching over the lever that drove the engine along its guides. He heard the apprehensive vague cry of innumerable men below.

Graham clutched the railing before him and gasped. The second seemed an age. The lower van of the aëropile passed within an ace of touching the people, who yelled and screamed and trampled one another below.

And then it rose.

For a moment it looked as if it could not possibly clear the opposite cliff, and then that it could not possibly clear the wind-wheel that rotated beyond.

And behold! it was clear and soaring, still heeling sideways, upward, upward into the wind-swept sky.

The suspense of the moment gave place to a fury of exasperation as the swarming people realised that Ostrog had escaped them. With belated activity they renewed their fire, until the rattling wove into a roar, until the whole area became dim and blue and the air pungent with the thin smoke of their weapons.

Too late! The aëropile dwindled smaller and smaller, and curved about and swept gracefully downward to the flying stage from which it had so lately risen. Ostrog had escaped.

For a while a confused babblement arose from the ruins, and then the universal attention came back to Graham, perched high among the scaffolding. He saw the faces of the people turned towards him, heard their shouts at his rescue. From the throat of the ways came the song of the revolt spreading like a breeze across that swaying sea of men.

The little group of men about him shouted congratulations on his escape. The man in yellow was close to him, with a set face and shining eyes. And the song was rising, louder and louder; tramp, tramp, tramp, tramp.

Slowly the realisation came of the full meaning of these things to him, the perception of the swift change in his position. Ostrog, who had stood beside him whenever he had faced that shouting multitude before, was beyond there—the antagonist. There was no one to rule for him any longer. Even the people about him, the leaders and organisers of the multitude, looked to see what he would do, looked to him to act, awaited his orders. He was King indeed. His puppet reign was at an end.

He was very intent to do the thing that was expected of him. His nerves and muscles were quivering, his mind was perhaps a little confused, but he felt neither fear nor anger. His hand that had been trodden upon throbbed and was hot. He was a little nervous about his bearing. He knew he was not afraid, but he was anxious not to seem afraid. In his former life he had often been more excited in playing games of skill. He was desirous of immediate action, he knew he must not think too much in detail of the huge complexity of the struggle about him lest he should be paralysed by the sense of its intricacy. Over there those square blue shapes, the flying stages, meant Ostrog; against Ostrog he was fighting for the world.

CHAPTER XXIII

WHILE THE AËROPLANES WERE COMING

FOR A TIME the Master of the Earth was not even master of his own mind. Even his will seemed a will not his own, his own acts surprised him and were but a part of the confusion of strange experiences that poured across his being. These things were definite, the aëroplanes were coming, Helen Wotton had warned the people of their coming, and he was Master of the Earth. Each of these facts seemed struggling for complete possession of his thoughts. They protruded from a background of swarming halls, elevated passages, rooms jammed with ward leaders in council, kinematograph and telephone rooms, and windows looking out on a seething sea of marching men. The man in yellow, and men whom he fancied were called Ward Leaders, were either propelling him forward or following him obediently; it was hard to tell. Perhaps they were doing a little of both. Perhaps some power unseen and unsuspected, propelled them all. He was aware that he was going to make a proclamation to the People of the Earth, aware of certain grandiose phrases floating in his mind as the thing he meant to say. Many little things happened, and then he found himself with the man in yellow entering a little room where this proclamation of his was to be made.

This room was grotesquely latter-day in its appointments. In the centre was a bright oval lit by shaded electric lights from above. The rest was in shadow, and the double finely fitting doors through which he came from the swarming Hall of the Atlas made the place very still. The dead thud of these as they closed behind him, the sudden cessation of the tumult in which he had been living for hours, the quivering circle of light, the whispers and quick noiseless movements of vaguely visible attendants in the shadows, had a strange effect upon Graham. The huge ears of a phonographic mechanism gaped in a battery for his words, the black eyes of great photographic cameras awaited his beginning, beyond metal rods and coils glittered dimly, and something whirled about with a droning hum. He walked into the centre of the light, and his shadow drew together black and sharp to a little blot at his feet.

The vague shape of the thing he meant to say was already in his mind. But this silence, this isolation, the sudden withdrawal from that contagious crowd, this silent audience of gaping, glaring machines had not been in his anticipation. All his supports seemed withdrawn together; he seemed to have dropped into this suddenly, suddenly to have discovered himself. In a moment he was changed. He found that he now feared to be inadequate, he feared to be theatrical, he feared the quality of his voice, the quality of his wit, astonished, he turned to the man in yellow with a propitiatory gesture. "For a moment," he said, "I must wait. I did not think it would be like this. I must think of the thing I have to say."

While he was still hesitating there came an agitated messenger with news that the foremost aëroplanes were passing over Arawan.

"Arawan?" he said. "Where is that? But anyhow, they are coming. They will be here. When?"

"By twilight."

"Great God! In only a few hours. What news of the flying stages?" he asked.

"The people of the south-west wards are ready."

"Ready!"

He turned impatiently to the blank circles of the lenses again.

"I suppose it must be a sort of speech. Would to God I knew certainly the thing that should be said! Aëroplanes at Arawan! They must have started before the main fleet. And the people only ready! Surely . . ."

"Oh! what does it matter whether I speak well or ill?" he said, and felt the light grow brighter.

He had framed some vague sentence of democratic sentiment when suddenly doubts overwhelmed him. His belief in his heroic quality and calling he found had altogether lost its assured conviction. The picture of a little strutting futility in a windy waste of incomprehensible destinies replaced it. Abruptly it was perfectly clear to him that this revolt against Ostrog was premature, foredoomed to failure, the impulse of passionate inadequacy against inevitable things. He thought of that swift flight of aëroplanes like the swoop of Fate towards him. He was astonished that he could have seen things in any other light. In that final emergency he debated, thrust debate resolutely aside, determined at all costs to go through with the thing he had undertaken. And he could find no word to begin. Even as he stood, awkward, hesitating, with an indiscrete apology for his inability trembling on his lips, came the noise of many people crying out, the running to and fro of feet. "Wait," cried someone, and a door opened. "She is coming," said the voices. Graham turned, and the watching lights waned.

Through the open doorway he saw a slight grey figure advancing across a spacious hall. His heart leapt. It was Helen Wotton. Behind and about her marched a riot of applause. The man in yellow came out of the nearer shadows into the circle of light.

"This is the girl who told us what Ostrog had done," he said.

Her face was aflame, and the heavy coils of her black hair fell about her shoulders. The folds of the soft silk robe she wore streamed from her and floated in the rhythm of her advance. She drew nearer and nearer, and his heart was beating fast. All his doubts were gone. The shadow of the doorway fell athwart her face and she was near him. "You have not betrayed us?" she cried. "You are with us?"

"Where have you been?" said Graham.

"At the office of the south-west wards. Until ten minutes since I did not know you had returned. I went to the office of the south-west wards to find the Ward Leaders in order that they might tell the people."

"I came back so soon as I heard——"

"I knew," she cried, "knew you would be with us. And it was I—it was I that told them. They have risen. All the world is rising. The people have awakened. Thank God that I did not act in vain! You are Master still."

"You told them," he said slowly, and he saw that in spite of her steady eyes her lips trembled and her throat rose and fell.

"I told them. I knew of the order. I was here. I heard that the troops were to come to London to guard you and to keep the people down—to keep you a prisoner. And I stopped it. I came out and told the people. And you are Master still."

Graham glanced at the black lenses of the cameras, the vast listening ears, and back to her face. "I am Master still," he said slowly, and the swift rush of a fleet of aëroplanes passed across his thoughts.

"And you did this? You, who are the niece of Ostrog."

"For you," she cried. "For you! That you for whom the world has waited should not be cheated of your power."

Graham stood for a space, wordless, regarding her. His doubts and questionings had fled before her presence. He remembered the things that he had meant to say. He faced the cameras again and the light about him grew brighter. He turned again towards her.

"You have saved me," he said; "you have saved my power. And the battle is beginning. God knows what this night will see—but not dishonour."

He paused. He addressed himself to the unseen multitudes who stared upon him through those grotesque black eyes. At first he spoke slowly.

"Men and women of the new age," he said; "You have arisen to do battle for the race! . . . There is no easy victory before us."

He stopped to gather words. The thoughts that had been in his mind before she came returned, but transfigured, no longer touched with the shadow of a possible irrelevance. "This night is a beginning," he cried. "This battle that is coming, this battle that rushes upon us to-night, is only a beginning. All your lives, it may be, you must fight. Take no thought though I am beaten, though I am utterly overthrown."

He found the thing in his mind too vague for words. He paused momentarily, and broke into vague exhortations, and then a rush of speech came upon him. Much that he said was but the humanitarian commonplace of a vanished age, but the conviction of his voice touched it to vitality. He stated the case of the old days to the people of the new age, to the woman at his side. "I come out of the past to you," he said, "with the memory of an age that hoped. My age was an age of dreams—of beginnings, an age of noble hopes; throughout the world we had made an end of slavery; throughout the world we had spread the desire and anticipation that wars might cease, that all men and women might live nobly, in freedom and peace. . . . So we hoped in the days that are past. And what of those hopes? How is it with man after two hundred years?

"Great cities, vast powers, a collective greatness beyond our dreams. For that we did not work, and that has come. But how is it with the little lives that make up this greater life? How is it with the common lives? As it has ever been—sorrow and labour, lives cramped and unfulfilled, lives tempted by power, tempted by wealth, and gone to waste and folly. The old faiths have faded and changed, the new faith—— Is there a new faith?"

Things that he had long wished to believe, he found that he believed. He plunged at belief and seized it, and clung for a time at her level. He spoke gustily, in broken incomplete sentences, but with all his heart and strength, of this new faith within him. He spoke of the greatness of self-abnegation, of his belief in an immortal life of Humanity in which we live and move and have our being. His voice rose and fell, and the recording appliances hummed their hurried applause, dim attendants watched him out of the shadow. Through all those doubtful places his sense of that silent spectator beside him sustained his sincerity. For a few glorious moments he was carried away; he felt no doubt of his heroic quality, no doubt of his heroic words, he had it all straight and plain. His eloquence limped no longer. And at last he made an end to speaking. "Here and now," he cried, "I make my will. All that is mine in the world I give to the people of the world. All that is mine in the world I give to the people of the world. I give it to you, and myself I give to you. And as God wills, I will live for you, or I will die."

He ended with a florid gesture and turned about. He found the light of his present exaltation reflected in the face of the girl. Their eyes met; her eyes were swimming with tears of enthusiasm. They seemed to be urged towards each other. They clasped hands and stood gripped, facing one another, in an eloquent silence. She whispered. "I knew," she whispered. "I knew." He could not speak, he crushed her hand in his. His mind was the theatre of gigantic passions.

The man in yellow was beside them. Neither had noted his coming. He was saying that the south-west wards were marching. "I never expected it so soon," he cried. "They have done wonders. You must send them a word to help them on their way."

Graham dropped Helen's hand and stared at him absent-mindedly. Then with a start he returned to his previous preoccupation about the flying stages.

"Yes," he said. "That is good, that is good." He weighed a message. "Tell them;—well done South West."

He turned his eyes to Helen Wotton again. His face expressed his struggle between conflicting ideas. "We must capture the flying stages," he explained. "Unless we can do that they will land. At all costs we must prevent that."

He felt even as he spoke that this was not what had been in his mind before the interruption. He saw a touch of surprise in her eyes. She seemed about to speak and a shrill bell drowned her voice.

It occurred to Graham that she expected him to lead these marching people, that that was the thing he had to do. He made the offer abruptly. He addressed the man in yellow, but he spoke to her. He saw her face respond. "Here I am doing nothing," he said.

"It is impossible," protested the man in yellow. "It is a fight in a warren. Your place is here."

He explained elaborately. He motioned towards the room where Graham must wait, he insisted no other course was possible. "We must know where you are," he said. "At any moment a crisis may arise needing your presence and decision." The room was a luxurious little apartment with news machines and a broken mirror that had once been *en rapport* with the crow's nest specula. It seemed a matter of course to Graham that Helen should stop with him.

A picture had drifted through his mind of such a vast dramatic struggle as the masses in the ruins had suggested. But here was no spectacular battle-field such as he imagined. Instead was seclusion—and suspense. It was only as the afternoon wore on that he pieced together a truer picture of the fight that was raging, inaudibly and invisibly, within four miles of him, beneath the Roehampton stage. A strange and unprecedented contest it was, a battle that was a hundred thousand little battles, a battle in a sponge of ways and channels, fought out of sight of sky or sun under the electric glare, fought out in a vast confusion by multitudes untrained in arms, led chiefly by acclamation, multitudes dulled by mindless labour and enervated by the tradition of two hundred years of servile security against multitudes demoralised by lives of venial privilege and sensual indulgence. They had no artillery, no differentiation into this force or that; the only weapon on either side was the little green metal carbine, whose secret manufacture and sudden distribution in enormous quantities had been one of Ostrog's culminating moves against the Council. Few had had any experience with this weapon, many had never discharged one, many who carried it came unprovided with ammunition; never was wilder firing in the history of warfare. It was a battle of amateurs, a hideous experimental warfare, armed rioters fighting armed rioters, armed rioters swept forward by the words and fury of a song, by the tramping sympathy of their numbers, pouring in countless myriads towards the smaller ways, the disabled lifts, the galleries slippery with blood, the halls and passages choked with smoke, beneath the flying stages, to learn there when retreat was hopeless the ancient mysteries of warfare. And overhead save for a few sharpshooters upon the roof spaces and for a few bands and threads of vapour that multiplied and darkened towards the evening, the day was a clear serenity. Ostrog it seems had no bombs at command and in all the earlier phases of the battle the aëropiles played no part. Not the smallest cloud was there to break the empty brilliance of the sky. It seemed as though it held itself vacant until the aëroplanes should come.

Ever and again there was news of these, drawing nearer, from this Mediterranean port and then that, and presently from the south of France. But of the new guns that Ostrog had made and which were known to be in the city came no news in spite of Graham's urgency, nor any report of successes from the dense felt of fighting strands about the flying stages. Section after section of the Labour Societies reported itself assembled, reported itself marching, and vanished from knowledge into the labyrinth of that warfare. What was happening there? Even the busy ward leaders did not know. In spite of the opening and closing of doors, the hasty messengers, the ringing of bells and the perpetual clitter-clack of recording implements, Graham felt isolated, strangely inactive, inoperative.

Their isolation seemed at times the strangest, the most unexpected of all the things that had happened since his awakening. It had something of the quality of that inactivity that comes in dreams. A tumult, the stupendous realisation of a world struggle between Ostrog and himself, and then this confined quiet little room with its mouthpieces and bells and broken mirror!

Now the door would be closed and they were alone together; they seemed sharply marked off then from all the unprecedented world storm that rushed together without, vividly aware of one another, only concerned with one another. Then the door would open again, messengers would enter, or a sharp bell would stab their quiet privacy, and it was like a window in a well built brightly lit house flung open suddenly to a hurricane. The dark hurry and tumult, the stress and vehemence of the battle rushed in and overwhelmed them. They were no longer persons but mere spectators, mere impressions of a tremendous convulsion. They became unreal even to themselves, miniatures of personality, indescribably small, and the two antagonistic realities, the only realities in being were first the city, that throbbed and roared yonder in a belated frenzy of defence and secondly the aëroplanes hurling inexorably towards them over the round shoulder of the world.

At first their mood had been one of exalted confidence, a great pride had possessed them, a pride in one another for the greatness of the issues they had challenged. At first he had walked the room eloquent with a transitory persuasion of his tremendous destiny. But slowly uneasy intimations of their coming defeat touched his spirit. There came a long period in which they were alone. He changed his theme, became egotistical, spoke of the wonder of his sleep, of the little life of his memories, remote yet minute and clear, like something seen through an inverted opera-glass, and all the brief play of desires and errors that had made his former life. She said little, but the emotion in her face followed the tones in his voice, and it seemed to him he had at last a perfect understanding. He reverted from pure reminiscence to that sense of greatness she imposed upon him. "And through it all, this destiny was before me," he said; "this vast inheritance of which I did not dream."

Insensibly their heroic preoccupation with the revolutionary struggle passed to the question of their relationship. He began to question her. She told him of the days before his awakening, spoke with a brief vividness of the girlish dreams that had given a bias to her life, of the incredulous emotions his awakening had aroused. She told him too of a tragic circumstance of her girlhood that had darkened her life, quickened her sense of injustice and opened her heart prematurely to the wider sorrows of the world. For a little time, so far as he was concerned, the great war about them was but the vast ennobling background to these personal things.

In an instant these personal relations were submerged. There came messengers to tell that a great fleet of aëroplanes was rushing between the sky and Avignon. He went to the crystal dial in the corner and assured himself that the thing was so. He went to the chart room and consulted a map to measure the distances of Avignon, New wan, Araand London. He made swift calculations. He went to the room of the Ward Leaders to ask for news of the fight for the stages—and there was no one there. After a time he came back to her.

His face had changed. It had dawned upon him that the struggle was perhaps more than half over, that Ostrog was holding his own, that the arrival of the aëroplanes would mean a panic that might leave him helpless. A chance phrase in the message had given him a glimpse of the reality that came. Each of these soaring giants bore its thousand half savage Police to the death grapple of the city. Suddenly his humanitarian enthusiasm showed flimsy. Only two of the Ward Leaders were in their room, when presently he repaired thither, the Hall of the Atlas seemed empty. He fancied a change in the bearing of the attendants in the outer rooms. A sombre disillusionment darkened his mind. She looked at him anxiously when he returned to her.

"No news," he said with an assumed carelessness, in answer to her eyes.

Then he was moved to frankness. "Or rather—bad news. We are losing. We are gaining no ground and the aëroplanes draw nearer and nearer."

He walked the length of the room and turned.

"Unless we can capture those flying stages in the next hour—there will be horrible things. We shall be beaten."

"No!" she said. "We have justice—we have the people. We have God on our side."

"Ostrog has discipline—he has plans. Do you know, out there just now I felt—— When I heard that these aëroplanes were a stage nearer. I felt as if I were fighting the machinery of fate."

She made no answer for a while. "We have done right," she said at last.

He looked at her doubtfully. "We have done what we could. But does this depend upon us? Is it not an older sin, a wider sin?"

"What do you mean?" she asked.

"These Africans are savages, ruled by force, used as force. And they have been under our rule two hundred years. Is it not a race quarrel? The race sinned—the race pays."

"But these labourers, these poor people of London——!"

"Vicarious atonement. To stand wrong is to share the guilt."

She looked keenly at him, astonished at the new aspect he presented.

Without came the shrill ringing of a bell, the sound of feet and the gabble of a phonographic message. The man in yellow appeared. "Yes?" said Graham.

"They are at Vichy."

"Where are the attendants who were in the great Hall of the Atlas?" asked Graham abruptly.

Presently the Babble Machine rang again. "We may win yet," said the man in yellow, going out to it. "If only we can find where Ostrog has hidden his guns. Everything hangs on that now. Perhaps this——"

Graham followed him. But the only news was of the aëroplanes. They had reached Orleans.

Graham returned to Helen. "No news," he said. "No news."

"And we can do nothing?"

"Nothing."

He paced impatiently. Suddenly the swift anger that was his nature swept upon him. "Curse this complex world!" he cried, "and all the inventions of men! That a man must die like a rat in a snare and never see his foe! Oh, for one blow! . . ."

He turned with an abrupt change in his manner. "That's nonsense," he said. "I am a savage."

He paced and stopped. "After all London and Paris are only two cities. All the temperate zone has risen. What if London is doomed and Paris destroyed? These are but accidents." Again came the mockery of news to call him to fresh enquiries. He returned with a graver face and sat down beside her.

"The end must be near," he said. "The people it seems have fought and died in tens of thousands, the ways about Roehampton must be like a smoked beehive. And they have died in vain. They are still only at the sub stage. The aëroplanes are near Paris. Even were a gleam of success to come now, there would be nothing to do, there would be no time to do anything before they were upon us. The guns that might have saved us are mislaid. Mislaid! Think of the disorder of things! Think of this foolish tumult, that cannot even find its weapons! Oh, for one aëropile —just one! For the want of that I am beaten. Humanity is beaten and our cause is lost! My kingship, my headlong foolish kingship will not last a night. And I have egged on the people to fight——"

"They would have fought anyhow."

"I doubt it. I have come among them——"

"No," she cried, "not that. If defeat comes—if you die—— But even that cannot be, it cannot be, after all these years."

"Ah! We have meant well. But—do you indeed believe——?"

"If they defeat you," she cried, "you have spoken. Your word has gone like a great wind through the world, fanning liberty into a flame. What if the flame sputters a little! Nothing can change the spoken word. Your message will have gone forth. . . ."

"To what end? It may be. It may be. You know I said, when you told me of these things—dear God! but that was scarcely a score of hours ago!—I said that I had not your faith. Well—at any rate there is nothing to do now. . . ."

"You have not my faith! Do you mean——? You are *sorry*?"

"No," he said hurriedly, "no! Before God—*no*!" His voice changed. "*But*—— I think—I have been indiscreet. I knew little—I grasped too hastily. . . ."

He paused. He was ashamed of this avowal. "There is one thing that makes up for all. I have known you. Across this gulf of time I have come to you. The rest is done. It is done. With you, too, it has been something more—or something less——"

He paused with his face searching hers, and without clamoured the unheeded message that the aëroplanes were rising into the sky of Amiens.

She put her hand to her throat, and her lips were white. She stared before her as if she saw some horrible possibility. Suddenly her features changed. "Oh, but I have been honest!" she cried, and then, "*Have* I been honest? I loved the world and freedom, I hated cruelty and oppression. Surely it was that."

"Yes," he said, "yes. And we have done what it lay in us to do. We have given our message, our message! We have started Armageddon! But now—— Now that we have, it may be our last hour, together, now that all these greater things are done. . . ."

He stopped. She sat in silence. Her face was a white riddle.

For a moment they heeded nothing of a sudden stir outside, a running to and fro, and cries. Then Helen started to an attitude of tense attention. "It is——" she cried and stood up, speechless, incredulous, triumphant. And Graham, too, heard. Metallic voices were shouting "Victory!" Yes it was "Victory!" He stood up also with the light of a desperate hope in his eyes.

Bursting through the curtains appeared the man in yellow, startled and dishevelled with excitement. "Victory," he cried, "victory! The people are winning. Ostrog's people have collapsed."

She rose. "Victory?" And her voice was hoarse and faint.

"What do you mean?" asked Graham. "Tell me! *What?*"

"We have driven them out of the under galleries at Norwood, Streatham is afire and burning wildly, and Roehampton is ours. *Ours!*—and we have taken the aëropile that lay thereon."

For an instant Graham and Helen stood in silence, their hearts were beating fast, they looked at one another. For one last moment there gleamed in Graham his dream of empire, of kingship, with Helen by his side. It gleamed, and passed.

A shrill bell rang. An agitated grey-headed man appeared from the room of the Ward Leaders. "It is all over," he cried.

"What matters it now that we have Roehampton? The aëroplanes have been sighted at Boulogne!"

"The Channel!" said the man in yellow. He calculated swiftly. "Half an hour."

"They still have three of the flying stages," said the old man.

"Those guns?" cried Graham.

"We cannot mount them—in half an hour."

"Do you mean they are found?"

"Too late," said the old man.

"If we could stop them another hour!" cried the man in yellow.

"Nothing can stop them now," said the old man. "They have near a hundred aëroplanes in the first fleet."

"Another hour?" asked Graham.

"To be so near!" said the Ward Leader. "Now that we have found those guns. To be so near—— If once we could get them out upon the roof spaces."

"How long would that take?" asked Graham suddenly.

"An hour—certainly."

"Too late," cried the Ward Leader, "too late."

"*Is* it too late?" said Graham. "Even now—— An hour!"

He had suddenly perceived a possibility. He tried to speak calmly, but his face was white. "There is one chance. You said there was an aëropile——?"

"On the Roehampton stage, Sire."

"Smashed?"

"No. It is lying crossways to the carrier. It might be got upon the guides—easily. But there is no aëronaut——"

Graham glanced at the two men and then at Helen. He spoke after a long pause. "*We* have no aëronauts?"

"None."

"The aëroplanes are clumsy," he said thoughtfully, "compared with the aëropiles."

He turned suddenly to Helen. His decision was made. "I must do it."

"Do what?"

"Go to this flying stage—to this aëropile."

"What do you mean?"

"I am an aëronaut. After all—— Those days for which you reproached me were not altogether wasted."

He turned to the old man in yellow. "Tell them to put the aëropile upon the guides."

The man in yellow hesitated.

"What do you mean to do?" cried Helen.

"This aëropile—it is a chance——"

"You don't mean——?"

"To fight—yes. To fight in the air. I have thought before—— An aëroplane is a clumsy thing. A resolute man——!"

"But—never since flying began——" cried the man in yellow.

"There has been no need. But now the time has come. Tell them now —send them my message—to put it upon the guides."

The old man dumbly interrogated the man in yellow, nodded, and hurried out.

Helen made a step towards Graham. Her face was white. "But—— How can one fight? You will be killed."

"Perhaps. Yet, not to do it—or to let someone else attempt it——"

He stopped, he could speak no more, he swept the alternative aside by a gesture, and they stood looking at one another.

"You are right," she said at last in a low tone. "You are right. If it can be done. . . . You must go."

He moved a step towards her, and she stepped back, her white face struggled against him and resisted him. "No," she gasped. "I cannot bear—— Go now."

He extended his hands stupidly. She clenched her fists. "Go now," she cried. "Go now."

He hesitated and understood. He threw his hands up in a queer half-theatrical gesture. He had no word to say. He turned from her.

The man in yellow moved towards the door with clumsy belated tact. But Graham stepped past him. He went striding through the room where the Ward Leader bawled at a telephone directing that the aëropile should be put upon the guides.

The man in yellow glanced at Helen's still figure, hesitated and hurried after him. Graham did not once look back, he did not speak until the curtain of the ante-chamber of the great Hall fell behind him. Then he turned his head with curt swift directions upon his bloodless lips.

CHAPTER XXIV

THE COMING OF THE AËROPLANES

TWO MEN in pale blue were lying in the irregular line that stretched along the edge of the captured Roehampton stage from end to end, grasping their carbines and peering into the shadows of the stage called Wimbledon Park. Now and then they spoke to one another. They spoke the mutilated English of their class and period. The fire of the Ostrogites had dwindled and ceased, and few of the enemy had been seen for some time. But the echoes of the fight that was going on now far below in the lower galleries of that stage, came every now and then between the staccato of shots from the popular side. One of these men was describing to the other how he had seen a man down below there dodge behind a girder, and had aimed at a guess and hit him cleanly as he dodged too far. "He's down there still," said the marksman. "See that little patch. Yes. Between those bars." A few yards behind them lay a dead stranger, face upward to the sky, with the blue canvas of his jacket smouldering in a circle about the neat bullet hole on his chest. Close beside him a wounded man, with a leg swathed about, sat with an expressionless face and watched the progress of that burning. Gigantic behind them, athwart the carrier, lay the captured aëropile.

"I can't see him *now*," said the second man in a tone of provocation. The marksman became foul-mouthed and high-voiced in his earnest endeavour to make things plain. And suddenly, interrupting him, came a noisy shouting from the substage.

"What's going on now," he said, and raised himself on one arm to stare at the stairheads in the central groove of the stage. A number of blue figures were coming up these, and swarming across the stage to the aëropile.

"We don't want all these fools," said his friend. "They only crowd up and spoil shots. What are they after?"

"Ssh!—they're shouting something."

The two men listened. The swarming new-comers had crowded densely about the aëropile. Three Ward Leaders, conspicuous by their black mantles and badges, clambered into the body and appeared above it. The rank and file flung themselves upon the vans, gripping hold of the edges, until the entire outline of the thing was manned, in some places three deep. One of the marksmen knelt up. "They're putting it on the carrier—that's what they're after."

He rose to his feet, his friend rose also. "What's the good?" said his friend. "We've got no aëronauts."

"That's what they're doing anyhow." He looked at his rifle, looked at the struggling crowd, and suddenly turning to the wounded man. "Mind these, mate," he said, handing his carbine and cartridge belt; and in a moment he was running towards the aëropile. For a quarter of an hour he was a perspiring Titan, lugging, thrusting, shouting and heeding shouts, and then the thing was done, and he stood with a multitude of others cheering their own achievement. By this time he knew, what indeed everyone in the city knew, that the Master, raw learner though he was, intended to fly this machine himself, was coming even now to take control of it, would let no other man attempt it. "He who takes the greatest danger, he who bears the heaviest burthen, that man is King," so the Master was reported to have spoken. And even as this man cheered, and while the beads of sweat still chased one another from the disorder of his hair, he heard the thunder of a greater tumult, and in fitful snatches the beat and impulse of the revolutionary song. He saw through a gap in the people that a thick stream of heads still poured up the stairway. "The Master is coming," shouted voices, "the Master is coming," and the crowd about him grew denser and denser. He began to thrust himself towards the central groove. "The Master is coming!" "The Sleeper, the Master!" "God and the Master!" roared the voices.

And suddenly quite close to him were the black uniforms of the revolutionary guard, and for the first and last time in his life he saw Graham, saw him quite nearly. A tall, dark man in a flowing black robe, with a white, resolute face and eyes fixed steadfastly before him; a man who for all the little things about him had neither ears nor eyes nor thoughts. . . . For all his days that man remembered the passing of Graham's bloodless face. In a moment it had gone and he was fighting in the swaying crowd. A lad weeping with terror thrust against him, pressing towards the stairways, yelling "Clear for the aëropile!" The bell that clears the flying stage became a loud unmelodious clanging.

With that clanging in his ears Graham drew near the aëropile, marched into the shadow of its tilting wing. He became aware that a number of people about him were offering to accompany him, and waved their offers aside. He wanted to think how one started the engine. The bell clanged faster and faster, and the feet of the retreating people roared faster and louder. The man in yellow was assisting him to mount through the ribs of the body. He clambered into the aëronaut's place, fixing himself very carefully and deliberately. What was it? The man in yellow was pointing to two aëropiles driving upward in the southern sky. No doubt they were looking for the coming aëroplanes. That—presently—the thing to do now was to start. Things were being shouted at him, questions, warnings. They bothered him. He wanted to think about the aëropile, to recall every item of his previous experience. He waved the people from him, saw the man in yellow dropping off through the ribs, saw the crowd cleft down the line of the girders by his gesture.

For a moment he was motionless, staring at the levers, the wheel by which the engine shifted, and all the delicate appliances of which he knew so little. His eye caught a spirit level with the bubble towards him, and he remembered something, spent a dozen seconds in swinging the engine forward until the bubble floated in the centre of the tube. He noted that the people were not shouting, knew they watched his deliberation. A bullet smashed on the bar above his head. Who fired? Was the line clear of people? He stood up to see and sat down again.

In another second the propeller was spinning, and he was rushing down the guides. He gripped the wheel and swung the engine back to lift the stem. Then it was the people shouted. In a moment he was throbbing with the quiver of the engine, and the shouts dwindled swiftly behind, rushed down to silence. The wind whistled over the edges of the screen, and the world sank away from him very swiftly.

Throb, throb, throb—throb, throb, throb; up he drove. He fancied himself free of all excitement, felt cool and deliberate. He lifted the stem still more, opened one valve on his left wing and swept round and up. He looked down with a steady head, and up. One of the Ostrogite aëropiles was driving across his course, so that he drove obliquely towards it and would pass below it at a steep angle. Its little aëronauts were peering down at him. What did they mean to do? His mind became active. One, he saw, held a weapon pointing, seemed prepared to fire. What did they think he meant to do? In a moment he understood their tactics, and his resolution was taken. His momentary lethargy was past. He opened two more valves to his left, swung round, end on to this hostile machine, closed his valves, and shot straight at it, stem and wind-screen shielding him from the shot. They tilted a little as if to clear him. He flung up his stem.

Throb, throb, throb—pause—throb, throb—he set his teeth, his face into an involuntary grimace, and crash! He struck it! He struck upward beneath the nearer wing.

Very slowly the wing of his antagonist seemed to broaden as the impetus of his blow turned it up. He saw the full breadth of it and then it slid downward out of his sight.

He felt his stem going down, his hands tightened on the levers, whirled and rammed the engine back. He felt the jerk of a clearance, the nose of the machine jerked upward steeply, and for a moment he seemed to be lying on his back. The machine was reeling and staggering, it seemed to be dancing on its screw. He made a huge effort, hung for a moment on the levers, and slowly the engine came forward again. He was driving upward but no longer so steeply. He gasped for a moment and flung himself at the levers again. The wind whistled about him. One further effort and he was almost level. He could breathe. He turned his head for the first time to see what had become of his antagonists. Turned back to the levers for a moment and looked again. For a moment he could have believed they were annihilated. And then he saw between the two stages to the east was a chasm, and down this something, a slender edge, fell swiftly and vanished, as a sixpence falls down a crack.

At first he did not understand, and then a wild joy possessed him. He shouted at the top of his voice, an inarticulate shout, and drove higher and higher up the sky. Throb, throb, throb, pause, throb, throb, throb. "Where was the other aëropile?" he thought. "They too——" As he looked round the empty heavens he had a momentary fear that this machine had risen above him, and then he saw it alighting on the Norwood stage. They had meant shooting. To risk being rammed headlong two thousand feet in the air was beyond their latter-day courage. The combat was declined.

For a little while he circled, then swooped in a steep descent towards the westward stage. Throb throb throb, throb throb throb. The twilight was creeping on apace, the smoke from the Streatham stage that had been so dense and dark, was now a pillar of fire, and all the laced curves of the moving ways and the translucent roofs and domes and the chasms between the buildings were glowing softly now, lit by the tempered radiance of the electric light that the glare of the day overpowered. The three efficient stages that the Ostrogites held—for Wimbledon Park was useless because of the fire from Roehampton, and Streatham was a furnace—were glowing with guide lights for the coming aëroplanes. As he swept over the Roehampton stage he saw the dark masses of the people thereon. He heard a clap of frantic cheering, heard a bullet from the Wimbledon Park stage tweet through the air, and went beating up above the Surrey wastes. He felt a breath of wind from the south-west, and lifted his westward wing as he had learnt to do, and so drove upward heeling into the rare swift upper air. Throb throb throb—throb throb throb.

Up he drove and up, to that pulsating rhythm, until the country beneath was blue and indistinct, and London spread like a little map traced in light, like the mere model of a city near the brim of the horizon. The south-west was a sky of sapphire over the shadowy rim of the world, and ever as he drove upward the multitude of stars increased.

And behold! In the southward, low down and glittering swiftly nearer, were two little patches of nebulous light. And then two more, and then a nebulous glow of swiftly driving shapes. Presently he could count them. There were four and twenty. The first fleet of aëroplanes had come! Beyond appeared a yet greater glow.

He swept round in a half circle, staring at this advancing fleet. It flew in a wedge-like shape, a triangular flight of gigantic phosphorescent shapes sweeping nearer through the lower air. He made a swift calculation of their pace, and spun the little wheel that brought the engine forward. He touched a lever and the throbbing effort of the engine ceased. He began to fall, fell swifter and swifter. He aimed at the apex of the wedge. He dropped like a stone through the whistling air. It seemed scarce a second from that soaring moment before he struck the foremost aëroplane.

No man of all that multitude saw the coming of his fate, no man among them dreamt of the hawk that struck downward upon him out of the sky. Those who were not limp in the agonies of air-sickness, were craning their necks and staring to see the filmy city that was rising out of the haze, the rich and splendid city to which "The Boss" had brought their obedient muscles. Teeth gleamed and faces shone. They had heard of

Paris. They knew they were to have lordly times among the "poor London" trash. And suddenly Graham struck them.

He had aimed at the body of the aëroplane, but at the very last instant a better idea had flashed into his mind. He twisted about and struck near the edge of the starboard wing with all his accumulated weight. He was jerked back as he struck. His prow went gliding across its smooth expanse towards the rim. He felt the forward rush of the huge fabric sweeping him and his aëropile along with it, and for a moment that seemed an age he could not tell what was happening. He heard a thousand throats yelling, and perceived that his machine was balanced on the edge of the gigantic float, and driving down, down; glanced over his shoulder and saw the backbone of the aëroplane and the opposite float swaying up. He had a vision through the ribs of sliding chairs, staring faces, and hands clutching at the tilting guide bars. The fenestrations in the further float flashed open as the aëronaut tried to right her. Beyond, he saw a second aëroplane leaping steeply to escape the whirl of its heeling fellow. The broad area of swaying wings seemed to jerk upward. He felt his aëropile had dropped clear, that the monstrous fabric, clean overturned, hung like a sloping wall above him.

He did not clearly understand that he had struck the side float of the aëroplane and slipped off, but he perceived that he was flying free on the down glide and rapidly nearing earth. What had he done? His heart throbbed like a noisy engine in his throat and for a perilous instant he could not move his levers because of the paralysis of his hands. He wrenched the levers to throw his engine back, fought for two seconds against the weight of it, felt himself righting, driving horizontally, set the engine beating again.

He looked upward and saw two aëroplanes glide shouting far overhead, looked back, and saw the main body of the fleet opening out and rushing upward and outward; saw the one he had struck fall edgewise on and strike like a gigantic knife-blade along the wind-wheels below it.

He put down his stern and looked again. He drove up heedless of his direction as he watched. He saw the wind-vanes give, saw the huge fabric strike the earth, saw its downward vans crumple with the weight of its descent, and then the whole mass turned over and smashed, upside down, upon the sloping wheels. Throb, throb, throb, pause. Suddenly from the heaving wreckage a thin tongue of white fire licked up towards the zenith. And then he was aware of a huge mass flying through the air towards him, and turned upwards just in time to escape the charge—if it was a charge—of a second aëroplane. It whirled by below, sucked him down a fathom, and nearly turned him over in the gust of its close passage.

He became aware of three others rushing towards him, aware of the urgent necessity of beating above them. Aëroplanes were all about him, circling wildly to avoid him, as it seemed. They drove past him, above, below, eastward and westward. Far away to the westward was the sound of a collision, and two falling flares. Far away to the southward a second squadron was coming. Steadily he beat upward. Presently all the aëroplanes were below him, but for a moment he doubted the height he had of them, and did not swoop again. And then he came down upon a second victim and all its load of soldiers saw him coming. The big machine heeled and swayed as the fear-maddened men scrambled to the stern for their weapons. A score of bullets sung through the air, and there flashed a star in the thick glass wind-screen that protected him. The aëroplane slowed and dropped to foil his stroke, and dropped too low. Just in time he saw the wind-wheels of Bromley hill rushing up towards him, and spun about and up as the aëroplane he had chased crashed among them. All its voices wove into a felt of yelling. The great fabric seemed to be standing on end for a second among the heeling and splintering vans, and then it flew to pieces. Huge splinters came flying through the air, its engines burst like shells. A hot rush of flame shot overhead into the darkling sky.

"*Two!*" he cried, with a bomb from overhead bursting as it fell, and forthwith he was beating up again. A glorious exhilaration possessed him now, a giant activity. His troubles about humanity, about his inadequacy, were gone for ever. He was a man in battle rejoicing in his power. Aëroplanes seemed radiating from him in every direction, intent only upon avoiding him, the yelling of their packed passengers came in short gusts as they swept by. He chose his third quarry, struck hastily and did but turn it on edge. It escaped him, to smash against the tall cliff of London wall. Flying from that impact he skimmed the darkling ground so nearly he could see a frightened rabbit bolting up a slope. He jerked up steeply, and found himself driving over south London with the air about him vacant. To the right of him a wild riot of signal rockets from the Ostrogites banged tumultuously in the sky. To the south the wreckage of half a dozen air ships flamed, and east and west and north the air ships fled before him. They drove away to the east and north, and went about in the south, for they could not pause in the air. In their present confusion any attempt at evolution would have meant disastrous collisions. He could scarcely realise the thing he had done. In every quarter aëroplanes were receding. They were receding. They dwindled smaller and smaller. They were in flight!

He passed two hundred feet or so above the Roehampton stage. It was black with people and noisy with their frantic shouting. But why was the Wimbledon Park stage black and cheering, too? The smoke and flame of Streatham now hid the three further stages. He curved about and rose

to see them and the northern quarters. First came the square masses of
Shooter's Hill into sight from behind the smoke, lit and orderly with the
aëroplane that had landed and its disembarking troops. Then came
Blackheath, and then under the corner of the reek the Norwood stage.
On Blackheath no aëroplane had landed but an aëropile lay upon the
guides. Norwood was covered by a swarm of little figures running to and
fro in a passionate confusion. Why? Abruptly he understood. The stubborn defence of the flying stages was over, the people were pouring into
the under-ways of these last strongholds of Ostrog's usurpation. And
then, from far away on the northern border of the city, full of glorious
import to him, came a sound, a signal, a note of triumph, the leaden thud
of a gun. His lips fell apart, his face was disturbed with emotion.

He drew an immense breath. "They win," he shouted to the empty
air; "the people win!" The sound of a second gun came like an answer.
And then he saw the aëropile on Blackheath was running down its
guides to launch. It lifted clean and rose. It shot up into the air, driving
straight southward and away from him.

In an instant it came to him what this meant. It must needs be Ostrog
in flight. He shouted and dropped towards it. He had the momentum of
his elevation and fell slanting down the air and very swiftly. It rose
steeply at his approach. He allowed for its velocity and drove straight
upon it.

It suddenly became a mere flat edge, and behold! he was past it, and
driving headlong down with all the force of his futile blow.

He was furiously angry. He reeled the engine back along its shaft and
went circling up. He saw Ostrog's machine beating up a spiral before him.
He rose straight towards it, won above it by virtue of the impetus of his
swoop and by the advantage and weight of a man. He dropped headlong
—dropped and missed again! As he rushed past he saw the face of Ostrog's aëronaut confident and cool and in Ostrog's attitude a wincing
resolution. Ostrog was looking steadfastly away from him—to the south.
He realised with a gleam of wrath how bungling his flight must be. Below
he saw the Croydon hills. He jerked upward and once more he gained on
his enemy.

He glanced over his shoulder and his attention was arrested by a
strange thing. The eastward stage, the one on Shooter's Hill, appeared
to lift; a flash changing to a tall grey shape, a cowled figure of smoke and
duct, jerked into the air. For a moment this cowled figure stood motionless, dropping huge masses of metal from its shoulders, and then it began
to uncoil a dense head of smoke. The people had blown it up, aëroplane
and all! As suddenly a second flash and grey shape sprang up from the
Norwood stage. And even as he stared at this came a dead report, and

the air wave of the first explosion struck him. He was flung up and sideways.

For a moment the aëropile fell nearly edgewise with her nose down, and seemed to hesitate whether to overset altogether. He stood on his wind-shield wrenching the wheel that swayed up over his head. And then the shock of the second explosion took his machine sideways.

He found himself clinging to one of the ribs of his machine, and the air was blowing past him and *upward*. He seemed to be hanging quite still in the air, with the wind blowing up past him. It occurred to him that he was falling. Then he was sure that he was falling. He could not look down.

He found himself recapitulating with incredible swiftness all that had happened since his awakening, the days of doubt the days of Empire, and at last the tumultuous discovery of Ostrog's calculated treachery. He was beaten but London was saved. London was saved!

The thought had a quality of utter unreality. Who was he? Why was he holding so tightly with his hands? Why could he not leave go? In such a fall as this countless dreams have ended. But in a moment he would wake. . . .

His thoughts ran swifter and swifter. He wondered if he should see Helen again. It seemed so unreasonable that he should not see her again. It *must* be a dream! Yet surely he would meet her. She at least was real. She was real. He would wake and meet her.

Although he could not look at it, he was suddenly aware that the earth was very near.

A STORY OF THE DAYS TO COME

By

H. G. WELLS

CONTENTS

THE CURE FOR LOVE

THE EXCELLENT Mr. Morris was an Englishman, and he lived in the days of Queen Victoria the Good. He was a prosperous and very sensible man; he read the *Times* and went to church, and as he grew towards middle age an expression of quiet contented contempt for all who were not as himself settled on his face. He was one of those people who do everything that is right and proper and sensible with inevitable regularity. He always wore just the right and proper clothes, steering the narrow way between the smart and the shabby, always subscribed to the right charities, just the judicious compromise between ostentation and meanness, and never failed to have his hair cut to exactly the proper length.

Everything that it was right and proper for a man in his position to possess, he possessed; and everything that it was not right and proper for a man in his position to possess, he did not possess.

And among other right and proper possessions, this Mr. Morris had a wife and children. They were the right sort of wife, and the right sort and number of children, of course; nothing imaginative or highty-flighty about any of them, so far as Mr. Morris could see; they wore perfectly correct clothing, neither smart nor hygienic nor faddy in any way, but just sensible; and they lived in a nice sensible house in the later Victorian sham Queen Anne style of architecture, with sham half-timbering of chocolate-painted plaster in the gables, Lincrusta Walton sham carved oak panels, a terrace of terra cotta to imitate stone, and cathedral glass in the front door. His boys went to good solid schools, and were put to respectable professions; his girls, in spite of a fantastic protest or so, were all married to suitable, steady, oldish young men with good prospects. And when it was a fit and proper thing for him to do so, Mr. Morris died. His tomb was of marble, and, without any art nonsense or laudatory inscription, quietly imposing—such being the fashion of his time.

He underwent various changes according to the accepted custom in these cases, and long before this story begins his bones even had become dust, and were scattered to the four quarters of heaven. And his sons and

his grandsons and his great-grandsons and his great-great
they too were dust and ashes, and were scattered likewise. It \
he could not have imagined, that a day would come when even
great-grandsons would be scattered to the four winds of heave
one had suggested it to him he would have resented it. He wa
those worthy people who take no interest in the future of mankin ̠ at all.
He had grave doubts, indeed, if there was any future for mankind after
he was dead.

It seemed quite impossible and quite uninteresting to imagine anything happening after he was dead. Yet the thing was so, and when even
his great-great-grandson was dead and decayed and forgotten, when the
sham half-timbered house had gone the way of all shams, and the *Times*
was extinct, and the silk hat a ridiculous antiquity, and the modestly
imposing stone that had been sacred to Mr. Morris had been burnt to
make lime for mortar, and all that Mr. Morris had found real and important was sere and dead, the world was still going on, and people were
still going about it, just as heedless and impatient of the Future, or,
indeed, of anything but their own selves and property, as Mr. Morris
had been.

And, strange to tell, and much as Mr. Morris would have been angered
if any one had foreshadowed it to him, all over the world there were
scattered a multitude of people, filled with the breath of life, in whose
veins the blood of Mr. Morris flowed. Just as some day the life which is
gathered now in the reader of this very story may also be scattered far
and wide about this world, and mingled with a thousand alien strains,
beyond all thought and tracing.

And among the descendants of this Mr. Morris was one almost as
sensible and clear-headed as his ancestor. He had just the same stout,
short frame as that ancient man of the nineteenth century, from whom
his name of Morris—he spelt it Mwres—came; he had the same half-
contemptuous expression of face. He was a prosperous person, too, as
times went, and he disliked the "new-fangled," and bothers about the
future and the lower classes, just as much as the ancestral Morris had
done. He did not read the *Times*: indeed, he did not know there ever had
been a *Times*—that institution had foundered somewhere in the intervening gulf of years; but the phonograph machine, that talked to him as
he made his toilet of a morning, might have been the voice of a reincarn-
ated Blowitz when it dealt with the world's affairs. This phonographic
machine was the size and shape of a Dutch clock, and down the front of
it were electric barometric indicators, and an electric clock and calendar,
and automatic engagement reminders, and where the clock would have
been was the mouth of a trumpet. When it had news the trumpet gobbled

like a turkey, "Galloop, galloop," and then brayed out its message as, let us say, a trumpet might bray. It would tell Mwres in full, rich, throaty tones about the overnight accidents to the omnibus flying-machines that plied around the world, the latest arrivals at the fashionable resorts in Tibet, and of all the great monopolist company meetings of the day before, while he was dressing. If Mwres did not like hearing what it said, he had only to touch a stud, and it would choke a little and talk about something else.

Of course his toilet differed very much from that of his ancestor. It is doubtful which would have been the more shocked and pained to find himself in the clothing of the other. Mwres would certainly have sooner gone forth to the world stark naked than in the silk hat, frock coat, grey trousers and watch-chain that had filled Mr. Morris with sombre self-respect in the past. For Mwres there was no shaving to do: a skilful operator had long ago removed every hair-root from his face. His legs he encased in pleasant pink and amber garments of an air-tight material, which with the help of an ingenious little pump he distended so as to suggest enormous muscles. Above this he also wore pneumatic garments beneath an amber silk tunic, so that he was clothed in air and admirably protected against sudden extremes of heat or cold. Over this he flung a scarlet cloak with its edge fantastically curved. On his head, which had been skilfully deprived of every scrap of hair, he adjusted a pleasant little cap of bright scarlet, held on by suction and inflated with hydrogen, and curiously like the comb of a cock. So his toilet was complete; and, conscious of being soberly and becomingly attired, he was ready to face his fellow-beings with a tranquil eye.

This Mwres—the civility of "Mr." had vanished ages ago—was one of the officials under the Wind Vane and Waterfall Trust, the great company that owned every wind wheel and waterfall in the world, and which pumped all the water and supplied all the electric energy that people in these latter days required. He lived in a vast hotel near that part of London called Seventh Way, and had very large and comfortable apartments on the seventeenth floor. Households and family life had long since disappeared with the progressive refinement of manners; and indeed the steady rise in rents and land values, the disappearance of domestic servants, the elaboration of cookery, had rendered the separate domicile of Victorian times impossible, even had any one desired such a savage seclusion. When his toilet was completed he went towards one of the two doors of his apartment—there were doors at opposite ends, each marked with a huge arrow pointing one one way and one the other—touched a stud to open it, and emerged on a wide passage, the centre of which bore chairs and was moving at a steady pace to the left. On some of these chairs were seated gaily-dressed men and women. He nodded to an acquaintance —it was not in those days etiquette to talk before breakfast—and seated himself on one of these chairs, and in a few seconds he had been carried to the doors of a lift, by which he descended to the great and splendid hall in which his breakfast would be automatically served.

It was a very different meal from a Victorian breakfast. The rude masses of bread needing to be carved and smeared over with animal fat before they could be made palatable, the still recognisable fragments of recently killed animals, hideously charred and hacked, the eggs torn ruthlessly from beneath some protesting hen—such things as these, though they constituted the ordinary fare of Victorian times, would have awakened only horror and disgust in the refined minds of the people of these latter days. Instead were pastes and cakes of agreeable and variegated design, without any suggestion in colour or form of the unfortunate animals from which their substances and juices were derived. They appeared on little dishes sliding out upon a rail from a little box at one side of the table. The surface of the table, to judge by touch and eye, would have appeared to a nineteenth-century person to be covered with fine white damask, but this was really an oxidised metallic surface, and could be cleaned instantly after a meal. There were hundreds of such little tables in the hall, and at most of them were other latter-day citizens singly or in groups. And as Mwres seated himself before his elegant repast, the invisible orchestra, which had been resting during an interval, resumed and filled the air with music.

But Mwres did not display any great interest either in his breakfast or the music; his eye wandered incessantly about the hall, as though he expected a belated guest. At last he rose eagerly and waved his hand, and simultaneously across the hall appeared a tall dark figure in a costume of yellow and olive green. As this person, walking amidst the tables with measured steps, drew near, the pallid earnestness of his face and the unusual intensity of his eyes became apparent. Mwres reseated himself and pointed to a chair beside him.

"I feared you would never come," he said. In spite of the intervening space of time, the English language was still almost exactly the same as it had been in England under Victoria the Good. The invention of the phonograph and suchlike means of recording sound, and the gradual replacement of books by such contrivances, had not only saved the human eyesight from decay, but had also by the establishment of a sure standard arrested the process of change in accent that had hitherto been so inevitable.

"I was delayed by an interesting case," said the man in green and yellow. "A prominent politician—ahem!—suffering from overwork."

He glanced at the breakfast and seated himself. "I have been awake for forty hours."

"Eh dear!" said Mwres: "fancy that! You hypnotists have your work to do."

The hypnotist helped himself to some attractive amber-coloured jelly. "I happen to be a good deal in request," he said modestly.

"Heaven knows what we should do without you."

"Oh! we're not so indispensable as all that," said the hypnotist, ruminating the flavour of the jelly. "The world did very well without us for some thousands of years. Two hundred years ago even—not one! In practice, that is. Physicians by the thousand, of course—frightfully clumsy brutes for the most part, and following one another like sheep—but doctors of the mind, except a few empirical flounderers there were none."

He concentrated his mind on the jelly.

"But were people so sane——?" began Mwres.

The hypnotist shook his head. "It didn't matter then if they were a bit silly or faddy. Life was so easy-going then. No competition worth speaking of—no pressure. A human being had to be very lopsided before anything happened. Then, you know, they clapped 'em away in what they called a lunatic asylum."

"I know," said Mwres. "In these confounded historical romances that every one is listening to, they always rescue a beautiful girl from an asylum or something of the sort. I don't know if you attend to that rubbish."

"I must confess I do," said the hypnotist. "It carries one out of oneself to hear of those quaint, adventurous, half-civilised days of the nineteenth century, when men were stout and women simple. I like a good swaggering story before all things. Curious times they were, with their smutty railways and puffing old iron trains, their rum little houses and their horse vehicles. I suppose you don't read books?"

"Dear, no!" said Mwres, "I went to a modern school and we had none of that old-fashioned nonsense. Phonographs are good enough for me."

"Of course," said the hypnotist, "of course"; and surveyed the table for his next choice. "You know," he said, helping himself to a dark blue confection that promised well, "in those days our business was scarcely thought of. I daresay if any one had told them that in two hundred years' time a class of men would be entirely occupied in impressing things upon the memory, effacing unpleasant ideas, controlling and overcoming instinctive but undesirable impulses, and so forth, by means of hypnotism, they would have refused to believe the thing possible. Few people knew that an order made during a mesmeric trance, even an order to forget or an order to desire, could be given so as to be obeyed after the trance was over. Yet there were men alive then who could have told them the thing was as absolutely certain to come about as—well, the transit of Venus."

"They knew of hypnotism, then?"

"Oh, dear, yes! They used it—for painless dentistry and things like that! This blue stuff is confoundedly good: what is it?"

"Haven't the faintest idea," said Mwres, "but I admit it's very good. Take some more."

The hypnotist repeated his praises, and there was an appreciative pause.

"Speaking of these historical romances," said Mwres, with an attempt at an easy, off-hand manner, "brings me—ah—to the matter I—ah—had in mind when I asked you—when I expressed a wish to see you." He paused and took a deep breath.

The hypnotist turned an attentive eye upon him, and continued eating.

"The fact is," said Mwres, "I have a—in fact a—daughter. Well, you know I have given her—ah—every educational advantage. Lectures— not a solitary lecturer of ability in the world but she has had a telephone direct, dancing, deportment, conversation, philosophy, art criticism. . . ." He indicated catholic culture by a gesture of his hand. "I had intended her to marry a very good friend of mine—Bindon of the Lighting Commission—plain little man, you know, and a bit unpleasant in some of his ways, but an excellent fellow really—an excellent fellow."

"Yes," said the hypnotist, "go on. How old is she?"

"Eighteen."

"A dangerous age. Well?"

"Well: it seems that she has been indulging in these historical romances —excessively. Excessively. Even to the neglect of her philosophy. Filled her mind with unutterable nonsense about soldiers who fight—what is it?—Etruscans?"

"Egyptians."

"Egyptians—very probably. Hack about with swords and revolvers and things—bloodshed galore—horrible!—and about young men on torpedo catchers who blow up—Spaniards, I fancy—and all sorts of irregular adventurers. And she has got it into her head that she must marry for Love, and that poor little Bindon——"

"I've met similar cases," said the hypnotist. "Who is the other young man?"

Mwres maintained an appearance of resigned calm. "You may well ask," he said. "He is"—and his voice sank with shame—"a mere attendant upon the stage on which the flying-machines from Paris alight. He has—as they say in the romances—good looks. He is quite young and very eccentric. Affects the antique—he can read and write! So can she. And instead of communicating by telephone, like sensible people, they write and deliver—what is it?"

"Notes?"

"No—not notes. . . . Ah—poems."

The hypnotist raised his eyebrows. "How did she meet him?"

"Tripped coming down from the flying-machine from Paris—and fell into his arms. The mischief was done in a moment!"

"Yes?"

"Well—that's all. Things must be stopped. That is what I want to consult you about. What must be done? What *can* be done? Of course I'm not a hypnotist; my knowledge is limited. But you——?"

"Hypnotism is not magic," said the man in green, putting both arms on the table.

"Oh, precisely! But still——!"

"People cannot be hypnotised without their consent. If she is able to stand out against marrying Bindon, she will probably stand out against being hypnotised. But if once she can be hypnotised—even by somebody else—the thing is done."

"You can——?"

"Oh, certainly! Once we get her amenable, then we can suggest that she *must* marry Bindon—that that is her fate; or that the young man is repulsive, and that when she sees him she will be giddy and faint, or any little thing of that sort. Or if we can get her into a sufficiently profound trance we can suggest that she should forget him altogether——"

"Precisely."

"But the problem is to get her hypnotised. Of course no sort of proposal or suggestion must come from you—because no doubt she already distrusts you in the matter."

The hypnotist leant his head upon his arm and thought.

"It's hard a man cannot dispose of his own daughter," said Mwres irrelevantly.

"You must give me the name and address of the young lady," said the hypnotist, "and any information bearing upon the matter. And, by the bye, is there any money in the affair?"

Mwres hesitated.

"There's a sum—in fact, a considerable sum—invested in the Patent Road Company. From her mother. That's what makes the thing so exasperating."

"Exactly," said the hypnotist. And he proceeded to cross-examine Mwres on the entire affair.

It was a lengthy interview.

And meanwhile "Elizebeθ Mwres," as she spelt her name, or "Elizabeth Morris" as a nineteenth-century person would have put it, was sitting in a quiet waiting-place beneath the great stage upon which the flying-machine from Paris descended. And beside her sat her slender, handsome lover reading her the poem he had written that morning while on duty upon the stage. When he had finished they sat for a time in silence; and then, as if for their special entertainment, the great machine that had come flying through the air from America that morning rushed down out of the sky.

At first it was a little oblong, faint and blue amidst the distant fleecy clouds; and then it grew swiftly large and white, and larger and whiter, until they could see the separate tiers of sails, each hundreds of feet wide, and the lank body they supported, and at last even the swinging seats of the passengers in a dotted row. Although it was falling it seemed to them to be rushing up the sky, and over the roof-spaces of the city below its shadow leapt towards them. They heard the whistling rush of the air about it and its yelling siren, shrill and swelling, to warn those who were on its landing-stage of its arrival. And abruptly the note fell down a couple of octaves, and it had passed, and the sky was clear and void, and she could turn her sweet eyes again to Denton at her side.

Their silence ended; and Denton, speaking in a little language of broken English that was, they fancied, their private possession—though lovers have used such little languages since the world began—told her how they too would leap into the air one morning out of all the obstacles and difficulties about them, and fly to a sunlit city of delight he knew of in Japan, half-way about the world.

She loved the dream, but she feared the leap; and she put him off with "Some day, dearest one, some day," to all his pleading that it might be soon; and at last came a shrilling of whistles, and it was time for him to go back to his duties on the stage. They parted—as lovers have been wont to part for thousands of years. She walked down a passage to a lift, and so came to one of the streets of that latter-day London, all glazed in with glass from the weather, and with incessant moving platforms that went to all parts of the city. And by one of these she returned to her apartments in the Hotel for Women where she lived, the apartments that were in telephonic communication with all the best lecturers in the world. But the sunlight of the flying stage was in her heart, and the wisdom of all the best lecturers in the world seemed folly in that light.

She spent the middle part of the day in the gymnasium, and took her midday meal with two other girls and their common chaperone—for it was still the custom to have a chaperone in the case of motherless girls of the more prosperous classes. The chaperone had a visitor that day, a man in green and yellow, with a white face and vivid eyes, who talked amazingly. Among other things, he fell to praising a new historical romance that one of the great popular story-tellers of the day had just put forth. It was, of course, about the spacious times of Queen Victoria; and the author, among other pleasing novelties, made a little argument before each section of the story, in imitation of the chapter headings of the old-fashioned books: as for example, "How the Cabmen of Pimlico stopped the Victoria Omnibuses, and of the Great Fight in Palace Yard," and "How the Piccadilly Policeman was slain in the midst of his Duty." The man in green and yellow praised this innovation. "These pithy sentences," he said, "are admirable. They show at a glance those head-long, tumultuous times, when men and animals jostled in the filthy streets, and death might wait for one at every corner. Life was life then! How great the world must have seemed then! How marvellous! There were still parts of the world absolutely unexplored. Nowadays we have almost abolished wonder, we lead lives so trim and orderly that courage, endurance, faith, all the noble virtues seem fading from mankind."

And so on, taking the girls' thoughts with him, until the life they led, life in the vast and intricate London of the twenty-second century, a life interspersed with soaring excursions to every part of the globe, seemed to them a monotonous misery compared with the dædal past.

At first Elizabeth did not join in the conversation, but after a time the subject became so interesting that she made a few shy interpolations. But he scarcely seemed to notice her as he talked. He went on to describe a new method of entertaining people. They were hypnotised, and then suggestions were made to them so skilfully that they seemed to be living in ancient times again. They played out a little romance in the past as vivid as reality, and when at last they awakened they remembered all they had been through as though it were a real thing.

"It is a thing we have sought to do for years and years," said the hypnotist. "It is practically an artificial dream. And we know the way at last. Think of all it opens out to us—the enrichment of our experience, the recovery of adventure, the refuge it offers from this sordid, competitive life in which we live! Think!"

"And you can do that!" said the chaperone eagerly.

"The thing is possible at last," the hypnotist said. "You may order a dream as you wish."

The chaperone was the first to be hypnotised, and the dream, she said, was wonderful, when she came to again.

The other two girls, encouraged by her enthusiasm, also placed them-selves in the hands of the hypnotist and had plunges into the romantic past. No one suggested that Elizabeth should try this novel entertainment; it was at her own request at last that she was taken into that land of dreams where there is neither any freedom of choice nor will. . . .

And so the mischief was done.

One day, when Denton went down to that quiet seat beneath the flying stage, Elizabeth was not in her wonted place. He was disappointed, and a little angry. The next day she did not come, and the next also. He was afraid. To hide his fear from himself, he set to work to write sonnets for her when she should come again. . . .

For three days he fought against his dread by such distraction, and then the truth was before him clear and cold, and would not be denied. She might be ill, she might be dead; but he would not believe that he had been betrayed. There followed a week of misery. And then he knew she was the only thing on earth worth having, and that he must seek her, however hopeless the search, until she was found once more.

He had some small private means of his own, and so he threw over his appointment on the flying stage, and set himself to find this girl who had become at last all the world to him. He did not know where she lived, and little of her circumstances; for it had been part of the delight of her girlish romance that he should know nothing of her, nothing of the difference of their station. The ways of the city opened before him east and west, north and south. Even in Victorian days London was a maze, that little London with its poor four millions of people; but the London he explored, the London of the twenty-second century, was a London of thirty million souls. At first he was energetic and headlong, taking time neither to eat nor sleep. He sought for weeks and months, he went through every imaginable phase of fatigue and despair, over-excitement and anger. Long after hope was dead, by the sheer inertia of his desire he still went to and fro, peering into faces and looking this way and that, in the incessant ways and lifts and passages of that interminable hive of men.

At last chance was kind to him, and he saw her.

It was in a time of festivity. He was hungry; he had paid the inclusive fee and had gone into one of the gigantic dining-places of the city; he was pushing his way among the tables and scrutinising by mere force of habit every group he passed.

He stood still, robbed of all power of motion, his eyes wide, his lips apart. Elizabeth sat scarcely twenty yards away from him, looking straight at him. Her eyes were as hard to him, as hard and expressionless and void of recognition, as the eyes of a statue.

She looked at him for a moment, and then her gaze passed beyond him.

Had he had only her eyes to judge by he might have doubted if it was indeed Elizabeth, but he knew her by the gesture of her hand, by the grace of a wanton little curl that floated over her ear as she moved her head. Something was said to her, and she turned smiling tolerantly to the man beside her, a little man in foolish raiment knobbed and spiked like some odd reptile with pneumatic horns—the Bindon of her father's choice.

For a moment Denton stood white and wild-eyed; then came a terrible faintness, and he sat before one of the little tables. He sat down with his back to her, and for a time he did not dare to look at her again. When at last he did, she and Bindon and two other people were standing up to go. The others were her father and her chaperone.

He sat as if incapable of action until the four figures were remote and small, and then he rose up possessed with the one idea of pursuit. For a space he feared he had lost them, and then he came upon Elizabeth and her chaperone again in one of the streets of moving platforms that intersected the city. Bindon and Mwres had disappeared.

He could not control himself to patience. He felt he must speak to her forthwith, or die. He pushed forward to where they were seated, and sat down beside them. His white face was convulsed with half-hysterical excitement.

He laid his hand on her wrist. "Elizabeth?" he said.

She turned in unfeigned astonishment. Nothing but the fear of a strange man showed in her face.

"Elizabeth," he cried, and his voice was strange to him: "dearest—you *know* me?"

Elizabeth's face showed nothing but alarm and perplexity. She drew herself away from him. The chaperone, a little grey-headed woman with mobile features, leant forward to intervene. Her resolute bright eyes examined Denton. "*What* do you say?" she asked.

"This young lady," said Denton—"she knows me."

"Do you know him, dear?"

"No," said Elizabeth in a strange voice, and with a hand to her forehead, speaking almost as one who repeats a lesson. "No, I do not know him. I *know*—I do not know him."

"But—but. . . . Not know me! It is I—Denton. Denton! To whom you used to talk. Don't you remember the flying stages? The little seat in the open air? The verses——"

"No," cried Elizabeth—"no. I do not know him. I do not know him. There is something. . . . But I don't know. All I know is that I do not know him." Her face was a face of infinite distress.

The sharp eyes of the chaperone flitted to and fro from the girl to the man. "You see?" she said, with the faint shadow of a smile. "She does not know you."

"I do not know you," said Elizabeth. "Of that I am sure."

"But, dear—the songs—the little verses——"

"She does not know you," said the chaperone. "You must not . . . You have made a mistake. You must not go on talking to us after that. You must not annoy us on the public ways."

"But——" said Denton, and for a moment his miserably haggard face appealed against fate.

"You must not persist, young man," protested the chaperone.

"*Elizabeth!*" he cried.

Her face was the face of one who is tormented. "I do not know you," she cried, hand to brow. "Oh, I do not know you!"

For an instant Denton sat stunned. Then he stood up and groaned aloud.

He made a strange gesture of appeal towards the remote glass roof of the public way, then turned and went plunging recklessly from one moving platform to another, and vanished amidst the swarms of people going to and fro thereon. The chaperone's eyes followed him, and then she looked at the curious faces about her.

"Dear," asked Elizabeth, clasping her hand, and too deeply moved to heed observation, "who was that man? Who *was* that man?"

The chaperone raised her eyebrows. She spoke in a clear, audible voice. "Some half-witted creature. I have never set eyes on him before."

"Never?"

"Never, dear. Do not trouble your mind about a thing like this."

And soon after this the celebrated hypnotist who dressed in green and yellow had another client. The young man paced his consulting-room, pale and disordered. "I want to forget," he cried. "I *must* forget."

The hypnotist watched him with quiet eyes, studied his face and clothes and bearing. "To forget anything—pleasure or pain—is to be, by so much—*less*. However, you know your own concern. My fee is high."

"If only I can forget——"

"That's easy enough with you. You wish it. I've done much harder things. Quite recently. I hardly expected to do it: the thing was done against the will of the hypnotised person. A love affair too—like yours. A girl. So rest assured."

The young man came and sat beside the hypnotist. His manner was a forced calm. He looked into the hypnotist's eyes. "I will tell you. Of course you will want to know what it is. There was a girl. Her name was Elizabeth Mwres. Well. . . ."

He stopped. He had seen the instant surprise on the hypnotist's face. In that instant he knew. He stood up. He seemed to dominate the seated figure by his side. He gripped the shoulder of green and gold. For a time he could not find words.

"*Give her me back!*" he said at last. "Give her me back!"

"What do you mean?" gasped the hypnotist.

"Give her me back."

"Give whom?"

"Elizabeth Mwres—the girl——"

The hypnotist tried to free himself; he rose to his feet. Denton's grip tightened.

"Let go!" cried the hypnotist, thrusting an arm against Denton's chest.

In a moment the two men were locked in a clumsy wrestle. Neither had the slightest training—for athleticism, except for exhibition and to afford opportunity for betting, had faded out of the earth—but Denton was not only the younger but the stronger of the two. They swayed across the room, and then the hypnotist had gone down under his antagonist. They fell together. . . .

Denton leaped to his feet, dismayed at his own fury; but the hypnotist lay still, and suddenly from a little white mark where his forehead had struck a stool shot a hurrying band of red. For a space Denton stood over him irresolute, trembling.

A fear of the consequences entered his gently nurtured mind. He turned towards the door. "No," he said aloud, and came back to the middle of the room. Overcoming the instinctive repugnance of one who had seen no act of violence in all his life before, he knelt down beside his antagonist and felt his heart. Then he peered at the wound. He rose quietly and looked about him. He began to see more of the situation.

When presently the hypnotist recovered his senses, his head ached severely, his back was against Denton's knees and Denton was sponging his face.

The hypnotist did not speak. But presently he indicated by a gesture that in his opinion he had been sponged enough. "Let me get up," he said.

"Not yet," said Denton.

"You have assaulted me, you scoundrel!"

"We are alone," said Denton, "and the door is secure."

There was an interval of thought.

"Unless I sponge," said Denton, "your forehead will develop a tremendous bruise."

"You can go on sponging," said the hypnotist sulkily.

There was another pause.

"We might be in the Stone Age," said the hypnotist. "Violence! Struggle!"

"In the Stone Age no man dared to come between man and woman," said Denton.

The hypnotist thought again.

"What are you going to do?" he asked.

"While you were insensible I found the girl's address on your tablets. I did not know it before. I telephoned. She will be here soon. Then——"

"She will bring her chaperone."

"That is all right."

"But what——? I don't see. What do you mean to do?"

"I looked about for a weapon also. It is an astonishing thing how few weapons there are nowadays. If you consider that in the Stone Age men owned scarcely anything *but* weapons. I hit at last upon this lamp. I have wrenched off the wires and things, and I hold it so." He extended it over the hypnotist's shoulders. "With that I can quite easily smash your skull. I *will*—unless you do as I tell you."

"Violence is no remedy," said the hypnotist, quoting from the "Modern Man's Book of Moral Maxims."

"It's an undesirable disease," said Denton.

"Well?"

"You will tell that chaperone you are going to order the girl to marry that knobby little brute with the red hair and ferrety eyes. I believe that's how things stand?"

"Yes—that's how things stand."

"And, pretending to do that, you will restore her memory of me."

"It's unprofessional."

"Look here! If I cannot have that girl I would rather die than not. I don't propose to respect your little fancies. If anything goes wrong you shall not live five minutes. This is a rude makeshift of a weapon, and it may quite conceivably be painful to kill you. But I will. It is unusual, I know, nowadays to do things like this—mainly because there is so little in life that is worth being violent about."

"The chaperone will see you directly she comes——"

"I shall stand in that recess. Behind you."

The hypnotist thought. "You are a determined young man," he said, "and only half civilised. I have tried to do my duty to my client, but in this affair you seem likely to get your own way. . . ."

"You mean to deal straightly."

"I'm not going to risk having my brains scattered in a petty affair like this."

"And afterwards?"

"There is nothing a hypnotist or doctor hates so much as a scandal. I at least am no savage. I am annoyed. . . . But in a day or so I shall bear no malice. . . ."

"Thank you. And now that we understand each other, there is no necessity to keep you sitting any longer on the floor."

CHAPTER II

THE VACANT COUNTRY

THE WORLD, they say, changed more between the year 1800 and the year 1900 than it had done in the previous five hundred years. That century, the nineteenth century, was the dawn of a new epoch in the history of mankind—the epoch of the great cities, the end of the old order of country life.

In the beginning of the nineteenth century the majority of mankind still lived upon the countryside, as their way of life had been for countless generations. All over the world they dwelt in little towns and villages then, and engaged either directly in agriculture, or in occupations that were of service to the agriculturist. They travelled rarely, and dwelt close to their work, because swift means of transit had not yet come. The few who travelled went either on foot, or in slow sailing-ships, or by means of jogging horses incapable of more than sixty miles a day. Think of it!— sixty miles a day. Here and there, in those sluggish times, a town grew a little larger than its neighbours, as a port or as a centre of government; but all the towns in the world with more than a hundred thousand inhabitants could be counted on a man's fingers. So it was in the beginning of the nineteenth century. By the end, the invention of railways, telegraphs, steamships, and complex agricultural machinery, had changed all these things: changed them beyond all hope of return. The vast shops, the varied pleasures, the countless conveniences of the larger towns were suddenly possible, and no sooner existed than they were brought into competition with the homely resources of the rural centres. Mankind were drawn to the cities by an overwhelming attraction. The demand for labour fell with the increase of machinery, the local markets were entirely superseded, and there was a rapid growth of the larger centres at the expense of the open country.

The flow of population townward was the constant preoccupation of Victorian writers. In Great Britain and New England, in India and China, the same thing was remarked: everywhere a few swollen towns were visibly replacing the ancient order. That this was an inevitable result of improved means of travel and transport—that, given swift means of transit, these things must be—was realised by few; and the most puerile schemes were devised to overcome the mysterious magnetism of the urban centres, and keep the people on the land.

Yet the developments of the nineteenth century were only the dawning of the new order. The first great cities of the new time were horribly inconvenient, darkened by smoky fogs, insanitary and noisy; but the discovery of new methods of building, new methods of heating, changed all this. Between 1900 and 2000 the march of change was still more rapid; and between 2000 and 2100 the continually accelerated progress of human invention made the reign of Victoria the Good seem at last an almost incredible vision of idyllic tranquil days.

The introduction of railways was only the first step in that development of those means of locomotion which finally revolutionised human life. By the year 2000 railways and roads had vanished together. The railways, robbed of their rails, had become weedy ridges and ditches upon the face of the world; the old roads, strange barbaric tracks of flint and soil, hammered by hand or rolled by rough iron rollers, strewn with miscellaneous filth, and cut by iron hoofs and wheels into ruts and puddles often many inches deep, had been replaced by patent tracks made of a substance called Eadhamite. This Eadhamite—it was named after its patentee—ranks with the invention of printing and steam as one of the epoch-making discoveries of the world's history.

When Eadham discovered the substance, he probably thought of it as a mere cheap substitute for india rubber; it cost a few shillings a ton. But you can never tell all an invention will do. It was the genius of a man named Warming that pointed to the possibility of using it, not only for the tires of wheels, but as a road substance, and who organised the enormous network of public ways that speedily covered the world.

These public ways were made with longitudinal divisions. On the outer on either side went foot cyclists and conveyances travelling at a less speed than twenty-five miles an hour; in the middle, motors capable of speed up to a hundred; and the inner, Warming (in the face of enormous ridicule) reserved for vehicles travelling at speeds of a hundred miles an hour and upward.

For ten years his inner ways were vacant. Before he died they were the most crowded of all, and vast light frameworks with wheels of twenty and thirty feet in diameter, hurled along them at paces that year after

year rose steadily towards two hundred miles an hour. And by the time
this revolution was accomplished, a parallel revolution had transformed
the ever-growing cities. Before the development of practical science the
fogs and filth of Victorian times vanished. Electric heating replaced fires
(in 2013 the lighting of a fire that did not absolutely consume its own
smoke was made an indictable nuisance), and all the city ways, all public
squares and places, were covered in with a recently invented glass-like
substance. The roofing of London became practically continuous. Certain short-sighted and foolish legislation against tall buildings was
abolished, and London, from a squat expanse of petty houses—feebly
archaic in design—rose steadily towards the sky. To the municipal
responsibility for water, light, and drainage, was added another, and that
was ventilation.

But to tell of all the changes in human convenience that these two
hundred years brought about, to tell of the long foreseen invention of
flying, to describe how life in households was steadily supplanted by life
in interminable hotels, how at last even those who were still concerned
in agricultural work came to live in the towns and to go to and fro to
their work every day, to describe how at last in all England only four
towns remained, each with many millions of people, and how there were
left no inhabited houses in all the countryside: to tell all this would take
us far from our story of Denton and his Elizabeth. They had been
separated and reunited, and still they could not marry. For Denton—it
was his only fault—had no money. Neither had Elizabeth until she was
twenty-one, and as yet she was only eighteen. At twenty-one all the
property of her mother would come to her, for that was the custom of
the time. She did not know that it was possible to anticipate her fortune,
and Denton was far too delicate a lover to suggest such a thing. So things
stuck hopelessly between them. Elizabeth said that she was very unhappy,
and that nobody understood her but Denton, and that when she was
away from him she was wretched; and Denton said that his heart longed
for her day and night. And they met as often as they could to enjoy the
discussion of their sorrows.

They met one day at their little seat upon the flying stage. The precise
site of this meeting was where in Victorian times the road from Wimbledon came out upon the common. They were, however, five hundred feet
above that point. Their seat looked far over London. To convey the
appearance of it all to a nineteenth-century reader would have been
difficult. One would have had to tell him to think of the Crystal Palace,
of the newly built "mammoth" hotels—as those little affairs were called
—of the larger railway stations of his time, and to imagine such buildings
enlarged to vast proportions and run together and continuous over the

whole metropolitan area. If then he was told that this continuous roof-space bore a huge forest of rotating wind-wheels, he would have begun very dimly to appreciate what to these young people was the commonest sight in their lives.

To their eyes it had something of the quality of a prison, and they were talking, as they had talked a hundred times before, of how they might escape from it and be at last happy together: escape from it, that is, before the appointed three years were at an end. It was, they both agreed, not only impossible but almost wicked, to wait three years. "Before that," said Denton—and the notes of his voice told of a splendid chest—"*we might both be dead!*"

Their vigorous young hands had to grip at this, and then Elizabeth had a still more poignant thought that brought the tears from her whole-some eyes and down her healthy cheeks. "*One* of us," she said, "*one* of us might be——"

She choked; she could not say the word that is so terrible to the young and happy.

Yet to marry and be very poor in the cities of that time was—for any one who had lived pleasantly—a very dreadful thing. In the old agricultural days that had drawn to an end in the eighteenth century there had been a pretty proverb of love in a cottage; and indeed in those days the poor of the countryside had dwelt in flower-covered, diamond-windowed cottages of thatch and plaster, with the sweet air and earth about them, amidst tangled hedges and the song of birds, and with the ever-changing sky overhead. But all this had changed (the change was already beginning in the nineteenth century), and a new sort of life was opening for the poor —in the lower quarters of the city.

In the nineteenth century the lower quarters were still beneath the sky; they were areas of land on clay or other unsuitable soil, liable to floods or exposed to the smoke of more fortunate districts, insufficiently supplied with water, and as insanitary as the great fear of infectious diseases felt by the wealthier classes permitted. In the twenty-second century, how-ever, the growth of the city storey above storey, and the coalescence of buildings, had led to a different arrangement. The prosperous people lived in a vast series of sumptuous hotels in the upper storeys and halls of the city fabric; the industrial population dwelt beneath in the tremen-dous ground-floor and basement, so to speak, of the place.

In the refinement of life and manners these lower classes differed little from their ancestors, the East-enders of Queen Victoria's time; but they had developed a distinct dialect of their own. In these under ways they lived and died, rarely ascending to the surface except when work took them there. Since for most of them this was the sort of life to which they had been born, they found no great misery in such circumstances; but for people like Denton and Elizabeth, such a plunge would have seemed more terrible than death.

"And yet what else is there?" asked Elizabeth.

Denton professed not to know. Apart from his own feeling of delicacy, he was not sure how Elizabeth would like the idea of borrowing on the strength of her expectations.

The passage from London to Paris even, said Elizabeth, was beyond their means; and in Paris, as in any other city in the world, life would be just as costly and impossible as in London.

Well might Denton cry aloud: "If only we had lived in those days, dearest! If only we had lived in the past!" For to their eyes even nineteenth-century Whitechapel was seen through a mist of romance.

"Is there *nothing*?" cried Elizabeth, suddenly weeping. "Must we really wait for those three long years? Fancy *three* years—six-and-thirty months!" The human capacity for patience had not grown with the ages.

Then suddenly Denton was moved to speak of something that had already flickered across his mind. He had hit upon it at last. It seemed to him so wild a suggestion that he made it only half seriously. But to put a thing into words has ever a way of making it seem more real and possible than it seemed before. And so it was with him.

"Suppose," he said, "we went into the country?"

She looked at him to see if he was serious in proposing such an adventure.

"The country?"

"Yes—beyond there. Beyond the hills."

"How could we live?" she said. "*Where* could we live?"

"It is not impossible," he said. "People used to live in the country."

"But then there were houses."

"There are the ruins of villages and towns now. On the clay lands they are gone, of course. But they are still left on the grazing land, because it does not pay the Food Company to remove them. I know that—for certain. Besides, one sees them from the flying machines, you know. Well, we might shelter in some one of these, and repair it with our hands. Do you know, the thing is not so wild as it seems. Some of the men who go out every day to look after the crops and herds might be paid to bring us food. . . ."

She stood in front of him. "How strange it would be if one really could. . . ."

"Why not?"

"But no one dares."

"That is no reason."

"It would be—oh! it would be so romantic and strange. If only it were possible."

"Why not possible?"

"There are so many things. Think of all the things we have, things that we should miss."

"Should we miss them? After all, the life we lead is very unreal—very artificial." He began to expand his idea, and as he warmed to his exposition the fantastic quality of his first proposal faded away.

She thought. "But I have heard of prowlers—escaped criminals."

He nodded. He hesitated over his answer because he thought it sounded boyish. He blushed. "I could get some one I know to make me a sword."

She looked at him with enthusiasm growing in her eyes. She had heard of swords, had seen one in a museum; she thought of those ancient days when men wore them as a common thing. His suggestion seemed an impossible dream to her, and perhaps for that reason she was eager for more detail. And inventing for the most part as he went along, he told her, how they might live in the country as the old-world people had done. With every detail her interest grew, for she was one of those girls for whom romance and adventure have a fascination.

His suggestion seemed, I say, an impossible dream to her on that day, but the next day they talked about it again, and it was strangely less impossible.

"At first we should take food," said Denton. "We could carry food for ten or twelve days." It was an age of compact artificial nourishment, and such a provision had none of the unwieldy suggestion it would have had in the nineteenth century.

"But—until our house," she asked—"until it was ready, where should we sleep?"

"It is summer."

"But . . . What do you mean?"

"There was a time when there were no houses in the world; when all mankind slept always in the open air."

"But for us! The emptiness! No walls—no ceiling!"

"Dear," he said, "in London you have many beautiful ceilings. Artists paint them and stud them with lights. But I have seen a ceiling more beautiful than any in London. . . ."

"But where?"

"It is the ceiling under which we two would be alone. . . ."

"You mean . . . ?"

"Dear," he said, "it is something the world has forgotten. It is Heaven and all the host of stars."

Each time they talked the thing seemed more possible and more desirable to them. In a week or so it was quite possible. Another week, and it was the inevitable thing they had to do. A great enthusiasm for the country seized hold of them and possessed them. The sordid tumult of the town, they said, overwhelmed them. They marvelled that this simple way out of their troubles had never come upon them before.

One morning near Midsummer-day, there was a new minor official upon the flying stage, and Denton's place was to know him no more.

Our two young people had secretly married, and were going forth manfully out of the city in which they and their ancestors before them had lived all their days. She wore a new dress of white cut in an old-fashioned pattern, and he had a bundle of provisions strapped athwart his back, and in his hand he carried—rather shame-facedly it is true, and under his purple cloak—an implement of archaic form, a cross-hilted thing of tempered steel.

Imagine that going forth! In their days the sprawling suburbs of Victorian times with their vile roads, petty houses, foolish little gardens of shrub and geranium, and all their futile, pretentious privacies, had disappeared: the towering buildings of the new age, the mechanical ways, the electric and water mains, all came to an end together, like a wall, like a cliff, near four hundred feet in height, abrupt and sheer. All about the city spread the carrot, swede, and turnip fields of the Food Company, vegetables that were the basis of a thousand varied foods, and weeds and hedgerow tangles had been utterly extirpated. The incessant expense of weeding that went on year after year in the petty, wasteful and barbaric farming of the ancient days, the Food Company had economised for ever more by a campaign of extermination. Here and there, however, neat rows of bramble standards and apple trees with whitewashed stems, intersected the fields, and at places groups of gigantic teazles reared their favoured spikes. Here and there huge agricultural machines hunched under waterproof covers. The mingled waters of the Wey and Mole and Wandle ran in rectangular channels; and wherever a gentle elevation of the ground permitted a fountain of deodorised sewage distributed its benefits athwart the land and made a rainbow of the sunlight.

By a great archway in that enormous city wall emerged the Eadhamite road to Portsmouth, swarming in the morning sunshine with an enormous traffic bearing the blue-clad servants of the Food Company to their toil. A rushing traffic, beside which they seemed two scarce-moving dots. Along the outer tracks hummed and rattled the tardy little old-fashioned motors of such as had duties within twenty miles or so of the city; the inner ways were filled with vaster mechanisms—swift monocycles bearing a score of men, lank multicycles, quadricycles sagging with heavy loads, empty gigantic produce carts that would come back again filled before the sun was setting, all with throbbing engines and noiseless wheels and a perpetual wild melody of horns and gongs.

Along the very verge of the outermost way our young people went in silence, newly wed and oddly shy of one another's company. Many were the things shouted to them as they tramped along, for in 2100 a foot-passenger on an English road was almost as strange a sight as a motor car would have been in 1800. But they went on with steadfast eyes into the country, paying no heed to such cries.

Before them in the south rose the Downs, blue at first, and as they came nearer changing to green, surmounted by the row of gigantic wind-wheels that supplemented the wind-wheels upon the roof-spaces of the city, and broken and restless with the long morning shadows of those whirling vanes. By midday they had come so near that they could see here and there little patches of pallid dots—the sheep the Meat Department of the Food Company owned. In another hour they had passed the clay and the root crops and the single fence that hedged them in, and the prohibition against trespass no longer held: the levelled roadway plunged into a cutting with all its traffic, and they could leave it and walk over the greensward and up the open hillside.

Never had these children of the latter days been together in such a lonely place.

They were both very hungry and footsore—for walking was a rare exercise—and presently they sat down on the weedless, close-cropped grass, and looked back for the first time at the city from which they had come, shining wide and splendid in the blue haze of the valley of the Thames. Elizabeth was a little afraid of the unenclosed sheep away up the slope—she had never been near big unrestrained animals before—but Denton reassured her. And overhead a white-winged bird circled in the blue.

They talked but little until they had eaten, and then their tongues were loosened. He spoke of the happiness that was now certainly theirs, of the folly of not breaking sooner out of that magnificent prison of latter-day life, of the old romantic days that had passed from the world for ever. And then he became boastful. He took up the sword that lay on the ground beside him, and she took it from his hand and ran a tremulous finger along the blade.

"And you could," she said, "*you*—could raise this and strike a man?"

"Why not? If there were need."

"But," she said, "it seems so horrible. It would slash. . . . There would be"—her voice sank—"*blood.*"

"In the old romances you have read often enough . . ."

"Oh, I know: in those—yes. But that is different. One knows it is not blood, but just a sort of red ink. . . . And *you*—killing!"

She looked at him doubtfully, and then handed him back the sword.

After they had rested and eaten, they rose up and went on their way towards the hills. They passed quite close to a huge flock of sheep, who stared and bleated at their unaccustomed figures. She had never seen sheep before, and she shivered to think such gentle things must needs be slain for food. A sheep-dog barked from a distance, and then a shepherd appeared amidst the supports of the wind-wheels, and came down towards them.

When he drew near he called out asking whither they were going.

Denton hesitated, and told him briefly that they sought some ruined house among the Downs, in which they might live together. He tried to speak in an off-hand manner, as though it was a usual thing to do. The man stared incredulously.

"Have you *done* anything?" he asked.

"Nothing," said Denton. "Only we don't want to live in a city any longer. Why should we live in cities?"

The shepherd stared more incredulously than ever. "You can't live here," he said.

"We mean to try."

The shepherd stared from one to the other. "You'll go back to-morrow," he said. "It looks pleasant enough in the sunlight. . . . Are you sure you've done nothing? We shepherds are not such *great* friends of the police."

Denton looked at him steadfastly. "No," he said. "But we are too poor to live in the city, and we can't bear the thought of wearing clothes of blue canvas and doing drudgery. We are going to live a simple life here, like the people of old."

The shepherd was a bearded man with a thoughtful face. He glanced at Elizabeth's fragile beauty.

"*They* had simple minds," he said.

"So have we," said Denton.

The shepherd smiled.

"If you go along here," he said, "along the crest beneath the wind-wheels, you will see a heap of mounds and ruins on your right-hand side. That was once a town called Epsom. There are no houses there, and the bricks have been used for a sheep pen. Go on, and another heap on the edge of the root-land is Leatherhead; and then the hill turns away along the border of a valley, and there are woods of beech. Keep along the crest. You will come to quite wild places. In some parts, in spite of all the weeding that is done, ferns and bluebells and other such useless plants are growing still. And through it all underneath the wind-wheels runs a straight lane paved with stones, a roadway of the Romans two thousand years old. Go to the right of that, down into the valley and follow it along by the banks of the river. You come presently to a street of houses, many with the roofs still sound upon them. There you may find shelter."

They thanked him.

"But it's a quiet place. There is no light after dark there, and I have heard tell of robbers. It is lonely. Nothing happens there. The phonographs of the story-tellers, the kinematograph entertainments, the news machines—none of them are to be found there. If you are hungry there is no food, if you are ill no doctor. . . ." He stopped.

"We shall try it," said Denton, moving to go on. Then a thought struck him, and he made an agreement with the shepherd, and learnt where they might find him, to buy and bring them anything of which they stood in need, out of the city.

And in the evening they came to the deserted village, with its houses that seemed so small and odd to them: they found it golden in the glory of the sunset, and desolate and still. They went from one deserted house to another, marvelling at their quaint simplicity, and debating which they should choose. And at last, in a sunlit corner of a room that had lost its outer wall, they came upon a wild flower, a little flower of blue that the weeders of the Food Company had overlooked.

That house they decided upon; but they did not remain in it long that night, because they were resolved to feast upon nature. And moreover the houses became very gaunt and shadowy after the sunlight had faded out of the sky. So after they had rested a little time they went to the crest of the hill again to see with their own eyes the silence of heaven set with stars, about which the old poets had had so many things to tell. It was a wonderful sight, and Denton talked like the stars, and when they went down the hill at last the sky was pale with dawn. They slept but little, and in the morning when they woke a thrush was singing in a tree.

So these young people of the twenty-second century began their exile. That morning they were very busy exploring the resources of this new home in which they were going to live the simple life. They did not explore very fast or very far, because they went everywhere hand-in-hand; but they found the beginnings of some furniture. Beyond the village was a store of winter fodder for the sheep of the Food Company, and Denton dragged great armfuls to the house to make a bed; and in several of the houses were old fungus-eaten chairs and tables—rough, barbaric, clumsy furniture, it seemed to them, and made of wood. They repeated many of the things they had said on the previous day, and towards evening they found another flower, a harebell. In the late afternoon some Company shepherds went down the river valley riding on a big multicycle; but they hid from them, because their presence, Elizabeth said, seemed to spoil the romance of this old-world place altogether.

In this fashion they lived a week. For all that week the days were cloudless, and the nights nights of starry glory, that were invaded each a little more by a crescent moon.

Yet something of the first splendour of their coming faded—faded imperceptibly day after day; Denton's eloquence became fitful, and lacked fresh topics of inspiration; the fatigue of their long march from London told in a certain stiffness of the limbs, and each suffered from a slight unaccountable cold. Moreover, Denton became aware of unoccupied time. In one place among the carelessly heaped lumber of the old times he found a rust-eaten spade, and with this he made a fitful attack on the razed and grass-grown garden—though he had nothing to plant or sow. He returned to Elizabeth with a sweat-streaming face, after half an hour of such work.

"There were giants in those days," he said, not understanding what wont and training will do. And their walk that day led them along the hills until they could see the city shimmering far away in the valley. "I wonder how things are going on there," he said.

And then came a change in the weather. "Come out and see the clouds," she cried; and behold! they were a sombre purple in the north and east, streaming up to ragged edges at the zenith. And as they went up the hill these hurrying streamers blotted out the sunset. Suddenly the wind set the beech-trees swaying and whispering, and Elizabeth shivered. And then far away the lightning flashed, flashed like a sword that is drawn suddenly, and the distant thunder marched about the sky, and even as they stood astonished, pattering upon them came the first headlong raindrops of the storm. In an instant the last streak of sunset was hidden by a falling curtain of hail, and the lightning flashed again, and the voice of the thunder roared louder, and all about them the world scowled dark and strange.

Seizing hands, these children of the city ran down the hill to their home, in infinite astonishment. And ere they reached it, Elizabeth was weeping with dismay, and the darkling ground about them was white and brittle and active with the pelting hail.

Then began a strange and terrible night for them. For the first time in their civilised lives they were in absolute darkness; they were wet and cold and shivering, all about them hissed the hail, and through the long neglected ceilings of the derelict home came noisy spouts of water and formed pools and rivulets on the creaking floors. As the gusts of the storm struck the worn-out building, it groaned and shuddered, and now a mass of plaster from the wall would slide and smash, and now some loosened tile would rattle down the roof and crash into the empty green-house below. Elizabeth shuddered, and was still; Denton wrapped his gay and flimsy city cloak about her, and so they crouched in the darkness. And ever the thunder broke louder and nearer, and ever more lurid flashed the lightning, jerking into a momentary gaunt clearness the steaming, dripping room in which they sheltered.

Never before had they been in the open air save when the sun was shining. All their time had been spent in the warm and airy ways and halls and rooms of the latter-day city. It was to them that night as if they were in some other world, some disordered chaos of stress and tumult, and almost beyond hoping that they should ever see the city ways again.

The storm seemed to last interminably, until at last they dozed between the thunderclaps, and then very swiftly it fell and ceased. And as the last patter of the rain died away they heard an unfamiliar sound.

"What is that?" cried Elizabeth.

It came again. It was the barking of dogs. It drove down the desert lane and passed; and through the window, whitening the wall before them and throwing upon it the shadow of the window-frame and of a tree in black silhouette, shone the light of the waxing moon. . . .

Just as the pale dawn was drawing the things about them into sight, the fitful barking of dogs came near again, and stopped. They listened. After a pause they heard the quick pattering of feet seeking round the house, and short, half-smothered barks. Then again everything was still.

"Ssh!" whispered Elizabeth, and pointed to the door of their room.

Denton went half-way towards the door, and stood listening. He came back with a face of affected unconcern. "They must be the sheep-dogs of the Food Company," he said. "They will do us no harm."

He sat down again beside her. "What a night it has been!" he said, to hide how keenly he was listening.

"I don't like dogs," answered Elizabeth, after a long silence.

"Dogs never hurt any one," said Denton. "In the old days—in the nineteenth century—everybody had a dog."

"There was a romance I heard once. A dog killed a man."

"Not this sort of dog," said Denton confidently. "Some of those romances—are exaggerated."

Suddenly a half bark and a pattering up the staircase; the sound of panting. Denton sprang to his feet and drew the sword out of the damp straw upon which they had been lying. Then in the doorway appeared a gaunt sheep-dog, and halted there. Behind it stared another. For an instant man and brute faced each other, hesitating.

Then Denton, being ignorant of dogs, made a sharp step forward. "Go away," he said, with a clumsy motion of his sword.

The dog started and growled. Denton stopped sharply. "Good dog!" he said.

The growling jerked into a bark.

"Good dog!" said Denton. The second dog growled and barked. A third out of sight down the staircase took up the barking also. Outside others gave tongue—a large number it seemed to Denton.

"This is annoying," said Denton, without taking his eye off the brutes before him. "Of course the shepherds won't come out of the city for hours yet. Naturally these dogs don't quite make us out."

"I can't hear," shouted Elizabeth. She stood up and came to him.

Denton tried again, but the barking still drowned his voice. The sound had a curious effect upon his blood. Odd disused emotions began to stir; his face changed as he shouted. He tried again; the barking seemed to mock him, and one dog danced a pace forward, bristling. Suddenly he turned, and uttering certain words in the dialect of the underways, words incomprehensible to Elizabeth, he made for the dogs. There was a sudden cessation of the barking, a growl and a snapping. Elizabeth saw the snarling head of the foremost dog, its white teeth and retracted ears, and the flash of the thrust blade. The brute leapt into the air and was flung back.

Then Denton, with a shout, was driving the dogs before him. The sword flashed above his head with a sudden new freedom of gesture, and then he vanished down the staircase. She made six steps to follow him, and on the landing there was blood. She stopped, and hearing the tumult of dogs and Denton's shouts pass out of the house, ran to the window.

Nine wolfish sheep-dogs were scattering, one writhed before the porch; and Denton, tasting that strange delight of combat that slumbers still in the blood of even the most civilised man, was shouting and running across the garden space. And then she saw something that for a moment he did not see. The dogs circled round this way and that, and came again. They had him in the open.

In an instant she divined the situation. She would have called to him. For a moment she felt sick and helpless, and then, obeying a strange impulse, she gathered up her white skirt and ran downstairs. In the hall was the rusting spade. That was it! She seized it and ran out.

She came none too soon. One dog rolled before him, well-nigh slashed in half; but a second had him by the thigh, a third gripped his collar behind, and a fourth had the blade of the sword between its teeth, tasting its own blood. He parried the leap of a fifth with his left arm.

It might have been the first century instead of the twenty-second, so far as she was concerned. All the gentleness of her eighteen years of city life vanished before this primordial need. The spade smote hard and sure, and cleft a dog's skull. Another, crouching for a spring, yelped with dismay at this unexpected antagonist, and rushed aside. Two wasted precious moments on the binding of a feminine skirt.

The collar of Denton's cloak tore and parted as he staggered back; and that dog too felt the spade, and ceased to trouble him. He sheathed his sword in the brute at his thigh.

"To the wall!" cried Elizabeth; and in three seconds the fight was at an end, and our young people stood side by side, while a remnant of five dogs, with ears and tails of disaster, fled shamefully from the stricken field.

For a moment they stood panting and victorious, and then Elizabeth, dropping her spade, covered her face, and sank to the ground in a paroxysm of weeping. Denton looked about him, thrust the point of his sword into the ground so that it was at hand, and stooped to comfort her.

At last their more tumultuous emotions subsided, and they could talk again. She leant upon the wall, and he sat upon it so that he could keep an eye open for any returning dogs. Two, at any rate, were up on the hillside and keeping up a vexatious barking.

She was tear-stained, but not very wretched now, because for half an hour he had been repeating that she was brave and had saved his life. But a new fear was growing in her mind.

"They are the dogs of the Food Company," she said. "There will be trouble."

"I am afraid so. Very likely they will prosecute us for trespass."

A pause.

"In the old times," he said, "this sort of thing happened day after day."

"Last night!" she said. "I could not live through another such night."

He looked at her. Her face was pale for want of sleep, and drawn and haggard. He came to a sudden resolution. "We must go back," he said.

She looked at the dead dogs, and shivered. "We cannot stay here," she said.

"We must go back," he repeated, glancing over his shoulder to see if the enemy kept their distance. "We have been happy for a time. . . . But the world is too civilised. Ours is the age of cities. More of this will kill us."

"But what are we to do? How can we live there?"

Denton hesitated. His heel kicked against the wall on which he sat. "It's a thing I haven't mentioned before," he said, and coughed; "but . . ."

"Yes?"

"You could raise money on your expectations," he said.

"Could I?" she said eagerly.

"Of course you could. What a child you are!"

She stood up, and her face was bright. "Why did you not tell me before?" she asked. "And all this time we have been here!"

He looked at her for a moment, and smiled. Then the smile vanished. "I thought it ought to come from you," he said. "I didn't like to ask for your money. And besides—at first I thought this would be rather fine."

There was a pause.

"It *has* been fine," he said; and glanced once more over his shoulder. "Until all this began."

"Yes," she said, "those first days. The first three days."

They looked for a space into one another's faces, and then Denton slid down from the wall and took her hand.

"To each generation," he said, "the life of its time. I see it all plainly now. In the city—that is the life to which we were born. To live in any other fashion . . . Coming here was a dream, and this—is the awakening."

"It was a pleasant dream," she said—"in the beginning."

For a long space neither spoke.

"If we would reach the city before the shepherds come here, we must start," said Denton. "We must get our food out of the house and eat as we go."

Denton glanced about him again, and, giving the dead dogs a wide berth, they walked across the garden space and into the house together. They found the wallet with their food, and descended the blood-stained stairs again. In the hall Elizabeth stopped. "One minute," she said. "There is something here."

She led the way into the room in which that one little blue flower was blooming. She stooped to it, she touched it with her hand.

"I want it," she said; and then, "I cannot take it. . . ."

Impulsively she stooped and kissed its petals.

Then silently, side by side, they went across the empty garden-space into the old high road, and set their faces resolutely towards the distant city—towards the complex mechanical city of those latter days, the city that had swallowed up mankind.

CHAPTER III

THE WAYS OF THE CITY

PROMINENT IF NOT paramount among world-changing inventions in the history of man is that series of contrivances in locomotion that began with the railway and ended for a century or more with the motor and the patent road. That these contrivances, together with the device of limited liability joint stock companies and the supersession of agricultural labourers by skilled men with ingenious machinery, would necessarily concentrate mankind in cities of unparalleled magnitude and work an entire revolution in human life, became, after the event, a thing so obvious that it is a matter of astonishment it was not more clearly anticipated. Yet that any steps should be taken to anticipate the miseries such a revolution might entail does not appear even to have been suggested; and the idea that the moral prohibitions and sanctions, the privileges and concessions, the conception of property and responsibility, of comfort and beauty, that had rendered the mainly agricultural states of the past prosperous and happy, would fail in the rising torrent of novel opportunities and novel stimulations, never seems to have entered the nineteenth-century mind. That a citizen, kindly and fair in his ordinary life, could as a shareholder become almost murderously greedy; that commercial methods that were reasonable and honourable on the old-fashioned countryside, should on an enlarged scale be deadly and overwhelming; that ancient charity was modern pauperisation, and ancient employment modern sweating; that, in fact, a revision and enlargement of the duties and rights of man had become urgently necessary, were things it could not entertain, nourished as it was on an archaic system of education and profoundly retrospective and legal in all its habits of thought. It was known that the accumulation of men in cities involved unprecedented dangers of pestilence; there was an energetic development of sanitation; but that the diseases of gambling and usury, of luxury and tyranny should become endemic, and produce horrible consequences was beyond the scope of nineteenth-century thought. And so, as if it were some inorganic process, practically unhindered by the creative will of man, the growth of the swarming unhappy cities that mark the twenty-first century accomplished itself.

The new society was divided into three main classes. At the summit slumbered the property owner, enormously rich by accident rather than design, potent save for the will and aim, the last *avatar* of Hamlet in the world. Below was the enormous multitude of workers employed by the gigantic companies that monopolised control; and between these two the dwindling middle class, officials of innumerable sorts, foremen, managers, the medical, legal, artistic, and scholastic classes, and the minor rich, a middle class whose members led a life of insecure luxury and precarious speculation amidst the movements of the great managers.

Already the love story and the marrying of two persons of this middle class have been told: how they overcame the obstacles between them, and how they tried the simple old-fashioned way of living on the countryside and came back speedily enough into the city of London. Denton had no means, so Elizabeth borrowed money on the securities that her father Mwres held in trust for her until she was one-and-twenty.

The rate of interest she paid was of course high, because of the uncertainty of her security, and the arithmetic of lovers is often sketchy and optimistic. Yet they had very glorious times after that return. They determined they would not go to a Pleasure city nor waste their days rushing through the air from one part of the world to the other, for in spite of one disillusionment, their tastes were still old-fashioned. They furnished their little room with quaint old Victorian furniture, and found a shop on the forty-second floor in Seventh Way where printed books of the old sort were still to be bought. It was their pet affectation to read print instead of hearing phonographs. And when presently there came a sweet little girl, to unite them further if it were possible, Elizabeth would not send it to a *crèche*, as the custom was, but insisted on nursing it at home. The rent of their apartments was raised on account of this singular proceeding, but that they did not mind. It only meant borrowing a little more.

Presently Elizabeth was of age, and Denton had a business interview with her father that was not agreeable. An exceedingly disagreeable interview with their money-lender followed, from which he brought home a white face. On his return Elizabeth had to tell him of a new and marvellous intonation of "Goo" that their daughter had devised, but Denton was inattentive. In the midst, just as she was at the cream of her description, he interrupted. "How much money do you think we have left, now that everything is settled?"

She stared and stopped her appreciative swaying of the Goo genius that had accompanied her description.

"You don't mean . . . ?"

"Yes," he answered. "Ever so much. We have been wild. It's the interest. Or something. And the shares you had, slumped. Your father did not mind. Said it was not his business, after what had happened. He's going to marry again. . . . Well—we have scarcely a thousand left!"

"Only a thousand?"

"Only a thousand."

And Elizabeth sat down. For a moment she regarded him with a white face, then her eyes went about the quaint, old-fashioned room, with its middle Victorian furniture and genuine oleographs, and rested at last on the little lump of humanity within her arms.

Denton glanced at her and stood downcast. Then he swung round on his heel and walked up and down very rapidly.

"I must get something to do," he broke out presently. "I am an idle scoundrel. I ought to have thought of this before. I have been a selfish fool. I wanted to be with you all day. . . ."

He stopped, looking at her white face. Suddenly he came and kissed her and the little face that nestled against her breast.

"It's all right, dear," he said, standing over her; "you won't be lonely now—now Dings is beginning to talk to you. And I can soon get something to do, you know. Soon. . . . Easily. . . . It's only a shock at first. But it will come all right. It's sure to come right. I will go out again as soon as I have rested, and find what can be done. For the present it's hard to think of anything . . ."

"It would be hard to leave these rooms," said Elizabeth; "but——"

"There won't be any need of that—trust me."

"They are expensive."

Denton waved that aside. He began talking of the work he could do. He was not very explicit what it would be; but he was quite sure that there was something to keep them comfortably in the happy middle class, whose way of life was the only one they knew.

"There are three-and-thirty million people in London," he said: "some of them *must* have need of me."

"Some *must*."

"The trouble is . . . Well—Bindon, that brown little old man your father wanted you to marry. He's an important person. . . . I can't go back to my flying-stage work, because he is now a Commissioner of the Flying Stage Clerks."

"I didn't know that," said Elizabeth.

"He was made that in the last few weeks . . . or things would be easy enough, for they liked me on the flying stage. But there's dozens of other things to be done—dozens. Don't you worry, dear. I'll rest a little while, and then we'll dine, and then I'll start on my rounds. I know lots of people—lots."

So they rested, and then they went to the public dining-room and dined, and then he started on his search for employment. But they soon realised that in the matter of one convenience the world was just as badly off as it had ever been, and that was a nice, secure, honourable, remunerative employment, leaving ample leisure for the private life, and demanding no special ability, no violent exertion nor risk, and no sacrifice of any sort for its attainment. He evolved a number of brilliant projects, and spent many days hurrying from one part of the enormous city to another in search of influential friends; and all his influential friends were glad to see him, and very sanguine until it came to definite proposals, and then they became guarded and vague. He would part with them coldly, and think over their behaviour, and get irritated on his way back, and stop at some telephone office and spend money on an animated but unprofitable quarrel. And as the days passed, he got so worried and irritated that even to seem kind and careless before Elizabeth cost him an effort—as she, being a loving woman, perceived very clearly.

After an extremely complex preface one day, she helped him out with a painful suggestion. He had expected her to weep and give way to despair when it came to selling all their joyfully bought early Victorian treasures, their quaint objects of art, their antimacassars, bead mats, repp curtains, veneered furniture, gold-framed steel engravings and pencil drawings, wax flowers under shades, stuffed birds, and all sorts of choice old things; but it was she who made the proposal. The sacrifice seemed to fill her with pleasure, and so did the idea of shifting to apartments ten or twelve floors lower in another hotel. "So long as Dings is with us, nothing matters," she said. "It's all experience." So he kissed her, said she was braver than when she fought the sheep-dogs, called her Boadicea, and abstained very carefully from reminding her that they would have to pay a considerably higher rent on account of the little voice with which Dings greeted the perpetual uproar of the city.

His idea had been to get Elizabeth out of the way when it came to selling the absurd furniture about which their affections were twined and tangled; but when it came to the sale it was Elizabeth who haggled with the dealer while Denton went about the running ways of the city, white and sick with sorrow and the fear of what was still to come. When they moved into their sparsely furnished pink-and-white apartments in a cheap hotel, there came an outbreak of furious energy on his part, and then nearly a week of lethargy during which he sulked at home. Through those days Elizabeth shone like a star, and at the end Denton's misery found a vent in tears. And then he went out into the city ways again, and —to his utter amazement—found some work to do.

His standard of employment had fallen steadily until at last it had reached the lowest level of independent workers. At first he had aspired to some high official position in the great Flying or Windvane or Water Companies, or to an appointment on one of the General Intelligence

Organisations that had replaced newspapers, or to some professional partnership, but those were the dreams of the beginning. From that he had passed to speculation, and three hundred gold "lions" out of Elizabeth's thousand had vanished one evening in the share market. Now he was glad his good looks secured him a trial in the position of salesman to the Suzannah Hat Syndicate, a Syndicate dealing in ladies' caps, hair decorations, and hats—for though the city was completely covered in, ladies still wore extremely elaborate and beautiful hats at the theatres and places of public worship.

It would have been amusing if one could have confronted a Regent Street shopkeeper of the nineteenth century with the development of his establishment in which Denton's duties lay. Nineteenth Way was still sometimes called Regent Street, but it was now a street of moving platforms and nearly eight hundred feet wide. The middle space was immovable and gave access by staircases descending into subterranean ways to the houses on either side. Right and left were an ascending series of continuous platforms each of which travelled about five miles an hour faster than the one internal to it, so that one could step from platform to platform until one reached the swiftest outer way and so go about the city. The establishment of the Suzannah Hat Syndicate projected a vast *façade* upon the outer way, sending out overhead at either end an overlapping series of huge white glass screens, on which gigantic animated pictures of the faces of well-known beautiful living women wearing novelties in hats were thrown. A dense crowd was always collected in the stationary central way watching a vast kinematograph which displayed the changing fashion. The whole front of the building was in perpetual chromatic change, and all down the *façade*—four hundred feet it measured—and all across the street of moving ways, laced and winked and glittered in a thousand varieties of colour and lettering the inscription—

SUZANNA! 'ETS! SUZANNA! 'ETS!

A broadside of gigantic phonographs drowned all conversation in the moving way and roared "*hats*" at the passer-by, while far down the street and up, other batteries counselled the public to "walk down for Suzannah," and queried, "Why *don't* you buy the girl a hat?"

For the benefit of those who chanced to be deaf—and deafness was not uncommon in the London of that age, inscriptions of all sizes were thrown from the roof above upon the moving platforms themselves, and on one's hand or on the bald head of the man before one, or on a lady's shoulders, or in a sudden jet of flame before one's feet, the moving finger wrote in unanticipated letters of fire "*'ets r chip t'de*," or simply "*'ets.*" And spite of all these efforts so high was the pitch at which the city lived, so trained became one's eyes and ears to ignore all sorts of advertisement, that many a citizen had passed that place thousands of times and was still unaware of the existence of the Suzannah Hat Syndicate.

To enter the building one descended the staircase in the middle way and walked through a public passage in which pretty girls promenaded, girls who were willing to wear a ticketed hat for a small fee. The entrance chamber was a large hall in which wax heads fashionably adorned rotated gracefully upon pedestals, and from this one passed through a cash office to an interminable series of little rooms, each room with its salesman, its three or four hats and pins, its mirrors, its kinematographs, telephones and hat slides in communication with the central depôt, its comfortable lounge and tempting refreshments. A salesman in such an apartment did Denton now become. It was his business to attend to any of the incessant stream of ladies who chose to stop with him, to behave as winningly as possible, to offer refreshment, to converse on any topic the possible customer chose, and to guide the conversation dexterously but not insistently towards hats. He was to suggest trying on various types of hat and to show by his manner and bearing, but without any coarse flattery, the enhanced impression made by the hats he wished to sell. He had several mirrors, adapted by various subtleties of curvature and tint to different types of face and complexion, and much depended on the proper use of these.

Denton flung himself at these curious and not very congenial duties with a good will and energy that would have amazed him a year before; but all to no purpose. The Senior Manageress, who had selected him for appointment and conferred various small marks of favour upon him, suddenly changed in her manner, declared for no assignable cause that he was stupid, and dismissed him at the end of six weeks of salesmanship. So Denton had to resume his ineffectual search for employment.

This second search did not last very long. Their money was at the ebb. To eke it out a little longer they resolved to part with their darling Dings, and took that small person to one of the public *crèches* that abounded in the city. That was the common use of the time. The industrial emancipation of women, the correlated disorganisation of the secluded "home," had rendered *crèches* a necessity for all but very rich and exceptionally-minded people. Therein children encountered hygienic and educational advantages impossible without such organisation. *Crèches* were of all classes and types of luxury, down to those of the Labour Company, where children were taken on credit, to be redeemed in labour as they grew up.

But both Denton and Elizabeth being, as I have explained, strange old-fashioned young people, full of nineteenth-century ideas, hated thes?

convenient *crèches* exceedingly and at last took their little daughter to
one with extreme reluctance. They were received by a motherly person
in a uniform who was very brisk and prompt in her manner until Elizabeth wept at the mention of parting from her child. The motherly person,
after a brief astonishment at this unusual emotion, changed suddenly
into a creature of hope and comfort, and so won Elizabeth's gratitude
for life. They were conducted into a vast room presided over by several
nurses and with hundreds of two-year-old girls grouped about the toy-
covered floor. This was the Two-year-old Room. Two nurses came forward, and Elizabeth watched their bearing towards Dings with jealous
eyes. They were kind—it was clear they felt kind, and yet . . .

Presently it was time to go. By that time Dings was happily established
in a corner, sitting on the floor with her arms filled, and herself, indeed,
for the most part hidden by an unaccustomed wealth of toys. She seemed
careless of all human relationships as her parents receded.

They were forbidden to upset her by saying good-bye.

At the door Elizabeth glanced back for the last time, and behold!
Dings had dropped her new wealth and was standing with a dubious
face. Suddenly Elizabeth gasped, and the motherly nurse pushed her
forward and closed the door.

"You can come again soon, dear," she said, with unexpected tenderness in her eyes. For a moment Elizabeth stared at her with a blank face.
"You can come again soon," repeated the nurse. Then with a swift
transition Elizabeth was weeping in the nurse's arms. So it was that
Denton's heart was won also.

And three weeks after our young people were absolutely penniless, and
only one way lay open. They must go to the Labour Company. So soon
as the rent was a week overdue their few remaining possessions were
seized, and with scant courtesy they were shown the way out of the hotel.
Elizabeth walked along the passage towards the staircase that ascended
to the motionless middle way, too dulled by misery to think. Denton
stopped behind to finish a stinging and unsatisfactory argument with the
hotel porter, and then came hurrying after her, flushed and hot. He
slackened his pace as he overtook her, and together they ascended to the
middle way in silence. There they found two seats vacant and sat down.

"We need not go there—*yet*?" said Elizabeth.

"No—not till we are hungry," said Denton.

They said no more.

Elizabeth's eyes sought a resting-place and found none. To the right
roared the eastward ways, to the left the ways in the opposite direction,
swarming with people. Backwards and forwards along a cable overhead
rushed a string of gesticulating men, dressed like clowns, each marked on

back and chest with one gigantic letter, so that altogether they spelt out:

"PURKINJE'S DIGESTIVE PILLS."

An anæmic little woman in horrible coarse blue canvas pointed a little girl to one of this string of hurrying advertisements.

"Look!" said the anæmic woman: "there's yer father."

"Which?" said the little girl.

"'Im wiv his nose coloured red," said the anæmic woman.

The little girl began to cry, and Elizabeth could have cried too.

"Ain't 'e kickin' 'is legs!—*just!*" said the anæmic woman in blue, trying to make things bright again. "Looky—*now!*"

On the *façade* to the right a huge intensely bright disc of weird colour span incessantly, and letters of fire that came and went spelt out—

"DOES THIS MAKE YOU GIDDY?"

Then a pause, followed by

"TAKE A PURKINJE'S DIGESTIVE PILL."

A vast and desolating braying began. "If you love Swagger Literature, put your telephone on to Bruggles, the Greatest Author of all Time. The Greatest Thinker of all Time. Teaches you Morals up to your Scalp! The very image of Socrates, except the back of his head, which is like Shakspeare. He has six toes, dresses in red, and never cleans his teeth. Hear HIM!"

Denton's voice became audible in a gap in the uproar. "I never ought to have married you," he was saying. "I have wasted your money, ruined you, brought you to misery. I am a scoundrel. . . . Oh, this accursed world!"

She tried to speak, and for some moments could not. She grasped his hand. "No," she said at last.

A half-formed desire suddenly became determination. She stood up. "Will you come?"

He rose also. "We need not go there yet."

"Not that. But I want you to come to the flying stages—where we met. You know? The little seat."

He hesitated. "*Can* you?" he said, doubtfully.

"Must," she answered.

He hesitated still for a moment, then moved to obey her will.

And so it was they spent their last half-day of freedom out under the open air in the little seat under the flying stages where they had been wont to meet five short years ago. There she told him, what she could not tell him in the tumultuous public ways, that she did not repent even now of their marriage—that whatever discomfort and misery life still had for them, she was content with the things that had been. The weather was kind to them, the seat was sunlit and warm, and overhead the shining aëroplanes went and came.

At last towards sunsetting their time was at an end, and they made their vows to one another and clasped hands, and then rose up and went back into the ways of the city, a shabby-looking, heavy-hearted pair, tired and hungry. Soon they came to one of the pale blue signs that marked a Labour Company Bureau. For a space they stood in the middle way regarding this and at last descended, and entered the waiting-room.

The Labour Company had originally been a charitable organisation; its aim was to supply food, shelter, and work to all comers. This it was bound to do by the conditions of its incorporation, and it was also bound to supply food and shelter and medical attendance to all incapable of work who chose to demand its aid. In exchange these incapables paid labour notes, which they had to redeem upon recovery. They signed these labour notes with thumb-marks, which were photographed and indexed in such a way that this world-wide Labour Company could identify any one of its two or three hundred million clients at the cost of an hour's inquiry. The day's labour was defined as two spells in a tread-mill used in generating electrical force, or its equivalent, and its due performance could be enforced by law. In practice the Labour Company found it advisable to add to its statutory obligations of food and shelter a few pence a day as an inducement to effort; and its enterprise had not only abolished pauperisation altogether, but supplied practically all but the very highest and most responsible labour throughout the world. Nearly a third of the population of the world were its serfs and debtors from the cradle to the grave.

In this practical, unsentimental way the problem of the unemployed had been most satisfactorily met and overcome. No one starved in the public ways, and no rags, no costume less sanitary and sufficient than the Labour Company's hygienic but inelegant blue canvas, pained the eye throughout the whole world. It was the constant theme of the phonographic newspapers how much the world had progressed since nineteenth-century days, when the bodies of those killed by the vehicular traffic or dead of starvation, were, they alleged, a common feature in all the busier streets.

Denton and Elizabeth sat apart in the waiting-room until their turn came. Most of the others collected there seemed limp and taciturn, but three or four young people gaudily dressed made up for the quietude of their companions. They were life clients of the Company, born in the

Company's *crèche* and destined to die in its hospital, and they had been out for a spree with some shillings or so of extra pay. They talked vociferously in a later development of the Cockney dialect, manifestly very proud of themselves.

Elizabeth's eyes went from these to the less assertive figures. One seemed exceptionally pitiful to her. It was a woman of perhaps forty-five, with gold-stained hair and a painted face, down which abundant tears had trickled; she had a pinched nose, hungry eyes, lean hands and shoulders, and her dusty worn-out finery told the story of her life. Another was a grey-bearded old man in the costume of a bishop of one of the high episcopal sects—for religion was now also a business, and had its ups and downs. And beside him a sickly, dissipated-looking boy of perhaps two-and-twenty glared at Fate.

Presently Elizabeth and then Denton interviewed the manageress—for the Company preferred women in this capacity—and found she possessed an energetic face, a contemptuous manner, and a particularly unpleasant voice. They were given various checks, including one to certify that they need not have their heads cropped; and when they had given their thumbmarks, learnt the number corresponding thereunto, and exchanged their shabby middle-class clothes for duly numbered blue canvas suits, they repaired to the huge plain dining-room for their first meal under these new conditions. Afterwards they were to return to her for instructions about their work.

When they had made the exchange of their clothing Elizabeth did not seem able to look at Denton at first; but he looked at her, and saw with astonishment that even in blue canvas she was still beautiful. And then their soup and bread came sliding on its little rail down the long table towards them and stopped with a jerk, and he forgot the matter. For they had had no proper meal for three days.

After they had dined they rested for a time. Neither talked—there was nothing to say; and presently they got up and went back to the manageress to learn what they had to do.

The manageress referred to a tablet. "Y'r rooms won't be here; it'll be in the Highbury Ward, ninety-seventh way, number two thousand and seventeen. Better make a note of it on y'r card. *You*, nought nought nought, type seven, sixty-four, b.c.d., *gamma* forty-one, female; you 'ave to go to the Metal-beating Company and try that for a day—fourpence bonus if ye're satisfactory; and *you*, nought seven one, type four, seven hundred and nine, g.f.b., *pi* five and ninety, male; you 'ave to go to the Photographic Company on Eighty-first way, and learn something or other—*I* don't know—thrippence. 'Ere's y'r cards. That's all. Next! *What?* Didn't catch it all? Lor! So suppose I must go over it all again.

Why don't you listen? Keerless, unprovident people! One'd think these things didn't matter."

Their ways to their work lay together for a time. And now they found they could talk. Curiously enough, the worst of their depression seemed over now that they had actually donned the blue. Denton could talk with interest even of the work that lay before them. "Whatever it is," he said, "it can't be so hateful as that hat shop. And after we have paid for Dings, we shall still have a whole penny a day between us even now. Afterwards —we may improve—get more money."

Elizabeth was less inclined to speech. "I wonder why work should seem so hateful," she said.

"It's odd," said Denton. "I suppose it wouldn't be if it were not the thought of being ordered about. . . . I hope we shall have decent managers."

Elizabeth did not answer. She was not thinking of that. She was tracing out some thoughts of her own.

"Of course," she said presently, "we have been using up work all our lives. It's only fair——"

She stopped. It was too intricate.

"We paid for it," said Denton, for at that time he had not troubled himself about these complicated things.

"We did nothing—and yet we paid for it. That's what I cannot understand."

"Perhaps we are paying," said Elizabeth presently—for her theology was old-fashioned and simple.

Presently it was time for them to part, and each went to the appointed work. Denton's was to mind a complicated hydraulic press that seemed almost an intelligent thing. This press worked by the sea-water that was destined finally to flush the city drains—for the world had long since abandoned the folly of pouring drinkable water into its sewers. This water was brought close to the eastward edge of the city by a huge canal, and then raised by an enormous battery of pumps into reservoirs at a level of four hundred feet above the sea, from which it spread by a billion arterial branches over the city. Thence it poured down, cleansing, sluicing, working machinery of all sorts, through an infinite variety of capillary channels into the great drains, the *cloacae maximae*, and so carried the sewage out to the agricultural areas that surrounded London on every side.

The press was employed in one of the processes of the photographic manufacture, but the nature of the process it did not concern Denton to understand. The most salient fact to his mind was that it had to be conducted in ruby light, and as a consequence the room in which he worked was lit by one coloured globe that poured a lurid and painful illumination about the room. In the darkest corner stood the press whose servant Denton had now become: it was a huge, dim, glittering thing with a projecting hood that had a remote resemblance to a bowed head, and, squatting like some metal Buddha in this weird light that ministered to its needs, it seemed to Denton in certain moods almost as if this must needs be the obscure idol to which humanity in some strange aberration had offered up his life. His duties had a varied monotony. Such items as the following will convey an idea of the service of the press. The thing worked with a busy clicking so long as things went well; but if the paste that came pouring through a feeder from another room and which it was perpetually compressing into thin plates, changed in quality the rhythm of its click altered and Denton hastened to make certain adjustments. The slightest delay involved a waste of paste and the docking of one or more of his daily pence. If the supply of paste waned—there were hand processes of a peculiar sort involved in its preparation, and sometimes the workers had convulsions which deranged their output—Denton had to throw the press out of gear. In the painful vigilance a multitude of such trivial attentions entailed, painful because of the incessant effort its absence of natural interest required, Denton had now to pass one-third of his days. Save for an occasional visit from the manager, a kindly but singularly foul-mouthed man, Denton passed his working hours in solitude.

Elizabeth's work was of a more social sort. There was a fashion for covering the private apartments of the very wealthy with metal plates beautifully embossed with repeated patterns. The taste of the time demanded, however, that the repetition of the patterns should not be exact —not mechanical, but "natural"—and it was found that the most pleasing arrangement of pattern irregularity was obtained by employing women of refinement and natural taste to punch out the patterns with small dies. So many square feet of plates was exacted from Elizabeth as a minimum, and for whatever square feet she did in excess she received a small payment. The room, like most rooms of women workers, was under a manageress: men had been found by the Labour Company not only less exacting but extremely liable to excuse favoured ladies from a proper share of their duties. The manageress was a not unkindly, taciturn person, with the hardened remains of beauty of the brunette type; and the other women workers, who of course hated her, associated her name scandalously with one of the metal-work directors in order to explain her position.

Only two or three of Elizabeth's fellow-workers were born labour serfs; plain, morose girls, but most of them corresponded to what the nineteenth century would have called a "reduced" gentlewoman. But the ideal of what constituted a gentlewoman had altered: the faint, faded, negative virtue, the modulated voice and restrained gesture of the old-fashioned gentlewoman had vanished from the earth. Most of her companions showed in discoloured hair, ruined complexions, and the texture of their reminiscent conversations, the vanished glories of a conquering youth. All of these artistic workers were much older than Elizabeth, and two openly expressed their surprise that any one so young and pleasant should come to share their toil. But Elizabeth did not trouble them with her old-world moral conceptions.

They were permitted, and even encouraged to converse with each other, for the directors very properly judged that anything that conduced to variations of mood made for pleasing fluctuations in their patterning; and Elizabeth was almost forced to hear the stories of these lives with which her own interwove: garbled and distorted they were by vanity indeed and yet comprehensible enough. And soon she began to appreciate the small spites and cliques, the little misunderstandings and alliances that enmeshed about her. One woman was excessively garrulous and descriptive about a wonderful son of hers; another had cultivated a foolish coarseness of speech, that she seemed to regard as the wittiest expression of originality conceivable; a third mused for ever on dress, and whispered to Elizabeth how she saved her pence day after day, and would presently have a glorious day of freedom, wearing . . . and then followed hours of description; two others sat always together, and called one another pet names, until one day some little thing happened, and they sat apart, blind and deaf as it seemed to one another's being. And always from them all came an incessant tap, tap, tap, tap, and the manageress listened always to the rhythm to mark if one fell away. Tap, tap, tap, tap: so their days passed, so their lives must pass. Elizabeth sat among them, kindly and quiet, gray-hearted, marvelling at Fate: tap, tap, tap; tap, tap, tap; tap, tap, tap.

So there came to Denton and Elizabeth a long succession of laborious days, that hardened their hands, wove strange threads of some new and sterner substance into the soft prettiness of their lives, and drew grave lines and shadows on their faces. The bright, convenient ways of the former life had receded to an inaccessible distance; slowly they learnt the lesson of the under-world—sombre and laborious, vast and pregnant. There were many little things happened: things that would be tedious and miserable to tell, things that were bitter and grievous to bear—indignities, tyrannies, such as must ever season the bread of the poor in cities; and one thing that was not little, but seemed like the utter blackening of life to them, which was that the child they had given life to sickened and died.

But that story, that ancient, perpetually recurring story, has been told so often, has been told so beautifully, that there is no need to tell it over again here. There was the same sharp fear, the same long anxiety, the deferred inevitable blow, and the black silence. It has always been the same; it will always be the same. It is one of the things that must be.

And it was Elizabeth who was the first to speak, after an aching, dull interspace of days: not, indeed, of the foolish little name that was a name no longer, but of the darkness that brooded over her soul. They had come through the shrieking, tumultuous ways of the city together; the clamour of trade, of yelling competitive religions, of political appeal, had beat upon deaf ears; the glare of focussed lights, of dancing letters, and fiery advertisements, had fallen upon the set, miserable faces unheeded. They took their dinner in the dining-hall at a place apart. "I want," said Elizabeth clumsily, "to go out to the flying stages—to that seat. Here, one can say nothing. . . ."

Denton looked at her. "It will be night," he said.

"I have asked—it is a fine night." She stopped.

He perceived she could find no words to explain herself. Suddenly he understood that she wished to see the stars once more, the stars they had watched together from the open downland in that wild honeymoon of theirs five years ago. Something caught at his throat. He looked away from her.

"There will be plenty of time to go," he said, in a matter-of-fact tone.

And at last they came out to their little seat on the flying stage, and sat there for a long time in silence. The little seat was in shadow, but the zenith was pale blue with the effulgence of the stage overhead, and all the city spread below them, squares and circles and patches of brilliance caught in a mesh-work of light. The little stars seemed very faint and small: near as they had been to the old-world watcher, they had become now infinitely remote. Yet one could see them in the darkened patches amidst the glare, and especially in the northward sky, the ancient constellations gliding steadfast and patient about the pole.

Long our two people sat in silence, and at last Elizabeth sighed.

"If I understood," she said, "if I could understand." When one is down there the city seems everything—the noise, the hurry, the voices—you must live, you must scramble. Here—it is nothing; a thing that passes. One can think in peace."

"Yes," said Denton. "How flimsy it all is! From here more than half of it is swallowed by the night. . . . It will pass."

"We shall pass first," said Elizabeth.

"I know," said Denton. "If life were not a moment, the whole of history would seem like the happening of a day. . . . Yes—we shall pass.

And the city will pass, and all the things that are to come. Man and the Overman and wonders unspeakable. And yet . . ."

He paused, and then began afresh. "I know what you feel. At least I fancy . . . Down there one thinks of one's work, one's little vexations and pleasures, one's eating and drinking and ease and pain. One lives, and one must die. Down there and everyday—our sorrow seemed the end of life. . . .

"Up here it is different. For instance, down there it would seem impossible almost to go on living if one were horribly disfigured, horribly crippled, disgraced. Up here—under these stars—none of those things would matter. They don't matter. . . . They are a part of something. One seems just to touch that something—under the stars. . . ."

He stopped. The vague, impalpable things in his mind, cloudy emotions half shaped towards ideas, vanished before the rough grasp of words. "It is hard to express," he said lamely.

They sat through a long stillness.

"It is well to come here," he said at last. "We stop—our minds are very finite. After all we are just poor animals rising out of the brute, each with a mind, the poor beginning of a mind. We are so stupid. So much hurts. And yet . . ."

"I know, I know—and some day we shall *see*.

"All this frightful stress, all this discord will resolve to harmony, and we shall know it. Nothing is but it makes for that. Nothing. All the failures—every little thing makes for that harmony. Everything is necessary to it, we shall find. We shall find. Nothing, not even the most dreadful thing, could be left out. Not even the most trivial. Every tap of your hammer on the brass, every moment of work, my idleness even. . . . Dear one! every movement of our poor little one . . . All these things go on for ever. And the faint impalpable things. We, sitting here together— Everything. . . .

"The passion that joined us, and what has come since. It is not passion now. More than anything else it is sorrow. *Dear* . . ."

He could say no more, could follow his thoughts no further.

Elizabeth made no answer—she was very still; but presently her hand sought his and found it.

CHAPTER IV

UNDERNEATH

UNDER THE STARS one may reach upward and touch resignation, whatever the evil thing may be, but in the heat and stress of the day's work we lapse again, come disgust and anger and intolerable moods. How little is all our magnanimity—an accident! a phase! The very Saints of old had first to flee the world. And Denton and his Elizabeth could not flee their world, no longer were there open roads to unclaimed lands where men might live freely—however hardly—and keep their souls in peace. The city had swallowed up mankind.

For a time these two Labour Serfs were kept at their original occupations, she at her brass stamping and Denton at his press; and then came a move for him that brought with it fresh and still bitterer experiences of life in the underways of the great city. He was transferred to the care of a rather more elaborate press in the central factory of the London Tile Trust.

In this new situation he had to work in a long vaulted room with a number of other men, for the most part born Labour Serfs. He came to this intercourse reluctantly. His upbringing had been refined, and, until his ill fortune had brought him to that costume, he had never spoken in his life, except by way of command or some immediate necessity, to the white-faced wearers of the blue canvas. Now at last came contact; he had to work beside them, share their tools, eat with them. To both Elizabeth and himself this seemed a further degradation.

His taste would have seemed extreme to a man of the nineteenth century. But slowly and inevitably in the intervening years a gulf had opened between the wearers of the blue canvas and the classes above, a difference not simply of circumstances and habits of life, but of habits of thought—even of language. The underways had developed a dialect of their own: above, too, had arisen a dialect, a code of thought, a language of "culture," which aimed by a sedulous search after fresh distinction to widen perpetually the space between itself and "vulgarity." The bond of a common faith, moreover, no longer held the race together. The last years of the nineteenth century were distinguished by the rapid development among the prosperous idle of esoteric perversions of the popular religion: glosses and interpretations that reduced the broad teachings of the carpenter of Nazareth to the exquisite narrowness of their lives. And, spite of their inclination towards the ancient fashion of living, neither Elizabeth nor Denton had been sufficiently original to escape the suggestion of their surroundings. In matters of common behaviour they had followed the ways of their class, and so when they fell at last to be Labour Serfs it seemed to them almost as though they were falling among offensive inferior animals; they felt as a nineteenth-century duke and duchess might have felt who were forced to take rooms in the Jago.

Their natural impulse was to maintain a "distance." But Denton's first idea of a dignified isolation from his new surroundings was soon rudely dispelled. He had imagined that his fall to the position of a Labour Serf was the end of his lesson, that when their little daughter had died he had plumbed the deeps of life; but indeed these things were only the beginning. Life demands something more from us than acquiescence. And now in a roomful of machine minders he was to learn a wider lesson, to make the acquaintance of another factor in life, a factor as elemental as the loss of things dear to us, more elemental even than toil.

His quiet discouragement of conversation was an immediate cause of offence—was interpreted, rightly enough I fear, as disdain. His ignorance of the vulgar dialect, a thing upon which he had hitherto prided himself, suddenly took upon itself a new aspect. He failed to perceive at once that his reception of the coarse and stupid but genially intended remarks that greeted his appearance must have stung the makers of these advances like blows in their faces. "Don't understand," he said rather coldly, and at hazard, "No, thank you."

The man who had addressed him stared, scowled, and turned away.

A second, who also failed at Denton's unaccustomed ear, took the trouble to repeat his remark, and Denton discovered he was being offered the use of an oil can. He expressed polite thanks, and this second man embarked upon a penetrating conversation. Denton, he remarked, had been a swell, and he wanted to know how he had come to wear the blue. He clearly expected an interesting record of vice and extravagance. Had Denton ever been at a Pleasure City? Denton was speedily to discover how the existence of these wonderful places of delight permeated and defiled the thought and honour of these unwilling, hopeless workers of the underworld.

His aristocratic temperament resented these questions. He answered "No" curtly. The man persisted with a still more personal question, and this time it was Denton who turned away.

"Gorblimey!" said his interlocutor, much astonished.

It presently forced itself upon Denton's mind that this remarkable conversation was being repeated in indignant tones to more sympathetic hearers, and that it gave rise to astonishment and ironical laughter. They looked at Denton with manifestly enhanced interest. A curious perception of isolation dawned upon him. He tried to think of his press and its unfamiliar peculiarities. . . .

The machines kept everybody pretty busy during the first spell, and then came a recess. It was only an interval for refreshment, too brief for any one to go out to a Labour Company dining-room. Denton followed his fellow-workers into a short gallery, in which were a number of bins of refuse from the presses.

Each man produced a packet of food. Denton had no packet. The manager, a careless young man who held his position by influence, had omitted to warn Denton that it was necessary to apply for this provision. He stood apart, feeling hungry. The others drew together in a group and talked in undertones, glancing at him ever and again. He became uneasy. His appearance of disregard cost him an increasing effort. He tried to think of the levers of his new press.

Presently one, a man shorter but much broader and stouter than Denton, came forward to him. Denton turned to him as unconcernedly as possible. "Here!" said the delegate—as Denton judged him to be— extending a cube of bread in a not too clean hand. He had a swart, broad-nosed face, and his mouth hung down towards one corner.

Denton felt doubtful for the instant whether this was meant for civility or insult. His impulse was to decline. "No, thanks," he said; and, at the man's change of expression, "I'm not hungry."

There came a laugh from the group behind. "Told you so," said the man who had offered Denton the loan of an oil can. "He's top side, he is. You ain't good enough for 'im."

The swart face grew a shade darker.

"Here," said its owner, still extending the bread, and speaking in a lower tone; "you got to eat this. See?"

Denton looked into the threatening face before him, and odd little currents of energy seemed to be running through his limbs and body.

"I don't want it," he said, trying a pleasant smile that twitched and failed.

The thickset man advanced his face, and the bread became a physical threat in his hand. Denton's mind rushed together to the one problem of his antagonist's eyes.

"Eat it," said the swart man.

There came a pause, and then they both moved quickly. The cube of bread described a complicated path, a curve that would have ended in Denton's face; and then his fist hit the wrist of the hand that gripped it, and it flew upward, and out of the conflict—its part played.

He stepped back quickly, fists clenched and arms tense. The hot, dark countenance receded, became an alert hostility, watching its chance.

Denton for one instant felt confident, and strangely buoyant and serene. His heart beat quickly. He felt his body alive, and glowing to the tips.

"Scrap, boys!" shouted some one, and then the dark figure had leapt forward, ducked back and sideways, and come in again. Denton struck out, and was hit. One of his eyes seemed to him to be demolished, and he felt a soft lip under his fist just before he was hit again—this time under the chin. A huge fan of fiery needles shot open. He had a momentary persuasion that his head was knocked to pieces, and then something hit his head and back from behind, and the fight became an uninteresting, an impersonal thing.

He was aware that time—seconds or minutes—had passed, abstract, uneventful time. He was lying with his head in a heap of ashes, and something wet and warm ran swiftly into his neck. The first shock broke up into discrete sensations. All his head throbbed; his eye and his chin throbbed exceedingly, and the taste of blood was in his mouth.

"He's all right," said a voice. "He's opening his eyes."

"Serve him —— well right," said a second.

His mates were standing about him. He made an effort and sat up. He put his hand to the back of his head, and his hair was wet and full of cinders. A laugh greeted the gesture. His eye was partially closed. He perceived what had happened. His momentary anticipation of a final victory had vanished.

"Looks surprised," said some one.

"'Ave any more?" said a wit; and then, imitating Denton's refined accent.

"No, thank you."

Denton perceived the swart man with a blood-stained handkerchief before his face, and somewhat in the background.

"Where's that bit of bread he's got to eat?" said a little ferret-faced creature; and sought with his foot in the ashes of the adjacent bin.

Denton had a moment of internal debate. He knew the code of honour requires a man to pursue a fight he has begun to the bitter end; but this was his first taste of the bitterness. He was resolved to rise again, but he felt no passionate impulse. It occurred to him—and the thought was no very violent spur—that he was perhaps after all a coward. For a moment his will was heavy, a lump of lead.

"'Ere it is," said the little ferret-faced man, and stooped to pick up a cindery cube. He looked at Denton, then at the others.

Slowly, unwillingly, Denton stood up.

A dirty-faced albino extended a hand to the ferret-faced man. "Gimme that toke," he said. He advanced threateningly, bread in hand, to Denton. "So you ain't 'ad your bellyful yet," he said. "Eh?"

Now it was coming. "No, I haven't," said Denton, with a catching of the breath, and resolved to try this brute behind the ear before he himself got stunned again. He knew he would be stunned again. He was astonished how ill he had judged himself beforehand. A few ridiculous lunges, and down he would go again. He watched the albino's eyes. The albino was grinning confidently, like a man who plans an agreeable trick. A sudden perception of impending indignities stung Denton.

"You leave 'im alone, Jim," said the swart man suddenly over the blood-stained rag. "He ain't done nothing to you."

The albino's grin vanished. He stopped. He looked from one to the other. It seemed to Denton that the swart man demanded the privilege of his destruction. The albino would have been better.

"You leave 'im alone," said the swart man. "See? 'E's 'ad 'is licks."

A clattering bell lifted up its voice and solved the situation. The albino hesitated. "Lucky for you," he said, adding a foul metaphor, and turned with the others towards the press-room again. "Wait for the end of the spell, mate," said the albino over his shoulder—an afterthought. The swart man waited for the albino to precede him. Denton realised that he had a reprieve.

The men passed towards an open door. Denton became aware of his duties, and hurried to join the tail of the queue. At the doorway of the vaulted gallery of presses a yellow-uniformed labour policeman stood ticking a card. He had ignored the swart man's hæmorrhage.

"Hurry up there!" he said to Denton.

"Hello!" he said, at the sight of his facial disarray. "Who's been hitting *you*?"

"That's my affair," said Denton.

"Not if it spiles your work, it ain't," said the man in yellow. "You mind that."

Denton made no answer. He was a rough—a labourer. He wore the blue canvas. The laws of assault and battery, he knew, were not for the likes of him. He went to his press.

He could feel the skin of his brow and chin and head lifting themselves to noble bruises, felt the throb and pain of each aspiring contusion. His nervous system slid down to lethargy; at each movement in his press adjustment he felt he lifted a weight. And as for his honour—that too throbbed and puffed. How did he stand? What precisely had happened in the last ten minutes? What would happen next? He knew that here was enormous matter for thought, and he could not think save in disordered snatches.

His mood was a sort of stagnant astonishment. All his conceptions were overthrown. He had regarded his security from physical violence as inherent, as one of the conditions of life. So, indeed, it had been while he wore his middle-class costume, had his middle-class property to serve for his defence. But who would interfere among Labour roughs fighting together? And indeed in those days no man would. In the Underworld there was no law between man and man; the law and machinery of the state had become for them something that held men down, fended them off from much desirable property and pleasure, and that was all. Violence, that ocean in which the brutes live for ever, and from which a thousand dykes and contrivances have won our hazardous civilised life, had flowed in again upon the sinking underways and submerged them. The fist ruled. Denton had come right down at last to the elemental—fist and trick and the stubborn heart and fellowship—even as it was in the beginning.

The ryhthm of his machine changed, and his thoughts were interrupted.

Presently he could think again. Strange how quickly things had happened! He bore these men who had thrashed him no very vivid ill-will. He was bruised and enlightened. He saw with absolute fairness now the reasonableness of his unpopularity. He had behaved like a fool. Disdain, seclusion, are the privilege of the strong. The fallen aristocrat still clinging to his pointless distinction is surely the most pitiful creature of pretence in all this claimant universe. Good heavens! what was there for him to despise in these men?

What a pity he had not appreciated all this better five hours ago!

What would happen at the end of the spell? He could not tell. He could not imagine. He could not imagine the thoughts of these men. He was sensible only of their hostility and utter want of sympathy. Vague possibilities of shame and violence chased one another across his mind. Could he devise some weapon? He recalled his assault upon the hypnotist, but there were no detachable lamps here. He could see nothing that he could catch up in his defence.

For a space he thought of a headlong bolt for the security of the public ways directly the spell was over. Apart from the trivial consideration of his self-respect, he perceived that this would be only a foolish postponement and aggravation of his trouble. He perceived the ferret-faced man and the albino talking together with their eyes towards him. Presently they were talking to the swart man, who stood with his broad back studiously towards Denton.

At last came the end of the second spell. The lender of oil cans stopped his press sharply and turned round, wiping his mouth with the back of his hand. His eyes had the quiet expectation of one who seats himself in a theatre.

Now was the crisis, and all the little nerves of Denton's being seemed leaping and dancing. He had decided to show fight if any fresh indignity was offered him. He stopped his press and turned. With an enormous affectation of ease he walked down the vault and entered the passage of the ash pits, only to discover he had left his jacket—which he had taken off because of the heat of the vault—beside his press. He walked back. He met the albino eye to eye.

He heard the ferret-faced man in expostulation. "'E reely ought, eat it," said the ferret-faced man. "'E did reely."

"No—you leave 'im alone," said the swart man.

Apparently nothing further was to happen to him that day. He passed out to the passage and staircase that led up to the moving platforms of the city.

He emerged on the livid brilliance and streaming movement of the public street. He became acutely aware of his disfigured face, and felt his swelling bruises with a limp, investigatory hand. He went up to the swiftest platform, and seated himself on a Labour Company bench.

He lapsed into a pensive torpor. The immediate dangers and stresses of his position he saw with a sort of static clearness. What would they do to-morrow? He could not tell. What would Elizabeth think of his brutalisation? He could not tell. He was exhausted. He was aroused presently by a hand upon his arm.

He looked up, and saw the swart man seated beside him. He started. Surely he was safe from violence in the public way!

The swart man's face retained no traces of his share in the fight; his expression was free from hostility—seemed almost deferential. "'Scuse me," he said, with a total absence of truculence. Denton realised that no assault was intended. He stared, awaiting the next development.

It was evident the next sentence was premeditated. "Whad—I—was—going—to say—was this," said the swart man, and sought through a silence for further words.

"Whad—I—was—going—to say—was this," he repeated.

Finally he abandoned that gambit. " *You're* aw right," he cried, laying a grimy hand on Denton's grimy sleeve. " *You're* aw right. You're a ge'man. Sorry—very sorry. Wanted to tell you that."

Denton realised that there must exist motives beyond a mere impulse to abominable proceedings in the man. He meditated, and swallowed an unworthy pride.

"I did not mean to be offensive to you," he said, "in refusing that bit of bread."

"Meant it friendly," said the swart man, recalling the scene; "but—in front of that blarsted Whitey and his snigger—Well—I 'ad to scrap."

"Yes," said Denton with sudden fervour: "I was a fool."

"Ah!" said the swart man, with great satisfaction. "*That's* aw right. Shake!"

And Denton shook.

The moving platform was rushing by the establishment of a face moulder, and its lower front was a huge display of mirror, designed to stimulate the thirst for more symmetrical features. Denton caught the reflection of himself and his new friend, enormously twisted and broadened. His own face was puffed, one-sided, and blood-stained; a grin of idiotic and insincere amiability distorted its latitude. A wisp of hair occluded one eye. The trick of the mirror presented the swart man as a gross expansion of lip and nostril. They were linked by shaking hands. Then abruptly this vision passed—to return to memory in the anæmic meditations of a waking dawn.

As he shook, the swart man made some muddled remark, to the effect that he had always known he could get on with a gentleman if one came his way. He prolonged the shaking until Denton, under the influence of the mirror, withdrew his hand. The swart man became pensive, spat impressively on the platform, and resumed his theme.

"Whad I was going to say was this," he said; was gravelled, and shook his head at his foot.

Denton became curious. "Go on," he said, attentive.

The swart man took the plunge. He grasped Denton's arm, became intimate in his attitude. "'Scuse me," he said. "Fact is, you done know '*ow* to scrap. Done know '*ow* to. Why—you done know 'ow to *begin*. You'll get killed if you don't mind. 'Ouldin' your 'ands—*There!*"

He reinforced his statement by objurgation, watching the effect of each oath with a wary eye.

"F'r instance. You're tall. Long arms. You get a longer reach than any one in the brasted vault. Gobblimey, but I thought I'd got a Tough on. 'Stead of which . . . 'Scuse me. I wouldn't have '*it* you if I'd known. It's like fighting sacks. 'Tisn' right. Y'r arms seemed 'ung on 'ooks. Reg'lar —'ung on 'ooks. There!"

Denton stared, and then surprised and hurt his battered chin by a sudden laugh. Bitter tears came into his eyes.

"Go on," he said.

The swart man reverted to his formula. He was good enough to say he liked the look of Denton, thought he had stood up "amazing plucky. On'y pluck ain't no good—ain't no brasted good—if you don't 'old your 'ands.

"Whad I was going to say was this," he said. "Lemme show you 'ow to scrap. Jest lemme. You're ig'nant, you ain't no class; but you might be a very decent scrapper—very decent. Shown. That's what I meant to say."

Denton hesitated. "But—" he said, "I can't give you anything——"

"That's the ge'man all over," said the swart man. "Who arst you to?"

"But your time?"

"If you don't get learnt scrapping you'll get killed—don't you make no bones of that."

Denton thought. "I don't know," he said.

He looked at the face beside him, and all its native coarseness shouted at him. He felt a quick revulsion from his transient friendliness. It seemed to him incredible that it should be necessary for him to be indebted to such a creature.

"The chaps are always scrapping," said the swart man. "Always. And, of course—if one gets waxy and 'its you vital . . .."

"By God!" cried Denton; "I wish one would."

"Of course, if you feel like that——"

"You don't understand."

"P'raps I don't," said the swart man; and lapsed into a fuming silence.

When he spoke again his voice was less friendly, and he prodded Denton by way of address. "Look see!" he said: "are you going to let me show you 'ow to scrap?"

"It's tremendously kind of you," said Denton; "but——"

There was a pause. The swart man rose and bent over Denton.

"Too much ge'man," he said—"eh? I got a red face. . . . By gosh! you are—you *are* a brasted fool!"

He turned away, and instantly Denton realised the truth of this remark.

The swart man descended with dignity to a cross way, and Denton, after a momentary impulse to pursuit, remained on the platform. For a time the things that had happened filled his mind. In one day his graceful system of resignation had been shattered beyond hope. Brute force, the final, the fundamental, had thrust its face through all his explanations and glosses and consolations and grinned enigmatically. Though he was hungry and tired, he did not go on directly to the Labour Hotel, where he would meet Elizabeth. He found he was beginning to think, he wanted very greatly to think; and so, wrapped in a monstrous cloud of meditation, he went the circuit of the city on his moving platform twice. You figure him, tearing through the glaring, thunder-voiced city at a pace of fifty miles an hour, the city upon the planet that spins along its chartless path through space many thousands of miles an hour, funking most terribly, and trying to understand why the heart and will in him should suffer and keep alive.

When at last he came to Elizabeth, she was white and anxious. He might have noted she was in trouble, had it not been for his own pre-occupation. He feared most that she would desire to know every detail of his indignities, that she would be sympathetic or indignant. He saw her eyebrows rise at the sight of him.

"I've had rough handling," he said, and gasped. "It's too fresh—too hot. I don't want to talk about it." He sat down with an unavoidable air of sullenness.

She stared at him in astonishment, and as she read something of the significant hieroglyphic of his battered face, her lips whitened. Her hand —it was thinner now than in the days of their prosperity, and her first finger was a little altered by the metal punching she did—clenched convulsively. "This horrible world!" she said, and said no more.

In these latter days they had become a very silent couple; they said scarcely a word to each other that night, but each followed a private train of thought. In the small hours, as Elizabeth lay awake, Denton started up beside her suddenly—he had been lying as still as a dead man.

"I cannot stand it!" cried Denton. "I *will* not stand it!"

She saw him dimly, sitting up; saw his arm lunge as if in a furious blow at the enshrouding night. Then for a space he was still.

"It is too much—it is more than one can bear!"

She could say nothing. To her, also, it seemed that this was as far as one could go. She waited through a long stillness. She could see that Denton sat with his arms about his knees, his chin almost touching them.

Then he laughed.

"No," he said at last, "I'm going to stand it. That's the peculiar thing. There isn't a grain of suicide in us—not a grain. I suppose all the people with a turn that way have gone. We're going through with it—to the end."

Elizabeth thought grayly, and realised that this also was true.

"We're going through with it. To think of all who have gone through with it: all the generations—endless—endless. Little beasts that snapped and snarled, snapping and snarling, snapping and snarling, generation after generation."

His monotone, ended abruptly, resumed after a vast interval.

"There were ninety thousand years of stone age. A Denton somewhere in all those years. Apostolic succession. The grace of going through. Let me see! Ninety—nine hundred—three nines, twenty-seven—*three thousand* generations of men!—men more or less. And each fought, and was bruised, and shamed, and somehow held his own—going through with it—passing it on. . . . And thousands more to come perhaps—thousands!

"Passing it on. I wonder if they will thank us."

His voice assumed an argumentative note. "If one could find something definite. . . . If one could say, 'This is why—this is why it goes on. . . .'"

He became still, and Elizabeth's eyes slowly separated him from the darkness until at last she could see how he sat with his head resting on his hand. A sense of the enormous remoteness of their minds came to her; that dim suggestion of another being seemed to her a figure of their mutual understanding. What could he be thinking now? What might he not say next? Another age seemed to elapse before he sighed and whispered: "No. I don't understand it. No!" Then a long interval, and he repeated this. But the second time it had the tone almost of a solution.

She became aware that he was preparing to lie down. She marked his movements, perceived with astonishment how he adjusted his pillow with a careful regard to comfort. He lay down with a sigh of contentment almost. His passion had passed. He lay still, and presently his breathing became regular and deep.

But Elizabeth remained with eyes wide open in the darkness, until the clamour of a bell and the sudden brilliance of the electric light warned them that the Labour Company had need of them for yet another day.

That day came a scuffle with the albino Whitey and the little ferret-faced man. Blunt, the swart artist in scrapping, having first let Denton grasp the bearing of his lesson, intervened, not without a certain quality of patronage. "Drop 'is 'air, Whitey, and let the man be," said his gross voice through a shower of indignities. "Can't you see 'e don't know 'ow to scrap?" And Denton, lying shamefully in the dust, realised that he must accept that course of instruction after all.

He made his apology straight and clean. He scrambled up and walked to Blunt. "I was a fool, and you are right," he said. "If it isn't too late . . ."

That night, after the second spell, Denton went with Blunt to certain waste and slime-soaked vaults under the Port of London, to learn the first beginnings of the high art of scrapping as it had been perfected in the great world of the underways: how to hit or kick a man so as to hurt him excruciatingly or make him violently sick, how to hit or kick "vital," how to use glass in one's garments as a club and to spread red ruin with various domestic implements, how to anticipate and demolish your adversary's intentions in other directions; all the pleasant devices, in fact, that had grown up among the disinherited of the great cities of the twentieth and twenty-first centuries, were spread out by a gifted exponent for Denton's learning. Blunt's bashfulness fell from him as the instruction proceeded, and he developed a certain expert dignity, a quality of fatherly consideration. He treated Denton with the utmost consideration, only "flicking him up a bit" now and then, to keep the interest hot, and roaring with laughter at a happy fluke of Denton's that covered his mouth with blood.

"I'm always keerless of my mouth," said Blunt, admitting a weakness. "Always. It don't seem to matter, like, just getting bashed in the mouth —not if your chin's all right. Tastin' blood does me good. Always. But I better not 'it you again."

Denton went home, to fall asleep exhausted and wake in the small hours with aching limbs and all his bruises tingling. Was it worth while that he should go on living? He listened to Elizabeth's breathing, and remembering that he must have awaked her the previous night, he lay very still. He was sick with infinite disgust at the new conditions of his life. He hated it all, hated even the genial savage who had protected him so generously. The monstrous fraud of civilisation glared stark before his eyes; he saw it as a vast lunatic growth, producing a deepening torrent of savagery below, and above ever more flimsy gentility and silly wastefulness. He could see no redeeming reason, no touch of honour, either in the life he had led or in this life to which he had fallen. Civilisation presented itself as some catastrophic product as little concerned with men —save as victims—as a cyclone or a planetary collision. He, and therefore all mankind, seemed living utterly in vain. His mind sought some strange expedients of escape, if not for himself then at least for Elizabeth. But he meant them for himself. What if he hunted up Mwres and told him of their disaster? It came to him as an astonishing thing how utterly Mwres and Bindon had passed out of his range. Where were they? What were they doing? From that he passed to thoughts of utter dishonour. And finally, not arising in any way out of this mental tumult, but ending it as dawn ends the night, came the clear and obvious conclusion of the night before: the conviction that he had to go through with things; that, apart from any remoter view and quite sufficient for all his thought and energy, he had to stand up and fight among his fellows and quit himself like a man.

The second night's instruction was perhaps less dreadful than the first; and the third was even endurable, for Blunt dealt out some praise. The fourth day Denton chanced upon the fact that the ferret-faced man was a coward. There passed a fortnight of smouldering days and feverish instruction at night; Blunt, with many blasphemies, testified that never had he met so apt a pupil; and all night long Denton dreamt of kicks and counters and gouges and cunning tricks. For all that time no further outrages were attempted, for fear of Blunt; and then came the second crisis. Blunt did not come one day—afterwards he admitted his deliberate intention—and through the tedious morning Whitey awaited the interval between the spells with an ostentatious impatience. He knew nothing of the scrapping lessons, and he spent the time in telling Denton and the vault generally of certain disagreeable proceedings he had in mind.

Whitey was not popular, and the vault disgorged to see him haze the new man with only a languid interest. But matters changed when Whitey's attempt to open the proceedings by kicking Denton in the face was met by an excellently executed duck, catch and throw, that completed the flight of Whitey's foot in its orbit and brought Whitey's head into the ash-heap that had once received Denton's. Whitey arose a shade whiter, and now blasphemously bent upon vital injuries. There were indecisive passages, foiled enterprises that deepened Whitey's evidently growing perplexity; and then things developed into a grouping of Denton uppermost with Whitey's throat in his hand, his knee on Whitey's chest, and tearful Whitey with a black face, protruding tongue and broken finger endeavouring to explain the misunderstanding by means of hoarse sounds. Moreover, it was evident that among the bystanders there had never been a more popular person than Denton.

Denton, with proper precaution, released his antagonist and stood up. His blood seemed changed to some sort of fluid fire, his limbs felt light and supernaturally strong. The idea that he was a martyr in the civilisation machine had vanished from his mind. He was a man in a world of men.

The little ferret-faced man was the first in the competition to pat him on the back. The lender of oil cans was a radiant sun of genial congratulation. . . . It seemed incredible to Denton that he had ever thought of despair.

Denton was convinced that not only had he to go through with things, but that he could. He sat on the canvas pallet expounding this new aspect to Elizabeth. One side of his face was bruised. She had not recently fought, she had not been patted on the back, there were no hot bruises upon her face, only a pallor and a new line or so about the mouth. She was taking the woman's share. She looked steadfastly at Denton in his new mood of prophecy. "I feel that there is something," he was saying, "something that goes on, a Being of Life in which we live and move and have our being, something that began fifty—a hundred million years ago, perhaps, that goes on—on: growing, spreading, to things beyond us— things that will justify us all. . . . That will explain and justify my fighting —these bruises, and all the pain of it. It's the chisel—yes, the chisel of the Maker. If only I could make you feel as I feel, if I could make you! You *will*, dear, I know you will."

"No," she said in a low voice. "No, I shall not."

"So I might have thought——"

She shook her head. "No," she said, "I have thought as well. What you say—doesn't convince me."

She looked at his face resolutely. "I hate it," she said, and caught at her breath. "You do not understand, you do not think. There was a time when you said things and I believed them. I am growing wiser. You are a man, you can fight, force your way. You do not mind bruises. You can be coarse and ugly, and still a man. Yes—it makes you. It makes you. You are right. Only a woman is not like that. We are different. We have let ourselves get civilised too soon. This underworld is not for us."

She paused and began again.

"I hate it! I hate this horrible canvas! I hate it more than—more than the worst that can happen. It hurts my fingers to touch it. It is horrible to the skin. And the women I work with day after day! I lie awake at nights and think how I may be growing like them. . . ."

She stopped. "I *am* growing like them," she cried passionately.

Denton stared at her distress. "But—— " he said and stopped.

"You don't understand. What have I? What have I to save me? *You* can fight. Fighting is man's work. But women—women are different. . . . I have thought it all out, I have done nothing but think night and day. Look at the colour of my face! I cannot go on. I cannot endure this life. . . . I cannot endure it."

She stopped. She hesitated.

"You do not know all," she said abruptly, and for an instant her lips had a bitter smile. "I have been asked to leave you."

"Leave me!"

She made no answer save an affirmative movement of the head.

Denton stood up sharply. They stared at one another through a long silence.

Suddenly she turned herself about, and flung face downward upon their canvas bed. She did not sob, she made no sound. She lay still upon her face. After a vast, distressful void her shoulders heaved and she began to weep silently.

"Elizabeth!" he whispered—"Elizabeth!"

Very softly he sat down beside her, bent down, put his arm across her in a doubtful caress, seeking vainly for some clue to this intolerable situation.

"Elizabeth," he whispered in her ear.

She thrust him from her with her hand. "I cannot bear a child to be a slave!" and broke out into loud and bitter weeping.

Denton's face changed—became blank dismay. Presently he slipped from the bed and stood on his feet. All the complacency had vanished from his face, had given place to impotent rage. He began to rave and curse at the intolerable forces which pressed upon him, at all the accidents and hot desires and heedlessness that mock the life of man. His little voice rose in that little room, and he shook his fist, this animalcule of the earth, at all that environed him about, at the millions about him, at his past and future and all the insensate vastness of the overwhelming city.

CHAPTER V

BINDON INTERVENES

IN BINDON'S younger days he had dabbled in speculation and made three brilliant flukes. For the rest of his life he had the wisdom to let gambling alone, and the conceit to believe himself a very clever man. A certain desire for influence and reputation interested him in the business intrigues of the giant city in which his flukes were made. He became at last one of the most influential shareholders in the company that owned the London flying-stages to which the aëroplanes came from all parts of the world. This much for his public activities. In his private life he was a man of pleasure. And this is the story of his heart.

But before proceeding to such depths, one must devote a little time to the exterior of this person. Its physical basis was slender, and short, and dark; and the face, which was fine-featured and assisted by pigments, varied from an insecure self-complacency to an intelligent uneasiness. His face and head had been depilated, according to the cleanly and hygienic fashion of the time, so that the colour and contour of his hair varied with his costume. This he was constantly changing.

At times he would distend himself with pneumatic vestments in the rococo vein. From among the billowy developments of this style, and beneath a translucent and illuminated head-dress, his eye watched jealously for the respect of the less fashionable world. At other times he emphasised his elegant slenderness in close-fitting garments of black satin. For effects of dignity he would assume broad pneumatic shoulders, from which hung a robe of carefully arranged folds of China silk, and a classical Bindon in pink tights was also a transient phenomenon in the eternal pageant of Destiny. In the days when he hoped to marry Elizabeth, he sought to impress and charm her, and at the same time to take off something of his burthen of forty years, by wearing the last fancy of the contemporary buck, a costume of elastic material with distensible warts and horns, changing in colour as he walked, by an ingenious arrangement of versatile chromatophores. And no doubt, if Elizabeth's affection had not been already engaged by the worthless Denton, and if her tastes had not had that odd bias for old-fashioned ways, this extremely *chic* conception would have ravished her. Bindon had consulted Elizabeth's father before presenting himself in this garb—he was one of those men who always invite criticism of their costume—and Mwres had pronounced him all that the heart of woman could desire. But the affair of the hypnotist proved that his knowledge of the heart of woman was incomplete.

Bindon's idea of marrying had been formed some little time before Mwres threw Elizabeth's budding womanhood in his way. It was one of Bindon's most cherished secrets that he had a considerable capacity for a pure and simple life of a grossly sentimental type. The thought imparted a sort of pathetic seriousness to the offensive and quite inconsequent and unmeaning excesses, which he was pleased to regard as dashing wickedness, and which a number of good people also were so unwise as to treat in that desirable manner. As a consequence of these excesses, and perhaps by reason also of an inherited tendency to early decay, his liver became seriously affected, and he suffered increasing inconvenience when travelling by aëroplane. It was during his convalescence from a protracted bilious attack that it occurred to him that in spite of all the terrible fascinations of Vice, if he found a beautiful, gentle, good young woman of a not too violently intellectual type to devote her life to him, he might yet be saved to Goodness, and even rear a spirited family in his likeness to solace his declining years. But like so many experienced men of the world, he doubted if there were any good women. Of such as he had heard tell he was outwardly sceptical and privately much afraid.

When the aspiring Mwres effected his introduction to Elizabeth, it seemed to him that his good fortune was complete. He fell in love with her at once. Of course, he had always been falling in love since he was sixteen, in accordance with the extremely varied recipes to be found in the accumulated literature of many centuries. But this was different. This was real love. It seemed to him to call forth all the lurking goodness in his nature. He felt that for her sake he could give up a way of life that had already produced the gravest lesions on his liver and nervous system. His imagination presented him with idyllic pictures of the life of the reformed rake. He would never be sentimental with her, or silly; but always a little cynical and bitter, as became the past. Yet he was sure she would have an intuition of his real greatness and goodness. And in due course he would confess things to her, pour his version of what he regarded as his wickedness—showing what a complex of Goethe, and Benvenuto Cellini, and Shelley, and all those other chaps he really was—into her shocked, very beautiful, and no doubt sympathetic ear. And preparatory to these things he wooed her with infinite subtlety and respect. And the reserve with which Elizabeth treated him seemed nothing more nor less than an exquisite modesty touched and enhanced by an equally exquisite lack of ideas.

Bindon knew nothing of her wandering affections, nor of the attempt made by Mwres to utilise hypnotism as a corrective to this digression of her heart; he conceived he was on the best of terms with Elizabeth, and had made her quite successfully various significant presents of jewellery and the more virtuous cosmetics, when her elopement with Denton threw the world out of gear for him. His first aspect of the matter was rage begotten of wounded vanity, and as Mwres was the most convenient person, he vented the first brunt of it upon him.

He went immediately and insulted the desolate father grossly, and then spent an active and determined day going to and fro about the city and interviewing people in a consistent and partly-successful attempt to ruin that matrimonial speculator. The effectual nature of these activities gave him a temporary exhilaration, and he went to the dining-place he had frequented in his wicked days in a devil-may-care frame of mind, and dined altogether too amply and cheerfully with two other golden youths in the early forties. He threw up the game; no woman was worth being good for, and he astonished even himself by the strain of witty cynicism he developed. One of the other desperate blades, warmed with wine, made a facetious allusion to his disappointment, but at the time this did not seem unpleasant.

The next morning found his liver and temper inflamed. He kicked his phonographic news machine to pieces, dismissed his valet, and resolved that he would perpetrate a terrible revenge upon Elizabeth. Or Denton. Or somebody. But anyhow, it was to be a terrible revenge; and the friend who had made fun at him should no longer see him in the light of a foolish girl's victim. He knew something of the little property that was due to her, and that this would be the only support of the young couple until Mwres should relent. If Mwres did not relent, and if unpropitious things should happen to the affair in which Elizabeth's expectations lay, they would come upon evil times and be sufficiently amenable to temptation of a sinister sort. Bindon's imagination, abandoning its beautiful idealism altogether, expanded the idea of temptation of a sinister sort. He figured himself as the implacable, the intricate and powerful man of wealth pursuing this maiden who had scorned him. And suddenly her image came upon his mind vivid and dominant, and for the first time in his life Bindon realised something of the real power of passion.

His imagination stood aside like a respectful footman who has done his work in ushering in the emotion.

"My God!" cried Bindon: "I will have her! If I have to kill myself to get her! And that other fellow——!"

After an interview with his medical man and a penance for his overnight excesses in the form of bitter drugs, a mitigated but absolutely resolute Bindon sought out Mwres. Mwres he found properly smashed, and impoverished and humble, in a mood of frantic self-preservation, ready to sell himself body and soul, much more any interest in a disobedient daughter, to recover his lost position in the world. In the reasonable discussion that followed, it was agreed that these misguided young people should be left to sink into distress, or possibly even assisted towards that improving discipline by Bindon's financial influence.

"And then?" said Mwres.

"They will come to the Labour Company," said Bindon. "They will wear the blue canvas."

"And then?"

"She will divorce him," he said, and sat for a moment intent upon that prospect. For in those days the austere limitations of divorce of Victorian times were extraordinarily relaxed, and a couple might separate on a hundred different scores.

Then suddenly Bindon astonished himself and Mwres by jumping to his feet. "She *shall* divorce him!" he cried. "I will have it so—I will work it so. By God! it shall be so. He shall be disgraced, so that she must. He shall be smashed and pulverised."

The idea of smashing and pulverising inflamed him further. He began a Jovian pacing up and down the little office. "I will have her," he cried. "I *will* have her! Heaven and Hell shall not save her from me!" His passion evaporated in its expression, and left him at the end simply histrionic. He struck an attitude and ignored with heroic determination a sharp twinge of pain about the diaphragm. And Mwres sat with his pneumatic cap deflated and himself very visibly impressed.

And so, with a fair persistency, Bindon set himself to the work of being Elizabeth's malignant providence, using with ingenious dexterity every particle of advantage wealth in those days gave a man over his fellow-creatures. A resort to the consolations of religion hindered these operations not at all. He would go and talk with an interesting, experienced and sympathetic Father of the Huysmanite sect of the Isis cult, about all the irrational little proceedings he was pleased to regard as his heaven dismaying wickedness, and the interesting, experienced and sympathetic Father representing Heaven dismayed, would with a pleasing affectation of horror, suggest simple and easy penances, and recommend a monastic foundation that was airy, cool, hygienic, and not vulgarised, for viscerally disordered penitent sinners of the refined and wealthy type. And

after these excursions, Bindon would come back to London quite active
and passionate again. He would machinate with really considerable
energy, and repair to a certain gallery high above the street of moving
ways, from which he could view the entrance to the barrack of the
Labour Company in the ward which sheltered Denton and Elizabeth.
And at last one day he saw Elizabeth go in, and thereby his passion was
renewed.

So in the fullness of time the complicated devices of Bindon ripened,
and he could go to Mwres and tell him that the young people were near
despair.

"It's time for you," he said, "to let your parental affections have play.
She's been in blue canvas some months, and they've been cooped together in one of those Labour dens, and the little girl is dead. She knows
now what his manhood is worth to her, by way of protection, poor girl.
She'll see things now in a clearer light. You go to her—I don't want to
appear in this affair yet—and point out to her how necessary it is that
she should get a divorce from him. . . ."

"She's obstinate," said Mwres doubtfully.

"Spirit!" said Bindon. "She's a wonderful girl—a wonderful girl!"

"She'll refuse."

"Of course she will. But leave it open to her. Leave it open to her. And
some day—in that stuffy den, in that irksome, toilsome life they can't
help it—*they'll have a quarrel*. And then——"

Mwres meditated over the matter, and did as he was told.

Then Bindon, as he had arranged with his spiritual adviser, went into
retreat. The retreat of the Huysmanite sect was a beautiful place, with
the sweetest air in London, lit by natural sunlight, and with restful quad-
rangles of real grass open to the sky, where at the same time the penitent
man of pleasure might enjoy all the pleasures of loafing and all the satisfaction of distinguished austerity. And, save for participation in the
simple and wholesome dietary of the place and in certain magnificent
chants, Bindon spent all his time in meditation upon the theme of Elizabeth, and the extreme purification his soul had undergone since he first
saw her, and whether he would be able to get a dispensation to marry her
from the experienced and sympathetic Father in spite of the approaching
"sin" of her divorce; and then . . . Bindon would lean against a pillar of
the quadrangle and lapse into reveries on the superiority of virtuous love
to any other form of indulgence. A curious feeling in his back and chest
that was trying to attract his attention, a disposition to be hot or shiver,
a general sense of ill-health and cutaneous discomfort he did his best to
ignore. All that of course belonged to the old life that he was shaking off.

When he came out of retreat he went at once to Mwres to ask for news of Elizabeth. Mwres was clearly under the impression that he was an exemplary father, profoundly touched about the heart by his child's unhappiness. "She was pale," he said, greatly moved; "She was pale. When I asked her to come away and leave him—and be happy—she put her head down upon the table"—Mwres sniffed—"and cried."

His agitation was so great that he could say no more.

"Ah!" said Bindon, respecting this manly grief. "Oh!" said Bindon quite suddenly, with his hand to his side.

Mwres looked up sharply out of the pit of his sorrows, startled. "What's the matter?" he asked, visibly concerned.

"A most violent pain. Excuse me! You were telling me about Elizabeth."

And Mwres, after a decent solicitude for Bindon's pain, proceeded with his report. It was even unexpectedly hopeful. Elizabeth, in her first emotion at discovering that her father had not absolutely deserted her, had been frank with him about her sorrows and disgusts.

"Yes," said Bindon, magnificently, "I shall have her yet." And then that novel pain twitched him for the second time.

For these lower pains the priest was comparatively ineffectual, inclining rather to regard the body and them as mental illusions amenable to contemplation; so Bindon took it to a man of a class he loathed, a medical man of extraordinary repute and incivility. "We must go all over you," said the medical man, and did so with the most disgusting frankness. "Did you ever bring any children into the world?" asked this gross materialist among other impertinent questions.

"Not that I know of," said Bindon, too amazed to stand upon his dignity.

"Ah!" said the medical man, and proceeded with his punching and sounding. Medical science in those days was just reaching the beginnings of precision. "You'd better go right away," said the medical man, "and make the Euthanasia. The sooner the better."

Bindon gasped. He had been trying not to understand the technical explanations and anticipations in which the medical man had indulged.

"I say!" he said. "But do you mean to say . . . Your science . . ."

"Nothing," said the medical man. "A few opiates. The thing is your own doing, you know, to a certain extent."

"I was sorely tempted in my youth."

"It's not that so much. But you come of a bad stock. Even if you'd have taken precautions you'd have had bad times to wind up with. The mistake was getting born. The indiscretions of the parents. And you've shirked exercise, and so forth."

"I had no one to advise me."

"Medical men are always willing."

"I was a spirited young fellow."

"We won't argue; the mischief's done now. You've lived. We can't start you again. You ought never to have started at all. Frankly—the Euthanasia!"

Bindon hated him in silence for a space. Every word of this brutal expert jarred upon his refinements. He was so gross, so impermeable to all the subtler issues of being. But it is no good picking a quarrel with a doctor. "My religious beliefs," he said, "I don't approve of suicide."

"You've been doing it all your life."

"Well, anyhow, I've come to take a serious view of life now."

"You're bound to, if you go on living. You'll hurt. But for practical purposes it's late. However, if you mean to do that—perhaps I'd better mix you a little something. You'll hurt a great deal. These little twinges . . ."

"Twinges!"

"Mere preliminary notices."

"How long can I go on? I mean, before I hurt—really."

"You'll get it hot soon. Perhaps three days."

Bindon tried to argue for an extension of time, and in the midst of his pleading gasped, put his hand to his side. Suddenly the extraordinary pathos of his life came to him clear and vivid. "It's hard," he said. "It's infernally hard! I've been no man's enemy but my own. I've always treated everybody quite fairly."

The medical man stared at him without any sympathy for some seconds. He was reflecting how excellent it was that there were no more Bindons to carry on that line of pathos. He felt quite optimistic. Then he turned to his telephone and ordered up a prescription from the Central Pharmacy.

He was interrupted by a voice behind him. "By God!" cried Bindon; "I'll have her yet."

The physician stared over his shoulder at Bindon's expression, and then altered the prescription.

So soon as this painful interview was over, Bindon gave way to rage. He settled that the medical man was not only an unsympathetic brute and wanting in the first beginnings of a gentleman, but also highly incompetent; and he went off to four other practitioners in succession, with a view to the establishment of this intuition. But to guard against surprises he kept that little prescription in his pocket. With each he began by expressing his grave doubts of the first doctor's intelligence, honesty and professional knowledge, and then stated his symptoms, suppressing only a few more material facts in each case. These were always subsequently elicited by the doctor. In spite of the welcome depreciation of another practitioner, none of these eminent specialists would give Bindon any hope of eluding the anguish and helplessness that loomed now close upon him. To the last of them he unburthened his mind of an accumulated disgust with medical science. "After centuries and centuries," he exclaimed hotly; "and you can do nothing—except admit your helplessness. I say, 'save me'—and what do you do?"

"No doubt it's hard on you," said the doctor. "But you should have taken precautions."

"How was I to know?"

"It wasn't our place to run after you," said the medical man, picking a thread of cotton from his purple sleeve. "Why should we save *you* in particular? You see—from one point of view—people with imaginations and passions like yours have to go—they have to go."

"Go?"

"Die out. It's an eddy."

He was a young man with a serene face. He smiled at Bindon. "We get on with research, you know; we give advice when people have the sense to ask for it. And we bide our time."

"Bide your time?"

"We hardly know enough yet to take over the management, you know."

"The management?"

"You needn't be anxious. Science is young yet. It's got to keep on growing for a few generations. We know enough now to know we don't know enough yet. . . . But the time is coming, all the same. *You* won't see the time. But, between ourselves, you rich men and party bosses, with your natural play of the passions and patriotism and religion and so forth, have made rather a mess of things; haven't you? These Underways! And all that sort of thing. Some of us have a sort of fancy that in time we may know enough to take over a little more than the ventilation and drains. Knowledge keeps on piling up, you know. It keeps on growing. And there's not the slightest hurry for a generation or so. Some day —some day, men will live in a different way." He looked at Bindon and meditated. "There'll be a lot of dying out before that day can come."

Bindon attempted to point out to this young man how silly and irrelevant such talk was to a sick man like himself, how impertinent and uncivil it was to him, an older man occupying a position in the official world of extraordinary power and influence. He insisted that a doctor was paid to cure people—he laid great stress on "*paid*"—and had no business to glance even for a moment at "those other questions." "But we do," said the young man, insisting upon facts, and Bindon lost his temper.

His indignation carried him home. That these incompetent imposters, who were unable to save the life of a really influential man like himself, should dream of some day robbing the legitimate property owners of social control, of inflicting one knew not what tyranny upon the world. Curse science! He fumed over the intolerable prospect for some time, and then the pain returned, and he recalled the made-up prescription of the first doctor, still happily in his pocket. He took a dose forthwith.

It calmed and soothed him greatly, and he could sit down in his most comfortable chair beside his library (of phonographic records), and think over the altered aspect of affairs. His indignation passed, his anger and his passion crumbled under the subtle attack of that prescription, pathos became his sole ruler. He stared about him, at his magnificent and voluptuously appointed apartment, at his statuary and discreetly veiled pictures, and all the evidences of a cultivated and elegant wickedness; he touched a stud and the sad pipings of Tristan's shepherd filled the air. His eye wandered from one object to another. They were costly and gross and florid—but they were his. They presented in concrete form his ideals, his conceptions of beauty and desire, his idea of all that is precious in life. And now—he must leave it all like a common man. He was, he felt, a slender and delicate flame, burning out. So must all life flame up and pass, he thought. His eyes filled with tears.

Then it came into his head that he was alone. Nobody cared for him, nobody needed him! at any moment he might begin to hurt vividly. He might even howl. Nobody would mind. According to all the doctors he would have excellent reason for howling in a day or so. It recalled what his spiritual adviser had said of the decline of faith and fidelity, the degeneration of the age. He beheld himself as a pathetic proof of this; he, the subtle, able, important, voluptuous, cynical, complex Bindon, possibly howling, and not one faithful simple creature in all the world to howl in sympathy. Not one faithful simple soul was there—no shepherd to pipe to him! Had all such faithful simple creatures vanished from this harsh and urgent earth? He wondered whether the horrid vulgar crowd that perpetually went about the city could possibly know what he thought of them. If they did he felt sure *some* would try to earn a better opinion. Surely the world went from bad to worse. It was becoming impossible for Bindons. Perhaps some day . . . He was quite sure that the one thing he had needed in life was sympathy. For a time he regretted that he left no sonnets—no enigmatical pictures or something of that sort behind him to carry on his being until at last the sympathetic mind should come . . .

It seemed incredible to him that this that came was extinction. Yet his sympathetic spiritual guide was in this matter annoyingly figurative and vague. Curse science! It had undermined all faith—all hope. To go out, to vanish from theatre and street, from office and dining-place, from the dear eyes of womankind. And not to be missed! On the whole to leave the world happier!

He reflected that he had never worn his heart upon his sleeve. Had he after all been *too* unsympathetic? Few people could suspect how subtly profound he really was beneath the mask of that cynical gaiety of his. They would not understand the loss they had suffered. Elizabeth, for example, had not suspected. . . .

He had reserved that. His thoughts having come to Elizabeth gravitated about her for some time. How *little* Elizabeth understood him!

That thought became intolerable. Before all other things he must set that right. He realised that there was still something for him to do in life, his struggle against Elizabeth was even yet not over. He could never overcome her now, as he had hoped and prayed. But he might still impress her!

From that idea he expanded. He might impress her profoundly—he might impress her so that she should for evermore regret her treatment of him. The thing that she must realise before everything else was his magnanimity. His magnanimity! Yes! he had loved her with amazing greatness of heart. He had not seen it so clearly before—but of course he was going to leave her all his property. He saw it instantly, as a thing determined and inevitable. She would think how good he was, how spaciously generous; surrounded by all that makes life tolerable from his hand, she would recall with infinite regret her scorn and coldness. And when she sought expression for that regret, she would find that occasion gone forever, she should be met by a locked door, by a disdainful stillness, by a white dead face. He closed his eyes and remained for a space imagining himself that white dead face.

From that he passed to other aspects of the matter, but his determination was assured. He meditated elaborately before he took action, for the drug he had taken inclined him to a lethargic and dignified melancholy. In certain respects he modified details. If he left all his property to Elizabeth it would include the voluptuously appointed room he occupied, and for many reasons he did not care to leave that to her. On the other hand, it had to be left to some one. In his clogged condition this worried him extremely.

In the end he decided to leave it to the sympathetic exponent of the fashionable religious cult, whose conversation had been so pleasing in the past. "*He* will understand," said Bindon with a sentimental sigh. "He knows what Evil means—he understands something of the Stupendous Fascination of the Sphinx of Sin. Yes—he will understand." By that phrase it was that Bindon was pleased to dignify certain unhealthy and undignified departures from sane conduct to which a misguided vanity and an ill-controlled curiosity had led him. He sat for a space thinking how very Hellenic and Italian and Neronic, and all those things, he had been. Even now—might one not try a sonnet? A penetrating voice to echo down the ages, sensuous, sinister, and sad. For a space he forgot Elizabeth. In the course of half an hour he spoilt three phonographic coils, got a headache, took a second dose to calm himself, and reverted to magnanimity and his former design.

At last he faced the unpalatable problem of Denton. It needed all his newborn magnanimity before he could swallow the thought of Denton; but at last this greatly misunderstood man, assisted by his sedative and the near approach of death, effected even that. If he was at all exclusive about Denton, if he should display the slightest distrust, if he attempted any specific exclusion of that young man, she might—*misunderstand*. Yes—she should have her Denton still. His magnanimity must go even to that. He tried to think only of Elizabeth in the matter.

He rose with a sigh, and limped across to the telephonic apparatus that communicated with his solicitor. In ten minutes a will duly attested and with its proper thumb-mark signature lay in the solicitor's office three miles away. And then for a space Bindon sat very still.

Suddenly he started out of a vague reverie and pressed an investigatory hand to his side.

Then he jumped eagerly to his feet and rushed to the telephone. The Euthanasia Company had rarely been called by a client in a greater hurry.

So it came at last that Denton and his Elizabeth, against all hope, returned unseparated from the labour servitude to which they had fallen. Elizabeth came out from her cramped subterranean den of metal-beaters and all the sordid circumstances of blue canvas, as one comes out of a nightmare. Back towards the sunlight their fortune took them; once the bequest was known to them, the bare thought of another day's hammering became intolerable. They went up long lifts and stairs to levels that they had not seen since the days of their disaster. At first she was full of this sensation of escape; even to think of the underways was intolerable; only after many months could she begin to recall with sympathy the faded women who were still below there, murmuring scandals and reminiscences and folly, and tapping away their lives.

Her choice of the apartments they presently took expressed the vehemence of her release. They were rooms upon the very verge of the city; they had a roof space and a balcony upon the city wall, wide open to the sun and wind, the country and the sky.

And in that balcony comes the last scene in this story. It was a summer sunsetting, and the hills of Surrey were very blue and clear. Denton leant upon the balcony regarding them, and Elizabeth sat by his side. Very wide and spacious was the view, for their balcony hung five hundred feet above the ancient level of the ground. The oblongs of the Food Company, broken here and there by the ruins—grotesque little holes and sheds— of the ancient suburbs, and intersected by shining streams of sewage, passed at last into a remote diapering at the foot of the distant hills. There once had been the squatting-place of the children of Uya. On those further slopes gaunt machines of unknown import worked slackly at the end of their spell, and the hill crest was set with stagnant wind vanes. Along the great south road the Labour Company's field workers in huge wheeled mechanical vehicles, were hurrying back to their meals, their last spell finished. And through the air a dozen little private aëropiles sailed down towards the city. Familiar scene as it was to the eyes of Denton and Elizabeth, it would have filled the minds of their ancestors with incredulous amazement. Denton's thoughts fluttered towards the future in a vain attempt at what that scene might be in another two hundred years, and, recoiling, turned towards the past.

He shared something of the growing knowledge of the time; he could picture the quaint smoke-grimed Victorian city with its narrow little roads of beaten earth, its wide common-land, ill-organised, ill-built suburbs, and irregular enclosures; the old countryside of the Stuart times, with its little villages and its petty London; the England of the monasteries, the far older England of the Roman dominion, and then before that a wild country with here and there the huts of some warring tribe. These huts must have come and gone and come again through a space of years that made the Roman camp and villa seem but yesterday; and before those years, before even the huts, there had been men in the valley. Even then —so recent had it all been when one judged it by the standards of geo- logical time—this valley had been here; and those hills yonder, higher, perhaps, and snow-tipped, had still been yonder hills, and the Thames had flowed down from the Cotswolds to the sea. But the men had been but the shapes of men, creatures of darkness and ignorance, victims of beasts and floods, storms and pestilence and incessant hunger. They had held a precarious foothold amidst bears and lions and all the monstrous violence of the past. Already some at least of these enemies were over- come. . . .

For a time Denton pursued the thoughts of this spacious vision, trying in obedience to his instinct to find his place and proportion in the scheme.

"It has been chance," he said, "it has been luck. We have come through. It happens we have come through. Not by any strength of our own. . . .

"And yet . . . No. I don't know."

He was silent for a long time before he spoke again.

"After all—there is a long time yet. There have scarcely been men for twenty thousand years—and there has been life for twenty millions. And what are generations? What are generations? It is enormous, and we are so little. Yet we know—we feel. We are not dumb atoms, we are part of it—part of it—to the limits of our strength and will. Even to die is part of it. Whether we die or live, we are in the making. . . .

"As time goes on—*perhaps*—men will be wiser. . . . Wiser. . . .

"Will they ever understand?"

He became silent again. Elizabeth said nothing to these things, but she regarded his dreaming face with infinite affection. Her mind was not very active that evening. A great contentment possessed her. After a time she laid a gentle hand on his beside her. He fondled it softly, still looking out upon the spacious gold-woven view. So they sat as the sun went down. Until presently Elizabeth shivered.

Denton recalled himself abruptly from these spacious issues of his leisure, and went in to fetch her a shawl.

THE
TIME MACHINE

By

H. G. WELLS

CONTENTS

INTRODUCTION

THE TIME TRAVELLER (for so it will be convenient to speak of him) was expounding a recondite matter to us. His grey eyes shone and twinkled, and his usually pale face was flushed and animated. The fire burnt brightly, and the soft radiance of the incandescent lights in the lilies of silver caught the bubbles that flashed and passed in our glasses. Our chairs, being his patents, embraced and caressed us rather than submitted to be sat upon, and there was that luxurious after-dinner atmosphere, when thought runs gracefully free of the trammels of precision. And he put it to us in this way—marking the points with a lean forefinger —as we sat and lazily admired his earnestness over this new paradox (as we thought it) and his fecundity.

"You must follow me carefully. I shall have to controvert one or two ideas that are almost universally accepted. The geometry, for instance, they taught you at school is founded on a misconception."

"Is not that rather a large thing to expect us to begin upon?" said Filby, an argumentative person with red hair.

"I do not mean to ask you to accept anything without reasonable ground for it. You will soon admit as much as I need from you. You know of course that a mathematical line, a line of thickness *nil*, has no real existence. They taught you that? Neither has a mathematical plane. These things are mere abstractions."

"That is all right," said the Psychologist.

"Nor, having only length, breadth, and thickness, can a cube have a real existence."

"There I object," said Filby. "Of course a solid body may exist. All real things——"

"So most people think. But wait a moment. Can an *instantaneous* cube exist?"

"Don't follow you," said Filby.

"Can a cube that does not last for any time at all, have a real existence?"

Filby became pensive. "Clearly," the Time Traveller proceeded, "any real body must have extension in *four* directions: it must have Length, Breadth, Thickness, and—Duration. But through a natural infirmity of the flesh, which I will explain to you in a moment, we incline to overlook this fact. There are really four dimensions, three which we call the three planes of Space, and a fourth, Time. There is, however, a tendency to draw an unreal distinction between the former three dimensions and the latter, because it happens that our consciousness moves intermittently in one direction along the latter from the beginning to the end of our lives."

"That," said a very young man, making spasmodic efforts to relight his cigar over the lamp; "that . . . very clear indeed."

"Now, it is very remarkable that this is so extensively overlooked," continued the Time Traveller, with a slight accession of cheerfulness. "Really this is what is meant by the Fourth Dimension, though some people who talk about the Fourth Dimension do not know they mean it. It is only another way of looking at Time. *There is no difference between Time and any of the three dimensions of Space except that our consciousness moves along it.* But some foolish people have got hold of the wrong side of that idea. You have all heard what they have to say about this Fourth Dimension?"

"*I* have not," said the Provincial Mayor.

"It is simply this. That Space, as our mathematicians have it, is spoken of as having three dimensions, which one may call Length, Breadth, and Thickness, and is always definable by reference to three planes, each at right angles to the others. But some philosophical people have been asking why *three* dimensions particularly—why not another direction at right angles to the other three?—and have even tried to construct a Four-Dimensional geometry. Professor Simon Newcomb was expounding this to the New York Mathematical Society only a month or so ago. You know how on a flat surface, which has only two dimensions, we can represent a figure of a three-dimensional solid, and similarly they think that by models of three dimensions they could represent one of four—if they could master the perspective of the thing. See?"

"I think so," murmured the Provincial Mayor; and, knitting his brows, he lapsed into an introspective state, his lips moving as one who repeats mystic words. "Yes, I think I see it now," he said after some time, brightening in a quite transitory manner.

"Well, I do not mind telling you I have been at work upon this geometry of Four Dimensions for some time. Some of my results are curious. For instance, here is a portrait of a man at eight years old, another at fifteen, another at seventeen, another at twenty-three, and so on. All these are evidently sections, as it were, Three-Dimensional representations of his Four-Dimensioned being, which is a fixed and unalterable thing."

"Scientific people," proceeded the Time Traveller, after the pause required for the proper assimilation of this, "know very well that Time is only a kind of Space. Here is a popular scientific diagram, a weather record. This line I trace with my finger shows the movement of the barometer. Yesterday it was so high, yesterday night it fell, then this morning it rose again, and so gently upward to here. Surely the mercury did not trace this line in any of the dimensions of Space generally recognized? But certainly it traced such a line, and that line, therefore, we must conclude was along the Time-Dimension."

"But," said the Medical Man, staring hard at a coal in the fire, "if Time is really only a fourth dimension of Space, why is it, and why has it always been, regarded as something different? And why cannot we move about in Time as we move about in the other dimensions of Space?"

The Time Traveller smiled. "Are you so sure we can move freely in Space? Right and left we can go, backward and forward freely enough, and men always have done so. I admit we move freely in two dimensions. But how about up and down? Gravitation limits us there."

"Not exactly," said the Medical Man. "There are balloons."

"But before the balloons, save for spasmodic jumping and the inequalities of the surface, man had no freedom of vertical movement."

"Still they could move a little up and down," said the Medical Man.

"Easier, far easier down than up."

"And you cannot move at all in Time, you cannot get away from the present moment."

"My dear sir, that is just where you are wrong. That is just where the whole world has gone wrong. We are always getting away from the present moment. Our mental existences, which are immaterial and have no dimensions, are passing along the Time-Dimension with a uniform velocity from the cradle to the grave. Just as we should travel *down* if we began our existence fifty miles above the earth's surface."

"But the great difficulty is this," interrupted the Psychologist. "You *can* move about in all directions of Space, but you cannot move about in Time."

"That is the germ of my great discovery. But you are wrong to say that we cannot move about in Time. For instance, if I am recalling an incident very vividly I go back to the instant of its occurrence: I become absent-minded, as you say. I jump back for a moment. Of course we have no means of staying back for any length of Time, any more than a savage or an animal has of staying six feet above the ground. But a civilized man is better off than the savage in this respect. He can go up against gravitaɔn in a balloon, and why should he not hope that ultimately he may be a le to stop or accelerate his drift along the Time-Dimension, or even tuın about and travel the other way?"

"Oh, *this*," began Filby, "is all——"

"Why not?" said the Time Traveller.

"It's against reason," said Filby.

"What reason?" said the Time Traveller.

"You can show black is white by argument," said Filby, "but you will never convince me."

"Possibly not," said the Time Traveller. "But now you begin to see the object of my investigations into the geometry of Four Dimensions. Long ago I had a vague inkling of a machine——"

"To travel through Time!" exclaimed the Very Young Man.

"That shall travel indifferently in any direction of Space and Time, as the driver determines."

Filby contented himself with laughter.

"But I have experimental verification," said the Time Traveller.

"It would be remarkably convenient for the historian," the Psychologist suggested. "One might travel back and verify the accepted account of the Battle of Hastings, for instance!"

"Don't you think you would attract attention?" said the Medical Man. "Our ancestors had no great tolerance for anachronisms."

"One might get one's Greek from the very lips of Homer and Plato," the Very Young Man thought.

"In which case they would certainly plough you for the Little-go. The German scholars have improved Greek so much."

"Then there is the future," said the Very Young Man. "Just think! One might invest all one's money, leave it to accumulate at interest, and hurry on ahead!"

"To discover a society," said I, "erected on a strictly communistic basis."

"Of all the wild extravagant theories!" began the Psychologist.

"Yes, so it seemed to me, and so I never talked of it until——"

"Experimental verification!" cried I. "You are going to verify *that*?"

"The experiment!" cried Filby, who was getting brain-weary.

"Let's see your experiment anyhow," said the Psychologist, "though it's all humbug, you know."

The Time Traveller smiled round at us. Then, still smiling faintly, and with his hands deep in his trousers pockets, he walked slowly out of the room, and we heard his slippers shuffling down the long passage to his laboratory.

The Psychologist looked at us. "I wonder what he's got?"

"Some sleight-of-hand trick or other," said the Medical Man, and Filby tried to tell us about a conjuror he had seen at Burslem, but before he had finished his preface the Time Traveller came back, and Filby's anecdote collapsed.

———————

CHAPTER II

THE MACHINE

THE THING the Time Traveller held in his hand was a glittering metallic framework, scarcely larger than a small clock, and very delicately made. There was ivory in it, and some transparent crystalline substance. And now I must be explicit, for this that follows—unless his explanation is to be accepted—is an absolutely unaccountable thing. He took one of the small octagonal tables that were scattered about the room, and set it in front of the fire, with two legs on the hearthrug. On this table he placed the mechanism. Then he drew up a chair, and sat down. The only other object on the table was a small shaded lamp, the bright light of which fell full upon the model. There were also perhaps a dozen candles about, two in brass candlesticks upon the mantel and several in sconces, so that the room was brilliantly illuminated. I sat in a low arm-chair nearest the fire, and I drew this forward so as to be almost between the Time Traveller and the fireplace. Filby sat behind him, looking over his shoulder. The Medical Man and the Provincial Mayor watched him in profile from the right, the Psychologist from the left. The Very Young Man stood behind the Psychologist. We were all on the alert. It appears incredible to me that any kind of trick, however subtly conceived and however adroitly done, could have been played upon us under these conditions.

The Time Traveller looked at us, and then at the mechanism. "Well?" said the Psychologist.

"This little affair," said the Time Traveller, resting his elbows upon the table and pressing his hands together above the apparatus, "is only a model. It is my plan for a machine to travel through time. You will notice that it looks singularly askew, and that there is an odd twinkling appearance about this bar, as though it was in some way unreal." He pointed to the part with his finger. "Also, here is one little white lever, and here is another."

The Medical Man got up out of his chair and peered into the thing. "It's beautifully made," he said.

"It took two years to make," retorted the Time Traveller. Then, when we had all imitated the action of the Medical Man, he said: "Now I want you clearly to understand that this lever, being pressed over, sends the machine gliding into the future, and this other reverses the motion. This saddle represents the seat of a time traveller. Presently I am going to press the lever, and off the machine will go. It will vanish, pass into future time, and disappear. Have a good look at the thing. Look at the table too, and satisfy yourselves there is no trickery. I don't want to waste this model, and then be told I'm a quack."

There was a minute's pause perhaps. The Psychologist seemed about to speak to me, but changed his mind. Then the Time Traveller put forth his finger towards the lever. "No," he said suddenly. "Lend me your hand." And turning to the Psychologist, he took that individual's hand in his own and told him to put out his forefinger. So that it was the Psychologist himself who sent forth the model Time Machine on its interminable voyage. We all saw the lever turn. I am absolutely certain there was no trickery. There was a breath of wind, and the lamp flame jumped. One of the candles on the mantel was blown out, and the little machine suddenly swung round, became indistinct, was seen as a ghost for a second perhaps, as an eddy of faintly glittering brass and ivory; and it was gone—vanished! Save for the lamp the table was bare.

Every one was silent for a minute. Then Filby said he was damned.

The Psychologist recovered from his stupor, and suddenly looked under the table. At that the Time Traveller laughed cheerfully. "Well?" he said, with a reminiscence of the Psychologist. Then, getting up, he went to the tobacco jar on the mantel, and with his back to us began to fill his pipe.

We stared at each other. "Look here," said the Medical Man, "are you in earnest about this? Do you seriously believe that that machine has travelled into time?"

"Certainly," said the Time Traveller, stooping to light a spill at the fire. Then he turned, lighting his pipe, to look at the Psychologist's face. (The Psychologist, to show that he was not unhinged, helped himself to a cigar and tried to light it uncut.) "What is more, I have a big machine nearly finished in there"—he indicated the laboratory—"and when that is put together I mean to have a journey on my own account."

"You mean to say that that machine has travelled into the future?" said Filby.

"Into the future or the past—I don't, for certain, know which."

After an interval the Psychologist had an inspiration. "It must have gone into the past if it has gone anywhere," he said.

"Why?" said the Time Traveller.

"Because I presume that it has not moved in space, and if it travelled into the future it would still be here all this time, since it must have travelled through this time."

"But," said I, "if it travelled into the past it would have been visible when we came first into this room; and last Thursday when we were here; and the Thursday before that; and so forth!"

"Serious objections," remarked the Provincial Mayor, with an air of impartiality, turning towards the Time Traveller.

"Not a bit," said the Time Traveller, and, to the Psychologist: "You think. *You* can explain that. It's presentation below the threshold, you know, diluted presentation."

"Of course," said the Psychologist, and reassured us. "That's a simple point in psychology. I should have thought of it. It's plain enough, and helps the paradox delightfully. We cannot see it, nor can we appreciate this machine, any more than we can the spoke of a wheel spinning, or a bullet flying through the air. If it is travelling through time fifty times or a hundred times faster than we are, if it gets through a minute while we get through a second, the impression it creates will of course be only one-fiftieth or one-hundredth of what it would make if it were not travelling in time. That's plain enough." He passed his hand through the space in which the machine had been. "You see?" he said, laughing.

We sat and stared at the vacant table for a minute or so. Then the Time Traveller asked us what we thought of it all.

"It sounds plausible enough to-night," said the Medical Man; "but wait until to-morrow. Wait for the common-sense of the morning."

"Would you like to see the Time Machine itself?" asked the Time Traveller. And therewith, taking the lamp in his hand, he led the way down the long, draughty corridor to his laboratory. I remember vividly the flickering light, his queer, broad head in silhouette, the dance of the shadows, how we all followed him, puzzled but incredulous, and how there in the laboratory we beheld a larger edition of the little mechanism which we had seen vanish from before our eyes. Parts were of nickel, parts of ivory, parts had certainly been filed or sawn out of rock crystal. The thing was generally complete, but the twisted crystalline bars lay unfinished upon the bench beside some sheets of drawings, and I took one up for a better look at it. Quartz it seemed to be.

"Look here," said the Medical Man, "are you perfectly serious? Or is this a trick—like that ghost you showed us last Christmas?"

"Upon that machine," said the Time Traveller, holding the lamp aloft, "I intend to explore time. Is that plain? I was never more serious in my life."

None of us quite knew how to take it.

I caught Filby's eye over the shoulder of the Medical Man, and he winked at me solemnly.

CHAPTER III

THE TIME TRAVELLER RETURNS

I THINK that at that time none of us quite believed in the Time Machine. The fact is, the Time Traveller was one of those men who are too clever to be believed: you never felt that you saw all round him; you always suspected some subtle reserve, some ingenuity in ambush, behind his lucid frankness. Had Filby shown the model and explained the matter in the Time Traveller's words, we should have shown *him* far less scepticism. For we should have perceived his motives: a pork-butcher could understand Filby. But the Time Traveller had more than a touch of whim among his elements, and we distrusted him. Things that would have made the fame of a less clever man seemed tricks in his hands. It is a mistake to do things too easily. The serious people who took him seriously never felt quite sure of his deportment: they were somehow aware that trusting their reputations for judgment with him was like furnishing a nursery with eggshell china. So I don't think any of us said very much about time travelling in the interval between that Thursday and the next, though its odd potentialities ran, no doubt, in most of our minds: its plausibility, that is, its practical incredibleness, the curious possibilities of anachronism and of utter confusion it suggested. For my own part, I was particularly preoccupied with the trick of the model. That I remember discussing with the Medical Man, whom I met on Friday at the Linnæan. He said he had seen a similar thing at Tübingen, and laid considerable stress on the blowing-out of the candle. But how the trick was done he could not explain.

The next Thursday I went again to Richmond—I suppose I was one of the Time Traveller's most constant guests—and, arriving late, found four or five men already assembled in his drawing-room. The Medical Man was standing before the fire with a sheet of paper in one hand and his watch in the other. I looked round for the Time Traveller, and—"It's half-past seven now," said the Medical Man. "I suppose we'd better have dinner?"

"Where's ——?" said I, naming our host.

"You've just come? It's rather odd. He's unavoidably detained. He asks me in this note to lead off with dinner at seven if he's not back. Says he'll explain when he comes."

"It seems a pity to let the dinner spoil," said the Editor of a well-known daily paper; and thereupon the Doctor rang the bell.

The Psychologist was the only person besides the Doctor and myself who had attended the previous dinner. The other men were Blank, the Editor afore-mentioned, a certain journalist, and another—a quiet, shy man with a beard—whom I didn't know, and who, as far as my observation went, never opened his mouth all the evening. There was some speculation at the dinner-table about the Time Traveller's absence, and I suggested time travelling, in a half jocular spirit. The Editor wanted that explained to him, and the Psychologist volunteered a wooden account of the "ingenious paradox and trick" we had witnessed that day week. He was in the midst of his exposition when the door from the corridor opened slowly and without noise. I was facing the door, and saw it first. "Hallo!" I said. "At last!" And the door opened wider, and the Time Traveller stood before us. I gave a cry of surprise. "Good heavens! man, what's the matter?" cried the Medical Man, who saw him next. And the whole tableful turned towards the door.

He was in an amazing plight. His coat was dusty and dirty, and smeared with green down the sleeves; his hair disordered, and as it seemed to me greyer—either with dust and dirt or because its colour had actually faded. His face was ghastly pale; his chin had a brown cut on it—a cut half-healed; his expression was haggard and drawn, as by intense suffering. For a moment he hesitated in the doorway, as if he had been dazzled by the light. Then he came into the room. He walked with just such a limp as I have seen in footsore tramps. We stared at him in silence, expecting him to speak.

He said not a word, but came painfully to the table, and made a motion towards the wine. The Editor filled a glass of champagne, and pushed it towards him. He drained it, and it seemed to do him good: for he looked round the table, and the ghost of his old smile flickered across his face. "What on earth have you been up to, man?" said the Doctor. The Time Traveller did not seem to hear. "Don't let me disturb you," he said, with a certain faltering articulation. "I'm all right." He stopped, held out his glass for more, and took it off at a draught. "That's good," he said. His eyes grew brighter, and a faint colour came into his cheeks. His glance flickered over our faces with a certain dull approval, and then went round the warm and comfortable room. Then he spoke again, still as it were feeling his way among his words. "I'm going to wash and dress, and then I'll come down and explain things. . . . Save me some of that mutton. I'm starving for a bit of meat."

He looked across at the Editor, who was a rare visitor, and hoped he was all right. The Editor began a question. "Tell you presently," said the Time Traveller. "I'm—funny! Be all right in a minute."

He put down his glass, and walked towards the staircase door. Again I remarked his lameness and the soft padding sound of his footfall, and standing up in my place, I saw his feet as he went out. He had nothing on them but a pair of tattered, blood-stained socks. Then the door closed upon him. I had half a mind to follow, till I remembered how he detested any fuss about himself. For a minute, perhaps, my mind was wool gathering. Then, "Remarkable Behaviour of an Eminent Scientist," I heard the Editor say, thinking (after his wont) in headlines. And this brought my attention back to the bright dinner-table.

"What's the game?" said the Journalist. "Has he been doing the Amateur Cadger? I don't follow." I met the eye of the Psychologist, and read my own interpretation in his face. I thought of the Time Traveller limping painfully upstairs. I don't think any one else had noticed his lameness.

The first to recover completely from this surprise was the Medical Man, who rang the bell—the Time Traveller hated to have servants waiting at dinner—for a hot plate. At that the Editor turned to his knife and fork with a grunt, and the silent man followed suit. The dinner was resumed. Conversation was exclamatory for a little while, with gaps of wonderment; and then the Editor got fervent in his curiosity. "Does our friend eke out his modest income with a crossing? or has he his Nebuchadnezzar phases?" he inquired. "I feel assured it's this business of the Time Machine," I said, and took up the Psychologist's account of our previous meeting. The new guests were frankly incredulous. The Editor raised objections. "What *was* this time travelling? A man couldn't cover himself with dust by rolling in a paradox, could he?" And then, as the idea came home to him, he resorted to caricature. Hadn't they any clothes-brushes in the Future? The Journalist, too, would not believe at any price, and joined the Editor in the easy work of heaping ridicule on the whole thing. They were both the new kind of journalist—very joyous, irreverent young men. "Our Special Correspondent in the Day after To-morrow reports," the Journalist was saying—or rather shouting—when the Time Traveller came back. He was dressed in ordinary evening clothes, and nothing save his haggard look remained of the change that had startled me.

"I say," said the Editor, hilariously, "these chaps here say you have been travelling into the middle of next week! ! Tell us all about little Rosebery, will you? What will you take for the lot?"

The Time Traveller came to the place reserved for him without a word. He smiled quietly, in his old way. "Where's my mutton?" he' said. "What a treat it is to stick a fork into meat again!"

"Story!" cried the Editor.

"Story be damned!" said the Time Traveller. "I want something to eat. I won't say a word until I get some peptone into my arteries. Thanks. And the salt."

"One word," said I. "Have you been time travelling?"

"Yes," said the Time Traveller, with his mouth full, nodding his head.

"I'd give a shilling a line for a verbatim note," said the Editor. The Time Traveller pushed his glass towards the Silent Man and rang it with his finger nail; at which the Silent Man, who had been staring at his face, started convulsively, and poured him wine. The rest of the dinner was uncomfortable. For my own part, sudden questions kept on rising to my lips, and I dare say it was the same with the others. The Journalist tried to relieve the tension by telling anecdotes of Hettie Potter. The Time Traveller devoted his attention to his dinner, and displayed the appetite of a tramp. The Medical Man smoked a cigarette, and watched the Time Traveller through his eyelashes. The Silent Man seemed even more clumsy than usual, and drank champagne with regularity and deter- mination out of sheer nervousness. At last the Time Traveller pushed his plate away, and looked round us. "I suppose I must apologize," he said. "I was simply starving. I've had a most amazing time." He reached out his hand for a cigar, and cut the end. "But come into the smoking-room. It's too long a story to tell over greasy plates." And ringing the bell in passing, he led the way into the adjoining room.

"You have told Blank, and Dash, and Chose about the machine?" he said to me, leaning back in his easy-chair and naming the three new guests.

"But the thing's a mere paradox," said the Editor.

"I can't argue to-night. I don't mind telling you the story, but I can't argue. I will," he went on, "tell you the story of what has happened to me, if you like, but you must refrain from interruptions. I want to tell it. Badly. Most of it will sound like lying. So be it! It's true—every word of it, all the same. I was in my laboratory at four o'clock, and since then . . . I've lived eight days . . . such days as no human being ever lived before! I'm nearly worn out, but I sha'n't sleep till I've told this thing over to you. Then I shall go to bed. But no interruptions! It is agreed?"

"Agreed," said the Editor, and the rest of us echoed "Agreed." And with that the Time Traveller began his story as I have set it forth. He sat back in his chair at first, and spoke like a weary man. Afterwards he got more animated. In writing it down I feel with only too much keenness the inadequacy of pen and ink—and, above all, my own inadequacy—to express its quality. You read, I will suppose, attentively enough; but you cannot see the speaker's white, sincere face in the bright circle of the little lamp, nor hear the intonation of his voice. You cannot know how his expression followed the turns of his story! Most of us hearers were in shadow, for the candles in the smoking-room had not been lighted, and only the face of the Journalist and the legs of the Silent Man from the knees downward were illuminated. At first we glanced now and again at each other. After a time we ceased to do that, and looked only at the Time Traveller's face.

CHAPTER IV

TIME TRAVELLING

"I TOLD some of you last Thursday of the principles of the Time Machine, and showed you the actual thing itself, incomplete in the workshop. There it is now, a little travel-worn, truly; and one of the ivory bars is cracked, and a brass rail bent; but the rest of it's sound enough. I expected to finish it on Friday; but on Friday, when the putting together was nearly done, I found that one of the nickel bars was exactly one inch too short, and this I had to get re-made; so that the thing was not complete until this morning. It was at ten o'clock to-day that the first of all Time Machines began its career. I gave it a last tap, tried all the screws again, put one more drop of oil on the quartz rod, and sat myself in the saddle. I suppose a suicide who holds a pistol to his skull feels much the same wonder at what will come next as I felt then. I took the starting lever in one hand and the stopping one in the other, pressed the first, and almost immediately the second. I seemed to reel; I felt a nightmare sensation of falling; and, looking round, I saw the laboratory exactly as before. Had anything happened? For a moment I suspected that my intellect had tricked me. Then I noted the clock. A moment before, as it seemed, it had stood at a minute or so past ten; now it was nearly half-past three!

"I drew a breath, set my teeth, gripped the starting lever with both hands, and went off with a thud. The laboratory got hazy and went dark. Mrs. Watchett came in, and walked, apparently without seeing me, towards the garden door. I suppose it took her a minute or so to traverse the place, but to me she seemed to shoot across the room like a rocket. I pressed the lever over to its extreme position. The night came like the turning out of a lamp, and in another moment came to-morrow. The laboratory grew faint and hazy, then fainter and ever fainter. To-morrow night came black, then day again, night again, day again, faster and faster still. An eddying murmur filled my ears, and a strange, dumb confusedness descended on my mind.

"I am afraid I cannot convey the peculiar sensations of time travelling. They are excessively unpleasant. There is a feeling exactly like that one has upon a switchback—of a helpless headlong motion! I felt the same horrible anticipation, too, of an imminent smash. As I put on pace, night followed day like the flapping of a black wing. The dim suggestion of the laboratory seemed presently to fall away from me, and I saw the sun hopping swiftly across the sky, leaping it every minute, and every minute marking a day. I supposed the laboratory had been destroyed and I had come into the open air. I had a dim impression of scaffolding, but I was already going too fast to be conscious of any moving things. The slowest snail that ever crawled dashed by too fast for me. The twinkling succession of darkness and light was excessively painful to the eye. Then, in the intermittent darknesses, I saw the moon spinning swiftly through her quarters from new to full, and had a faint glimpse of the circling stars. Presently, as I went on, still gaining velocity, the palpitation of night and day merged into one continuous greyness; the sky took on a wonderful deepness of blue, a splendid luminous colour like that of early twilight; the jerking sun became a streak of fire, a brilliant arch, in space, the moon a fainter fluctuating band; and I could see nothing of the stars, save now and then a brighter circle flickering in the blue.

"The landscape was misty and vague. I was still on the hill-side upon which this house now stands, and the shoulder rose above me grey and dim. I saw trees growing and changing like puffs of vapour, now brown, now green: they grew, spread, shivered, and passed away. I saw huge buildings rise up faint and fair, and pass like dreams. The whole surface of the earth seemed changed—melting and flowing under my eyes. The little hands upon the dials that registered my speed raced round faster and faster. Presently I noted that the sun-belt swayed up and down, from solstice to solstice, in a minute or less, and that, consequently, my pace was over a year a minute; and minute by minute the white snow flashed across the world, and vanished, and was followed by the bright, brief green of spring.

"The unpleasant sensations of the start were less poignant now. They merged at last into a kind of hysterical exhilaration. I remarked, indeed, a clumsy swaying of the machine, for which I was unable to account. But my mind was too confused to attend to it, so with a kind of madness growing upon me, I flung myself into futurity. At first I scarce thought of stopping, scarce thought of anything but these new sensations. But presently a fresh series of impressions grew up in my mind—a certain curiosity and therewith a certain dread—until at last they took complete possession of me. What strange developments of humanity, what wonderful advances upon our rudimentary civilization, I thought, might not appear when I came to look nearly into the dim elusive world that raced and fluctuated before my eyes! I saw great and splendid architecture rising about me, more massive than any buildings of our own time, and yet, as it seemed, built of glimmer and mist. I saw a richer green flow up the hill-side, and remain there without any wintry intermission. Even through the veil of my confusion the earth seemed very fair. And so my mind came round to the business of stopping.

"The peculiar risk lay in the possibility of my finding some substance in the space which I, or the machine, occupied. So long as I travelled at a high velocity through time, this scarcely mattered: I was, so to speak, attenuated—was slipping like a vapour through the interstices of intervening substances! But to come to a stop involved the jamming of myself, molecule by molecule, into whatever lay in my way: meant bringing my atoms into such intimate contact with those of the obstacle that a profound chemical reaction—possibly a far-reaching explosion—would result, and blow myself and my apparatus out of all possible dimensions —into the Unknown. This possibility had occurred to me again and again while I was making the machine; but then I had cheerfully accepted it as an unavoidable risk—one of the risks a man has got to take! Now the risk was inevitable, I no longer saw it in the same cheerful light. The fact is that, insensibly, the absolute strangeness of everything, the sickly jarring and swaying of the machine, above all, the feeling of prolonged falling, had absolutely upset my nerve. I told myself that I could never stop, and with a gust of petulance I resolved to stop forthwith. Like an impatient fool, I lugged over the lever, and incontinently the thing went reeling over, and I was flung headlong through the air.

"There was the sound of a clap of thunder in my ears. I may have been stunned for a moment. A pitiless hail was hissing round me, and I was sitting on soft turf in front of the overset machine. Everything still seemed grey, but presently I remarked that the confusion in my ears was gone. I looked round me. I was on what seemed to be a little lawn in a garden, surrounded by rhododendron bushes, and I noticed that their mauve and purple blossoms were dropping in a shower under the beating of the hailstones. The rebounding, dancing hail hung in a little cloud over the machine, and drove along the ground like smoke. In a moment I was wet to the skin. 'Fine hospitality,' said I, 'to a man who has travelled innumerable years to see you.'

"Presently I thought what a fool I was to get wet. I stood up and looked round me. A colossal figure, carved apparently in some white stone, loomed indistinctly beyond the rhododendrons through the hazy downpour. But all else of the world was invisible.

"My sensations would be hard to describe. As the columns of hail grew thinner, I saw the white figure more distinctly. It was very large, for a silver birch tree touched its shoulder. It was of white marble, in shape something like a winged sphinx, but the wings, instead of being carried vertically at the sides, were spread so that it seemed to hover. The pedestal, it appeared to me, was of bronze, and was thick with verdigris. It chanced that the face was towards me; the sightless eyes seemed to watch me; there was the faint shadow of a smile on the lips. It was greatly weather-worn, and that imparted an unpleasant suggestion of disease. I stood looking at it for a little space—half-a-minute, perhaps, or half-an-hour. It seemed to advance and to recede as the hail drove before it denser or thinner. At last I tore my eyes from it for a moment, and saw that the hail curtain had worn threadbare, and that the sky was lightening with the promise of the sun.

"I looked up again at the crouching white shape, and the full temerity of my voyage came suddenly upon me. What might appear when that hazy curtain was altogether withdrawn? What might not have happened to men? What if cruelty had grown into a common passion? What if in this interval the race had lost its manliness, and had developed into something inhuman, unsympathetic, and overwhelmingly powerful? I might seem some old-world savage animal, only the more dreadful and disgusting for our common likeness—a foul creature to be incontinently slain.

"Already I saw other vast shapes—huge buildings with intricate parapets and tall columns, with a wooded hill-side dimly creeping in upon me through the lessening storm. I was seized with a panic fear. I turned frantically to the Time Machine, and strove hard to readjust it. As I did so the shafts of the sun smote through the thunder-storm. The grey downpour was swept aside and vanished like the trailing garments of a ghost. Above me, in the intense blue of the summer sky, some faint brown shreds of cloud whirled into nothingness. The great buildings about me stood out clear and distinct, shining with the wet of the thunderstorm, and picked out in white by the unmelted hailstones piled along their courses. I felt naked in a strange world. I felt as perhaps a bird may feel in the clear air, knowing the hawk wins above and will swoop. My fear grew to frenzy. I took a breathing space, set my teeth, and again grappled fiercely, wrist and knee, with the machine. It gave under my desperate onset and turned over. It struck my chin violently. One hand on the saddle, the other on the lever, I stood panting heavily in attitude to mount again.

"But with this recovery of a prompt retreat my courage recovered. I looked more curiously and less fearfully at this world of the remote future. In a circular opening, high up in the wall of the nearer house, I saw a group of figures clad in rich soft robes. They had seen me, and their faces were directed towards me.

"Then I heard voices approaching me. Coming through the bushes by the White Sphinx were the heads and shoulders of men running. One of these emerged in a pathway leading straight to the little lawn upon which I stood with my machine. He was a slight creature—perhaps four feet high—clad in a purple tunic, girdled at the waist with a leather belt. Sandals or buskins—I could not clearly distinguish which—were on his feet; his legs were bare to the knees, and his head was bare. Noticing that, I noticed for the first time how warm the air was.

"He struck me as being a very beautiful and graceful creature, but indescribably frail. His flushed face reminded me of the more beautiful kind of consumptive—that hectic beauty of which we used to hear so much. At the sight of him I suddenly regained confidence. I took my hands from the machine.

CHAPTER V

IN THE GOLDEN AGE

"IN ANOTHER moment we were standing face to face, I and this fragile thing out of futurity. He came straight up to me and laughed into my eyes. The absence from his bearing of any sign of fear struck me at once. Then he turned to the two others who were following him and spoke to them in a strange and very sweet and liquid tongue.

"There were others coming, and presently a little group of perhaps eight or ten of these exquisite creatures were about me. One of them addressed me. It came into my head, oddly enough, that my voice was too harsh and deep for them. So I shook my head, and pointing to my ears, shook it again. He came a step forward, hesitated, and then touched my hand. Then I felt other soft little tentacles upon my back and shoulders. They wanted to make sure I was real. There was nothing in this at all alarming. Indeed, there was something in these pretty little people that inspired confidence—a graceful gentleness, a certain childlike ease. And besides, they looked so frail that I could fancy myself flinging the whole dozen of them about like nine-pins. But I made a sudden motion to warn them when I saw their little pink hands feeling at the Time Machine. Happily then, when it was not too late, I thought of a danger I had hitherto forgotten, and reaching over the bars of the machine, I unscrewed the little levers that would set it in motion, and put these in my pocket. Then I turned again to see what I could do in the way of communication.

"And then, looking more nearly into their features, I saw some further peculiarities in their Dresden china type of prettiness. Their hair, which was uniformly curly, came to a sharp end at the neck and cheek; there was not the faintest suggestion of it on the face, and their ears were singularly minute. The mouths were small, with bright red, rather thin lips, and the little chins ran to a point. The eyes were large and mild; and —this may seem egotism on my part—I fancied even then that there was a certain lack of the interest I might have expected in them.

"As they made no effort to communicate with me, but simply stood round me smiling and speaking in soft cooing notes to each other, I begun the conversation. I pointed to the Time Machine and to myself. Then, hesitating for a moment how to express Time, I pointed to the sun. At once a quaintly pretty little figure in chequered purple and white followed my gesture, and then astonished me by imitating the sound of thunder.

"For a moment I was staggered, though the import of his gesture was plain enough. The question had come into my mind abruptly: were these creatures fools? You may hardly understand how it took me. You see I had always anticipated that the people of the year Eight Hundred and Two Thousand odd would be incredibly in front of us in knowledge, art, everything. Then one of them suddenly asked me a question that showed him to be on the intellectual level of one of our five-year-old children— asked me, in fact, if I had come from the sun in a thunderstorm! It let loose the judgment I had suspended upon their clothes, their frail light limbs and fragile features. A flow of disappointment rushed across my mind. For a moment I felt that I had built the Time Machine in vain.

"I nodded, pointed to the sun, and gave them such a vivid rendering of a thunderclap as startled them. They all withdrew a pace or so and bowed. Then came one laughing towards me, carrying a chain of beautiful flowers altogether new to me, and put it about my neck. The idea was received with melodious applause; and presently they were all running to and fro for flowers, and laughingly flinging them upon me until I was almost smothered with blossom. You who have never seen the like can scarcely imagine what delicate and wonderful flowers countless years of culture had created. Then some one suggested that their plaything should be exhibited in the nearest building, and so I was led past the sphinx of white marble, which had seemed to watch me all the while with a smile at my astonishment, towards a vast grey edifice of fretted stone. As I went with them the memory of my confident anticipations of a profoundly grave and intellectual posterity came, with irresistible merriment, to my mind.

"The building had a huge entry, and was altogether of colossal dimensions. I was naturally most occupied with the growing crowd of little people, and with the big open portals that yawned before me shadowy and mysterious. My general impression of the world I saw over their heads was of a tangled waste of beautiful bushes and flowers, a long-neglected and yet weedless garden. I saw a number of tall spikes of strange white flowers, measuring a foot perhaps across the spread of the waxen petals. They grew scattered, as if wild, among the variegated shrubs, but, as I say, I did not examine them closely at this time. The Time Machine was left deserted on the turf among the rhododendrons.

"The arch of the doorway was richly carved, but naturally I did not observe the carving very narrowly, though I fancied I saw suggestions of old Phœnician decorations as I passed through, and it struck me that they were very badly broken and weather-worn. Several more brightly-clad people met me in the doorway, and so we entered, I, dressed in dingy nineteenth-century garments, looking grotesque enough, garlanded with flowers, and surrounded by an eddying mass of bright, soft-coloured robes and shining white limbs, in a melodious whirl of laughter and laughing speech.

"The big doorway opened into a proportionately great hall hung with brown. The roof was in shadow, and the windows, partially glazed with coloured glass and partially unglazed, admitted a tempered light. The floor was made up of huge blocks of some very hard white metal, not plates nor slabs—blocks, and it was so much worn, as I judged by the going to and fro of past generations, as to be deeply channelled along the more frequented ways. Transverse to the length were innumerable tables made of slabs of polished stone, raised, perhaps, a foot from the floor, and upon these were heaps of fruits. Some I recognized as a kind of hypertrophied raspberry and orange, but for the most part they were strange.

"Between the tables was scattered a great number of cushions. Upon these my conductors seated themselves, signing for me to do likewise. With a pretty absence of ceremony they began to eat the fruit with their hands, flinging peel and stalks, and so forth, into the round openings in the sides of the tables. I was not loth to follow their example, for I felt thirsty and hungry. As I did so I surveyed the hall at my leisure.

"And perhaps the thing that struck me most was its dilapidated look. The stained-glass windows, which displayed only a geometrical pattern, were broken in many places, and the curtains that hung across the lower end were thick with dust. And it caught my eye that the corner of the marble table near me was fractured. Nevertheless, the general effect was extremely rich and picturesque. There were, perhaps, a couple of hundred people dining in the hall, and most of them, seated as near to me as they could come, were watching me with interest, their little eyes shining over the fruit they were eating. All were clad in the same soft, and yet strong, silky material.

"Fruit, by the bye, was all their diet. These people of the remote future were strict vegetarians, and while I was with them, in spite of some carnal cravings, I had to be frugivorous also. Indeed, I found afterwards that horses, cattle, sheep, dogs, had followed the Ichthyosaurus into extinction. But the fruits were very delightful; one, in particular, that seemed to be in season all the time I was there—a floury thing in a three-sided husk—was especially good, and I made it my staple. At first I was puzzled by all these strange fruits, and by the strange flowers I saw, but later I began to perceive their import.

"However, I am telling you of my fruit dinner in the distant future now. So soon as my appetite was a little checked, I determined to make a resolute attempt to learn the speech of these new men of mine. Clearly that was the next thing to do. The fruits seemed a convenient thing to begin upon, and holding one of these up I began a series of interrogative sounds and gestures. I had some considerable difficulty in conveying my meaning. At first my efforts met with a stare of surprise or inextinguishable laughter, but presently a fair-haired little creature seemed to grasp my intention and repeated a name. They had to chatter and explain their business at great length to each other, and my first attempts to make their exquisite little sounds of the language caused an immense amount of genuine, if uncivil, amusement. However, I felt like a school-master amidst children, and persisted, and presently I had a score of noun substantives at least at my command; and then I got to demonstrative pronouns, and even the verb "to eat." But it was slow work, and the little people soon tired and wanted to get away from my interrogations, so I determined, rather of necessity, to let them give their lessons in little doses when they felt inclined. And very little doses I found they were before long, for I never met people more indolent or more easily fatigued.

CHAPTER VI

THE SUNSET OF MANKIND

"A QUEER THING I soon discovered about my little hosts, and that was their lack of interest. They would come to me with eager cries of astonishment, like children, but, like children, they would soon stop examining me, and wander away after some other toy. The dinner and my conversational beginnings ended, I noted for the first time that almost all those who had surrounded me at first were gone. It is odd, too, how speedily I came to disregard these little people. I went out through the portal into the sunlit world again so soon as my hunger was satisfied. I was continually meeting more of these men of the future, who would follow me a little distance, chatter and laugh about me, and, having smiled and gesticulated in a friendly way, leave me again to my own devices.

"The calm of evening was upon the world as I emerged from the great hall, and the scene was lit by the warm glow of the setting sun. At first things were very confusing. Everything was so entirely different from the world I had known—even the flowers. The big building I had left was situate on the slope of a broad river valley, but the Thames had shifted, perhaps, a mile from its present position. I resolved to mount to the summit of a crest, perhaps a mile and a half away, from which I could get a wider view of this our planet in the year Eight Hundred and Two Thousand Seven Hundred and One, A.D. For that, I should explain, was the date the little dials of my machine recorded.

"As I walked I was watchful for every impression that could possibly help to explain the condition of ruinous splendour in which I found the world—for ruinous it was. A little way up the hill, for instance, was a great heap of granite, bound together by masses of aluminium, a vast labyrinth of precipitous walls and crumbled heaps, amidst which were thick heaps of very beautiful pagoda-like plants—nettles possibly—but wonderfully tinted with brown about the leaves, and incapable of stinging. It was evidently the derelict remains of some vast structure, to what end built I could not determine. It was here that I was destined, at a later date, to have a very strange experience—the first intimation of a still stranger discovery—but of that I will speak in its proper place.

"Looking round, with a sudden thought, from a terrace on which I rested for awhile, I realized that there were no small houses to be seen. Apparently, the single house, and possibly even the household, had vanished. Here and there among the greenery were palace-like buildings, but the house and the cottage, which form such characteristic features of our own English landscape, had disappeared.

" 'Communism,' said I to myself.

"And on the heels of that came another thought. I looked at the half-dozen little figures that were following me. Then, in a flash, I perceived that all had the same form of costume, the same soft hairless visage, and the same girlish rotundity of limb. It may seem strange, perhaps, that I had not noticed this before. But everything was so strange. Now, I saw the fact plainly enough. In costume, and in all the differences of texture and bearing that now mark off the sexes from each other, these people of the future were alike. And the children seemed to my eyes to be but the miniatures of their parents. I judged then that the children of that time were extremely precocious, physically at least, and I found afterwards abundant verification of my opinion.

"Seeing the ease and security in which these people were living, I felt that this close resemblance of the sexes was after all what one would expect; for the strength of a man and the softness of a woman, the institution of the family, and the differentiation of occupations are mere militant necessities of an age of physical force. Where population is balanced and abundant, much child-bearing becomes an evil rather than a blessing to the State: where violence comes but rarely and offspring are secure, there is less necessity—indeed there is no necessity—of an efficient family, and the specialization of the sexes with reference to their children's needs disappears. We see some beginnings of this even in our own time, and in this future age it was complete. This, I must remind you, was my speculation at the time. Later, I was to appreciate how far it fell short of the reality.

"While I was musing upon these things, my attention was attracted by a pretty little structure, like a well under a cupola. I thought in a transitory way of the oddness of wells still existing, and then resumed the thread of my speculations. There were no large buildings towards the top of the hill, and as my walking powers were evidently miraculous, I was presently left alone for the first time. With a strange sense of freedom and adventure I pushed on up to the crest.

"There I found a seat of some yellow metal that I did not recognize, corroded in places with a kind of pinkish rust and half-smothered in soft moss, the arm-rests cast and filed into the resemblance of griffins' heads. I sat down on it, and I surveyed the broad view of our old world under the sunset of that long day. It was as sweet and fair a view as I have ever seen. The sun had already gone below the horizon and the west was flaming gold, touched with some horizontal bars of purple and crimson. Below was the valley of the Thames, in which the river lay like a band of burnished steel. I have already spoken of the great palaces dotted about among the variegated greenery, some in ruins and some still occupied. Here and there rose a white or silvery figure in the waste garden of the earth, here and there came the sharp vertical line of some cupola or obelisk. There were no hedges, no signs of proprietary rights, no evidences of agriculture; the whole earth had become a garden.

"So watching, I began to put my interpretation upon the things I had seen, and as it shaped itself to me that evening, my interpretation was something in this way. (Afterwards I found I had got only a half truth—or only a glimpse of one facet of the truth):

"It seemed to me that I had happened upon humanity upon the wane. The ruddy sunset set me thinking of the sunset of mankind. For the first time I began to realize an odd consequence of the social effort in which we are at present engaged. And yet, come to think, it is a logical consequence enough. Strength is the outcome of need: security sets a premium on feebleness. The work of ameliorating the conditions of life—the true civilizing process that makes life more and more secure—had gone steadily on to a climax. One triumph of a united humanity over Nature had followed another. Things that are now mere dreams had become projects deliberately put in hand and carried forward. And the harvest was what I saw!

"After all, the sanitation and the agriculture of to-day are still in the rudimentary stage. The science of our time has attacked but a little department of the field of human disease, but, even so, it spreads its operations very steadily and persistently. Our agriculture and horticulture destroy a weed just here and there and cultivate perhaps a score or so of wholesome plants, leaving the greater number to fight out a balance as they can. We improve our favourite plants and animals—and how few they are—gradually by selective breeding; now a new and better peach, now a seedless grape, now a sweeter and larger flower, now a more con-venient breed of cattle. We improve them gradually, because our ideals are vague and tentative, and our knowledge is very limited; because Nature, too, is shy and slow in our clumsy hands. Some day all this will be better organized, and still better. That is the drift of the current in spite of the eddies. The whole world will be intelligent, educated, and co-operating; things will move faster and faster towards the subjugation of Nature. In the end, wisely and carefully we shall readjust the balance of animal and vegetable life to suit our human needs.

"This adjustment, I say, must have been done, and done well: done indeed for all time, in the space of Time across which my machine had leapt. The air was free from gnats, the earth from weeds or fungi; every-where were fruits and sweet and delightful flowers; brilliant butterflies flew hither and thither. The ideal of preventive medicine was attained. Diseases had been stamped out. I saw no evidence of any contagious diseases during all my stay. And I shall have to tell you later that even the processes of putrefaction and decay had been profoundly affected by these changes.

"Social triumphs, too, had been effected. I saw mankind housed in splendid shelters, gloriously clothed, and as yet I had found them engaged in no toil. There were no signs of struggle, neither social nor economical struggle. The shop, the advertisement, traffic, all that commerce which constitutes the body of our world, was gone. It was natural on that golden evening that I should jump at the idea of a social paradise. The difficulty of increasing population had been met, I guessed, and popula-tion had ceased to increase.

"But with this change in condition comes inevitably adaptations to the change. What, unless biological science is a mass of errors, is the cause of human intelligence and vigour? Hardship and freedom: conditions under which the active, strong, and subtle survive and the weaker go to the wall; conditions that put a premium upon the loyal alliance of cap-able men, upon self-restraint, patience, and decision. And the institution of the family, and the emotions that arise therein, the fierce jealousy, the tenderness for offspring, parental self-devotion, all found their justifica-tion and support in the imminent dangers of the young. *Now*, where are these imminent dangers? There is a sentiment arising, and it will grow, against connubial jealousy, against fierce maternity, against passion of all sorts; unnecessary things now, and things that make us uncomfort-able, savage survivals, discords in a refined and pleasant life.

"I thought of the physical slightness of the people, their lack of intelli-gence, and those big abundant ruins, and it strengthened my belief in a perfect conquest of Nature. For after the battle comes Quiet. Humanity had been strong, energetic, and intelligent, and had used all its abundant vitality to alter the conditions under which it lived. And now came the reaction of the altered conditions.

"Under the new conditions of perfect comfort and security, that restless energy, that with us is strength, would become weakness. Even in our own time certain tendencies and desires, once necessary to survival, are a constant source of failure. Physical courage and the love of battle, for instance, are no great help—may even be hindrances—to a civilized man. And in a state of physical balance and security, power, intellectual as well as physical, would be out of place. For countless years I judged there had been no danger of war or solitary violence, no danger from wild beasts, no wasting disease to require strength of constitution, no need of toil. For such a life, what we should call the weak are as well equipped as the strong, are indeed no longer weak. Better equipped indeed they are, for the strong would be fretted by an energy for which there was no outlet. No doubt the exquisite beauty of the buildings I saw was the outcome of the last surgings of the now purposeless energy of mankind before it settled down into perfect harmony with the conditions under which it lived—the flourish of that triumph which began the last great peace. This has ever been the fate of energy in security; it takes to art and to eroticism, and then come languor and decay.

"Even this artistic impetus would at last die away—had almost died in the Time I saw. To adorn themselves with flowers, to dance, to sing in the sunlight; so much was left of the artistic spirit, and no more. Even that would fade in the end into a contented inactivity. We are kept keen on the grindstone of pain and necessity, and, it seemed to me, that here was that hateful grindstone broken at last!

"As I stood there in the gathering dark I thought that in this simple explanation I had mastered the problem of the world—mastered the whole secret of these delicious people. Possibly the checks they had devised for the increase of population had succeeded too well, and their numbers had rather diminished than kept stationary. That would account for the abandoned ruins. Very simple was my explanation, and plausible enough—as most wrong theories are!

CHAPTER VII

A SUDDEN SHOCK

"AS I STOOD there musing over this too perfect triumph of man, the full moon, yellow and gibbous, came up out of an overflow of silver light in the north-east. The bright little figures ceased to move about below, a noiseless owl flitted by, and I shivered with the chill of the night. I determined to descend and find where I could sleep.

"I looked for the building I knew. Then my eye travelled along to the figure of the White Sphinx upon the pedestal of bronze, growing distinct as the light of the rising moon grew brighter. I could see the silver birch against it. There was the tangle of rhododendron bushes, black in the pale light, and there was the little lawn. I looked at the lawn again. A queer doubt chilled my complacency. 'No,' I said stoutly to myself, 'that was not the lawn.'

"But it *was* the lawn. For the white leprous face of the sphinx was towards it. Can you imagine what I felt as this conviction came home to me? But you cannot. The Time Machine was gone!

"At once, like a lash across the face, came the possibility of losing my own age, of being left helpless in this strange new world. The bare thought of it was an actual physical sensation. I could feel it grip me at the throat and stop my breathing. In another moment I was in a passion of fear, and running with great leaping strides down the slope. Once I fell headlong and cut my face; I lost no time in stanching the blood, but jumped up and ran on, with a warm trickle down my cheek and chin. All the time I ran I was saying to myself, 'They have moved it a little, pushed it under the bushes out of the way.' Nevertheless, I ran with all my might. All the time, with the certainty that sometimes comes with excessive dread, I knew that such assurance was folly, knew instinctively that the machine was removed out of my reach. My breath came with pain. I suppose I covered the whole distance from the hill crest to the little lawn, two miles, perhaps, in ten minutes. And I am not a young man. I cursed aloud, as I ran, at my confident folly in leaving the machine, wasting good breath thereby. I cried aloud, and none answered. Not a creature seemed to be stirring in that moonlit world.

"When I reached the lawn my worst fears were realized. Not a trace of the thing was to be seen. I felt faint and cold when I faced the empty space, among the black tangle of bushes. I ran round it furiously, as if the thing might be hidden in a corner, and then stopped abruptly, with my hands clutching my hair. Above me towered the sphinx, upon the bronze pedestal, white, shining, leprous, in the light of the rising moon. It seemed to smile in mockery of my dismay.

"I might have consoled myself by imagining the little people had put the mechanism in some shelter for me, had I not felt assured of their physical and intellectual inadequacy. That is what dismayed me: the sense of some hitherto unsuspected power, through whose intervention my invention had vanished. Yet, of one thing I felt assured: unless some other age had produced its exact duplicate, the machine could not have moved in time. The attachment of the levers—I will show you the method later—prevented any one from tampering with it in that way when they were removed. It had moved, and was hid, only in space. But then, where could it be?

"I think I must have had a kind of frenzy. I remember running violently in and out among the moonlit bushes all round the sphinx, and startling some white animal that, in the dim light, I took for a small deer. I remember, too, late that night, beating the bushes with my clenched fists until my knuckles were gashed and bleeding from the broken twigs. Then, sobbing and raving in my anguish of mind, I went down to the great building of stone. The big hall was dark, silent, and deserted. I slipped on the uneven floor, and fell over one of the malachite tables, almost breaking my shin. I lit a match and went on past the dusty curtains, of which I have told you.

"There I found a second great hall covered with cushions, upon which, perhaps, a score or so of the little people were sleeping. I have no doubt they found my second appearance strange enough, coming suddenly out of the quiet darkness with inarticulate noises and the splutter and flare of a match. For they had forgotten about matches. 'Where is my Time Machine?' I began, bawling like an angry child, laying hands upon them and shaking them up together. It must have been very queer to them. Some laughed, most of them looked sorely frightened. When I saw them standing round me, it came into my head that I was doing as foolish a thing as it was possible for me to do under the circumstances, in trying to revive the sensation of fear. For, reasoning from their daylight behaviour, I thought that fear must be forgotten.

"Abruptly, I dashed down the match, and knocking one of the people over in my course, went blundering across the big dining-hall again, out under the moonlight. I heard cries of terror and their little feet running and stumbling this way and that. I do not remember all I did as the moon crept up the sky. I suppose it was the unexpected nature of my loss that maddened me. I felt hopelessly cut off from my own kind—a strange animal in an unknown world. I must have raved to and fro, screaming and crying upon God and Fate. I have a memory of horrible fatigue, as the long night of despair wore away; of looking in this impossible place and that; of groping among moonlit ruins and touching strange creatures in the black shadows; at last, of lying on the ground near the sphinx, and weeping with absolute wretchedness, even anger at the folly of leaving the machine having leaked away with my strength. I had nothing left but misery. Then I slept, and when I woke again it was full day, and a couple of sparrows were hopping round me on the turf within reach of my arm.

"I sat up in the freshness of the morning, trying to remember how I had got there, and why I had such a profound sense of desertion and despair. Then things came clear in my mind. With the plain, reasonable daylight, I could look my circumstances fairly in the face. I saw the wild folly of my frenzy overnight, and I could reason with myself. Suppose the worst? I said. Suppose the machine altogether lost—perhaps destroyed? It behoves me to be calm and patient, to learn the way of the people, to get a clear idea of the method of my loss, and the means of getting materials and tools; so that in the end, perhaps, I may make another. That would be my only hope, a poor hope, perhaps, but better than despair. And, after all, it was a beautiful and curious world.

"But probably the machine had only been taken away. Still, I must be calm and patient, find its hiding-place, and recover it by force or cunning. And with that I scrambled to my feet and looked about me, wondering where I could bathe. I felt weary, stiff, and travel-soiled. The freshness of the morning made me desire an equal freshness. I had exhausted my emotion. Indeed, as I went about my business, I found myself wondering at my intense excitement overnight. I made a careful examination of the ground about the little lawn. I wasted some time in futile questionings, conveyed, as well as I was able, to such of the little people as came by. They all failed to understand my gestures: some were simply stolid; some thought it was a jest, and laughed at me. I had the hardest task in the world to keep my hands off their pretty laughing faces. It was a foolish impulse, but the devil begotten of fear and blind anger was ill curbed, and still eager to take advantage of my perplexity. The turf gave better counsel. I found a groove ripped in it, about midway between the pedestal of the sphinx and the marks of my feet where, on arrival, I had struggled with the overturned machine. There were other signs of removal about, with queer narrow footprints like those I could imagine made by a sloth. This directed my closer attention to the pedestal. It was, as I think I have said, of bronze. It was not a mere block, but highly decorated with deep framed panels on either side. I went and rapped at these. The pedestal was hollow. Examining the panels with care I found them discontinuous with the frames. There were no handles or keyholes, but possibly the panels, if they were doors as I supposed, opened from within. One thing was clear enough to my mind. It took no very great mental effort to infer that my Time Machine was inside that pedestal. But how it got there was a different problem.

" I saw the heads of two orange-clad people coming through the bushes and under some blossom-covered apple-trees towards me. I turned smiling to them, and beckoned them to me. They came, and then, pointing to the bronze pedestal, I tried to intimate my wish to open it. But at my first gesture towards this they behaved very oddly. I don't know how to convey their expression to you. Suppose you were to use a grossly improper gesture to a delicate-minded woman—it is how she would look. They went off as if they had received the last possible insult. I tried a sweet-looking little chap in white next, with exactly the same result. Somehow, his manner made me feel ashamed of myself. But, as you know, I wanted the Time Machine, and I tried him once more. As he turned off, like the others, my temper got the better of me. In three strides I was after him, had him by the loose part of his robe round the neck, and began dragging him towards the sphinx. Then I saw the horror and repugnance of his face, and all of a sudden I let him go.

"But I was not beaten yet. I banged with my fist at the bronze panels. I thought I heard something stir inside—to be explicit, I thought I heard a sound like a chuckle—but I must have been mistaken. Then I got a big pebble from the river, and came and hammered till I had flattened a coil in the decorations, and the verdigris came off in powdery flakes. The delicate little people must have heard me hammering in gusty outbreaks a mile away on either hand, but nothing came of it. I saw a crowd of them upon the slopes, looking furtively at me. At last, hot and tired, I sat down to watch the place. But I was too restless to watch long; I am too Occidental for a long vigil. I could work at a problem for years, but to wait inactive for twenty-four hours—that is another matter.

"I got up after a time, and began walking aimlessly through the bushes towards the hill again. 'Patience,' said I to myself. 'If you want your machine again you must leave that sphinx alone. If they mean to take your machine away, it's little good your wrecking their bronze panels, and if they don't, you will get it back as soon as you can ask for it. To sit among all those unknown things before a puzzle like that is hopeless. That way lies monomania. Face this world. Learn its ways, watch it, be careful of too hasty guesses at its meaning. In the end you will find clues to it all.' Then suddenly the humour of the situation came into my mind: the thought of the years I had spent in study and toil to get into the future age, and now my passion of anxiety to get out of it. I had made myself the most complicated and the most hopeless trap that ever a man devised. Although it was at my own expense, I could not help myself. I laughed aloud.

"Going through the big palace, it seemed to me that the little people avoided me. It may have been my fancy, or it may have had something to do with my hammering at the gates of bronze. Yet I felt tolerably sure of the avoidance. I was careful, however, to show no concern, and to abstain from any pursuit of them, and in the course of a day or two things got back to the old footing. I made what progress I could in the language, and, in addition, I pushed my explorations here and there. Either I missed some subtle point, or their language was excessively simple— almost exclusively composed of concrete substantives and verbs. There seemed to be few, if any, abstract terms, or little use of figurative language. Their sentences were usually simple and of two words, and I failed to convey or understand any but the simplest propositions. I determined to put the thought of my Time Machine, and the mystery of the bronze doors under the sphinx, as much as possible in a corner of memory, until my growing knowledge would lead me back to them in a natural way. Yet a certain feeling, you may understand, tethered me in a circle of a few miles round the point of my arrival.

CHAPTER VIII

EXPLANATION

"SO FAR as I could see, all the world displayed the same exuberant richness as the Thames valley. From every hill I climbed I saw the same abundance of splendid buildings, endlessly varied in material and style; the same clustering thickets of evergreens, the same blossom-laden trees and tree ferns. Here and there water shone like silver, and beyond, the land rose into blue undulating hills, and so faded into the serenity of the sky. A peculiar feature, which presently attracted my attention, was the presence of certain circular wells, several, as it seemed to me, of a very great depth. One lay by the path up the hill, which I had followed during my first walk. Like the others, it was rimmed with bronze, curiously wrought, and protected by a little cupola from the rain. Sitting by the side of these wells, and peering down into the shafted darkness, I could see no gleam of water, nor could I start any reflection with a lighted match. But in all of them I heard a certain sound: a thud—thud—thud, like the beating of some big engine; and I discovered, from the flaring of my matches, that a steady current of air set down the shafts. Further, I threw a scrap of paper into the throat of one; and, instead of fluttering slowly down, it was at once sucked swiftly out of sight.

"After a time, too, I came to connect these wells with tall towers standing here and there upon the slopes; for above them there was often just such a flicker in the air as one sees on a hot day above a sun-scorched beach. Putting things together, I reached a strong suggestion of an extensive system of subterranean ventilation, whose true import it was difficult to imagine. I was at first inclined to associate it with the sanitary apparatus of these people. It was an obvious conclusion, but it was absolutely wrong.

"And here I must admit that I learned very little of drains and bells and modes of conveyance, and the like conveniences, during my time in this real future. In some of these visions of Utopias and coming times which I have read, there is a vast amount of detail about building, and social arrangements, and so forth. But while such details are easy enough to obtain when the whole world is contained in one's imagination, they are altogether inaccessible to a real traveller amid such realities as I found here. Conceive the tale of London which a negro, fresh from Central Africa, would take back to his tribe! What would he know of railway companies, of social movements, of telephone and telegraph wires, of the Parcels Delivery Company, and postal orders and the like? Yet we, at least, should be willing enough to explain these things to him! And even of what he knew, how much could he make his untravelled friend either apprehend or believe? Then, think how narrow the gap between a negro and a white man of our own times, and how wide the interval between myself and these of the Golden Age! I was sensible of much which was unseen, and which contributed to my comfort; but, save for a general impression of automatic organization, I fear I can convey very little of the difference to your mind.

"In the matter of sepulture, for instance, I could see no signs of crematoria nor anything suggestive of tombs. But it occurred to me that, possibly, there might be cemeteries (or crematoria) somewhere beyond the range of my explorings. This, again, was a question I deliberately put to myself, and my curiosity was at first entirely defeated upon the point. The thing puzzled me, and I was led to make a further remark, which puzzled me still more: that aged and infirm among this people there were none.

"I must confess that my satisfaction with my first theories of an automatic civilization and a decadent humanity did not long endure. Yet I could think of no other. Let me put my difficulties. The several big palaces I had explored were mere living places, great dining-halls and sleeping apartments. I could find no machinery, no appliances of any kind. Yet these people were clothed in pleasant fabrics that must at times need renewal, and their sandals, though undecorated, were fairly complex specimens of metal-work. Somehow such things must be made. And the little people displayed no vestige of a creative tendency. There were no shops, no workshops, no sign of importations among them. They spent all their time in playing gently, in bathing in the river, in making love in a half-playful fashion, in eating fruit and sleeping. I could not see how things were kept going.

"Then, again, about the Time Machine: something, I knew not what, had taken it into the hollow pedestal of the White Sphinx. *Why?* For the life of me I could not imagine. Those waterless wells, too, those flickering pillars. I felt I lacked a clue. I felt—how shall I put it? Suppose you found an inscription, with sentences here and there in excellent plain English, and, interpolated therewith, others made up of words, of letters even, absolutely unknown to you? Well, on the third day of my visit, that was how the world of Eight Hundred and Two Thousand Seven Hundred and One presented itself to me!

"That day, too, I made a friend—of a sort. It happened that, as I was watching some of the little people bathing in a shallow, one of them was seized with cramp, and began drifting down stream. The main current ran rather swiftly, but not too strongly for even a moderate swimmer. It will give you an idea, therefore, of the strange deficiency in these creatures, when I tell you that none made the slightest attempt to rescue the weakly-crying little thing which was drowning before their eyes. When I realized this, I hurriedly slipped off my clothes, and, wading in at a point lower down, I caught the poor mite, and drew her safe to land. A little rubbing of the limbs soon brought her round, and I had the satisfaction of seeing she was all right before I left her. I had got to such a low estimate of her kind that I did not expect any gratitude from her. In that, however, I was wrong.

"This happened in the morning. In the afternoon I met my little woman, as I believe it was, as I was returning towards my centre from an exploration: and she received me with cries of delight, and presented me with a big garland of flowers—evidently made for me and me alone. The thing took my imagination. Very possibly I had been feeling desolate. At any rate I did my best to display my appreciation of the gift. We were soon seated together in a little stone arbour, engaged in conversation, chiefly of smiles. The creature's friendliness affected me exactly as a child's might have done. We passed each other flowers, and she kissed my hands. I did the same to hers. Then I tried talk, and found that her name was Weena, which, though I don't know what it meant, somehow seemed appropriate enough. That was the beginning of a queer friendship which lasted a week, and ended—as I will tell you!

"She was exactly like a child. She wanted to be with me always. She tried to follow me everywhere, and on my next journey out and about it went to my heart to tire her down, and leave her at last, exhausted and calling after me rather plaintively. But the problems of the world had to be mastered. I had not, I said to myself, come into the future to carry on a miniature flirtation. Yet her distress when I left her was very great, her expostulations at the parting were sometimes frantic, and I think, altogether, I had as much trouble as comfort from her devotion. Nevertheless she was, somehow, a very great comfort. I thought it was mere childish affection that made her cling to me. Until it was too late, I did not clearly know what I had inflicted upon her when I left her. Nor until it was too late did I clearly understand what she was to me. For, by merely seeming fond of me, and showing in her weak futile way that she cared for me, the little doll of a creature presently gave my return to the neighbourhood of the White Sphinx almost the feeling of coming home; and I would watch for her tiny figure of white and gold so soon as I came over the hill.

"It was from her, too, that I learnt that fear had not yet left the world. She was fearless enough in the daylight, and she had the oddest confidence in me; for once, in a foolish moment, I made threatening grimaces at her, and she simply laughed at them. But she dreaded the dark, dreaded shadows, dreaded black things. Darkness to her was the one thing dreadful. It was a singularly passionate emotion, and it set me thinking and observing. I discovered, then, among other things, that these little people gathered into the great houses after dark, and slept in droves. To enter upon them without a light was to put them into a tumult of apprehension. I never found one out of doors, or one sleeping alone within doors, after dark. Yet I was still such a blockhead that I missed the lesson of that fear, and, in spite of Weena's distress, I insisted upon sleeping away from these slumbering multitudes.

"It troubled her greatly, but in the end her odd affection for me triumphed, and for five of the nights of our acquaintance, including the last night of all, she slept with her head pillowed on my arm. But my story slips away from me as I speak of her. It must have been the night before her rescue that I was awakened about dawn. I had been restless, dreaming most disagreeably that I was drowned, and that sea-anemones were feeling over my face with their soft palps. I woke with a start, and with an odd fancy that some greyish animal had just rushed out of the chamber.

I tried to get to sleep again, but I felt restless and uncomfortable. It was that dim grey hour when things are just creeping out of darkness, when everything is colourless and clear cut, and yet unreal. I got up, and went down into the great hall, and so out upon the flagstones in front of the palace. I thought I would make a virtue of necessity, and see the sunrise.

"The moon was setting, and the dying moonlight and the first pallor of dawn were mingled in a ghastly half-light. The bushes were inky black, the ground a sombre grey, the sky colourless and cheerless. And up the hill I thought I could see ghosts. There several times, as I scanned the slope, I saw white figures. Twice I fancied I saw a solitary white, ape-like creature running rather quickly up the hill, and once near the ruins I saw a leash of them carrying some dark body. They moved hastily. I did not see what became of them. It seemed that they vanished among the bushes. The dawn was still indistinct, you must understand. I was feeling that chill, uncertain, early-morning feeling you may have known. I doubted my eyes.

"As the eastern sky grew brighter, and the light of the day came on and its vivid colouring returned upon the world once more, I scanned the view keenly. But I saw no vestige of my white figures. They were mere creatures of the half-light. 'They must have been ghosts,' I said; 'I wonder whence they dated.' For a queer notion of Grant Allen's came into my head, and amused me. If each generation die and leave ghosts, he argued, the world at last will get overcrowded with them. On that theory they would have grown innumerable some Eight Hundred Thousand Years hence, and it was no great wonder to see four at once. But the jest was unsatisfying, and I was thinking of these figures all the morning, until Weena's rescue drove them out of my head. I associated them in some indefinite way with the white animal I had startled in my first passionate search for the Time Machine. But Weena was a pleasant substitute. Yet all the same, they were soon destined to take far deadlier possession of my mind.

"I think I have said how much hotter than our own was the weather of this Golden Age. I cannot account for it. It may be that the sun was hotter, or the earth nearer the sun. It is usual to assume that the sun will go on cooling steadily in the future. But people, unfamiliar with such speculations as those of the younger Darwin, forget that the planets must ultimately fall back one by one into the parent body. As these catastrophes occur, the sun will blaze with renewed energy; and it may be that some inner planet had suffered this fate. Whatever the reason, the fact remains that the sun was very much hotter than we know it.

"Well, one very hot morning—my fourth, I think—as I was seeking shelter from the heat and glare in a colossal ruin near the great house where I slept and fed, there happened this strange thing. Clambering among these heaps of masonry, I found a narrow gallery, whose end and side windows were blocked by fallen masses of stone. By contrast with the brilliancy outside, it seemed at first impenetrably dark to me. I entered it groping, for the change from light to blackness made spots of colour swim before me. Suddenly I halted spellbound. A pair of eyes, luminous by reflection against the daylight without, was watching me out of the darkness.

"The old instinctive dread of wild beasts came upon me. I clenched my hands and steadfastly looked into the glaring eyeballs. I was afraid to turn. Then the thought of the absolute security in which humanity appeared to be living came to my mind. And then I remembered that strange terror of the dark. Overcoming my fear to some extent, I advanced a step and spoke. I will admit that my voice was harsh and ill-controlled. I put out my hand and touched something soft. At once the eyes darted sideways, and something white ran past me. I turned with my heart in my mouth, and saw a queer little ape-like figure, its head held down in a peculiar manner, running across the sunlit space behind me. It blundered against a block of granite, staggered aside, and in a moment was hidden in a black shadow beneath another pile of ruined masonry.

"My impression of it is, of course, imperfect; but I know it was a dull white, and had strange large greyish-red eyes; also that there was flaxen hair on its head and down its back. But, as I say, it went too fast for me to see distinctly. I cannot even say whether it ran on all fours, or only with its fore-arms held very low. After an instant's pause I followed it into the second heap of ruins. I could not find it at first; but, after a time in the profound obscurity, I came upon one of those round well-like openings of which I have told you, half closed by a fallen pillar. A sudden thought came to me. Could this Thing have vanished down the shaft? I lit a match, and, looking down, I saw a small, white moving creature, with large bright eyes which regarded me steadfastly as it retreated. It made me shudder. It was so like a human spider! It was clambering down the wall, and now I saw for the first time a number of metal foot- and hand-rests forming a kind of ladder down the shaft. Then the light burned my fingers and fell out of my hand, going out as it dropped, and when I had lit another the little monster had disappeared.

"I do not know how long I sat peering down that well. It was not for some time that I could succeed in persuading myself that the thing I had seen was human. But, gradually, the truth dawned on me: that Man had not remained one species, but had differentiated into two distinct animals: that my graceful children of the Upper World were not the sole descendants of our generation, but that this bleached, obscene, nocturnal Thing, which had flashed before me, was also heir to all the ages.

"I thought of the flickering pillars and of my theory of an underground ventilation. I began to suspect their true import. And what, I wondered, was this Lemur doing in my scheme of a perfectly balanced organization? How was it related to the indolent serenity of the beautiful Overworlders? And what was hidden down there, at the foot of that shaft? I sat upon the edge of the well telling myself that, at any rate, there was nothing to fear, and that there I must descend for the solution of my difficulties. And withal I was absolutely afraid to go! As I hesitated, two of the beautiful upperworld people came running in their amorous sport across the daylight into the shadow. The male pursued the female, flinging flowers at her as he ran.

"They seemed distressed to find me, my arm against the overturned pillar, peering down the well. Apparently it was considered bad form to remark these apertures; for when I pointed to this one, and tried to frame a question about it in their tongue, they were still more visibly distressed and turned away. But they were interested by my matches, and I struck some to amuse them. I tried them again about the well, and again I failed. So presently I left them, meaning to go back to Weena, and see what I could get from her. But my mind was already in revolution; my guesses and impressions were slipping and sliding to a new adjustment. I had now a clue to the import of these wells, to the ventilating towers, to the mystery of the ghosts: to say nothing of a hint at the meaning of the bronze gates and the fate of the Time Machine! And very vaguely there came a suggestion towards the solution of the economic problem that had puzzled me.

"Here was the new view. Plainly, this second species of Man was subterranean. There were three circumstances in particular which made me think that its rare emergence above ground was the outcome of a long-continued underground habit. In the first place, there was the bleached look common in most animals that live largely in the dark—the white fish of the Kentucky caves, for instance. Then, those large eyes, with that capacity for reflecting light, are common features of nocturnal things—witness the owl and the cat. And last of all, that evident confusion in the sunshine, that hasty yet fumbling and awkward flight towards dark shadow, and that peculiar carriage of the head while in the light—all reinforced the theory of an extreme sensitiveness of the retina.

"Beneath my feet then the earth must be tunnelled enormously, and these tunnellings were the habitat of the New Race. The presence of ventilating-shafts and wells along the hill slopes—everywhere, in fact, except along the river valley—showed how universal were its ramifications. What so natural, then, as to assume that it was in this artificial Underworld that such work as was necessary to the comfort of the daylight race was done? The notion was so plausible that I at once accepted it, and went on to assume the *how* of this splitting of the human species. I dare say you will anticipate the shape of my theory, though, for myself, I very soon felt that it fell far short of the truth.

"At first, proceeding from the problems of our own age, it seemed clear as daylight to me that the gradual widening of the present merely temporary and social difference between the Capitalist and the Labourer, was the key to the whole position. No doubt it will seem grotesque enough to you—and wildly incredible!—and yet even now there are existing circumstances to point that way. There is a tendency to utilize underground space for the less ornamental purposes of civilization; there is the Metropolitan Railway in London, for instance, there are new electric railways, there are subways, there are underground workrooms and restaurants, and they increase and multiply. Evidently, I thought, this tendency had increased till Industry had gradually lost its birthright in the sky. I mean that it had gone deeper and deeper into larger and ever larger underground factories, spending a still-increasing amount of its time therein, till, in the end——! Even now, does not an East-end worker live in such artificial conditions as practically to be cut off from the natural surface of the earth?

"Again, the exclusive tendency of richer people—due, no doubt, to the increasing refinement of their education, and the widening gulf between them and the rude violence of the poor—is already leading to the closing, in their interest, of considerable portions of the surface of the land. About London, for instance, perhaps half the prettier country is shut in against intrusion. And this same widening gulf—which is due to the length and expense of the higher educational process and the increased facilities for and temptations towards refined habits on the part of the rich—will make that exchange between class and class, that promotion by intermarriage which at present retards the splitting of our species along lines of social stratification, less and less frequent. So, in the end, above ground you must have the Haves, pursuing pleasure and comfort and beauty, and below ground the Have-nots; the Workers getting continually adapted to the conditions of their labour. Once they were there, they would, no doubt, have to pay rent, and not a little of it, for the ventilation of their caverns; and if they refused, they would starve or be suffocated for arrears. Such of them as were so constituted as to be miserable and rebellious would die; and, in the end, the balance being permanent, the survivors would become as well adapted to the conditions of underground life, and as happy in their way, as the Overworld people were to theirs. As it seemed to me, the refined beauty and the etiolated pallor followed naturally enough.

"The great triumph of Humanity I had dreamed of took a different shape in my mind. It had been no such triumph of moral education and general co-operation as I had imagined. Instead, I saw a real aristocracy, armed with a perfected science and working to a logical conclusion the industrial system of to-day. Its triumph had not been simply a triumph over nature, but a triumph over nature and the fellow-man. This, I must warn you, was my theory at the time. I had no convenient cicerone in the pattern of the Utopian books. My explanation may be absolutely wrong. I still think it is the most plausible one. But even on this supposition the balanced civilization that was at last attained must have long since passed its zenith, and was now far fallen into decay. The too-perfect security of the Overworlders had led them to a slow movement of de-generation, to a general dwindling in size, strength, and intelligence. That I could see clearly enough already. What had happened to the Undergrounders I did not yet suspect; but, from what I had seen of the Morlocks—that, by the bye, was the name by which these creatures were called—I could imagine that the modification of the human type was even far more profound than among the 'Eloi,' the beautiful race that I already knew.

"Then came troublesome doubts. Why had the Morlocks taken my Time Machine? For I felt sure it was they who had taken it. Why, too, if the Eloi were masters, could they not restore the machine to me? And why were they so terribly afraid of the dark? I proceeded, as I have said, to question Weena about this Underworld, but here again I was dis-appointed. At first she would not understand my questions, and presently she refused to answer them. She shivered as though the topic was un-endurable. And when I pressed her, perhaps a little harshly, she burst into tears. They were the only tears, except my own, I ever saw in that Golden Age. When I saw them I ceased abruptly to trouble about the Morlocks, and was only concerned in banishing these signs of her human inheritance from Weena's eyes. And very soon she was smiling and clapping her hands, while I solemnly burnt a match.

CHAPTER IX

THE MORLOCKS

"IT MAY seem odd to you, but it was two days before I could follow up the new-found clue in what was manifestly the proper way. I felt a peculiar shrinking from those pallid bodies. They were just the half-bleached colour of the worms and things one sees preserved in spirit in a zoological museum. And they were filthily cold to the touch. Probably my shrinking was largely due to the sympathetic influence of the Eloi, whose disgust of the Morlocks I now began to appreciate.

"The next night I did not sleep well. Probably my health was a little disordered. I was oppressed with perplexity and doubt. Once or twice I had a feeling of intense fear for which I could perceive no definite reason. I remember creeping noiselessly into the great hall where the little people were sleeping in the moonlight—that night Weena was among them—and feeling reassured by their presence. It occurred to me, even then, that in the course of a few days the moon must pass through its last quarter, and the nights grow dark, when the appearances of these unpleasant creatures from below, these whitened Lemurs, this new vermin that had replaced the old, might be more abundant. And on both these days I had the restless feeling of one who shirks an inevitable duty. I felt assured that the Time Machine was only to be recovered by boldly penetrating these mysteries of underground. Yet I could not face the mystery. If only I had had a companion it would have been different. But I was so horribly alone, and even to clamber down into the darkness of the well appalled me. I don't know if you will understand my feeling, but I never felt quite safe at my back.

"It was this restlessness, this insecurity, perhaps, that drove me further and further afield in my exploring expeditions. Going to the south-westward towards the rising country that is now called Combe Wood, I observed far off, in the direction of nineteenth-century Banstead, a vast green structure, different in character from any I had hitherto seen. It was larger than the largest of the palaces or ruins I knew, and the façade had an Oriental look: the face of it having the lustre, as well as the pale-green tint, a kind of bluish-green, of a certain type of Chinese porcelain. This difference in aspect suggested a difference in use, and I was minded to push on and explore. But the day was growing late, and I had come upon the sight of the place after a long and tiring circuit; so I resolved to hold over the adventure for the following day, and I returned to the welcome and the caresses of little Weena. But next morning I perceived clearly enough that my curiosity regarding the Palace of Green Porcelain was a piece of self-deception, to enable me to shirk, by another day, an experience I dreaded. I resolved I would make the descent without further waste of time, and started out in the early morning towards a well near the ruins of granite and aluminium.

"Little Weena ran with me. She danced beside me to the well, but when she saw me lean over the mouth and look downward, she seemed strangely disconcerted. 'Good-bye, little Weena,' I said, kissing her; and then, putting her down, I began to feel over the parapet for the climbing hooks. Rather hastily, I may as well confess, for I feared my courage might leak away! At first she watched me in amazement. Then she gave a most piteous cry, and, running to me, began to pull at me with her little hands. I think her opposition nerved me rather to proceed. I shook her off, perhaps a little roughly, and in another moment I was in the throat of the well. I saw her agonized face over the parapet, and smiled to reassure her. Then I had to look down at the unstable hooks to which I clung.

"I had to clamber down a shaft of perhaps two hundred yards. The descent was effected by means of metallic bars projecting from the sides of the well, and these being adapted to the needs of a creature much smaller and lighter than myself, I was speedily cramped and fatigued by the descent. And not simply fatigued! One of the bars bent suddenly under my weight, and almost swung me off into the blackness beneath. For a moment I hung by one hand, and after that experience I did not dare to rest again. Though my arms and back were presently acutely painful, I went on clambering down the sheer descent with as quick a motion as possible. Glancing upward, I saw the aperture, a small blue disk, in which a star was visible, while little Weena's head showed as a round black projection. The thudding sound of a machine below grew louder and more oppressive. Everything save that little disk above was profoundly dark, and when I looked up again Weena had disappeared.

"I was in an agony of discomfort. I had some thought of trying to go up the shaft again, and leave the Underworld alone. But even while I turned this over in my mind I continued to descend. At last, with intense relief, I saw dimly coming up, a foot to the right of me, a slender loophole in the wall. Swinging myself in, I found it was the aperture of a narrow horizontal tunnel in which I could lie down and rest. It was not too soon. My arms ached, my back was cramped, and I was trembling with the prolonged terror of a fall. Besides this, the unbroken darkness had had a distressing effect upon my eyes. The air was full of the throb-and-hum of machinery pumping air down the shaft.

"I do not know how long I lay. I was roused by a soft hand touching my face. Starting up in the darkness I snatched at my matches and, hastily striking one, I saw three stooping white creatures similar to the one I had seen above ground in the ruin, hastily retreating before the light. Living, as they did, in what appeared to me impenetrable darkness, their eyes were abnormally large and sensitive, just as are the pupils of the abysmal fishes, and they reflected the light in the same way. I have no doubt they could see me in that rayless obscurity, and they did not seem to have any fear of me apart from the light. But, so soon as I struck a match in order to see them, they fled incontinently, vanishing into dark gutters and tunnels, from which their eyes glared at me in the strangest fashion.

"I tried to call to them, but the language they had was apparently different from that of the overworld people; so that I was needs left to my own unaided efforts, and the thought of flight before exploration was even then in my mind. But I said to myself, 'You are in for it now,' and, feeling my way along the tunnel, I found the noise of machinery grow louder. Presently the walls fell away from me, and I came to a large open space, and, striking another match, saw that I had entered a vast arched cavern, which stretched into utter darkness beyond the range of my light. The view I had of it was as much as one could see in the burning of a match.

"Necessarily my memory is vague. Great shapes like big machines rose out of the dimness, and cast grotesque black shadows, in which dim spectral Morlocks sheltered from the glare. The place, by the bye, was very stuffy and oppressive, and the faint halitus of freshly-shed blood was in the air. Some way down the central vista was a little table of white metal, laid with what seemed a meal. The Morlocks at any rate were carnivorous! Even at the time, I remember wondering what large animal could have survived to furnish the red joint I saw. It was all very indistinct: the heavy smell, the big unmeaning shapes, the obscene figures lurking in the shadows, and only waiting for the darkness to come at me again! Then the match burnt down, and stung my fingers, and fell, a wriggling red spot in the blackness.

"I have thought since how particularly ill-equipped I was for such an experience. When I had started with the Time Machine, I had started with the absurd assumption that the men of the Future would certainly be infinitely ahead of ourselves in all their appliances. I had come without arms, without medicine, without anything to smoke—at times I missed tobacco frightfully!—even without enough matches. If only I had thought of a Kodak! I could have flashed that glimpse of the Underworld in a second, and examined it at leisure. But, as it was, I stood there with only the weapons and the powers that Nature had endowed me with— hands, feet, and teeth; these, and four safety matches thàt still remained to me.

"I was afraid to push my way in among all this machinery in the dark, and it was only with my last glimpse of light I discovered that my store of matches had run low. It had never occurred to me until that moment that there was any need to economize them, and I had wasted almost half the box in astonishing the Overworlders, to whom fire was a novelty.

Now, as I say, I had four left, and while I stood in the dark, a hand touched mine, lank fingers came feeling over my face, and I was sensible of a peculiar unpleasant odour. I fancied I heard the breathing of a crowd of those dreadful little beings about me. I felt the box of matches in my hand being gently disengaged, and other hands behind me plucking at my clothing. The sense of these unseen creatures examining me was indescribably unpleasant. The sudden realization of my ignorance of their ways of thinking and doing came home to me very vividly in the darkness. I shouted at them as loudly as I could. They started away, and then I could feel them approaching me again. They clutched at me more boldly, whispering odd sounds to each other. I shivered violently, and shouted again—rather discordantly. This time they were not so seriously alarmed, and they made a queer laughing noise as they came back at me. I will confess I was horribly frightened. I determined to strike another match and escape under the protection of its glare. I did so, and eking out the flicker with a scrap of paper from my pocket, I made good my retreat to the narrow tunnel. But I had scarce entered this when my light was blown out, and in the blackness I could hear the Morlocks rustling like wind among leaves, and pattering like the rain, as they hurried after me.

"In a moment I was clutched by several hands, and there was no mistaking that they were trying to haul me back. I struck another light, and waved it in their dazzled faces. You can scarce imagine how nauseatingly inhuman they looked—those pale, chinless faces and great, lidless, pinkish-grey eyes!—as they stared in their blindness and bewilderment. But I did not stay to look, I promise you: I retreated again, and when my second match had ended, I struck my third. It had almost burnt through when I reached the opening into the shaft. I lay down on the edge, for the throb of the great pump below made me giddy. Then I felt sideways for the projecting hooks, and, as I did so, my feet were grasped from behind, and I was violently tugged backward. I lit my last match . . . and it incontinently went out. But I had my hand on the climbing bars now, and, kicking violently, I disengaged myself from the clutches of the Morlocks, and was speedily clambering up the shaft, while they stayed peering and blinking up at me: all but one little wretch who followed me for some way, and well-nigh secured my boot as a trophy.

"That climb seemed interminable to me. With the last twenty or thirty feet of it a deadly nausea came upon me. I had the greatest difficulty in keeping my hold. The last few yards was a frightful struggle against this faintness. Several times my head swam, and I felt all the sensations of falling. At last, however, I got over the well-mouth somehow, and staggered out of the ruin into the blinding sunlight. I fell upon my face. Even the soil smelt sweet and clean. Then I remember Weena kissing my hands and ears, and the voices of others among the Eloi. Then, for a time, I was insensible.

***

CHAPTER X

WHEN THE NIGHT CAME

"NOW, INDEED, I seemed in a worse case than before. Hitherto, except during my night's anguish at the loss of the Time Machine, I had felt a sustaining hope of ultimate escape, but that hope was staggered by these new discoveries. Hitherto I had merely thought myself impeded by the childish simplicity of the little people, and by some unknown forces which I had only to understand to overcome; but there was an altogether new element in the sickening quality of the Morlocks—a something inhuman and malign. Instinctively I loathed them. Before, I had felt as a man might feel who had fallen into a pit: my concern was with the pit and how to get out of it. Now I felt like a beast in a trap, whose enemy would come upon him soon.

"The enemy I dreaded may surprise you. It was the darkness of the new moon. Weena had put this into my head by some at first incomprehensible remarks about the Dark Nights. It was not now such a very difficult problem to guess what the coming Dark Nights might mean. The moon was on the wane: each night there was a longer interval of darkness. And I now understood to some slight degree at least the reason of the fear of the little upper-world people for the dark. I wondered vaguely what foul villainy it might be that the Morlocks did under the new moon. I felt pretty sure now that my second hypothesis was all wrong. The upper-world people might once have been the favoured aristocracy, and the Morlocks their mechanical servants; but that had long since passed away. The two species that had resulted from the evolution of man were sliding down towards, or had already arrived at, an altogether new relationship. The Eloi, like the Carlovignan kings, had decayed to a mere beautiful futility. They still possessed the earth on sufferance: since the Morlocks, subterranean for innumerable generations, had come at last to find the daylit surface intolerable. And the Morlocks made their garments, I inferred, and maintained them in their habitual needs, perhaps through the survival of an old habit of service.

They did it as a standing horse paws with his foot, or as a man enjoys killing animals in sport: because ancient and departed necessities had impressed it on the organism. But, clearly, the old order was already in part reversed. The Nemesis of the delicate ones was creeping on apace. Ages ago, thousands of generations ago, man had thrust his brother man out of the ease and the sunshine. And now that brother was coming back —changed! Already the Eloi had begun to learn one old lesson anew. They were becoming re-acquainted with Fear. And suddenly there came into my head the memory of the meat I had seen in the under-world. It seemed odd how it floated into my mind: not stirred up as it were by the current of my meditations, but coming in almost like a question from outside. I tried to recall the form of it. I had a vague sense of something familiar, but I could not tell what it was at the time.

"Still, however helpless the little people in the presence of their mysterious Fear, I was differently constituted. I came out of this age of ours, this ripe prime of the human race, when Fear does not paralyze and mystery has lost its terrors. I at least would defend myself. Without further delay I determined to make myself arms and a fastness where I might sleep. With that refuge as a base, I could face this strange world with some of that confidence I had lost in realizing to what creatures night by night I lay exposed. I felt I could never sleep again until my bed was secure from them. I shuddered with horror to think how they must already have examined me.

"I wandered during the afternoon along the valley of the Thames, but found nothing that commended itself to my mind as inaccessible. All the buildings and trees seemed easily practicable to such dexterous climbers as the Morlocks, to judge by their wells, must be. Then the tall pinnacles of the Palace of Green Porcelain and the polished gleam of its walls came back to my memory; and in the evening, taking Weena like a child upon my shoulder, I went up the hills towards the south-west. The distance, I had reckoned, was seven or eight miles, but it must have been nearer eighteen. I had first seen the place on a moist afternoon when distances are deceptively diminished. In addition, the heel of one of my shoes was loose, and a nail was working through the sole—they were comfortable old shoes I wore about indoors—so that I was lame. And it was already long past sunset when I came in sight of the palace, silhouetted black against the pale yellow of the sky.

"Weena had been hugely delighted when I began to carry her, but after a time she desired me to let her down, and ran along by the side of me, occasionally darting off on either hand to pick flowers to stick in my pockets. My pockets had always puzzled Weena, but at the last she had concluded that they were an eccentric kind of vases for floral decoration.

At least she utilized them for that purpose. And that reminds me! In changing my jacket I found . . ."

The Time Traveller paused, put his hand into his pocket, and silently placed two withered flowers, not unlike very large white mallows, upon the little table. Then he resumed his narrative.

"As the hush of evening crept over the world and we proceeded over the hill crest towards Wimbledon, Weena grew tired and wanted to return to the house of grey stone. But I pointed out the distant pinnacles of the Palace of Green Porcelain to her, and contrived to make her understand that we were seeking a refuge there from her Fear. You know that great pause that comes upon things before the dusk? Even the breeze stops in the trees. To me there is always an air of expectation about that evening stillness. The sky was clear, remote, and empty save for a few horizontal bars far down in the sunset. Well, that night the expectation took the colour of my fears. In that darkling calm my senses seemed preternaturally sharpened. I fancied I could even feel the hollowness of the ground beneath my feet: could, indeed, almost see through it the Morlocks on their ant-hill going hither and thither and waiting for the dark. In my excitement I fancied that they would receive my invasion of their burrows as a declaration of war. And why had they taken my Time Machine?

"So we went on in the quiet, and the twilight deepened into night. The clear blue of the distance faded, and one star after another came out. The ground grew dim and the trees black. Weena's fears and her fatigue grew upon her. I took her in my arms and talked to her and caressed her. Then, as the darkness grew deeper, she put her arms round my neck, and, closing her eyes, tightly pressed her face against my shoulder. So we went down a long slope into a valley, and there in the dimness I almost walked into a little river. This I waded, and went up the opposite side of the valley, past a number of sleeping-houses, and by a statue—a Faun, or some such figure, *minus* the head. Here, too, were acacias. So far I had seen nothing of the Morlocks, but it was yet early in the night, and the darker hours before the old moon rose were still to come.

"From the brow of the next hill I saw a thick wood spreading wide and black before me. I hesitated at this. I could see no end to it, either to the right or the left. Feeling tired—my feet in particular, were very sore—I carefully lowered Weena from my shoulder as I halted, and sat down upon the turf. I could no longer see the Palace of Green Porcelain, and I was in doubt of my direction. I looked into the thickness of the wood and thought of what it might hide. Under that dense tangle of branches one would be out of sight of the stars. Even were there no other lurking danger—a danger I did not care to let my imagination loose upon—

there would still be all the roots to stumble over and the tree boles to strike against. I was very tired, too, after the excitements of the day; so I decided that I would not face it, but would pass the night upon the open hill.

"Weena, I was glad to find, was fast asleep. I carefully wrapped her in my jacket, and sat down beside her to wait for the moonrise. The hill-side was quiet and deserted, but from the black of the wood there came now and then a stir of living things. Above me shone the stars, for the night was very clear. I felt a certain sense of friendly comfort in their twinkling. All the old constellations had gone from the sky, however: that slow movement which is imperceptible in a hundred human lifetimes, had long since re-arranged them in unfamiliar groupings. But the Milky Way, it seemed to me, was still the same tattered streamer of star-dust as of yore. Southward (as I judged it) was a very bright red star that was new to me: it was even more splendid than our own green Sirius. And amid all these scintillating points of light one bright planet shone kindly and steadily like the face of an old friend.

"Looking at these stars suddenly dwarfed my own troubles and all the gravities of terrestrial life. I thought of their unfathomable distance, and the slow inevitable drift of their movements out of the unknown past into the unknown future. I thought of the great precessional cycle that the pole of the earth describes. Only forty times had that silent revolution occurred during all the years that I had traversed. And during these few revolutions all the activity, all the traditions, the complex organizations, the nations, languages, literatures, aspirations, even the mere memory of Man as I knew him, had been swept out of existence. Instead were these frail creatures who had forgotten their high ancestry, and the white Things of which I went in terror. Then I thought of the Great Fear that was between the two species, and for the first time, with a sudden shiver, came the clear knowledge of what the meat I had seen might be. Yet it was too horrible! I looked at little Weena sleeping beside me, her face white and starlike under the stars, and forthwith dismissed the thought.

"Through that long night I held my mind off the Morlocks as well as I could, and whiled away the time by trying to fancy I could find signs of the old constellations in the new confusion. The sky kept very clear, except for a hazy cloud or so. No doubt I dozed at times. Then, as my vigil wore on, came a faintness in the eastward sky, like the reflection of some colourless fire, and the old moon rose, thin and peaked and white. And close behind, and overtaking it, and overflowing it, the dawn came, pale at first, and then growing pink and warm. No Morlocks had approached us. Indeed, I had seen none upon the hill that night. And in the confidence of renewed day it almost seemed to me that my fear had been unreasonable. I stood up and found my foot with the loose heel swollen at the ankle and painful under the heel; so I sat down again, took off my shoes, and flung them away.

"I awakened Weena, and we went down into the wood, now green and pleasant instead of black and forbidding. We found some fruit wherewith to break our fast. We soon met others of the dainty ones, laughing and dancing in the sunlight as though there was no such thing in nature as the night. And then I thought once more of the meat that I had seen. I felt assured now of what it was, and from the bottom of my heart I pitied this last feeble rill from the great flood of humanity. Clearly, at some time in the Long-Ago of human decay the Morlocks' food had run short. Possibly they had lived on rats and suchlike vermin. Even now man is far less discriminating and exclusive in his food than he was—far less than any monkey. His prejudice against human flesh is no deep-seated instinct. And so these inhuman sons of men——! I tried to look at the thing in a scientific spirit. After all, they were less human and more remote than our cannibal ancestors of three or four thousand years ago. And the intelligence that would have made this state of things a torment had gone. Why should I trouble myself? These Eloi were mere fatted cattle, which the ant-like Morlocks preserved and preyed upon—probably saw to the breeding of. And there was Weena dancing at my side!

"Then I tried to preserve myself from the horror that was coming upon me, by regarding it as a rigorous punishment of human selfishness. Man had been content to live in ease and delight upon the labours of his fellow-man, had taken Necessity as his watchword and excuse, and in the fulness of time Necessity had come home to him. I even tried a Carlyle-like scorn of this wretched aristocracy-in-decay. But this attitude of mind was impossible. However great their intellectual degradation, the Eloi had kept too much of the human form not to claim my sympathy, and to make me perforce a sharer in their degradation and their Fear.

"I had at that time very vague ideas as to the course I should pursue. My first was to secure some safe place of refuge, and to make myself such arms of metal or stone as I could contrive. That necessity was immediate. In the next place, I hoped to procure some means of fire, so that I should have the weapon of a torch at hand, for nothing, I knew, would be more efficient against these Morlocks. Then I wanted to arrange some con-trivance to break open the doors of bronze under the White Sphinx. I had in mind a battering-ram. I had a persuasion that if I could enter these doors and carry a blaze of light before me I should discover the Time Machine and escape. I could not imagine the Morlocks were strong enough to move it far away. Weena I had resolved to bring with me to our own time. And turning such schemes over in my mind I pursued our way towards the building which my fancy had chosen as our dwelling.

———————◆———————

CHAPTER XI

THE PALACE OF GREEN PORCELAIN

"I FOUND the Palace of Green Porcelain, when we approached it about noon, deserted and falling into ruin. Only ragged vestiges of glass remained in its windows, and great sheets of the green facing had fallen away from the corroded metallic framework. It lay very high upon a turfy down, and looking north-eastward before I entered it, I was surprised to see a large estuary, or even creek, where I judged Wandsworth and Battersea must once have been. I thought then—though I never followed up the thought—of what might have happened, or might be happening, to the living things in the sea.

"The material of the Palace proved on examination to be indeed porcelain, and along the face of it I saw an inscription in some unknown character. I thought, rather foolishly, that Weena might help me to interpret this, but I only learnt that the bare idea of writing had never entered her head. She always seemed to me, I fancy, more human than she was, perhaps because her affection was so human.

"Within the big valves of the door—which were open and broken—we found, instead of the customary hall, a long gallery lit by many side windows. At the first glance I was reminded of a museum. The tiled floor was thick with dust, and a remarkable array of miscellaneous objects was shrouded in the same grey covering. Then I perceived, standing strange and gaunt in the centre of the hall, what was clearly the lower part of a huge skeleton. I recognized by the oblique feet that it was some extinct creature after the fashion of the Megatherium. The skull and the upper bones lay beside it in the thick dust, and in one place, where rain-water had dropped through a leak in the roof, the thing itself had been worn away. Further in the gallery was the huge skeleton barrel of a Brontosaurus. My museum hypothesis was confirmed. Going towards the side I found what appeared to be sloping shelves, and, clearing away the thick dust, I found the old familiar glass cases of our own time. But they must have been air-tight, to judge from the fair preservation of some of their contents.

"Clearly we stood among the ruins of some latter-day South Kensington! Here, apparently, was the Palæontological Section, and a very splendid array of fossils it must have been, though the inevitable process of decay that had been staved off for a time, and had, through the extinction of bacteria and fungi, lost ninety-nine hundredths of its force, was, nevertheless, with extreme sureness if with extreme slowness at work again upon all its treasures. Here and there I found traces of the little people in the shape of rare fossils broken to pieces or threaded in strings upon reeds. And the cases had in some instances been bodily removed—by the Morlocks as I judged. The place was very silent. The thick dust deadened our footsteps. Weena, who had been rolling a sea-urchin down the sloping glass of a case, presently came, as I stared about me, and very quietly took my hand and stood beside me.

"And at first I was so much surprised by this ancient monument of an intellectual age, that I gave no thought to the possibilities it presented. Even my pre-occupation about the Time Machine receded a little from my mind.

"To judge from the size of the place, this Palace of Green Porcelain had a great deal more in it than a Gallery of Palæontology; possibly historical galleries; it might be, even a library! To me, at least in my present circumstances, these would be vastly more interesting than this spectacle of old-time geology in decay. Exploring, I found another short gallery running transversely to the first. This appeared to be devoted to minerals, and the sight of a block of sulphur set my mind running on gunpowder. But I could find no saltpetre; indeed, no nitrates of any kind. Doubtless they had deliquesced ages ago. Yet the sulphur hung in my mind, and set up a train of thinking. As for the rest of the contents of that gallery, though, on the whole, they were the best preserved of all I saw, I had little interest. I am no specialist in mineralogy, and I went on down a very ruinous aisle running parallel to the first hall I had entered. Apparently this section had been devoted to natural history, but everything had long since passed out of recognition. A few shrivelled and blackened vestiges of what had once been stuffed animals, desiccated mummies in jars that had once held spirit, a brown dust of departed plants: that was all! I was sorry for that, because I should have been glad to trace the patient re-adjustments by which the conquest of animated nature had been attained. Then we came to a gallery of simply colossal proportions, but singularly ill-lit, the floor of it running downward at a slight angle from the end at which I entered. At intervals white globes hung from the ceiling—many of them cracked and smashed—which suggested that originally the place had been artificially lit. Here I was more in my element, for rising on either side of me were the huge bulks of big machines, all greatly corroded and many broken down, but some still fairly complete. You know I have a certain weakness for mechanism, and I was inclined to linger among these: the more so as for the most part they had the interest of puzzles, and I could make only the vaguest guesses at what they were for. I fancied that if I could solve their puzzles I should find myself in possession of powers that might be of use against the Morlocks.

"Suddenly Weena came very close to my side. So suddenly that she startled me. Had it not been for her I do not think I should have noticed that the floor of the gallery sloped at all.[1] The end I had come in at was quite above ground, and was lit by rare slit-like windows. As you went down the length, the ground came up against these windows, until at last there was a pit like the 'area' of a London house before each, and only a narrow line of daylight at the top. I went slowly along, puzzling about the machines, and had been too intent upon them to notice the gradual diminution of the light, until Weena's increasing apprehensions drew my attention. Then I saw that the gallery ran down at last into a thick darkness. I hesitated, and then, as I looked round me, I saw that the dust was less abundant and its surface less even. Further away towards the dimness, it appeared to be broken by a number of small narrow footprints. My sense of the immediate presence of the Morlocks revived at that. I felt that I was wasting my time in this academic examination of machinery. I called to mind that it was already far advanced in the afternoon, and that I had still no weapon, no refuge, and no means of making a fire. And then down in the remote blackness of the gallery I heard a peculiar pattering, and the same odd noises I had heard down the well.

"I took Weena's hand. Then, struck with a sudden idea, I left her and turned to a machine from which projected a lever not unlike those in a signal-box. Clambering upon the stand, and grasping this lever in my hands, I put all my weight upon it sideways. Suddenly Weena, deserted in the central aisle, began to whimper. I had judged the strength of the lever pretty correctly, for it snapped after a minute's strain, and I rejoined her with a mace in my hand more than sufficient, I judged, for any Morlock skull I might encounter. And I longed very much to kill a Morlock or so. Very inhuman, you may think, to want to go killing one's own descendants! But it was impossible, somehow, to feel any humanity in the things. Only my disinclination to leave Weena, and a persuasion that if I began to slake my thirst for murder my Time Machine

---

[1] It may be, of course, that the floor did not slope, but that the museum was built into the side of a hill.—ED.

might suffer, restrained me from going straight down the gallery and killing the brutes I heard.

"Well, mace in one hand and Weena in the other, I went out of that gallery and into another and still larger one, which at the first glance reminded me of a military chapel hung with tattered flags. The brown and charred rags that hung from the sides of it, I presently recognized as the decaying vestiges of books. They had long since dropped to pieces, and every semblance of print had left them. But here and there were warped boards and cracked metallic clasps that told the tale well enough. Had I been a literary man I might, perhaps, have moralized upon the futility of all ambition. But as it was, the thing that struck me with keenest force was the enormous waste of labour to which this sombre wilderness of rotting paper testified. At the time I will confess that I thought chiefly of the *Philosophical Transactions* and my own seventeen papers upon physical optics.

"Then, going up a broad staircase, we came to what may once have been a gallery of technical chemistry. And here I had not a little hope of useful discoveries. Except at one end where the roof had collapsed, this gallery was well preserved. I went eagerly to every unbroken case. And at last, in one of the really air-tight cases, I found a box of matches. Very eagerly I tried them. They were perfectly good. They were not even damp. I turned to Weena. 'Dance,' I cried to her in her own tongue. For now I had a weapon indeed against the horrible creatures we feared. And so, in that derelict museum, upon the thick soft carpeting of dust, to Weena's huge delight, I solemnly performed a kind of composite dance, whistling *The Land of the Leal* as cheerfully as I could. In part it was a modest *can-can*, in part a step dance, in part a skirt dance (so far as my tail-coat permitted), and in part original. For I am naturally inventive, as you know.

"Now, I still think that for this box of matches to have escaped the wear of time for immemorial years was a most strange, as for me it was a most fortunate, thing. Yet, oddly enough, I found a far unlikelier sub-stance, and that was camphor. I found it in a sealed jar, that by chance, I suppose, had been really hermetically sealed. I fancied at first that it was paraffin wax, and smashed the glass accordingly. But the odour of camphor was unmistakable. In the universal decay this volatile substance had chanced to survive, perhaps through many thousands of centuries. It reminded me of a sepia painting I had once seen done from the ink of a fossil Belemnite that must have perished and become fossilized millions of years ago. I was about to throw it away, but I remembered that it was inflammable and burnt with a good bright flame—was, in fact, an ex-cellent candle—and I put it in my pocket. I found no explosives, however, nor any means of breaking down the bronze doors. As yet my iron crow-bar was the most helpful thing I had chanced upon. Nevertheless I left that gallery greatly elated.

"I cannot tell you all the story of that long afternoon. It would require a great effort of memory to recall my explorations in at all the proper order. I remember a long gallery of rusting stands of arms, and how I hesitated between my crowbar and a hatchet or a sword. I could not carry both, however, and my bar of iron promised best against the bronze gates. There were numbers of guns, pistols, and rifles. The most were masses of rust, but many were of some new metal, and still fairly sound. But any cartridges or powder there may once have been had rotted into dust. One corner I saw was charred and shattered: perhaps, I thought, by an explosion among the specimens. In another place was a vast array of idols—Polynesian, Mexican, Grecian, Phœnician, every country on earth I should think. And here, yielding to an irresistible impulse, I wrote my name upon the nose of a steatite monster from South America that particularly took my fancy.

"As the evening drew on, my interest waned. I went through gallery after gallery, dusty, silent, often ruinous, the exhibits sometimes mere heaps of rust and lignite, sometimes fresher. In one place I suddenly found myself near the model of a tin mine, and then by the merest accident I discovered, in an air-tight case, two dynamite cartridges! I shouted 'Eureka,' and smashed the case with joy. Then came a doubt. I hesitated. Then, selecting a little side gallery, I made my essay. I never felt such a disappointment as I did in waiting five, ten, fifteen minutes for an explosion that never came. Of course the things were dummies, as I might have guessed from their presence. I really believe that, had they not been so, I should have rushed off incontinently and blown Sphinx, bronze doors, and (as it proved) my chances of finding the Time Machine, all together into non-existence.

"It was after that, I think, that we came to a little open court within the palace. It was turfed, and had three fruit-trees. So we rested and re-freshed ourselves. Towards sunset I began to consider our position. Night was creeping upon us, and my inaccessible hiding-place had still to be found. But that troubled me very little now. I had in my possession a thing that was, perhaps, the best of all defences against the Morlocks —I had matches! I had the camphor in my pocket, too, if a blaze were needed. It seemed to me that the best thing we could do would be to pass the night in the open, protected by a fire. In the morning there was the getting of the Time Machine. Towards that, as yet, I had only my iron mace. But now, with my growing knowledge, I felt very differently towards those bronze doors. Up to this, I had refrained from forcing them, largely because of the mystery on the other side. They had never impressed me as being very strong, and I hoped to find my bar of iron not altogether inadequate for the work.

———

CHAPTER XII

IN THE DARKNESS

"WE EMERGED from the Palace while the sun was still in part above the horizon. I was determined to reach the White Sphinx early the next morning, and ere the dusk I purposed pushing through the woods that had stopped me on the previous journey. My plan was to go as far as possible that night, and then, building a fire, to sleep in the protection of its glare. Accordingly, as we went along I gathered any sticks or dried grass I saw, and presently had my arms full of such litter. Thus loaded, our progress was slower than I had anticipated, and besides Weena was tired. And I, also, began to suffer from sleepiness too; so that it was full night before we reached the wood. Upon the shrubby hill of its edge Weena would have stopped, fearing the darkness before us; but a singular sense of impending calamity, that should indeed have served me as a warning, drove me onward. I had been without sleep for a night and two days, and I was feverish and irritable. I felt sleep coming upon me, and the Morlocks with it.

"While we hesitated, among the black bushes behind us, and dim against their blackness, I saw three crouching figures. There was scrub and long grass all about us, and I did not feel safe from their insidious approach. The forest, I calculated, was rather less than a mile across. If we could get through it to the bare hill-side, there, as it seemed to me, was an altogether safer resting-place: I thought that with my matches and my camphor I could contrive to keep my path illuminated through the woods. Yet it was evident that if I was to flourish matches with my hands I should have to abandon my firewood: so, rather reluctantly, I put it down. And then it came into my head that I would amaze our friends behind by lighting it. I was to discover the atrocious folly of this proceeding, but it came to my mind as an ingenious move for covering our retreat.

"I don't know if you have ever thought what a rare thing flame must be in the absence of man and in a temperate climate. The sun's heat is rarely strong enough to burn, even when it is focussed by dewdrops, as is sometimes the case in more tropical districts. Lightning may blast and blacken, but it rarely gives rise to wide-spread fire. Decaying vegetation may occasionally smoulder with the heat of its fermentation, but this rarely results in flame. In this decadence, too, the art of fire-making had been forgotten on the earth. The red tongues that went licking up my heap of wood were an altogether new and strange thing to Weena.

"She wanted to run to it and play with it. I believe she would have cast herself into it had I not restrained her. But I caught her up, and, in spite of her struggles, plunged boldly before me into the wood. For a little way the glare of my fire lit the path. Looking back presently, I could see, through the crowded stems, that from my heap of sticks the blaze had spread to some bushes adjacent, and a curved line of fire was creeping up the grass of the hill. I laughed at that, and turned again to the dark trees before me. It was very black, and Weena clung to me convulsively, but there was still, as my eyes grew accustomed to the darkness, sufficient light for me to avoid the stems. Overhead it was simply black, except where a gap of remote blue sky shone down upon us here and there. I lit none of my matches because I had no hands free. Upon my left arm I carried my little one, in my right hand I had my iron bar.

"For some way I heard nothing but the crackling twigs under my feet, the faint rustle of the breeze above, and my own breathing and the throb of the blood-vessels in my ears. Then I seemed to know of a pattering about me. I pushed on grimly. The pattering grew more distinct, and then I caught the same queer sounds and voices I had heard in the under-world. There were evidently several of the Morlocks, and they were closing in upon me. Indeed, in another minute I felt a tug at my coat, then something at my arm. And Weena shivered violently, and became quite still.

"It was time for a match. But to get one I must put her down. I did so, and, as I fumbled with my pocket, a struggle began in the darkness about my knees, perfectly silent on her part and with the same peculiar cooing sounds from the Morlocks. Soft little hands, too, were creeping over my coat and back, touching even my neck. Then the match scratched and fizzed. I held it flaring, and saw the white backs of the Morlocks in flight amid the trees. I hastily took a lump of camphor from my pocket, and prepared to light it as soon as the match should wane. Then I looked at Weena. She was lying clutching my feet and quite motionless, with her face to the ground. With a sudden fright I stooped to her. She seemed scarcely to breathe. I lit the block of camphor and flung it to the ground, and as it split and flared up and drove back the Morlocks and the shadows, I knelt down and lifted her. The wood behind seemed full of the stir and murmur of a great company!

"She seemed to have fainted. I put her carefully upon my shoulder and rose to push on, and then there came a horrible realization. In manœuvring with my matches and Weena, I had turned myself about several times, and now I had not the faintest idea in what direction lay my path. For all I knew, I might be facing back towards the Palace of Green Porcelain. I found myself in a cold sweat. I had to think rapidly what to do. I determined to build a fire and encamp where we were. I put Weena, still motionless, down upon a turfy bole, and very hastily, as my first lump of camphor waned, I began collecting sticks and leaves. Here and there out of the darkness round me the Morlocks' eyes shone like carbuncles.

"The camphor flickered and went out. I lit a match, and as I did so, two white forms that had been approaching Weena dashed hastily away. One was so blinded by the light that he came straight for me and I felt his bones grind under the blow of my fist. He gave a whoop of dismay, staggered a little way, and fell down. I lit another piece of camphor, and went on gathering my bonfire. Presently I noticed how dry was some of the foliage above me, for since my arrival on the Time Machine, a matter of a week, no rain had fallen. So, instead of casting about among the trees for fallen twigs, I began leaping up and dragging down branches. Very soon I had a choking smoky fire of green wood and dry sticks, and could economize my camphor. Then I turned to where Weena lay beside my iron mace. I tried what I could to revive here, but she lay like one dead. I could not even satisfy myself whether or not she breathed.

"Now, the smoke of the fire beat over towards me, and it must have made me heavy of a sudden. Moreover, the vapour of camphor was in the air. My fire would not need replenishing for an hour or so. I felt very weary after my exertion, and sat down. The wood, too, was full of a slumbrous murmur that I did not understand. I seemed just to nod and open my eyes. But all was dark, and the Morlocks had their hands upon me. Flinging off their clinging fingers I hastily felt in my pocket for the match-box, and—it had gone! Then they gripped and closed with me again. In a moment I knew what had happened. I had slept, and my fire had gone out, and the bitterness of death came over my soul. The forest seemed full of the smell of burning wood. I was caught by the neck, by the hair, by the arms, and pulled down. It was indescribably horrible in the darkness to feel all these soft creatures heaped upon me. I felt as if I was in a monstrous spider's web. I was overpowered, and went down. I felt little teeth nipping at my neck. I rolled over, and as I did so my hand came against my iron lever. It gave me strength. I struggled up, shaking the human rats from me, and, holding the bar short, I thrust where I judged their faces might be. I could feel the succulent giving of flesh and bone under my blows, and for a moment I was free.

"The strange exultation that so often seems to accompany hard fighting came upon me. I knew that both I and Weena were lost, but I determined to make the Morlocks pay for their meat. I stood with my back to a tree, swinging the iron bar before me. The whole wood was full of the stir and cries of them. A minute passed. Their voices seemed to rise to a higher pitch of excitement, and their movements grew faster. Yet none came within reach. I stood glaring at the blackness. Then suddenly came hope. What if the Morlocks were afraid? And close on the heels of that came a strange thing. The darkness seemed to grow luminous. Very dimly I began to see the Morlocks about me—three battered at my feet— and then I recognized, with incredulous surprise, that the others were running, in an incessant stream, as it seemed, from behind me, and away through the wood in front. And their backs seemed no longer white, but reddish. As I stood agape, I saw a little red spark go drifting across a gap of starlight between the branches, and vanish. And at that I understood the smell of burning wood, the slumbrous murmur that was growing now into a gusty roar, the red glow, and the Morlocks' flight.

"Stepping out from behind my tree and looking back, I saw, through the black pillars of the nearer trees, the flames of the burning forest. It was my first fire coming after me. With that I looked for Weena, but she was gone. The hissing and crackling behind me, the explosive thud as each fresh tree burst into flame, left little time for reflection. My iron bar still gripped, I followed in the Morlocks' path. It was a close race. Once the flames crept forward so swiftly on my right as I ran, that I was outflanked, and had to strike off to the left. But at last I emerged upon a small open space, and as I did so, a Morlock came blundering towards me, and past me, and went on straight into the fire!

"And now I was to see the most weird and horrible thing, I think, of all that I beheld in that future age. This whole space was as bright as day with the reflection of the fire. In the centre was a hillock or tumulus, surmounted by a scorched hawthorn. Beyond this was another arm of the burning forest, with yellow tongues already writhing from it, completely encircling the space with a fence of fire. Upon the hill-side were some thirty or forty Morlocks, dazzled by the light and heat, and blundering hither and thither against each other in their bewilderment. At first I did not realize their blindness, and struck furiously at them with my bar, in a frenzy of fear, as they approached me, killing one and crippling several more. But when I had watched the gestures of one of them groping under the hawthorn against the red sky, and heard their moans, I was assured of their absolute helplessness and misery in the glare, and I struck no more of them.

"Yet every now and then one would come straight towards me, setting loose a quivering horror that made me quick to elude him. At one time the flames died down somewhat, and I feared the foul creatures would presently be able to see me. I was even thinking of beginning the fight by killing some of them before this should happen; but the fire burst out again brightly, and I stayed my hand. I walked about the hill among them and avoided them, looking for some trace of Weena. But Weena was gone.

"At last I sat down on the summit of the hillock, and watched this strange incredible company of blind things groping to and fro, and making uncanny noises to each one, as the glare of the fire beat on them. The coiling uprush of smoke streamed across the sky, and through the rare tatters of that red canopy, remote as though they belonged to another universe, shone the little stars. Two or three Morlocks came blundering into me, and I drove them off with blows of my fists, trembling as I did so.

"For the most part of that night I was persuaded it was a nightmare. I bit myself and screamed in a passionate desire to awake. I beat the ground with my hands, and got up and sat down again, and wandered here and there, and again sat down. Then I would fall to rubbing my eyes and calling upon God to let me awake. Thrice I saw Morlocks put their heads down in a kind of agony and rush into the flames. But, at last, above the subsiding red of the fire, above the streaming masses of black smoke and the whitening and blackening tree stumps, and the diminishing numbers of these dim creatures, came the white light of the day.

"I searched again for traces of Weena, but there were none. It was plain that they had left her poor little body in the forest. I cannot describe how it relieved me to think that it had escaped the awful fate to which it seemed destined. As I thought of that, I was almost moved to begin a massacre of the helpless abominations about me, but I contained myself. The hillock, as I have said, was a kind of island in the forest. From its summit I could now make out through a haze of smoke the Palace of Green Porcelain, and from that I could get my bearings for the White Sphinx. And so, leaving the remnant of these damned souls still going hither and thither and moaning, as the day grew clearer, I tied some grass about my feet and limped on across smoking ashes and among black stems that still pulsated internally with fire, towards the hiding-place of the Time Machine. I walked slowly, for I was almost exhausted, as well as lame, and I felt the intensest wretchedness for the horrible death of little Weena. It seemed an overwhelming calamity. Now, in this old familiar room, it is more like the sorrow of a dream than an actual loss. But that morning it left me absolutely lonely again—terribly alone. I began to think of this house of mine, of this fireside, of some of you, and with such thoughts came a longing that was pain.

"But, as I walked over the smoking ashes under the bright morning sky, I made a discovery. In my trouser pocket were still some loose matches. The box must have leaked before it was lost.

CHAPTER XIII

THE TRAP OF THE WHITE SPHINX

"ABOUT EIGHT or nine in the morning I came to the same seat of yellow metal from which I had viewed the world upon the evening of my arrival. I thought of my hasty conclusions upon that evening, and could not refrain from laughing bitterly at my confidence. Here was the same beautiful scene, the same abundant foliage, the same splendid palaces and magnificent ruins, the same silver river running between its fertile banks. The gay robes of the beautiful people moved hither and thither among the trees. Some were bathing in exactly the place where I had saved Weena, and that suddenly gave me a keen stab of pain. And like blots upon the landscape rose the cupolas above the ways to the under-world. I understood now what all the beauty of the over-world people covered. Very pleasant was their day, as pleasant as the day of the cattle in the field. Like the cattle, they knew of no enemies, and provided against no needs. And their end was the same.

"I grieved to think how brief the dream of the human intellect had been. It had committed suicide. It had set itself steadfastly towards comfort and ease, a balanced society with security and permanency as its watchword, it had attained its hopes—to come to this at last. Once, life and property must have reached almost absolute safety. The rich had been assured of his wealth and comfort, the toiler assured of his life and work. No doubt in that perfect world there had been no unemployed problem, no social question left unsolved. And a great quiet had followed.

"It is a law of nature we overlook, that intellectual versatility is the compensation for change, danger, and trouble. An animal perfectly in harmony with its environment is a perfect mechanism. Nature never appeals to intelligence until habit and instinct are useless. There is no intelligence where there is no change and no need of change. Only those animals partake of intelligence that have to meet a huge variety of needs and dangers.

"So, as I see it, the upper-world man had drifted towards his feeble prettiness, and the under-world to mere mechanical industry. But that perfect state had lacked one thing even for mechanical perfection—absolute permanency. Apparently as time went on, the feeding of the under-world, however it was effected, had become disjointed. Mother Necessity, who had been staved off for a few thousand years, came back again, and she began below. The under-world being in contact with machinery, which, however perfect, still needs some little thought outside habit, had probably retained perforce rather more initiative, if less of every other human character, than the upper. And when other meat failed them, they turned to what old habit had hitherto forbidden. So I say I saw it in my last view of the world of Eight Hundred and Two Thousand Seven Hundred and One. It may be as wrong an explanation as mortal wit could invent. It is how the thing shaped itself to me, and as that I give it to you.

"After the fatigues, excitements, and terrors of the past days, and in spite of my grief, this seat and the tranquil view and the warm sunlight were very pleasant. I was very tired and sleepy, and soon my theorizing passed into dozing. Catching myself at that, I took my own hint, and spreading myself out upon the turf I had a long and refreshing sleep.

"I awoke a little before sunsetting. I now felt safe against being caught napping by the Morlocks, and, stretching myself, I came on down the hill towards the White Sphinx. I had my crowbar in one hand, and the other hand played with the matches in my pocket.

"And now came a most unexpected thing. As I approached the pedestal of the sphinx I found the bronze valves were open. They had slid down into grooves.

"At that I stopped short before them, hesitating to enter.

"Within was a small apartment, and on a raised place in the corner of this was the Time Machine. I had the small levers in my pocket. So here, after all my elaborate preparations for the siege of the White Sphinx, was a meek surrender. I threw my iron bar away, almost sorry not to use it.

"A sudden thought came into my head as I stooped towards the portal. For once, at least, I grasped the mental operations of the Morlocks. Suppressing a strong inclination to laugh, I stepped through the bronze frame and up to the Time Machine. I was surprised to find it had been carefully oiled and cleaned. I have suspected since that the Morlocks had even partially taken it to pieces while trying in their dim way to grasp its purpose.

"Now as I stood and examined it, finding a pleasure in the mere touch of the contrivance, the thing I had expected happened. The bronze panels suddenly slid up and struck the frame with a clang. I was in the dark— trapped. So the Morlocks thought. At that I chuckled gleefully.

"I could already hear their murmuring laughter as they came towards me. Very calmly I tried to strike the match. I had only to fix on the levers and depart then like a ghost. But I had overlooked one little thing. The matches were of that abominable kind that light only on the box.

"You may imagine how all my calm vanished. The little brutes were close upon me. One touched me. I made a sweeping blow in the dark at them with the levers, and began to scramble into the saddle of the machine. Then came one hand upon me and then another. Then I had simply to fight against their persistent fingers for my levers, and at the same time feel for the studs over which these fitted. One, indeed, they almost got away from me. As it slipped from my hand, I had to butt in the dark with my head—I could hear the Morlock's skull ring—to re- cover it. It was a nearer thing than the fight in the forest, I think, this last scramble.

"But at last the lever was fixed and pulled over. The clinging hands slipped from me. The darkness presently fell from my eyes. I found my- self in the same grey light and tumult I have already described.

CHAPTER XIV

THE FURTHER VISION

"I HAVE already told you of the sickness and confusion that comes with time travelling. And this time I was not seated properly in the saddle, but sideways and in an unstable fashion. For an indefinite time I clung to the machine as it swayed and vibrated, quite unheeding how I went, and when I brought myself to look at the dials again I was amazed to find where I had arrived. One dial records days, another thousands of days, another millions of days, and another thousands of millions. Now, instead of reversing the levers I had pulled them over so as to go forward with them, and when I came to look at these indicators I found that the thousands hand was sweeping round as fast as the seconds hands of a watch—into futurity. Very cautiously, for I remembered my former headlong fall, I began to reverse my motion. Slower and slower went the circling hands until the thousands one seemed motionless and the daily one was no longer a mere mist upon its scale. Still slower, until the grey haze around me became distincter and dim outlines of an undulating waste grew visible.

"I stopped. I was on a bleak moorland, covered with a sparse vegetation, and grey with a thin hoarfrost. The time was midday, the orange sun, shorn of its effulgence, brooded near the meridian in a sky of drabby grey. Only a few black bushes broke the monotony of the scene. The great buildings of the decadent men among whom, it seemed to me, I had been so recently, had vanished and left no trace: not a mound even marked their position. Hill and valley, sea and river—all, under the wear and work of the rain and frost, had melted into new forms. No doubt, too, the rain and snow had long since washed out the Morlock tunnels. A nipping breeze stung my hands and face. So far as I could see there were neither hills, nor trees, nor rivers: only an uneven stretch of cheerless plateau.

"Then suddenly a dark bulk rose out of the moor, something that gleamed like a serrated row of iron plates, and vanished almost immediately in a depression. And then I became aware of a number of faint-grey things, coloured to almost the exact tint of the frost-bitten soil, which were browsing here and there upon its scanty grass, and running to and fro. I saw one jump with a sudden start, and then my eye detected perhaps a score of them. At first I thought they were rabbits, or some small breed of kangaroo. Then, as one came hopping near me, I perceived that it belonged to neither of these groups. It was plantigrade, its hind legs rather the longer; it was tailless, and covered with a straight greyish hair that thickened about the head into a Skye terrier's mane. As I had understood that in the Golden Age man had killed out almost all the other animals, sparing only a few of the more ornamental, I was naturally curious about the creatures. They did not seem afraid of me, but browsed on, much as rabbits would do in a place unfrequented by men; and it occurred to me that I might perhaps secure a specimen.

"I got off the machine, and picked up a big stone. I had scarcely done so when one of the little creatures came within easy range. I was so lucky as to hit it on the head, and it rolled over at once and lay motionless. I ran to it at once. It remained still, almost as if it were killed. I was surprised to see that the thing had five feeble digits to both its fore and hind feet—the fore feet, indeed, were almost as human as the fore feet of a frog. It had, moreover, a roundish head, with a projecting forehead and forward-looking eyes, obscured by its lank hair. A disagreeable apprehension flashed across my mind. As I knelt down and seized my capture, intending to examine its teeth and other anatomical points which might show human characteristics, the metallic-looking object, to which I have already alluded, reappeared above a ridge in the moor, coming towards me and making a strange clattering sound as it came. Forthwith the grey animals about me began to answer with a short, weak yelping— as if of terror—and bolted off in a direction opposite to that from which this new creature approached. They must have hidden in burrows or behind bushes and tussocks, for in a moment not one of them was visible.

"I rose to my feet, and stared at this grotesque monster. I can only describe it by comparing it to a centipede. It stood about three feet high, and had a long segmented body, perhaps thirty feet long, with curiously overlapping greenish-black plates. It seemed to crawl upon a multitude of feet, looping its body as it advanced. Its blunt round head, with a polygonal arrangement of black eye spots, carried two flexible, writhing, horn-like antennæ. It was coming along, I should judge, at a pace of about eight or ten miles an hour, and it left me little time for thinking. Leaving my grey animal, or grey man, whichever it was, on the ground, I set off for the machine. Halfway I paused, regretting that abandonment, but a glance over my shoulder destroyed any such regret. When I gained the machine the monster was scarce fifty yards away. It was certainly not a vertebrated animal. It had no snout, and its mouth was fringed with jointed dark-coloured plates. But I did not care for a nearer view.

"I traversed one day and stopped again, hoping to find the colossus gone and some vestige of my victim; but, I should judge, the giant centipede did not trouble itself about bones. At any rate both had vanished. The faintly human touch of these little creatures perplexed me greatly. If you come to think, there is no reason why a degenerate humanity should not come at last to differentiate into as many species as the descendants of the mud fish who fathered all the land vertebrates. I saw no more of any insect colossus, as to my thinking the segmented creature must have been. Evidently the physiological difficulty that at present keeps all the insects small had been surmounted at last, and this division of the animal kingdom had arrived at the long-awaited supremacy which its enormous energy and vitality deserve. I made several attempts to kill or capture another of the greyish vermin, but none of my missiles were so successful as my first; and, after perhaps a dozen disappointing throws, that left my arm aching, I felt a gust of irritation at my folly in coming so far into futurity without weapons or equipment. I resolved to run on for one glimpse of the still remoter future—one peep into the deeper abysm of time—and then to return to you and my own epoch. Once more I remounted the machine, and once more the world grew hazy and grey.

"As I drove on, a peculiar change crept over the appearance of things. The palpitating greyness grew darker; then—though I was still travelling with prodigious velocity—the blinking succession of day and night, which was usually indicative of a slower pace, returned, and grew more and more marked. This puzzled me very much at first. The alternations of night and day grew slower and slower, and so did the passage of the sun across the sky, until they seemed to stretch through centuries. At last a steady twilight brooded over the earth, a twilight only broken now and then when a comet glared across the darkling sky. The band of light that had indicated the sun had long since disappeared; for the sun had ceased to set—it simply rose and fell in the west, and grew ever broader and more red. All trace of the moon had vanished. The circling of the stars, growing slower and slower, had given place to creeping points of light. At last, some time before I stopped, the sun, red and very large, halted motionless upon the horizon, a vast dome glowing with a dull heat, and now and then suffering a momentary extinction. At one time it had for a little while glowed more brilliantly again, but it speedily reverted to its sullen red-heat. I perceived by this slowing down of its rising and setting that the work of the tidal drag was done. The earth had come to rest with one face to the sun, even as in our own time the moon faces the earth. Very cautiously, for I remembered my former headlong fall, I began to reverse my motion. Slower and slower went the circling hands until the thousands one seemed motionless, and the daily one was no longer a mere mist upon its scale. Still slower, until the dim outlines of a desolate beach grew visible.

"I stopped very gently and sat upon the Time Machine, looking round. The sky was no longer blue. North-eastward it was inky black, and out of the blackness shone brightly and steadily the pale white stars. Overhead it was a deep Indian red and starless, and south-eastward it grew brighter to a glowing scarlet where, cut by the horizon, lay the huge hull of the sun, red and motionless. The rocks about me were of a harsh reddish colour, and all the trace of life that I could see at first was the intensely green vegetation that covered every projecting point on their south-eastern face. It was the same rich green that one sees on forest moss or on the lichen in caves: plants which like these grow in a perpetual twilight.

"The machine was standing on a sloping beach. The sea stretched away to the south-west, to rise into a sharp bright horizon against the wan sky. There were no breakers and no waves, for not a breath of wind was stirring. Only a slight oily swell rose and fell like a gentle breathing, and showed that the eternal sea was still moving and living. And along the margin where the water sometimes broke was a thick incrustation of salt—pink under the lurid sky. There was a sense of oppression in my head, and I noticed that I was breathing very fast. The sensation reminded me of my only experience of mountaineering, and from that I judged the air to be more rarefied than it is now.

"Far away up the desolate slope I heard a harsh scream, and saw a thing like a huge white butterfly go slanting and fluttering up into the sky and, circling, disappear over some low hillocks beyond. The sound of its voice was so dismal that I shivered and seated myself more firmly upon the machine. Looking round me again, I saw that, quite near, what I had taken to be a reddish mass of rock was moving slowly towards me. Then I saw the thing was really a monstrous crab-like creature. Can you imagine a crab as large as yonder table, with its many legs moving slowly and uncertainly, its big claws swaying, its long antennæ, like carters' whips, waving and feeling, and its stalked eyes gleaming at you on either side of its metallic front? Its back was corrugated and ornamented with ungainly bosses, and a greenish incrustation blotched it here and there. I could see the many palps of its complicated mouth flickering and feeling as it moved.

"As I stared at this sinister apparition crawling towards me, I felt a tickling on my cheek as though a fly had lighted there. I tried to brush it away with my hand, but in a moment it returned, and almost immediately came another by my ear. I struck at this, and caught something thread-like. It was drawn swiftly out of my hand. With a frightful qualm, I turned, and saw that I had grasped the antenna of another monster crab that stood just behind me. Its evil eyes were wriggling on their stalks, its mouth was all alive with appetite, and its vast ungainly claws, smeared with an algal slime, were descending upon me. In a moment my hand was on the lever, and I had placed a month between myself and these monsters. But I was still on the same beach, and I saw them distinctly now as soon as I stopped. Dozens of them seemed to be crawling here and there, in the sombre light, among the foliated sheets of intense green.

"I cannot convey the sense of abominable desolation that hung over the world. The red eastern sky, the northward blackness, the salt Dead Sea, the stony beach crawling with these foul, slow-stirring monsters, the uniform poisonous-looking green of the lichenous plants, the thin air that hurts one's lungs: all contributed to an appalling effect. I moved on a hundred years, and there was the same red sun—a little larger, a little duller—the same dying sea, the same chill air, and the same crowd of earthy crustacea creeping in and out among the green weed and the red rocks. And in the westward sky I saw a curved pale line like a vast new moon.

"So I travelled, stopping ever and again, in great strides of a thousand years or more, drawn on by the mystery of the earth's fate, watching with a strange fascination the sun grow larger and duller in the westward sky, and the life of the old earth ebb away. At last, more than thirty million years hence, the huge red-hot dome of the sun had come to obscure nearly a tenth part of the darkling heavens. Then I stopped once more, for the crawling multitude of crabs had disappeared, and the red beach, save for its livid green liverworts and lichens, seemed lifeless. And now it was flecked with white. A bitter cold assailed me. Rare white flakes ever and again came eddying down. To the north-eastward, the glare of snow lay under the starlight of the sable sky, and I could see an undulating crest of hillocks pinkish-white. There were fringes of ice along the sea margin, with drifting masses further out; but the main expanse of that salt ocean, all bloody under the eternal sunset, was still unfrozen.

" I looked about me to see if any traces of animal-life remained. A certain indefinable apprehension still kept me in the saddle of the machine. But I saw nothing moving, in earth or sky or sea. The green slime on the rocks alone testified that life was not extinct. A shallow sandbank had appeared in the sea and the water had receded from the beach. I fancied I saw some black object flopping about upon this bank, but it became motionless as I looked at it, and I judged that my eye had been deceived, and that the black object was merely a rock. The stars in the sky were intensely bright and seemed to me to twinkle very little.

"Suddenly I noticed that the circular westward outline of the sun had changed; that a concavity, a bay, had appeared in the curve. I saw this grow larger. For a minute perhaps I stared aghast at this blackness that was creeping over the day, and then I realized that an eclipse was beginning. Either the moon or the planet Mercury was passing across the sun's disk. Naturally, at first I took it to be the moon, but there is much to incline me to believe that what I really saw was the transit of an inner planet passing very near to the earth.

"The darkness grew apace; a cold wind began to blow in freshening gusts from the east, and the showering white flakes in the air increased in number. From the edge of the sea came a ripple and whisper. Beyond these lifeless sounds the world was silent. Silent? It would be hard to convey the stillness of it. All the sounds of man, the bleating of sheep, the cries of birds, the hum of insects, the stir that makes the background of our lives—all that was over. As the darkness thickened, the eddying flakes grew more abundant, dancing before my eyes; and the cold of the air more intense. At last, one by one, swiftly, one after the other, the white peaks of the distant hills vanished into blackness. The breeze rose to a moaning wind. I saw the black central shadow of the eclipse sweeping towards me. In another moment the pale stars alone were visible. All else was rayless obscurity. The sky was absolutely black.

"A horror of this great darkness came on me. The cold, that smote to my marrow, and the pain I felt in breathing overcame me. I shivered, and a deadly nausea seized me. Then like a red-hot bow in the sky appeared the edge of the sun. I got off the machine to recover myself. I felt giddy and incapable of facing the return journey. As I stood sick and confused I saw again the moving thing upon the shoal—there was no mistake now that it was a moving thing—against the red water of the sea. It was a round thing, the size of a football perhaps, or, it may be, bigger, and tentacles trailed down from it; it seemed black against the weltering blood-red water, and it was hopping fitfully about. Then I felt I was fainting. But a terrible dread of lying helpless in that remote and awful twilight sustained me while I clambered upon the saddle.

CHAPTER XV

THE TIME TRAVELLER'S RETURN

"SO I CAME back. For a long time I must have been insensible upon the machine. The blinking succession of the days and nights was resumed, the sun got golden again, the sky blue. I breathed with greater freedom. The fluctuating contours of the land ebbed and flowed. The hands spun backward upon the dials. At last I saw again the dim shadows of houses, the evidences of decadent humanity. These, too, changed and passed, and others came. Presently, when the million dial was at zero, I slackened speed. I began to recognize our own petty and familiar architecture, the thousands hand ran back to the starting-point, the night and day flapped slower and slower. Then the old walls of the laboratory came round me. Very gently, now, I slowed the mechanism down.

"I saw one little thing that seemed odd to me. I think I have told you that when I set out, before my velocity became very high, Mrs. Watchett had walked across the room, travelling, as it seemed to me, like a rocket. As I returned, I passed again across that minute when she traversed the laboratory. But now her every motion appeared to be the exact inversion of her previous ones. The door at the lower end opened, and she glided quietly up the laboratory, back foremost, and disappeared behind the door by which she had previously entered. Just before that I seemed to see Hillyer for a moment; but he passed like a flash.

"Then I stopped the machine, and saw about me again the old familiar laboratory, my tools, my appliances just as I had left them. I got off the thing very shakily, and sat down upon my bench. For several minutes I trembled violently. Then I became calmer. Around me was my old work-shop again, exactly as it had been. I might have slept there, and the whole thing have been a dream.

"And yet, not exactly! The thing had started from the south-east corner of the laboratory. It had come to rest again in the north-west, against the wall where you saw it. That gives you the exact distance from my little lawn to the pedestal of the White Sphinx, into which the Mor-locks had carried my machine.

"For a time my brain went stagnant. Presently I got up and came through the passage here, limping, because my heel was still painful, and feeling sorely begrimed. I saw the *Pall Mall Gazette* on the table by the door. I found the date was indeed to-day, and looking at the timepiece, saw the hour was almost eight o'clock. I heard your voices and the clatter of plates. I hesitated—I felt so sick and weak. Then I sniffed good whole-some meat, and opened the door on you. You know the rest. I washed, and dined, and now I am telling you the story."

CHAPTER XVI

AFTER THE STORY

"I KNOW," he said, after a pause, "that all this will be absolutely incredible to you, but to me the one incredible thing is that I am here to-night in this old familiar room, looking into your friendly faces, and telling you all these strange adventures." He looked at the Medical Man. "No. I cannot expect you to believe it. Take it as a lie—or a prophecy. Say I dreamed it in the workshop. Consider I have been speculating upon the destinies of our race, until I have hatched this fiction. Treat my assertion of its truth as a mere stroke of art to enhance its interest. And taking it as a story, what do you think of it?"

He took up his pipe, and began, in his old accustomed manner, to tap with it nervously upon the bars of the grate. There was a momentary stillness. Then chairs began to creak and shoes to scrape upon the carpet. I took my eyes off the Time Traveller's face, and looked round at his audience. They were in the dark, and little spots of colour swam before them. The Medical Man seemed absorbed in the contemplation of our host. The Editor was looking hard at the end of his cigar—the sixth. The Journalist fumbled for his watch. The others, as far as I remember, were motionless.

The Editor stood up with a sigh. "What a pity it is you're not a writer of stories!" he said, putting his hand on the Time Traveller's shoulder.

"You don't believe it?"

"Well——"

"I thought not."

The Time Traveller turned to us. "Where are the matches?" he said. He lit one and spoke over his pipe, puffing. "To tell you the truth . . . I hardly believe it myself. . . . And yet . . ."

His eye fell with a mute inquiry upon the withered white flowers upon the little table. Then he turned over the hand holding his pipe, and I saw he was looking at some half-healed scars on his knuckles.

The Medical Man rose, came to the lamp, and examined the flowers. "The gynæceum's odd," he said. The Psychologist leant forward to see, holding out his hand for a specimen.

"I'm hanged if it isn't a quarter to one," said the Journalist. "How shall we get home?"

"Plenty of cabs at the station," said the Psychologist.

"It's a curious thing," said the Medical Man; "but I certainly don't know the natural order of these flowers. May I have them?"

The Time Traveller hesitated. Then suddenly, "Certainly not."

"Where did you really get them?" said the Medical Man.

The Time Traveller put his hand to his head. He spoke like one who was trying to keep hold of an idea that eluded him. "They were put into my pocket by Weena, when I travelled into Time." He stared round the room. "I'm damned if it isn't all going. This room and you and the atmosphere of every day is too much for my memory. Did I ever make a Time Machine, or a model of a Time Machine? Or is it all only a dream? They say life is a dream, a precious poor dream at times—but I can't stand another that won't fit. It's madness. And where did the dream come from? . . . I must look at that machine. If there *is* one!"

He caught up the lamp swiftly, and carried it, flaring red, through the door into the corridor. We followed him. There in the flickering light of the lamp was the machine sure enough, squat, ugly, and askew, a thing of brass, ebony, ivory, and translucent glimmering quartz. Solid to the touch—for I put out my hand and felt the rail of it—and with brown spots and smears upon the ivory, and bits of grass and moss upon the lower parts, and one rail bent awry.

The Time Traveller put the lamp down on the bench, and ran his hand along the damaged rail. "It's all right now," he said. "The story I told you was true. I'm sorry to have brought you out here in the cold." He took up the lamp, and, in an absolute silence, we returned to the smoking-room.

He came into the hall with us, and helped the Editor on with his coat. The Medical Man looked into his face and, with a certain hesitation, told him he was suffering from overwork, at which he laughed hugely. I remember him standing in the open doorway, bawling good-night.

I shared a cab with the Editor. He thought the tale a "gaudy lie." For my own part I was unable to come to a conclusion. The story was so fantastic and incredible, the telling so credible and sober. I lay awake most of the night thinking about it. I determined to go next day, and see the Time Traveller again. I was told he was in the laboratory, and being on easy terms in the house, I went up to him. The laboratory, however, was empty. I stared for a minute at the Time Machine and put out my hand and touched the lever. At that the squat substantial-looking mass swayed like a bough shaken by the wind. Its instability startled me extremely, and I had a queer reminiscence of the childish days when I used to be forbidden to meddle. I came back through the corridor. The Time Traveller met me in the smoking-room. He was coming from the house. He had a small camera under one arm and a knapsack under the other. He laughed when he saw me, and gave me an elbow to shake. "I'm frightfully busy," said he, "with that thing in there."

"But is it not some hoax?" I said. "Do you really travel through time?"

"Really and truly I do." And he looked frankly into my eyes. He hesitated. His eye wandered about the room. "I only want half an hour," he said. "I know why you came, and it's awfully good of you. There's some magazines here. If you'll stop to lunch I'll prove you this time travelling up to the hilt, specimens and all. If you'll forgive my leaving you now?"

I consented, hardly comprehending then the full import of his words, and he nodded and went on down the corridor. I heard the door of the laboratory slam, seated myself in a chair, and took up a daily paper. What was he going to do before lunch-time? Then suddenly I was reminded by an advertisement that I had promised to meet Richardson, the publisher, at two. I looked at my watch, and saw that I could barely save that engagement. I got up and went down the passage to tell the Time Traveller.

As I took hold of the handle of the door I heard an exclamation, oddly truncated at the end, and a click and a thud. A gust of air whirled round me as I opened the door, and from within came the sound of broken glass falling on the floor. The Time Traveller was not there. I seemed to see a ghostly, indistinct figure sitting in a whirling mass of black and brass for a moment—a figure so transparent that the bench behind with its sheets of drawings was absolutely distinct; but this phantasm vanished as I rubbed my eyes. The Time Machine had gone. Save for a subsiding stir of dust, the further end of the laboratory was empty. A pane of the sky-light had, apparently, just been blown in.

I felt an unreasonable amazement. I knew that something strange had happened, and for the moment could not distinguish what the strange thing might be. As I stood staring, the door into the garden opened, and the man-servant appeared.

We looked at each other. Then ideas began to come. "Has Mr. —— gone out that way?" said I.

"No, sir. No one has come out this way. I was expecting to find him here."

At that I understood. At the risk of disappointing Richardson I stayed on, waiting for the Time Traveller: waiting for the second, perhaps still stranger story, and the specimens and photographs he would bring with him. But I am beginning now to fear that I must wait a lifetime. The Time Traveller vanished three years ago. And, as everybody knows now, he has never returned.

EPILOGUE

ONE CANNOT choose but wonder. Will he ever return? It may be that he swept back into the past, and fell among the blood-drinking, hairy savages of the Age of Unpolished Stone; into the abysses of the Cretaceous Sea; or among the grotesque saurians, the huge reptilian brutes of the Jurassic times. He may even now—if I may use the phrase

—be wandering on some plesiosaurus-haunted Oolitic coral reef, or beside the lonely saline seas of the Triassic Age. Or did he go forward, into one of the nearer ages, in which men are still men, but with the riddles of our own time answered and its wearisome problems solved? Into the manhood of the race: for I, for my own part, cannot think that these latter days of weak experiment, fragmentary theory, and mutual discord are indeed man's culminating time! I say, for my own part. He, I know—for the question had been discussed among us long before the Time Machine was made—thought but cheerlessly of the Advancement of Mankind, and saw in the growing pile of civilization only a foolish heaping that must inevitably fall back upon and destroy its makers in the end. If that is so, it remains for us to live as though it were not so. But to me the future is still black and blank—is a vast ignorance, lit at a few casual places by the memory of his story. And I have by me, for my comfort, two strange white flowers—shrivelled now, and brown and flat and brittle—to witness that even when mind and strength had gone, gratitude and a mutual tenderness still lived on in the heart of man.

A CATALOGUE OF SELECTED DOVER BOOKS
IN ALL FIELDS OF INTEREST

A CATALOGUE OF SELECTED DOVER BOOKS
IN ALL FIELDS OF INTEREST

THE DEVIL'S DICTIONARY, Ambrose Bierce. Barbed, bitter, brilliant witticisms in the form of a dictionary. Best, most ferocious satire America has produced. 145pp.　　　　　　　　　　　　　　　　　　　　　　20487-1 Pa. $1.50

ABSOLUTELY MAD INVENTIONS, A.E. Brown, H.A. Jeffcott. Hilarious, useless, or merely absurd inventions all granted patents by the U.S. Patent Office. Edible tie pin, mechanical hat tipper, etc. 57 illustrations. 125pp.　　　22596-8 Pa. $1.50

AMERICAN WILD FLOWERS COLORING BOOK, Paul Kennedy. Planned coverage of 48 most important wildflowers, from Rickett's collection; instructive as well as entertaining. Color versions on covers. 48pp. 8¼ x 11.　　　20095-7 Pa. $1.35

BIRDS OF AMERICA COLORING BOOK, John James Audubon. Rendered for coloring by Paul Kennedy. 46 of Audubon's noted illustrations: red-winged blackbird, cardinal, purple finch, towhee, etc. Original plates reproduced in full color on the covers. 48pp. 8¼ x 11.　　　　　　　　　　　　　　23049-X Pa. $1.35

NORTH AMERICAN INDIAN DESIGN COLORING BOOK, Paul Kennedy. The finest examples from Indian masks, beadwork, pottery, etc. — selected and redrawn for coloring (with identifications) by well-known illustrator Paul Kennedy. 48pp. 8¼ x 11.　　　　　　　　　　　　　　　　　　　　21125-8 Pa. $1.35

UNIFORMS OF THE AMERICAN REVOLUTION COLORING BOOK, Peter Copeland. 31 lively drawings reproduce whole panorama of military attire; each uniform has complete instructions for accurate coloring. (Not in the Pictorial Archives Series). 64pp. 8¼ x 11.　　　　　　　　　　　　　　　21850-3 Pa. $1.50

THE WONDERFUL WIZARD OF OZ COLORING BOOK, L. Frank Baum. Color the Yellow Brick Road and much more in 61 drawings adapted from W.W. Denslow's originals, accompanied by abridged version of text. Dorothy, Toto, Oz and the Emerald City. 61 illustrations. 64pp. 8¼ x 11.　　　　　20452-9 Pa. $1.50

CUT AND COLOR PAPER MASKS, Michael Grater. Clowns, animals, funny faces . . . simply color them in, cut them out, and put them together, and you have 9 paper masks to play with and enjoy. Complete instructions. Assembled masks shown in full color on the covers. 32pp. 8¼ x 11.　　　　23171-2 Pa. $1.50

STAINED GLASS CHRISTMAS ORNAMENT COLORING BOOK, Carol Belanger Grafton. Brighten your Christmas season with over 100 Christmas ornaments done in a stained glass effect on translucent paper. Color them in and then hang at windows, from lights, anywhere. 32pp. 8¼ x 11.　　　　20707-2 Pa. $1.75

CREATIVE LITHOGRAPHY AND HOW TO DO IT, Grant Arnold. Lithography as art form: working directly on stone, transfer of drawings, lithotint, mezzotint, color printing; also metal plates. Detailed, thorough. 27 illustrations. 214pp.
21208-4 Pa. $3.00

DESIGN MOTIFS OF ANCIENT MEXICO, Jorge Enciso. Vigorous, powerful ceramic stamp impressions — Maya, Aztec, Toltec, Olmec. Serpents, gods, priests, dancers, etc. 153pp. 6⅛ x 9¼.
20084-1 Pa. $2.50

AMERICAN INDIAN DESIGN AND DECORATION, Leroy Appleton. Full text, plus more than 700 precise drawings of Inca, Maya, Aztec, Pueblo, Plains, NW Coast basketry, sculpture, painting, pottery, sand paintings, metal, etc. 4 plates in color. 279pp. 8⅜ x 11¼.
22704-9 Pa. $4.50

CHINESE LATTICE DESIGNS, Daniel S. Dye. Incredibly beautiful geometric designs: circles, voluted, simple dissections, etc. Inexhaustible source of ideas, motifs. 1239 illustrations. 469pp. 6⅛ x 9¼.
23096-1 Pa. $5.00

JAPANESE DESIGN MOTIFS, Matsuya Co. Mon, or heraldic designs. Over 4000 typical, beautiful designs: birds, animals, flowers, swords, fans, geometric; all beautifully stylized. 213pp. 11⅜ x 8¼.
22874-6 Pa. $4.95

PERSPECTIVE, Jan Vredeman de Vries. 73 perspective plates from 1604 edition; buildings, townscapes, stairways, fantastic scenes. Remarkable for beauty, surrealistic atmosphere; real eye-catchers. Introduction by Adolf Placzek. 74pp. 11⅜ x 8¼.
20186-4 Pa. $2.75

EARLY AMERICAN DESIGN MOTIFS, Suzanne E. Chapman. 497 motifs, designs, from painting on wood, ceramics, appliqué, glassware, samplers, metal work, etc. Florals, landscapes, birds and animals, geometrics, letters, etc. Inexhaustible. Enlarged edition. 138pp. 8⅜ x 11¼.
22985-8 Pa. $3.50
23084-8 Clothbd. $7.95

VICTORIAN STENCILS FOR DESIGN AND DECORATION, edited by E.V. Gillon, Jr. 113 wonderful ornate Victorian pieces from German sources; florals, geometrics; borders, corner pieces; bird motifs, etc. 64pp. 9⅜ x 12¼.
21995-X Pa. $2.50

ART NOUVEAU: AN ANTHOLOGY OF DESIGN AND ILLUSTRATION FROM THE STUDIO, edited by E.V. Gillon, Jr. Graphic arts: book jackets, posters, engravings, illustrations, decorations; Crane, Beardsley, Bradley and many others. Inexhaustible. 92pp. 8⅛ x 11.
22388-4 Pa. $2.50

ORIGINAL ART DECO DESIGNS, William Rowe. First-rate, highly imaginative modern Art Deco frames, borders, compositions, alphabets, florals, insectals, Wurlitzer-types, etc. Much finest modern Art Deco. 80 plates, 8 in color. 8⅜ x 11¼.
22567-4 Pa. $3.00

HANDBOOK OF DESIGNS AND DEVICES, Clarence P. Hornung. Over 1800 basic geometric designs based on circle, triangle, square, scroll, cross, etc. Largest such collection in existence. 261pp.
20125-2 Pa. $2.50

How to Solve Chess Problems, Kenneth S. Howard. Practical suggestions on problem solving for very beginners. 58 two-move problems, 46 3-movers, 8 4-movers for practice, plus hints. 171pp. 20748-X Pa. $2.00

A Guide to Fairy Chess, Anthony Dickins. 3-D chess, 4-D chess, chess on a cylindrical board, reflecting pieces that bounce off edges, cooperative chess, retrograde chess, maximummers, much more. Most based on work of great Dawson. Full handbook, 100 problems. 66pp. 7⅞ x 10¾. 22687-5 Pa. $2.00

Win at Backgammon, Millard Hopper. Best opening moves, running game, blocking game, back game, tables of odds, etc. Hopper makes the game clear enough for anyone to play, and win. 43 diagrams. 111pp. 22894-0 Pa. $1.50

Bidding a Bridge Hand, Terence Reese. Master player "thinks out loud" the binding of 75 hands that defy point count systems. Organized by bidding problem—no-fit situations, overbidding, underbidding, cueing your defense, etc. 254pp. EBE 22830-4 Pa. $2.50

The Precision Bidding System in Bridge, C.C. Wei, edited by Alan Truscott. Inventor of precision bidding presents average hands and hands from actual play, including games from 1969 Bermuda Bowl where system emerged. 114 exercises. 116pp. 21171-1 Pa. $1.75

Learn Magic, Henry Hay. 20 simple, easy-to-follow lessons on magic for the new magician: illusions, card tricks, silks, sleights of hand, coin manipulations, escapes, and more —all with a minimum amount of equipment. Final chapter explains the great stage illusions. 92 illustrations. 285pp. 21238-6 Pa. $2.95

The New Magician's Manual, Walter B. Gibson. Step-by-step instructions and clear illustrations guide the novice in mastering 36 tricks; much equipment supplied on 16 pages of cut-out materials. 36 additional tricks. 64 illustrations. 159pp. 6⅝ x 10. 23113-5 Pa. $3.00

Professional Magic for Amateurs, Walter B. Gibson. 50 easy, effective tricks used by professionals —cards, string, tumblers, handkerchiefs, mental magic, etc. 63 illustrations. 223pp. 23012-0 Pa. $2.50

Card Manipulations, Jean Hugard. Very rich collection of manipulations; has taught thousands of fine magicians tricks that are really workable, eye-catching. Easily followed, serious work. Over 200 illustrations. 163pp. 20539-8 Pa. $2.00

Abbott's Encyclopedia of Rope Tricks for Magicians, Stewart James. Complete reference book for amateur and professional magicians containing more than 150 tricks involving knots, penetrations, cut and restored rope, etc. 510 illustrations. Reprint of 3rd edition. 400pp. 23206-9 Pa. $3.50

The Secrets of Houdini, J.C. Cannell. Classic study of Houdini's incredible magic, exposing closely-kept professional secrets and revealing, in general terms, the whole art of stage magic. 67 illustrations. 279pp. 22913-0 Pa. $2.50

EGYPTIAN MAGIC, E.A. Wallis Budge. Foremost Egyptologist, curator at British Museum, on charms, curses, amulets, doll magic, transformations, control of demons, deific appearances, feats of great magicians. Many texts cited. 19 illustrations. 234pp.   USO 22681-6 Pa. $2.50

THE LEYDEN PAPYRUS: AN EGYPTIAN MAGICAL BOOK, edited by F. Ll. Griffith, Herbert Thompson. Egyptian sorcerer's manual contains scores of spells: sex magic of various sorts, occult information, evoking visions, removing evil magic, etc. Transliteration faces translation. 207pp.   22994-7 Pa. $2.50

THE MALLEUS MALEFICARUM OF KRAMER AND SPRENGER, translated, edited by Montague Summers. Full text of most important witchhunter's "Bible," used by both Catholics and Protestants. Theory of witches, manifestations, remedies, etc. Indispensable to serious student. 278pp. 6⅝ x 10.   USO 22802-9 Pa. $3.95

LOST CONTINENTS, L. Sprague de Camp. Great science-fiction author, finest, fullest study: Atlantis, Lemuria, Mu, Hyperborea, etc. Lost Tribes, Irish in pre-Columbian America, root races; in history, literature, art, occultism. Necessary to everyone concerned with theme. 17 illustrations. 348pp.   22668-9 Pa. $3.50

THE COMPLETE BOOKS OF CHARLES FORT, Charles Fort. Book of the Damned, Lo!, Wild Talents, New Lands. Greatest compilation of data: celestial appearances, flying saucers, falls of frogs, strange disappearances, inexplicable data not recognized by science. Inexhaustible, painstakingly documented. Do not confuse with modern charlatanry. Introduction by Damon Knight. Total of 1126pp.
23094-5 Clothbd. $15.00

FADS AND FALLACIES IN THE NAME OF SCIENCE, Martin Gardner. Fair, witty appraisal of cranks and quacks of science: Atlantis, Lemuria, flat earth, Velikovsky, orgone energy, Bridey Murphy, medical fads, etc. 373pp.   20394-8 Pa. $3.00

HOAXES, Curtis D. MacDougall. Unbelievably rich account of great hoaxes: Locke's moon hoax, Shakespearean forgeries, Loch Ness monster, Disumbrationist school of art, dozens more; also psychology of hoaxing. 54 illustrations. 338pp.   20465-0 Pa. $3.50

THE GENTLE ART OF MAKING ENEMIES, James A.M. Whistler. Greatest wit of his day deflates Wilde, Ruskin, Swinburne; strikes back at inane critics, exhibitions. Highly readable classic of impressionist revolution by great painter. Introduction by Alfred Werner. 334pp.   21875-9 Pa. $4.00

THE BOOK OF TEA, Kakuzo Okakura. Minor classic of the Orient: entertaining, charming explanation, interpretation of traditional Japanese culture in terms of tea ceremony. Edited by E.F. Bleiler. Total of 94pp.   20070-1 Pa. $1.25

Prices subject to change without notice.
Available at your book dealer or write for free catalogue to Dept. GI, Dover Publications, Inc., 180 Varick St., N.Y., N.Y. 10014. Dover publishes more than 150 books each year on science, elementary and advanced mathematics, biology, music, art, literary history, social sciences and other areas.

40
53
63
85.
86
93
94
95
½
137
141

194

$ 800/oz